TAKE HART

ALSO BY JAIME PARKER STICKLE

Corey in Los Angeles

Vicious Cycle

PRAISE FOR JAIME PARKER STICKLE

Vicious Cycle

"Stickle buttresses her well-executed mystery plot with sharp wit . . . Readers will be hungry to hear more."

—*Publishers Weekly*

"Jaime Stickle's debut, *Vicious Cycle*, is a layer cake of enjoyment. Any former reporter can investigate murder, but Stickle's protagonist, Corey Tracey-Lieberman, does it with a baby strapped to her chest while fighting postpartum anxiety. Funny in spots, heartbreaking in spots, Stickle brings the humanity—and lands the plane without nary a bump."

—Tracy Clark, award-winning author of the Cass Raines and Detective Harriet Foster series

"Jaime Parker Stickle's debut is both a love letter to the everyday people of Los Angeles and a kick-ass mystery. Corey Tracey-Lieberman is a vibrant, often-delirious, and surprisingly moving investigator who never stops being herself, even in the most hilarious and harrowing circumstances. *Vicious Cycle* is an absolute delight."

—Tod Goldberg, *New York Times* bestselling author

TAKE HART

A Thriller

JAIME PARKER STICKLE

THOMAS & MERCER

Published by Thomas & Mercer, Seattle

www.apub.com

EU product safety contact:
Amazon Media EU S. à r.l.
38, avenue John F. Kennedy, L-1855 Luxembourg
amazonpublishing-gpsr@amazon.com

ISBN-13: 9781662531750 (paperback)
ISBN-13: 9781662531767 (digital)

Cover design and illustration by Jarrod Taylor

Printed in the United States of America

To my sweet son, who inspires all my work.

Take Hart is a story with strong themes that may be triggering for some readers. These themes include violence against women, mental health, and thoughts of self-harm. It is also about courage, community, and rebuilding after loss.

1

I pull away from the kiss, more confused than ever.

"I-I'm sorry," I say.

"Corey, I'm not going to give up on you. Or us," Evan says. The dark circles under his eyes are visible even now, in the twilight of early morning. The growth of a beard defines his chiseled jaw. The lines on his forehead are a little deeper, adding to the rugged nature of his new look—Outdoorsy Guy. Mountain Man. He could pass as a host for any Mount Everest travel show. It's such a contrast from his Monday work look—skinny work slacks and button-down—his marketing job uniform. It also contrasts with his new electric Volvo. Predictable, stable, handsome—the first three words that come to mind when I talk about Evan in therapy.

But then there's the judgment. Quick to make sure I know who he believes is solely at fault for our separation. *I'm not going to give up on you.* He believes, maybe he has to, that it is me who is broken, and so I need to be fixed. It is me doing this to our family—to him. I'm the problem in our marriage. And he is *not going to give up on* me.

"Jacob is going to be up soon. I need to get ready for work—" Before I can finish my sentence, my phone buzzes in my pocket. I pull it out and read without hesitating.

Chris: There's a missing woman.

Me: Where?

Chris: From Highland Park. No last whereabouts yet. Son reported it.

That hits me in the chest. Her son reported her missing. I say a quick prayer in my head to the universe, and to any god and goddess listening, to please never burden my son with the need to call the police to report me missing.

Chris: Corey, I know her.

I'm not surprised—the community is small, and Chris is even more connected to it than I am. But how well does he know her? And *Is she more than a friend?* is the question.

Me: You okay?

Chris: Yep. Sending you a link to look at right now.

From Evan's watch I hear Jacob babbling. He's awake, in his crib where he should be. I clock that Evan is still monitoring the house on his watch. What else is he accessing? Does he leave Jacob's channel open when he's not here? I'm suddenly feeling very vulnerable and need him to go.

"Well, that's my cue," I say. "Thank you for stopping by with coffee. That was very nice. Do you have everything you need?"

"I'm all set. Tell Jacob I said hi and that I love him," Evan says. Without a goodbye to me, Evan heads toward the driveway, to his car, and I walk into the house alone, and I close the door behind me.

2

"Hello, my love. Good morning," I say, finding myself straining to pick up a disheveled-haired baby from his crib—his growth spurts are anything but small. "Did you sleep well?" Jacob's response is a garbled mouthful of sounds that are closer to sentences than even a week ago.

He has entered the phase of starting to walk, and every time I pick him up now, he thrusts his whole body into an athletic rock back and forth in my arms. As though he may get enough momentum to literally take off flying. It's lovely to watch and brutal on my hips and back.

"Do you want to go check out the window with me? We can check to see if Daddy has gone yet," I say, knowing that Jacob understands Daddy leaves in a car but always comes back. I walk toward the upstairs hallway window that looks directly down on the driveway to see if Evan has left yet. His impromptu visits in the evenings are one thing, but this early on a Monday is another.

"Da!" Jacob says while striking the glass of the window with his balled-up fist. I jerk us back and into the bathroom before Evan can see us. Unpredictable, that is what Jacob has become at fifteen months old. Unpredictable.

"Daddy is leaving. We will see him later," I say. "Bye-bye, Daddy, see you later." I hold Jacob's wrist and help him make the motion of a goodbye wave. *See you later* is almost a promise I make to Jacob. A promise with a hint of regret because later isn't specific. Evan may pop over before Jacob's bedtime, or he may come in the morning again, but at breakfast. Evan doesn't adhere to a schedule, and I haven't enforced one. It doesn't seem right to, since I need to keep Jacob with me full-time, and my psychiatrist agrees that Jacob should be with me in the home full-time. I've been letting my guilt over it guide me. I feel like the bad guy, making Evan sleep somewhere else for a bit. Really, live somewhere else. It was supposed to be for just a month, but the longer Evan is gone, the better I feel.

Staring at the counter, I notice the orange pill bottle waiting for me. A Paxil a day keeps all my demons away—the ones that tell me I'm a bad mom. Dr. Rosenberg sounded like one of those drug commercials when he explained it. Taking a single Paxil every day would help control the intrusive thoughts—the obsessive-compulsive part of my panic disorder—and alleviate my anxiety, bringing my baseline closer to *normal*, but it could be accompanied by a loss of impulse control, weight gain, and brain fog. Next to the Paxil is a second orange bottle—Klonopin. That one is to catch the demons immediately if there's even a hint of them coming for an attack. That is my break-glass-in-case-of-emergency pill, when the Paxil isn't cutting it. Depending on how bad my spinout is, a single Klonopin might make me chill out, or it might put me to sleep. Or if it's really bad, I might need two or three to stop the merry-go-round of my intrusive thoughts. Some days it's enough just knowing I have the Klonopin. Knowing that I can shut out the thoughts before a panic attack hits or before one can escalate. The recommended dose is one Paxil per day and Klonopin as needed to stay ahead of the anxiety. There were many days in the past months when I needed one or two or three Klonopins. Yesterday, when Evan was out with Jacob, I almost took one, nearly breaking my monthlong streak of not needing any Klonopin at all. When Jacob isn't within arm's reach, it's a trigger. And yeah, this morning's daily Paxil will probably work . . . mostly, but that 1 percent of the time it doesn't work is scary as hell. I've never hit the four-pills-a-day Klonopin maximum, but I've come close. I grab the bottle of Klonopin and take it to my bedroom. I open the top drawer, an overloaded mess of socks, bras, and underwear. I dig to the bottom of the pile of socks, under one pair of black tights, and tuck the Klonopin underneath them all, making it harder for me to grab one. I don't need them anymore. I'm okay. I'm fine. I'm really doing better.

"Ouchie," I say, grabbing the fist that Jacob is about to land on my head for a second time. "Mommy is sorry she spaced out. Let's go get breakfast, okay?" *Breakfast, snack, cookie, banana,* these are all magic words for Jacob. I had a dog once that loved the same words. I hope I never say *good boy* to Jacob.

My phone vibrates aggressively against my leg. The Cyclone Spin Studio, where I work part-time as an instructor and an assistant manager, issued us all black leggings that suck me in like a girdle, making the phone vibration tingle deep inside my thigh. Or the quadriceps, as Monique, my boss and the studio's owner, likes to rebrand thighs.

I manage to unwrap the phone from the painted-on pocket with one hand and know it's either Chris, my partner in crime—literally, well, my boss in crime fighting—or Detective Lopez, my other partner . . . or other boss. We're still working out our relationship hierarchy. It's Chris.

Chris: Did you look at the link? Thoughts?

Shit. I forgot. Saying goodbye to Evan, grabbing Jacob. That's the other thing with the Paxil—too many tasks at once, and I forget what I'm doing. My brain doesn't have the space for all the information since the meds kicked in.

Me: Looking at it now.

Chris: . . .

Those three dots always keep me hanging on. Waiting for another message from Chris. Is he going to say something about work? About us? But the dots disappear, and nothing more is typed for the moment. I hate the dots. Loathe them.

I'm out of bananas, so I open a banana-smoothie pouch for Jacob, grab my laptop with my free hand, and head out to the porch. We have one of those massive porches that looks like it may wrap around the whole house but doesn't. I put Jacob in the baby swing Evan and I set up on the porch, and I sit in the perfect position to watch my street.

My 1903-built Craftsman sits atop a plateau, affording me the privilege of looking down at the whole street with an unencumbered view of the homes and of the mountains to the east and west. All the homes are different. Designed by different architects or built by each owner's two hands. That's the thing with Highland Park, both things are true because it is one of the oldest neighborhoods in Los Angeles. The house on the opposite corner of mine is coated in a mauve-beige paint forced on the homeowner by the HPOZ, the Historic Preservation Overlay Zone of Highland Park. It's a Craftsman that was built in the 1920s, and because it sits right next to the railroad track and it's the largest and nicest home on the block, my assumption has always been that it belonged to someone working for the big rail company. The older woman who currently owns the property rarely leaves her home. I can usually see her through an unshaded window in the afternoons, but not today. The house across from hers leans a little to the left, maybe due to an earthquake or just another faulty foundation. It was purchased before we moved in, painted stark white with black trim, now coated by a layer of dust drifting down from Mount Washington. A security gate around the front gives the impression the property offers security from the rest of the block. My porch is high enough that I can see the pebble-and-succulent landscaping of the front yard. I've never met the owner. It operates as a short-term rental property, but I rarely see any renters. They must enter through the alley in the back because it's always booked—I checked the site.

I sit in front of the swing that Jacob gently sways in and open my laptop, continually glancing between the screen and my baby. I copy the link Chris sent me—it takes me to a Facebook post.

MISSING: SONJA HART

There's a recent picture and stats—forty-two years old, five feet four, 140 pounds. Last spoken to on Saturday, March 14. She is someone's mom. Moved back to Northeast Los Angeles recently. She's currently attending South Pasadena Community College. The picture posted does her no favors. Her brows will be considered too thin, her pixie-cut bleached hair with black roots criminal, the tank top reveals too much cleavage, and the tattoos scream trouble—she fits an old stereotype that says she is asking for something bad to happen, maybe that she runs with a rough crowd. She needs a better picture to make any headway with the general population and the police. She doesn't present well as a victim. She's good on paper, but not on socials. But even more disturbing are the comments under the post:

Fake News. This reads just like the last time everyone forwarded a missing woman.

It's just a scam. Delete.

Scam Alert.

I want to write back, *IT'S NOT A SCAM! PAY ATTENTION!! WOMEN ARE GOING MISSING!* But then there is the kicker of a comment:

> There's nothing in the news about this woman locally or otherwise. If she were really missing, then the news would be reporting on it. Please don't share—this is a scam.

The misinformed. The way I'd like to take the time to talk to every person that believes the news is covering every missing woman. The way I'd like to inform them that not every child abduction makes it to the Amber Alerts either. There's a type that makes good coverage, and then there's everybody else.

I scroll further down to another post made about a month ago. It's a video. I press play and watch as a semidifferent version of Sonja Hart is on a tiny makeshift stage, a single mic set up in front of her. It looks like a small space with windows behind her that look out to a small parking lot. It's not a theater, maybe a coffee shop, maybe a bar. I turn my volume up, peek up at Jacob, and give him a small smile and a tiny push on the swing and then watch as Sonja Hart recites what I think is poetry. I am transfixed by her voice: the increase in volume, the breath work, the speed at the parts that are difficult, but it's not a struggle—she's performing. She is good.

Her hair is longer in the video and more toned down, no black roots. She's in a boyfriend-baggy chambray button-down cinched with a belt in the middle. It looks like her pants are green in the video, maybe linen, flowy, and she's got on a pair of black Converse that pull the whole look together. She is beautiful. She commands the space she takes up on that little stage, and in Sonja, in her performance, her words speak about humanity. The lack of caring for the unhoused, the mentally ill, the aging in our communities, who are left to fend for themselves. She doesn't label us bad, instead overwhelmed, underserved, and desperate for human connection and compassion. Her performance is angry and tender at the same time. I see every woman that is taking a chance and doing something new, big, and hard. I touch my face and realize I'm crying. I watch Sonja's performance again. I watch the way her body moves when she ends a sentence. I listen to the crowd applauding, whistling, cheering when she finishes. It is earned, but I am listening for something else. I am listening for the voice of the person recording the performance—are they a part of the cheering crowd, or do they stay silent while recording? Who was there with Sonja last month, that night?

Was Chris there?

3

Me: I'm ready. Breakfast at the diner?

Chris: See you there.

I scroll further down Sonja's page for more. More videos, more posts, any birthday greetings sent by friends, but there isn't much of that. It's all reposts of fundraisers for local charity events. I glance back up at Jacob in his swing and know it's time to shut the laptop and give him my undivided attention. I want him to know he is my focus, my priority.

Chris and I haven't been working around the clock like I anticipated after we helped resolve the deaths of three women five months ago.

The cold case Detective Lopez hired me to investigate is more than two decades old. I've been relying on old newspaper articles, and they have all been slanted, each one more egregious than the last. Nobody cares about the victims, just the killer and whether or not they were serial in their behavior. Now we have someone current who needs us. Needs me. And her name is Sonja Hart.

I push Jacob and watch him light up while giving little shrieks at the thrill of the swing, and I think about my assignment, the unsolved double homicide of a mother and her toddler from twenty-five years ago. Only one article from the time has been made available online. My calls to other news sources to look through their paper archives have been met with repeated brush-offs. One crime reporter who was around at the time the homicides took place has theories, but you can't write a crime report on personal theory. And his fear of being misrepresented makes him refuse to share his suspicions. His article, posted a year after the homicides, is just a hodgepodge of information he took from interviewing beat cops and detectives that had been at the scene or assigned the case. The information is more contradictory in nature than helpful. It reads more like a story about what went wrong in the investigation but without the conviction to say the investigation was messy.

The victims, twenty-seven-year-old Renee Flores and her two-year-old son, Martin, had just arrived home. Her husband was still at work when her neighbor saw an unidentified male walk into the house with them. Later that evening Renee's husband returned home to police cruisers, fire trucks, and yellow tape. The killer had tried to burn the house down to cover up their crime. The first scent of smoke had the entire block calling the fire department, and when the fire was extinguished, Renee was found propped up on the couch, Martin in his mother's arms. They had been strangled. Dead before the fire had begun. The case, or maybe it's the Paxil, has left me numb. Unwilling some days to dive deeper like I normally would. Some days I feel stuck staring at the same page of text and never quite digesting the information.

In my therapy sessions with Dr. Rosenberg, he asserts that I'm identifying with the victims, a mother and son murdered, and I counter that I'm not. I complain that the Paxil is preventing me from investing deeply in the case. That I need to take a break from the medicine, that my panic is under control. At this point he removes his spectacles and pinches the bridge of his nose in a move that has become all too familiar, meaning—no dice, not yet.

The LAPD says, "No homicide investigated will ever be closed until it is resolved," and I want that too. I want that so I can tell Renee's parents they can rest now, we've caught the person and have delivered the justice they have relentlessly pursued all these years. Weekly calls for twenty-five years to the police department for any new information or leads. I know that's why I'm here now, so Lopez can say, *We've hired a private consultant, we're doing something more.*

I want to find this Sonja Hart whose son has reported her missing before she becomes an unsolved case that's too old to give justice. I need to work on this because it's time sensitive, and I know I can do it. I can find that place that gives me purpose.

4

I grab a teething biscuit for Jacob to suck on while we make our quick commute to the Cyclone Spin Studio. I always take the same route even though I know better than to do that—changing up your route is safety 101. I love the way Avenue 51 winds around the neighborhood north of York Boulevard. The mid-century revitalized homes with their Etsy-customized metal house numbers in Helvetica fonts, their designer hardscaped front yards, and plastic white picket fences that largely negate the style. It's hard to imagine any of the people in the homes spend time sitting in the front yards around the firepit in the colorful Adirondack chairs, but then again, maybe it's all staged for short-term renters. That is what's been happening for so long now. And the minute I begin to resent the homes north of York, I hit the top of the tiny mountain we've been climbing and see out across the city, and it stuns me. The beauty, the height, the expanse of it all. Like the bird's-eye view of Northeast LA on a postcard. The blended colors of the morning sky's oranges to blue meet the earth and the miniature-looking rooftops. Then we come down the mountain and land right in front of the studio.

Jacob and I arrive at Cyclone ten minutes before my seven a.m. class starts. I park underground in the garage, an upgrade since accepting the position of part-time assistant manager. Only managers have the privilege of parking in one of the three spots designated to the studio. Sometimes I wonder if the easy and gated parking is why I keep the job, but then I also wonder if it's the free workouts. Or, my inability to quit and have utter faith in my work as an independent investigator and part-time journalist. I'm afraid I'll be so reliant on Evan's financial support that I won't be able to leave him. Where would we go? I imagine Jacob and me sleeping in my car in this very garage, depending on the gates to protect us from the threats of the world. Or us wandering into a women's shelter, Jacob in my arms and my shoulders straining under a backpack with all I could carry of his—nothing of my own.

Another car horn beeps as their owner remotely locks it. The sudden sound in the echoey space snaps me out of the spiral, and I quickly exit the car before it can pull me back in.

I quietly slip inside the back entrance of the studio and behind the class in session to get to the front desk. I glance over at the unfamiliar voice leading the class. It's a newbie, teaching/auditioning, which means Monique will be at the desk. She looks and sounds like a recording of one of the online, live cycling instructors that have become so popular with at-home riders. It's made a not great dent in the Cyclone Studio's attendance. She probably memorized the routine and copied it to teach with. Everything she's doing is mechanical and rehearsed, more unnatural than the last one we tried out. I feel sorry for her. Monique will not hold back on her assessment.

I park Jacob in his stroller at the front desk next to me but don't see Monique. I take the opportunity and log in to the computer. I log in to my fake Facebook account and search for Sonja Hart. I'm looking for a connection to the missing woman that isn't Chris. I find Sonja's profile and click through her small list of friends—a task that I had bailed on earlier this morning . . . only 126 friends, and none of them is Chris.

I look at Jacob in his stroller and ask, "Jacob, how is your biscuit?" He slaps the tray of his stroller with glee. "Is it okay we're here at Mommy's work?" I ask. One day he'll be able to answer, and I'm not totally ready for what that answer will be. At the moment he's cherishing his biscuit.

I look back to the computer screen and start clicking on each person.

I get lucky on number eleven. Los Angeles is a big city, but a very small world, and Highland Park is basically a giant high school. There it is, a woman that has checked into classes at the Cyclone Spin Studio is, minimally, Facebook friends with Sonja Hart—Anne Silva. She hasn't left any comment on the missing-person post.

I log out of Facebook and into the Cyclone client portal to look up the woman that knows Sonja Hart. I scroll to Silva, Anne.

"Lieberman, you're early," Monique, short for Monica, says. She moves past Jacob's stroller and slips behind the desk where I'm reviewing client information on the computer.

"What are you doing, looking up client files?"

Monique will never not be on my case about my work. My life, my style, my baby. She's twenty-eight, dates hot women, and pulls off a grunge, rocker vibe better than I'm pulling off the mom vibe. She is also my boss, and I like her.

"Do you know Anne Silva?" I scroll through the previous week's schedule to see when Anne comes to the studio. She is clearly not a regular because I go back three weeks and can't find her signed in to a single class, but we make everyone fill out paperwork, thank god. I can't say I remember her name from ever being her instructor, and I remember everyone's name and face, always. Which tells me she's not a morning workout girlie either. She probably came once—to take advantage of our first-class-is-free offer.

"Lieberman, what are you doing?"

"Just checking when was the last time a client came to class."

"Stop."

"She may know something about a missing woman. I need to find where she lives."

"Lieberman! You can't look people up in the system for your reporter work. It violates a million privacy laws. I'm going to lock you out of the system." She presses the button, and the monitor goes black. "I should fire you."

"I'm done, sorry." I have enough information to find her.

"Why, what for, who . . . Corey, what do you need from Anne Silva?" Monique's voice is low enough the booming music mutes it from any clients' hearing as sweaty stragglers from the six a.m. class make their way out and fresh new riders file in.

"There's a missing woman," I say. There's as much emphasis in my voice as there is when I'm ordering coffee. If it's not a missing woman, it's a dead one. The inundation of information from all sources—social media, alerts, news, and true crime everything—has made dead and missing women as mundane as the weather report. The more I plug in, the more tolerance I find myself developing for the inhumane. The unconscionable. The downright violence—like a natural progression of every American western filmed. It's almost as if the world wants us to be numb to the value of life.

"Is she suspected of something? Should I ban her from the studio? I won't go through that again."

Six months ago, the studio lost its other owner, Monique's business partner, Kat. An accidental death—she was only twenty-six. Kat was hiking with another instructor from the Cyclone Studio. She was also sleeping with the instructor's estranged husband. An argument at the top of a cliff led to a shove, trip, and fall off the side. The problem that still plagues the community is that the woman never told anyone about Kat's fall. The entire community was looking for a missing Kat. Charges have yet to be filed by the DA for anything—involuntary manslaughter, obstruction, anything at all.

"No, no. Nothing like that, I don't think. Both live in the neighborhood, Facebook friends, and I saw that this Anne Silva checked into Cyclone on her page. I wanted to see if she's a current member of the studio." I look at the piece of paper I've written down too much of Anne's information on, hoping Monique can't read it upside down.

Monique rolls her eyes. "Go teach your class, Lieberman, before your baby learns to walk and leaves."

"Who's the new trainer? Do we like her?" I say as I place the latest mommy blogger–loved noise-canceling headphones over Jacob's ears.

They make him look more like a DJ than a baby at work with his mom, but it's a spin class at a boutique fitness facility, so he kind of fits the vibe.

Monique gives me a thumbs-down regarding the new instructor. I smile a little to myself as I roll the stroller with me toward the instructor's bike. I like that Monique likes me. Her not liking other people feels like it increases my value.

I notice my class is smaller than usual. A few empty bikes to my left and right. If I were concerned about losing this job, it would not be over customer retention. It would definitely be for spying on people. Classes fluctuate, and it happens in waves. When Kat died, we were empty for a month. Once her case was solved, we had more riders than bikes and couldn't accept walk-ins for weeks. I assumed the influx was in large part due to rubberneckers and overly curious influencers wanting to exploit a tragedy for follower bumps.

I change the music over to my own playlist and start the class with a slow, mellow beat. Something to ease our legs into the ride. I know Monique is sighing and rolling her eyes the minute she hears it, but not all classes are made for techno and electronic dance music. "Okay, everybody, we're here to move, so let's get on with it. Add a little resistance, and let's roll out those legs." I scan the faces of the women. All of them familiar. My regulars, none of them are named Anne, I know. I wonder if Chris also knows Anne. The hairs on my arm stand up. I should have known about Sonja first, not Chris, but I'm working on cold cases, and Lopez is on homicide—so, I guess it's a good thing. Maybe I can find her in time . . . alive.

"Let's take it up and out of the saddle," I say, and my speaking voice booms through the speakers. I look over at Jacob. He's already rotated the headphones so they're barely on his ears. I have to hop off the bike and adjust them while giving commands to the riders. "We're going to give that dial a quarter of a turn up, let's go in three, two, one, and climb."

5

As soon as the class ends, I bolt out the back door with barely a goodbye to Monique. I need to get to the diner and see Chris. Jacob is antsy from the forty-five minutes confined in his stroller. I spent most of the class off the bike teaching while holding the noise-canceling headphones on his ears. Much to Monique's chagrin. Sometimes I think I'm the only person Monique trusts, and that's why she keeps me around. Otherwise, she would be well within her rights to fire me for momming my son every class.

I strap Jacob in, throw my bag onto the passenger seat, and pull out of the parking garage. The minute I turn into the flow of traffic, Jacob shrieks, and my breasts fill. Fuck—my shirt. Ruined by an enormous wave of emotion stimulating all the milk that was supposed to be lessening, not still engorging.

"Buddy, are you okay?" I look at him in my rearview mirror. His cheeks are ruddy, his nose a little runny. "You look tired," I tell him, and he won't know what I mean by that for years to come yet. I hope he's not sick, and I hope I didn't miss any of the signs of sickness last night. I scan through my memories of yesterday, bedtime, and first breakfast, check, check, check, nothing out of the ordinary. He was with Evan alone for only a few hours. I should text him and ask. I don't want to. I'd rather just monitor the situation.

"Ten more minutes in the car, and then we'll be at the diner, okay?" I want him to answer me back sometimes. Just to let me know in a very verbal way exactly how he is doing. The guessing and wondering if this is an instance that will land us at Children's Hospital or just growing pains is gentle torture. It worries me to the point I feel the poke of my anxiety in the pit of my stomach. I sense my throat slightly constrict.

I pull into the parking lot of the diner. I park and look at my shirt. It's a lost cause. I check the diaper bag, nothing, no clean shirt for me or for Jacob, no nipple pads, nothing. I grab the muslin baby blanket I keep in the car and tie it around my neck like a scarf. A baby-elephant-patterned scarf that just covers the wet marks from my leaking breasts. I made a weak attempt to stop breastfeeding, but my body won't stop producing all the milk. They leak daily, and binding them only exacerbates my panic disorder. Constricting my breath isn't something I need help with. As it is, I'm buying sports bras twice my size just to make it through teaching spin.

"Well, you hungry?" I say to Jacob, sitting in his new four-in-one, front-facing car seat. He mumbles a string of distinct sounds—almost English, but still more baby words—back at me while waving a chewed-on, wet-from-drool book at me. Teething.

"Yeah, is that a good book? *ABCs with Tiger*? Looks yummy, dude, but I need you to empty these things quick for Mommy." I get into the back seat of the car and lock the doors. It's the vulnerable moments that I fear the most. I pull him from his seat. He smacks me in the face with the book and then his hand. "Listen, I thought we had some time before this conversation would be necessary, but you do not hit women. No, sir. Not nice. Not ever." I lift my T-shirt and unhinge my bra and gently push him on to my right nipple. He resists for a moment but relents quickly. The familiar a comfort to us both. I grab my phone and text.

Me: I'm running a little late. Be there in a bit.

My phone erupts with alarms:

NelaScanBoy on XX tweeted:

House fire in Progress HLP AVE 52

Oh shit, that's behind the Groceries for Less. That's the running path to Debs Park.

NelaScanBoy on X tweeted:

One person reported dead

Chris: Did you get my alert about the fire? I have to head over there—Can I see you after?

Chris, a.k.a. NelaScanBoy, and I meet at the diner for work—office hours, but it's been less and less frequent since I've been working on my cold case, and he's actively watching and reporting on all current events in the area. We both stay on top of the stories of victims that are plaguing our corner of Los Angeles—NELA—Northeast Los Angeles. Chris and I had been partners in television broadcast news for years, before I was fired. And after a few years off, working as a spin instructor and having a baby, I jumped back into investigating stories with him. In the years we've worked together, since we were in our twenties, it's like he hasn't aged at all—tall, tan skin, dark, wavy hair groomed to a medium length, a trace of gray now framing his face, beautiful teeth. His looks can and do satisfy multiple generations of women. We are partners—chasing stories, interviews, informants, police contacts—we do all the heavy lifting together. I also bring Jacob on this job with me. Jacob is full-time. Chris turned his NelaScanBoy status into *The Eastsider Times*, and we report the stories—all of them—even the ones that don't make the local or national headlines. Every dead body in Highland Park, in Northeast LA, has a story, and we tell it.

Me: I'll meet you there—in a bit.

I pull Jacob from one nipple, and he latches to the second one without assistance. Now he knows how to gingerly grab my soft breast with his two little hands and hold it in his mouth like a bottle. It doesn't hurt anymore either. The biting stopped, trained out of him. His favorite food now is noodles. All the noodles. I try mixing them with expensive baby pouches of mushed vegetables, but he isn't interested. It makes eating on the go difficult, except for breastfeeding. And the breastfeeding fixes my issues with leaks and his issues as a fussy eater.

I give Jacob six minutes to eat. I would have measured that as roughly two songs on the radio in the past if I was following, watching, waiting to catch someone I wanted to interview (catch/nab) by surprise. But the radio isn't on today, and I'm in the back seat nursing my baby, too far to reach the buttons, so I sit and listen to the gentle sounds of Jacob eating. It's soothing and meditative when it's just the two of us, and I can let the world around me fall away.

I pull him off, a little less than satisfied, but we, no—me, I can't do this forever. I head east from Los Feliz back to Highland Park. A dead woman in a blazing house waits. I wonder if it's Sonja Hart. God help me if it is. Two cases of women burning and too far apart in years to be related. I always wonder if one thing is connected to the other. More often than we like—it is. There are very few coincidences. Just like every issue I've had since Jacob's birth. *It's just a coincidence*, my doctor always says. I should find a new doctor, but the time it takes feels too big. And, calling to have my records transferred is letting them know I've fired them, and that feels bad too. And the more I think about it, the more I feel my throat tighten, and my breathing gets constricted, and the whole thing is too much, so I stop. Just thinking about the panic is making me anxious. I look in my bag for my pill bottle, the Klonopin, my emergency pill. I shake the bottle. The pills rattle inside. I take a deep breath. Sometimes, just knowing I have a few pills close by, I can calm down the attack before it locks me in its grasp. It's like a living, breathing thing of its own inside me. It wraps its hands around my rib cage and squeezes until my lungs don't work. I concentrate on relaxing. All my thoughts to this panic are *I am fine*. But the more I try to convince it that I'm fine, the harder it squeezes, and the less I feel like I can breathe. I wish the meditation I read about, listened to podcasts about, have tried, would work. I would meditate every morning. Maybe the meditation method would save my relationship with Evan, but it doesn't work. And neither does my marriage.

6

Figueroa Boulevard is a traffic nightmare with late-morning commuters, breakfast food trucks, and full bus stops. As I approach Avenue 52 I am stopped by a traffic cop and forced back into the congestion of Fig. I make an illegal U-turn and see the usual crime scene crowd: an audience of pedestrians as well as police, fire trucks, and news media. There will for sure be a thirty-second-on-the-scene spot with a lower-ranked field reporter, and then the story will be buried and forgotten. I'll have to dig for more information, but there will be none from the usual news channels. I'll be getting my information straight from Detective Lopez, my source at the LAPD Northeast Division. She is always on duty, doesn't slack or sleep, and treats everyone the same, like she's mothering teenagers—a role she plays when she is off duty. Lopez always wears her hair back in a tight, low ponytail. She wears makeup, but only enough to enhance all the natural gifts she was given: high cheekbones, round eyes with long lashes, and a hint of red on her lips. Lopez is a formidable detective.

I park in the Groceries for Less parking lot and pull Jacob into the ergo-friendly baby carrier. Velcro him in easily and walk around the block to watch the end of the fire being doused. The air is still thick with heat and the smell of campfire—though it is anything but a kumbaya moment. The homes are all holdovers—families generations deep keeping what they have and holding tight. No one selling. Perpendicular to Avenue 52 is a block with brand-new townhomes and condos. There are balloons and signs and garish flash everywhere, obscene for a neighborhood block, begging people to come look at the million-dollar-price-tagged units presented and built by neLA Living. A corporate entity that has taken homes on every block of Highland Park and turned them into multiplex developments. This is a place where greed crushes communities. And now a woman is dead. She may not be Sonja, but it's one more precious dream gone all the same.

The public schools are losing funding. Funding that goes toward sports programs, art programs, music, all because their enrollment numbers have dropped with evictions and unaffordable housing. The new families spending millions on the homes send their kids to charter schools, taking the public funding away from the public schools of the families that have invested in the neighborhood for generations. There are families who've lost their homes to these developers and are now living in RVs and tents in the area, just to be able to continue to send their children to school. All the sports and arts programs? They kept those kids feeling tethered to a community. There are local groups helping to support families with school supplies and backpacks and meals. Self-organized, community-led groups trying to raise funds through posts and outreach on the Highland Park Facebook group.

With deep, endless pockets, corporations like neLA Living can afford to look the other way when it comes to the displacement of the families who own the homes and the rise in the unhoused in the neighborhood. I am convinced they have a team that scouts the neighborhood for homes in violation of LA housing codes. Homes where the families have been in residence so long and take their time rebuilding and fixing their properties when they're not working seven days a week, and neLA reports their findings. When a homeowner cannot make repairs or pay the fine, they must sell. That's when neLA Living swoops in with a cash offer. It's dirty and not illegal, but certainly immoral. I hate them and cannot wait until they mess with the wrong homeowner.

I look for Chris in the crowd. Spot the back of him, undeniable in any large group, inside the police line. He's talking to a cop I don't recognize. I push my way through. "Excuse me. I need to get through with my baby, excuse me." The crowd parts for me and Jacob, like it usually does when they see a woman with a baby walk into a crime scene. Part shock, part manners—trying to figure it out would break my brain. I am close enough to smell the chemicals melted from the fire now—similar to hot tar being laid on the street. It is noxious. I should mask Jacob—or leave.

"Corey!" Chris runs over. I notice he has a bandanna tied around his face as a makeshift mask. "You need to take Jacob out of here. It's not safe for him or—" He doesn't finish. He knows better than to tell me what is safe or not for me. "I'll swing by your place after and download you."

I don't want to know the information secondhand. I want to stay, but I look at Jacob, eyes watering from the environment, and agree. "Okay, get names. Ages. What was in the house? Was it a rental? Get all the information—"

"Mama—Mama." Jacob is beating his fists against my chest and sobbing. Interrupting my thoughts. I put my arms around the baby carrier and cradle and squeeze him to me in a bear hug. I pull the baby blanket from around my neck and loosely drape it over his face like I do when he's asleep.

"Corey." Chris pulls the bandanna down from his nose and mouth. He looks at me with concern stretching across the soft lines of his face. He starts to untie the bandanna. He's going to try to put it over my mouth and nose.

"I'm going," I say, before he finishes untying the knot on the bandanna. He nods and waits to watch me until I leave. I feel his eyes on my back—conscious of my walk, I hurry. Each step awkward—a body I should be used to, fifteen months after giving birth, but I'm not, not by a long shot. I'm not used to the hips, or the large breasts, or my gait when I carry a constantly growing baby—not quite old enough or just too lazy to assist with his weight while being held.

I turn the corner back to the Groceries for Less parking lot—two feet from my car when a man approaches—dirty. He looks like he's come from the ashes of the fire. Dirt crusts under his too-long nails. Filth deepens and darkens the furrow of his brow. He could be thirty or fifty. He could be homeless or a day laborer or both. He could have been in the fire.

"Got any change?" he asks.

"I'm sorry, I don't—I have a bottle of water in the car. Would that help?" After I offer it I am suddenly aware that this man I don't know is following me, with my baby, to my car. He will know what I drive. Have my license plate number. He could hit me in the head and shove me in the back when the tailgate is up. He could steal Jacob and never return. What would that Amber Alert look like:

> Missing fifteen-month-old boy. Silver Subaru license plate number 6CJT167. Person unknown.

It's too late. The man nods and begins to follow me. Is Chris still watching? I glance back over my shoulder but am met with the gaze of the man in need of water. I cannot see past him to where Chris was standing moments ago. Water, that's what we are going to my car to get. I adjust Jacob, who is much calmer than he was a minute ago, as much as I can in the baby carrier so that he is away from the stranger that walks just behind my left shoulder. I keep my body tense in case I need to strike with my free hand. I pop the tailgate and pull out a liter bottle from the tray I keep in the car. Next to the tray is a box of baby smoothie pouches that Jacob refuses. I pull out two pouches and hand them to the man. And while he's distracted, pocketing the items, I palm the black MAGLITE that's next to my emergency earthquake bag. It's heavy and feels strong in my hand. I have Evan to thank for this preparedness. I turn toward the man, the MAGLITE hanging by my side.

"Thanks." The man is closer now. His clothes look dirty from work, not homelessness. Age still indistinguishable in the beating sunlight, but if I had to put something down on a police report, I'd say forty to fifty-five.

"Did you happen to see the fire?" I ask. "When it started or while it was burning?"

"No—I was sleeping. Over there." He points to an RV set up in the corner of the store's parking lot.

"I'm not a cop," I say. "I live just around the block. I'm just curious, that's all. I have no interest in trouble."

"I was sleeping when it started. Heard screaming and sirens, so I came out. Saw the flames shooting up—thought someone let off a firework, and it landed on a roof or something."

It makes sense. The fireworks are always going off at all hours all the time—or so it seems. It's some sort of pastime that never goes out of style. The message boards on Facebook are filled with animal lovers begging all the "assholes" in town to stop. The "assholes" write back *Shut the hell up, Gentrifier*. The war between the gentrifiers and the Indigenous People of Highland Park is like a heartbeat—up and down, up and down. Half the time it's the locals complaining about the noise and their dogs, and then the comment threads really heat up—sympathizers, traitors. It is endless. As long as historical murals and buildings and homes are bulldozed, painted over, and claimed by corporate, capitalist greed, there will be no unification.

"Yeah, maybe. It's pretty bad over there. Looks like the whole place is a loss," I say.

"You know, it's one of those old-school triplexes."

"So, you got close enough to see?" I've caught him. Of course he went to look. It's our human fucking nature.

Right then Jacob's diaper fills. I hear the bubbles—I knew it was coming, I'd just fed him. He looks at me with relief etched across his face and smiles. "Mama."

"I looked from the corner. My cousin used to live in that back house twenty years ago. I think some of them flippers bought it a few years back. Fixed it up nice. Don't know who lives in 'em now."

"Thank you," I say. "I need to get this guy home and changed. Mind if I check in on you this week? Maybe if you hear anything else you can let me know?"

He nods. "Can't say I'll still be here. Not allowed to stay all night—they tow."

"Right, of course. Well, um, I'm Corey, Corey Tracey-Lieberman," I say. He looks at Jacob, and I feel pressure to introduce him. I binge TikToks and Instagram stories that say we can keep our child's autonomy by not introducing them to strangers and not forcing them to hug grandparents. So instead, I ask him, "What's your name?" I hope I don't offend him or show my card—the one that says I don't trust him.

"Dave. You got a card? I got a phone. I can call you."

I rip a piece of cardboard off the water bottle tray. I have a pen in the front console. I walk over to the driver's side door and lean in, squishing Jacob between me and the steering wheel. I scribble down my number and name and hand it over.

"Thank you. Thank you so much," I say.

Dave walks toward the crowd gathered near the fire where Chris is watching me, us. I nod at Chris, then get Jacob strapped into his car seat. I throw the MAGLITE into the back and push down the tailgate. I hop in the driver's seat, and Jacob and I drive off in the direction of home. There is one missing woman, one dead woman from a fire, and it is only Monday. It's going to be a long week.

7

I pull up to a cacophony of noise at the house. A loud scrape of plastic on cement screams at Jacob and me. Across the street a car too low for the steep driveway just lost all the paint off the bottom side of their bumper.

Evan is parked in our driveway and waves at me. I check the clock. It is technically still lunchtime, albeit late lunch. I guess we're having lunches during the workweek now too. He gets out of the car and walks over to Jacob and me, smiling. He looks genuinely excited.

"Looks like maybe we have new neighbors moving in," he says. "Should we go say hi?"

Before I can tell him *no*, that he needs to go because I have work to do, and it's Jacob's nap time, and for the love of god he lives in a rental a few blocks away, so we can figure ourselves out, and his unpredictable visits are setting us back, and that impromptu kiss this morning was over the line, and—the new neighbors spot us. We are standing in the most visible spot—the sidewalk. Dammit.

"Hello!" The man across the street shouts before he kneels to check the damage he's done to his bumper.

"Hi! Moving in?" Evan belts back across the street. His excitement growing at the prospect of a new friend.

Before I know it's happening, I'm walking with Evan across the street, Jacob in my arms, to meet them.

"Hi, I'm Ben, and this is my wife, Julia," the man says. His arm extends before he even reaches us. Ben is tall, thin, white. He looks the age every white couple spending a million-plus dollars on these small 849-square-foot homes looks—thirtyish to fortyish. Julia, the wife, walks an inch behind him and stands just as tall, and just as white, and just as thirtyish to fortyish. I wonder if it's generational wealth or tech-bro money funding them.

"Welcome to the street, I'm Evan and this is—"

"Corey." I take the pause to say it myself. "Jacob, these are our new neighbors, Ben and Julia," I say.

"Hi, Jacob, it is so nice to meet you," Julia says. She walks over and squats down close to Jacob's face. "You are so handsome," she says. Her voice goes up an octave as she talks to him. She sounds like a cartoon princess, and I detect the faint aroma of day-old whiskey on her breath, or perhaps from her pores.

"Thank you," I say for Jacob. "Where are you moving from?" I know it's abrupt, but let's get to it. I want to know who they are, why they moved here, and if it wasn't easily internet searchable, I would ask how much they paid for the house.

"Brooklyn," Julia says. She tucks a strand of dark-blonde hair behind her ear. A move that looks so natural she must have rehearsed it a thousand times before. "We couldn't take the winters anymore, so we decided to move west."

It's such a trite comment, but I am compelled to smile.

"She's only teasing," Ben says when there's no laughter. "I'm a commercial director. Decided it was time to make the leap to film." It comes out almost like a LinkedIn announcement. Like, if we had a job opportunity, he'd fill it or, minimally, be interested. "Julia's an actress."

My face is flat, expressionless. I can feel it in all its dullness. I am unimpressed. It is Los Angeles, but I also know that the Paxil has left me numb, and I need to make an effort to pretend to emote like a normal, functioning human being. Not a muted mother with postpartum panic disorder. So I smile. I know it must look forced, but they don't know me at all, so maybe I'm passing it off as normal. "That's cool. Maybe I've heard of your work. What was your last name?" I try my hardest to sound in awe of a *big-time* actress and director moving in across the street, but my god, I'm not. I want their name only so I can do my due diligence on who exactly is moving in across the street from me and my child.

"I doubt it. Julia's a Broadway actress, not film or television—"

"I've booked a few costars in the past—" Julia starts.

"Guest stars, babe, you booked *guest stars*." Ben rubs Julia's lower back and continues at Evan and me. "She had to turn down several series regular parts because she was locked into long Broadway runs." He looks at Julia before saying, "Now you're going to be the Hollywood star the world has been waiting for." Ben kisses Julia on the temple and pulls her into him by the waist. I cannot tell if it's sincere. Is this the way they communicate regularly, or is there more happening? Maybe Julia was happy being a Broadway star. She doesn't look particularly excited about starting over in Hollywood now—or maybe that's just the way her face looks all the time.

"I'm so sorry. I missed the last name again?" I say, watching Julia stare off at the mountains to the east.

"Sorry, I got so excited—I do that. Ben and Julia Palmer," Ben says.

Evan's phone and mine abruptly start screaming at us. The sound is evocative of the tornado sirens of my youth in Michigan. Only, this is an Amber Alert, not a tornado warning. The message on my home screen says:

> Downey, CA AMBER Alert: LIC/7XXX777 (CA) 2012
> Red Toyota Prius

My heart lurches. I look down at Jacob and then up to the house. I assess all the points of entry to ensure I didn't leave a single window open before leaving today. I could never live without my baby.

"Those alerts are terrifying. I shut them off in my notifications," Ben says, drawing my attention back to the group. To him.

"I have a baby." I look to Jacob, again. "I like to think everyone gets the alerts and pays attention to them," I say. It is so flat and unapologetic. I can feel Evan staring at me, see him in my peripheral vision. I'm not sure whether it's pity or pain. I force a smile. I feel it come off as smug, but it looks like everyone else is buying it as sincere.

"How old is your baby?" Julia says, cutting through the tension I created or imagine.

"Just over a year," Evan says.

"Fifteen months," I say.

"He is the best thing in the world," Evan says with so much force I think he's trying to convince *me* of the sentiment. He rubs the top of Jacob's head and asks the Palmers, "Do you have kids?"

"Not yet," Ben says.

My phone alert goes off again. The Amber Alert has been canceled. "The child has been found, thank god," I say. I announce it as I stare at my phone, so it's directed at no one.

"Good news," Ben says.

Jacob is ready to play and be active. His patience with me is learned and not natural. I do worry his aloofness, his laid-back chill might be my medicine and not his natural personality, even though I'm assured it's not. But I sure as hell am sluggish all the time on the Paxil. I think about coming off it now that the daily, hourly panic attacks have mostly abated. The low levels of anxiety are still present, but the intrusive thoughts are gone. And I test those regularly. I intentionally think about knives, ropes, plastic bags. Nothing happens. There's no thought that latches on and plays out like a horror story in my head. I am relieved. Relieved my brain doesn't recycle the same shitty thought over and over and over again. Like a front-load washer, and all I can do is just watch the clothes on rinse.

"I think our guy is in need of a diaper change," Evan says. Of course he would notice. He probably smelled it while I was walking up the block. It's a perfect excuse for me to leave.

"A diaper change and a nap," I say to the group.

"Mama," he says.

"That's right, baby, Mama. Yes, Mama." I am transfixed when he says it. How does he know who I am so easily? My heart leaps into my throat, but no tears come. That's also the Paxil. It snuffs out the emotions before they can release. I feel them deep down and know I should let them out, but they never quite make it to the surface. Sometimes it's uncomfortable, but I like it better than the bad thoughts, the obsessive-compulsive thoughts that were dominating my life only a few months ago.

"Nice meeting you both," I say to Ben and Julia before I head for the house. Before I can get up the driveway, Evan is next to me.

"Aren't you going to say goodbye? I'm taking my lunch hour to see you and Jacob," Evan says.

"You should have texted first or called. I'm working. You can't just show up in the middle of the day—it's, it's presumptuous." It sounds harsh, but I want it to sound firm, like a boundary he's crossed, not a law that's been broken.

"Is that what you need? A heads-up every time I want to see my kid and pop over to *our house*?"

"Yes, Evan. I need that. This is the second time in the same day, and it's only Monday—you had him yesterday! We are living separately, and unannounced visits aren't part of the rules."

"Oh, so now there are rules. Now I know, and I will make sure to have mine ready for you before I take Jacob next time."

"Please don't make this a fight," I say. "You caught me off guard, and you know I'm struggling with this cold case I've been on for months. I just need time to work, and when you disrupt the flow of my day with unannounced visits, I—it's hard for me to get back on track."

"Yeah, that's life, Corey. I'm sorry, but you don't get to tell me when I can and cannot see my son. It's killing me not to be here all the time. We bought this home together. Jacob is ours, and this, this thing we're doing because the family therapist said to, isn't a divorce. You cannot dictate the rules." Evan looks pleased with his argument. If I give in now, maybe he'll just go away.

"You're right, I'm sorry. I just want to get Jacob down for his nap, and he's had a full diaper since before I pulled up to the house. You're welcome to come in and change him"—I lift Jacob's rear up to Evan's nose—"or you can let me handle this one, and you can come back to see him later." I give Evan an apologetic smile even though it's a mask. I'm not sorry for anything.

"Thank you," he says. "I will let you take care of business, and I'll see you both later." He bends down and kisses Jacob on the head and then leans in to kiss my cheek. I accept the gesture instead of pulling away abruptly—I'm too damn tired to fight, thank you, Paxil.

I sit on the porch with my laptop and watch the moving truck that must have arrived when I was putting Jacob down. From every angle of my porch and yard I can see Ben and Julia's house.

The house Ben and Julia are moving into has always looked small from the outside. The front yard is all cement and painted green. The color green a child would use to color grass or trees in art class. There isn't much of a porch, just two steps up into the front door. It shares a driveway with the house on its left, but there are two distinct, separate garages—one is in need of paint and maybe a new foundation, as it looks close to collapsing. And then there is Ben and Julia's garage. Its fresh coat of paint, new roof, windows, and glass French doors give it the appearance of an additional living unit on the property. On the other side of Ben and Julia's house, to their right, or to the left if I'm looking at them from my porch, is Pete's house. Pete is like a cockroach. He's got a criminal past, and he makes you jump when you see him. We all, the entire neighborhood, work hard to get along with him. Ben and Julia have no idea what's in store for them with Pete next door. He could take a shine to them and offer them the largest avocados from his ancient tree. Or he could dislike them and passive aggressively block all the parking in front of their house with a parade of cars he mysteriously comes home with.

"Hey, neighbor."

I flinch before Elsie, my immediate neighbor, makes it to my side. "You nearly gave me a heart attack," I say.

"Engrossed in the newbies?" she asks. "I've spent the last hour watching them try to get that couch in the house with the movers. And now that it's in—oof. They've barely smiled at each other. Probably realizing the house wasn't worth their life savings plus inheritance, if they can't even fit a couch in it."

"I've watched him try to hug her three times, but she keeps brushing him off—like he's prickly. Something's not going well for them, and I don't think it's the house. I barely smile at Evan anymore, and I promise you it's not our little home," I say. Even when we were living together, I couldn't fake a smile regularly. A persistent anxiousness consumed me when his car arrived after work, and I stayed anxious until he left in the mornings. On repeat every day until this month. It's my fault. I chose this life with him. And I barely smile now when he arrives and leaves because he's usually there to take my baby for the day, and my stomach, heart, breasts cannot handle it. Elsie rubs my back. It's comforting, and it feels good. Touch feels good. I've been snappish for so long—since I was pregnant with Jacob if I'm honest. But this, this gentle, safe small rub on my back is mothering, and I want to curl up into it. Like a cat, I want to curl up small like a cat and be stroked on the back just like this. Just like this but with someone else. Someone else named Chris. The more I try to not think about him, the more I do. I think about our kiss a few months ago. How I wish it would happen again. Also, about how guilty I feel because that kiss happened when Evan and I weren't separated yet. And though this separation of ours is called a trial, I have no intention of moving back in together in the foreseeable future.

Chris and I both called the kiss a mistake, I think. I can't remember entirely because of the Klonopin I was taking at the time, and the Paxil in my system now makes me foggy, but I do remember, at least, that Chris said it was a mistake. I also remember the absolute want I felt when our lips touched. I wanted to wrap my arms and legs around him and not let go. I wanted to devour his face that night. I also remember the taste of peppermint on his tongue. It was subtle and sweet, like he'd taken a striped peppermint candy from the diner and eaten it just before seeing me. Not like a fresh piece of gum that's spicy and too strong.

I remember he smelled like clean clothes and soap, no cologne or fruit-scented hair gels. It was such a calming scent. I could have stayed in that kiss for hours, but it was only a few seconds. And I'm married. And it was on my front porch. And it was a *mistake.*

I hear Jacob yell on the baby monitor. "Wait here and watch them while I go get Jacob. Watch how he approaches her, and she shrugs him off. I'll be right back." Elsie nods and takes a seat. When I get to the front door, I look down at the house and the movers once more. Before I look away, Julia is at the window, waving hello to me. She can see me, on my porch from her living room window. My private porch where no one should be able to see me. I wave back. I've been caught staring.

Jacob yells for Elsie's attention when we get back outside, and she lifts him from my arms.

"Hola, guapo. Qué pasa?" Elsie smiles huge, right in Jacob's face, and he giggles with so much gusto it's contagious. "Tu es mucho guapo. Qué pasa, bebé? Qué pasa?"

He can't control himself now. The giggles are sure to lead to hiccups, but I don't stop the joy. I let Jacob enjoy his moment with Elsie while I grow anxious about the hiccups that will make nap time a nightmare. I start to allow the anxiety to spiral a bit. The hiccups could lead to him choking on his dinner. I check my phone to ensure I still have the correct first aid choking video for fifteen-month-old babies downloaded and at the ready. I know I can just nurse him later. Would that still be enough food? I know he has to be on solids now, even if they are a choking hazard. But missing one meal of solids for breast milk would not be the end of the world. Though, I am trying to reduce the amount of milk I produce so I'm not even sure at this point if I could feed him until he's full since he just drained them a bit ago. Is there enough left for a meal or just comfort? I just don't know anymore because I don't pump at all now. I still have a few bottles in the freezer left from a few months ago. Will I end up needing to call Evan for assistance? And what if I do because I can't get the choking hazard out of his throat? Will it be too late by the time Evan shows up? What if I have a panic attack, which I haven't had in five whole glorious months, but what if this is the moment I have one, and it does kill me? Who will Jacob become if his mother dies? This spiral is happening fast.

"They're going to have a baby," Elsie says, interrupting my thoughts.

"Who?" I say.

"The new neighbors."

"They told you that?" I ask.

"No, I went to say hello earlier, but they didn't answer the door, so I took a peek inside while the movers were in the truck. Saw the baby furniture."

"Elsie, that's—"

"Shh, it's neighborly. I dropped off a coffee cake with a note."

"She's definitely not pregnant yet," I say.

"How do you know?"

"Her breath smelled like whiskey from what can only be late-night drinking or possibly morning drinks, but I suspect the former from the bloodshot eyes and day-old mascara smudged underneath them."

"Oh dear." Elsie shakes her head. "Nothing we can say or do about that . . . can we?" I shrug in response. "What we can do something about is this young man. He needs food, and you should go in and eat something too. You look thin."

I laugh so hard I forget to say thank you, not that I would. Thin, yeah, right.

"Hey, did you hear about the fire today behind the Groceries for Less?" I ask.

"Yeah, I'm not surprised. I remember there being fires all the time back in the day, but I'm sure that was only what it felt like. Houses going up in flames, but just the abandoned ones usually. Sad."

"Right, yeah." Are house fires a thing again, and how did that not register on my radar? "Do you remember the murder of a woman named Renee Flores and her son? It was over twenty years ago."

"I barely remember my prom. Why?" Elsie asks.

"It's this cold case I'm working on right now. She and her son were murdered, and their house was lit on fire. The police believe the fire was to cover up the murders."

"I'm not sure I'm ready to talk about the death of another woman yet," Elsie says. Her eyes give me an apologetic sorry.

I lay my hand over hers. "That's totally fair and reasonable. I'm sorry I asked, I should have been more thoughtful." After all, Elsie's daughter had two close friends die just six months prior. They were murdered at just seventeen years old.

She hands Jacob back over to me. "I need to go clean up and make sure no one in my house is burning anything down. Please don't go over to look at that burned-down squatter's place. I mean it, Corey. Let the police come tell you what they have."

"I won't. Promise," I say. "Wait, how do you know it was a squatter's place?"

"I don't—I'm just assuming, promise. I have no information."

Elsie gives me a wink and heads to her house. I watch her slip behind her privacy gate and only when I hear her screen door bounce on its hinges do I head into my quiet home with Jacob. The home that is just mine and Jacob's. Well, not technically, but we are alone in it for now.

Chris: Are you home?

Me: . . .

It isn't a hard question, but I don't know what to write. Do I say *Yes, come over*? I can't leave because Jacob needs food and a nap. And, can I have Chris come over? What if Evan happens to pop in? What will he say? He knows we work together, but we don't work here. At the house I share with Evan. But, Chris is my partner not my boyfriend, and I haven't even told Evan about the kiss from six months ago. There's a missing woman, a dead woman from a fire, and a double homicide that's twenty-five years old, and the pressure to give something to Lopez on the case is building.

Me: Yes.

Chris: I'm around the corner. Good time to stop by?

Shit.
Yes.

Me: Of course. I'm about to feed Jacob. Now is fine.

"Jacob, I am going to heat you up some noodles, and it's going to be so good. I also have to work a little. And then we can go for a walk." Jacob claps his hands and smiles as I set him into his highchair. I'm glad I have a giant bowl of macaroni noodles ready to be nuked in the microwave for ten seconds. I also pull out a mixed-berry-with-spinach smoothie pack, hoping he may suck it down. Before I can uncap it, Chris is already at the door. He must have literally been right around the block to already be here. I pass Jacob the smoothie.

"Be right back," I tell him.

"Hi." I answer the door and let Chris in. It's weird to have him here at the house and not at the diner.

"Hey, smells good. What are you cooking?" Chris says.

"I'm heating up plain noodles in the microwave for Jacob, but I'm sure he'd be happy to share."

Chris laughs at the joke, but in all honesty, I would heat him up plain noodles if he wanted them. I'm an absolute puddle without focus. It's been happening so much lately I have to believe it's the Paxil. I need to call Dr. Rosenberg and schedule an appointment. I can't be unfocused like this. I'd slap myself if I didn't have an audience right now.

"I'm good, but if you had coffee, I'd definitely take a cup," he says.

"Yes, of course. This way." I lead Chris into the kitchen where Jacob has been waiting for his noodles. The mixed-berry-and-spinach smoothie is smeared around his highchair tray and down the front of his bibless shirt. "You didn't like that flavor either?" I ask Jacob.

"No," Jacob says. *No* is his favorite word and the third one he learned.

"Okay, noodles coming up." I take the bowl of noodles out of the microwave and watch Chris sit down in front of Jacob. I blow on the noodles and watch as Chris takes his finger and swipes up some of the splattered smoothie from the highchair tray and eats it.

"Oh, yum. Jacob, this is delicious," he says.

Jacob starts to laugh. Chris swipes up more smoothie and eats it with his finger.

"It's so good. Are you sure you don't like it?" he asks Jacob.

"No," Jacob says.

"Okay if I eat it then?"

"No," Jacob says and laughs.

Chris takes another swipe and licks it from his finger. Then Jacob starts to mimic him. In no time at all, Jacob is sucking on the smoothie pack as I stand aside, holding a bowl of plain, boring noodles.

Jacob finishes, and I hold him in my lap so Chris and I can work. The minute I start gently bouncing him in my arms, he yawns like another nap is coming. I look at my watch. It's only been an hour or so, but it wouldn't be the first time a second nap came on quick.

"Give me a minute to take him upstairs. I'll make us some coffee when I get back."

"No rush," Chris says.

By the time I lay Jacob on his back in his crib, he's out. I partially close his blackout curtains, letting a sliver of sunlight in—I don't want him to sleep all afternoon, or he'll never go to bed. I turn on the baby monitor that connects to my phone, and I pause. Is Evan using the same app right now? Can he hear me or *see* me? I slip out of the room and debate closing the door for privacy from my could-be eavesdropper but can't bring myself to do it, so I leave Jacob's door ajar as I exit and head downstairs.

On my way down, I smell coffee. I know I didn't start it before I went upstairs. I can remember that much even if I'm foggy brained. I walk into the kitchen, and Chris is sitting at the table with two steaming mugs.

"Thank you," I say. "I'm sorry, I should have made it before I put him down. I'm so sorry. That was—"

"No, no, I thought I'd get a head start. Make you a cup. You're great, Corey."

I hope I'm not blushing. I'm probably not. That's another bonus of the Paxil—because strong displays of emotions are muted, my blushing has been under control. However, my impulse control is not—I have to watch everything I'm eating carefully, or I'm likely to just stand in front of the cupboard and eat the whole inventory.

"Thank you," I say and sit across from him. I look at my coffee. He's already poured the half-and-half, and I know when I take a sip I will taste about a teaspoon of sugar. I smile to myself. "Okay, let's talk about the arson, the body, and the missing woman."

8

"We have to wait on the fire. It could have been an electrical issue. The house did have a squatter." I knew Elsie was holding back something.

Chris continues. "She was an older woman, been living there for the past year. Not paying rent, no utilities in her name. She may have tried to turn the gas oven on and light a match to start it since the fire does appear to have started in the kitchen."

"Did you get all this from your cousin?" I ask.

"No—the fire investigators were there. My cousin was able to get me a few minutes with them. They cleared everyone out when the arson team arrived, so he's going to get back to me with any new developments."

"This woman, do they know who she is?"

"Not yet, just what the neighbors know about her. It seems like she may have been a recluse, at least that's what the neighbors' opinions are. She took up residence when the last tenants abandoned the place. The house was empty except for the front room and kitchen. Front room had a mattress, lots of blankets, and boxes of miscellaneous junk—books, mail for the previous tenants, newspapers."

"I thought it was a triplex?" I say.

"There was a back unit, a converted garage—could have, at some point, been a split-level main house. A tenant on top and one on bottom. Doesn't matter, no one's been in the back unit in years either, according to the neighbors. Last known owner currently resides in

Florida. Interestingly, the house isn't even on the market to sell or rent. The woman that was squatting, she could have probably lived there the rest of her life without anyone bothering her."

"She did live there the rest of her life. She died in that house," I say.

Chris looks grim. The situation *is* grim.

"I have a question, where are people acquiring these RVs they're living in around the city?" I ask. I can't imagine spending money on one of the run-down RVs, especially if I can't afford housing. But, would I squat in a house over acquiring an RV?

"Auctions, organizations working to assist with the housing crisis, vanlords," Chris says.

"Vanlords?"

"Yep, there are landlords that cheaply buy up the RVs at auctions and then rent them out to the unhoused folks around LA," Chris says.

"Wait, how? Do they charge people to rent the RVs?" I cannot wrap my head around the fact that anyone would pay a monthly fee to be in constant movement around the city, no hookups for the utilities, and that includes bathrooms. Plus, the RVs were sold at auctions. The history of the vehicle could be anything, including death traps.

"They do. I've heard anywhere from four hundred bucks a month upward to eight hundred."

"I'm sorry, what? How? There's no permanent address—how do they collect rent? What means do these folks have to pay that? They're not even legally allowed to be in one place for more than twenty-four hours, and the rules are constantly changing. That's outrageous."

"Yeah, but if you have kids, at least they have a roof over their head, and they can stay in school. And they must be registered to one school in one district. That makes it easy for a landlord to find you, and you'll pay."

I feel fucking sick to my stomach. I want to cry and realize how fucking shitty I am for not even knowing what the situation with the RVs is, except that at last count there were over a thousand housing people who were displaced around the city. The devastation sinks deeper into my emotions than I want it to.

Chris looks at my mug of coffee that I haven't tried yet. "Is there enough sugar?" he asks.

I lift the mug to my lips to sip. It's perfect. Creamy and sweet but still tastes like coffee. "Thank you. How do you remember how I drink my coffee?"

"I remember a lot of things, Corey Tracey. It's my job." He says my name, and it sounds like poetry the way it comes out of his mouth. I notice he doesn't add the Lieberman, and I cannot tell if it's on purpose or just forgetful. I cannot recall a time when he's ever used my hyphenate, Lieberman, to be honest.

"Well, thank you, Mr. Villar, I do so appreciate your attention to and memory for detail." Chris smirks, and there's a single beat of staring at each other in silence that feels purposeful. I break the contact and take another sip of the coffee. It is absolutely perfect. I linger in this personal moment before pivoting back to work. "Okay, so where are we with Sonja Hart?"

"I did get her address here in Highland Park. She has a son. He lives in Oregon, and he's the one that reported his mom missing. I've been chatting with him on the phone, getting as much information as possible. He gave me her address. It's just down the street. Those original art deco apartments on Avenue 50 across the train tracks. That's why I came straight here. I thought we could go over there together."

"Absolutely—I just have to wait until Jacob's nap is over."

"I know. He's full-time." Chris repeats the words to me I'd used on him months ago.

I pause for a moment before I ask, "How did you know Sonja?"

"We volunteered together a few times. I didn't know her well, but she was always at community events raising funds for homeless students, feeding the community, at meetings about the whitewashing of the community murals." He shakes his head and looks at his coffee.

"She was a nice person. All I really knew was that she had roots here and came back to build a new life for herself."

"Did you know about her poetry performances?" I ask.

"No, we weren't close like that. I only knew she had a kid in college or college age."

I pull up the video on my phone and hand it to Chris to watch while I get up to pour myself another cup of coffee. When Jacob is in college, will I feel lonely?

My mother said I would feel lonely waking up in a king-size bed alone. She said living by myself with a baby is not a safe place for a woman of my age. The best years behind me and all. She said that Evan and I had been together long enough that it would feel strange not to be together—but I am never alone.

Jacob has never not come to work with me. It's a thing that wears on my marriage with Evan. In the end, he can't deny the huge savings in childcare costs. Babysitters range from twenty-five to fifty dollars an hour. And child day cares require too much of a commitment. You aren't allowed to drop off for an hour and then pick up. Jacob is required to stay for the half day or full day—with week-in-advance notice. No week-of changes to schedules. Plus, you have to pay the monthly tuition regardless of how many days or hours a week you need. And those costs are equal to what we pay on our mortgage monthly.

Evan can't bring him to his job—it's a large corporate office, very last century. And my mom and dad told us to view them as "holiday parents," meaning they would see us on holidays—if we travel to Michigan . . . and plan to stay at a rental house or hotel. There would be no visits to California. Too difficult for them to find a pet sitter. At fifteen months old Jacob has still not met his maternal grandparents. My mom argues that's not true, because they've chatted face-to-face on the phone.

Evan's parents firmly believe in nannies and au pairs, and if you cannot afford these things, then you're doing something wrong. And if you can afford them and choose not to use them, then your priorities are wrong. They're usually traveling, mostly to Europe, for long extended stays, so even a last-minute emergency isn't really an option.

The lack of parental presence in our lives really did bond Evan and me in the beginning. I had so much trouble dating men whose parents wanted to meet me, invite me over, have dinner. It was something I would never be able to offer in return and not something I wanted dissected by a partner: *Why are your parents so distant?* Evan didn't care. He had his own set of boundaries with his mom and dad. His parents are local, and I didn't meet them until we were engaged.

I've won my case with Evan. Jacob comes to work with me and has been since he was three months old.

I shouldn't have told my mother what was going on, but the Paxil, it just numbs my inhibitions. The anxiety that causes the panic that keeps me from speaking is mostly muted—it's awesome and horrible at the same time.

But what I can confidently say and have told my mother multiple times is *I do not feel lonely.* Instead I feel like me. For the first time in over a year, I feel more in control and confident and free of judgment. Did Sonja feel this way when she was reading her poetry?

I hear a car pull into the driveway, and my eyes dart to the clock on the microwave. Four thirty p.m. Too early for another surprise visit from Evan after work. Nonetheless, I jump up from my seat and run to the window. It's the fastest I've moved since before I was pregnant. Fear that Evan has just shown up without texting, calling, or planning it with me first pumps adrenaline through me. I'm terrified. Terrified of being caught with Chris in the house. Terrified of a fight that I don't think I can win while taking Paxil—too slow. Terrified of him grabbing Jacob from his crib and just leaving with him.

Chris follows me, and I gently push him away. In case Evan is close enough to see in the window.

"Corey, is everything okay?" Chris asks.

I put up my finger to ask for a minute. I close my eyes and pray to the gods and goddesses and whomever else one prays to. Do not let it be Evan, please. And when I peer outside I see my new neighbors across the street idling in the apron of my driveway.

I turn to Chris and let out a huge sigh. "Everything is fine," I say. "I just thought, you know what? I don't know what I thought. But, it looks like my new neighbors from across the street are stuck in my driveway."

Chris peers through the window and watches next to me. "Should we try to help?" he asks.

And as if on cue, I hear Jacob calling. He doesn't usually cry when he wakes up. He has in the past, but now he pulls himself up and stands, leaning his body into the guardrail of the crib, and talks. If I don't get to him immediately, he'll say Mama over and over, and I can almost picture him grown, calling me on the phone, doing the same thing.

"You go see what's going on. I'll grab Jacob and meet you outside. And we can walk over to the apartments from there. Good?" I say.

"Good." The way he holds my eyes with his gaze sends sparks through me. "See you in a minute."

There's a moment where I feel myself leaning in to kiss Chris goodbye, like I would Evan whenever he walked out the door. I stop myself from the muscle memory, but the lack of control for that split second is too much. I definitely need space. From both men in my life, but it isn't possible in either case. Evan is going to come see Jacob every day. And Chris and I work together. The door shuts behind Chris, and I'm still frozen to the spot. I can't believe I almost kissed him. Again.

"Mammma," Jacob calls. It brings me back to the moment, and I run up the stairs to him.

"Hello, love of my life," I say. Before anything else, I turn off the monitor. "Did you have a good nap?" Jacob smiles and bounces his feet on his mattress. I scoop him up out of the crib and know we need a fast diaper change before we leave. Evan is the master at changing diapers. It's a race for him where he gives himself points for speed and perfection. I'm slow and deliberate and chat with Jacob while I have his undivided attention. "Do you want to go on a little walk now?" I ask him. "That sounds like fun, right?" Jacob claps. Whether it's the tone of my voice or whether he understands what I'm saying, I'm not always certain. But, he does like a good walk.

With his diaper changed, I clip on the baby carrier and pop Jacob inside. I grab my tote bag and make sure there's a bottle of water for Jacob and me in it, plus a stuffie if he's fussy on the five-minute walk. I am better at preparing to have a baby with me all day since I've been on the Paxil. Wearing Jacob on my chest, I walk out the front door and see Chris squatting in the driveway, looking at the neighbor's car.

"What's going on?" I ask as I walk over to Chris, Ben, and Julia all huddled where Chris is squatting.

"A stray cat ran under the car while they were backing out of your driveway. Julia thought she ran it over, but the cat looks okay other than the fact that it is currently giving birth under the car right now," Chris says.

"You honestly could not make a story like this up," Ben says. "I mean, if it were Brooklyn, it'd be a rat, and I'd probably keep driving." Julia hits Ben in the arm both affectionately and in the way that implies *Shut up*. "Well, I may have run over a few rats in Brooklyn. I'm just saying."

"It looks like your car may be here awhile," Chris says, standing now.

"We're so sorry, Corey. We were just turning around," Julia says.

"It's okay. I don't really use the driveway, Evan does." Julia looks frantic. Her eyes are darting around to her house, under the car to the cat, to her husband. "Well, why don't you leave the car, and we'll check on the mama and kitties in a little bit. Do you have an empty moving box? We can put a towel in one and set it up on this side of the car. Maybe she'll move into it with her babies, and we can relocate them all."

"Do you think it's someone's lost cat?" Julia asks. "Should we knock on doors?"

I head over to the car and squat down indelicately with Jacob on me and look. It's one of the feral white cats everyone feeds that lives a free, wild existence. Full of fleas, bigger than a house cat, just this side of smaller than a mountain lion. I'm glad I parked on the street.

"No, she's feral. Just leave her be. She'll know what to do if you grab a box and towel," I say. "We need to run a quick errand, but I'll check on her when I get back. Hope you don't need your car for the rest of the day."

It looks like Julia is staring at me, but I follow her gaze to Jacob.

"Jacob, can you say hi to Julia?" I ask him like he's a circus performer.

"Hi, Jacob," Julia says.

Jacob smiles at her. We need to go.

Julia rises and walks back to Ben. "Yes, we'll go grab that box and set it up. Who knows, maybe we'll get a kitten now."

I turn and roll my eyes.

Chris, Jacob, and I leave and head over to Sonja Hart's apartment complex.

"The new neighbors are—"

"Interesting. Look like brother and sister. Rich," I say. "Very white gentrify-ey. Did I mention rich?"

"From New York," Chris says. He chuckles. "Corey, you're a white gentrifier too, you're just not rich."

I laugh until I snort.

"Fair," I say. "Well, he's a film director, and she's an actress."

We're about to cross the metro railroad tracks, and I freeze. I haven't walked over them since having Jacob. The metro line comes quick, and even though there are gates and lights and noise that alert you to the train coming, I've had the intrusive thought of what if, what if I just stepped in front of the train? I don't want to die. I start to sweat, and as I look at the tracks, I think about the thought, but nothing happens. There's no thought. It's not happening. The intrusive idea that would monopolize the space where rational thinking should live is quiet. The Paxil is doing its job.

"Corey? You okay?" Chris asks.

He doesn't know about the postpartum disorder. He knows I have anxiety and that I need medicine, but I haven't told him about the intrusive thoughts and the panic disorder diagnosis. What if it's too much for him? What if he doesn't want to work with me anymore because I'm this? Evan treats me like I'm broken. Made of glass. And the spidering of my glass needs all his tape to hold me together. But, I'm not.

"Yeah, all good," I say. "Just thinking." And that is the truth.

I walk across the track, and we're standing in front of the building. The entrance is open, or the security lock is broken. Both things could be true.

"What's her apartment number?" I say.

"Two zero eight," Chris says.

Second floor. I don't know what I'm expecting. "I'm sure the police have been here, but I need to confirm with Detective Lopez. See what she can tell us."

"Stairs," Chris says, and he takes them two at a time. Normally I would as well, but carrying Jacob on the front of me makes it nearly impossible.

At the top is a long hall of units. We walk until we reach apartment 208. I knock, and we wait. There's no answer. Chris knocks harder, louder, and there's still no answer. An older man in a custodial outfit walks by.

"Police already came and knocked," the custodian says. "They called me to unlock it when no one answered then. I think she left. Last time I seen her, she had a suitcase."

"When was that?" I ask. "The last time you saw her?"

"It was early—six a.m.? I get my paper and coffee from Chicos on the corner every morning."

"Did you ever see anyone else here with her? Un novio?" Chris says. I know enough Spanish and enough questioning to know he's asking about a boyfriend while letting the man know he's a Spanish speaker. It's a little thing Chris does in case the person we're talking to feels more comfortable speaking Spanish.

"It's okay. English is fine, friend. No, never seen her with a man or no one else. She was a nice lady, kept to herself. Left in the mornings, came home in the evenings. That's it. Left with a suitcase this morning."

"Did you tell the police that?" I ask. "That she left with a suitcase?" I ask with more force or panic—they sometimes sound the same.

"Yeah, told them right away. Said she had a suitcase with her when she left this morning. You friends? Family?"

Jacob starts to whine. When he's in the baby carrier, he wants me to keep moving or he gets fidgety. I probably would too. I start to bounce up and down, like he does now, and try to give him some movement.

"Friends of the family," Chris says. "Just checking in, wanted to make sure she was doing okay."

"What kind of car was she driving?" I ask. I know this man is not buying that we are friends or family. The police have already been here. He knows we're fishing, and I don't care. He's not showing any concern, so it doesn't seem that Sonja was accustomed to having the wrong kind of people visit her . . . At least not here at her apartment.

"A white Prius. I think. My memory isn't always a hundred percent." He takes a step closer to the three of us, and I tense. "You two made one hell of a beautiful baby there."

"Thank you." I don't correct him. "Can I give you my number, and if she shows up, will you call me?" I ask. It's a weird request, but the cops have already been here, so the situation is undeniable. She's not communicating, and someone wants to know she's okay.

"Sure thing. Want me to give her your number to call you?"

He's caught me. Not family. He's not going to call us out—maybe we look worried enough.

"Yeah, that too. But, please, if you see her, call me." I rummage through my bag and grab a business card I had snagged from a new locally owned café, and a pen. I scribble out the café's information and, on the back, write my name and number. I pass it to the man, and he walks back in the direction he was headed.

"Do you think she went somewhere?" I ask Chris.

"Have you ever left town and not told someone? A friend, your grown child, your parent?"

"What if she did tell someone, but that person isn't known to the rest of her family? She had a suitcase when she left," I say.

"Right, so we need to find a friend."

"I think I have, she's local. I looked through all her Facebook friends, and one has something in common with me."

"Only in Highland Park," Chris says.

"Only in Highland Park. She's a client at Cyclone. I snagged her address and info from the computer at work this morning."

Jacob babbles along with us. We leave the apartment ready to check in with Sonja's friend Anne Silva tomorrow. I wish my gut was relieved by the custodian's story, but it isn't. I'm more worried now. The state is huge, the country is vast, and Mexico is a two-hour drive south. Where would she go, whom would she go with, and where's her car? I need to get to Lopez and see if she can pull some favors. And because Sonja is a missing person, not dead, she won't be Lopez's problem. And since the custodian saw her ten hours ago, her missing-person report may be voided. So no one in Los Angeles is looking for Sonja now but me, Chris, and Jacob.

9

Jacob and I part ways with Chris at his car, parked a few houses away. Like he knows to be discreet. He knows to not add to my anxiety with Evan. And I don't need to explain.

When I get back to the house with Jacob, I see Evan, Ben, and Julia are squatting in the driveway with a moving cardboard box. As we get closer I hear them cooing to the cat, asking her to "Get in the box, sweet mama." I roll my eyes, again. The audacity of these three people speaking to a mother in labor and asking her to do more. It's so incredibly symbolic of the world we live in I want to scream. Jesus Christ. I jog, carrying Jacob in my arms the rest of the way to them.

"Stop," I say. "Stop asking her to come to you and back up. My god. She's in the middle of labor." I grab the box and towels and tilt it, so the open part is up against the car. "When we leave, and she's done, and she's ready to move—she will do it on her own."

"The coyotes will come and eat her and the babies. I can't let that happen. I can't let anything happen to those babies," Julia says. She's trembling as she says it. Ben puts his arm around her, and she buries her face in his shoulder. Her outburst feels dramatic, and I feel Evan's invisible recoil from the palpable emotion of a stranger. Of a woman. But a part of me recognizes the misfire of her fight-or-flight instinct. The panic. Driving her into the shoulder of the only source of familiarity and comfort she knows in this strange new land.

"Before Brooklyn we both grew up in Manhattan—Upper East Side. Our backyard was Central Park. This is a lot of newness for us. When we decided to move to LA, we weren't expecting a wildlife crisis in the middle of the city. I think it's been a long week with the drive and today with the movers—we're tired," Ben says.

"That's on me," Evan says, looking directly at me. "I'm worried about the coyotes getting to her and the babies and said it out loud."

Fuck. The coyotes. One more predator in the world a mother has to worry about. They'd smell her and the open wound that would be the birth of her babies and come hunting tonight. Usually we hear them right after dinner, before the sun is set. They've been seen roaming earlier and earlier for some time. Their nocturnal instincts regressing. The local community groups online are filled with sightings of coyotes all day long. Healthy, no-mange coyotes walking the streets like stray dogs.

"Okay, well, I guess some of us are going to be outside for a while. I'll get a lawn chair," I say.

"I can order some pizzas," Ben says. "If you know a place?"

"How about I order the pizzas, and you guys can bring over some drinks," Evan says. And just like that he's created a dinner party. Without asking, without permission. At my house.

"How long have you two been married?" Julia asks.

We've been sitting outside a few feet away from the car and the kittens for about two hours now. Pizza has been consumed, and Evan, Julia, and Ben have been drinking red wine—a third bottle is being uncorked. Every time they pour a new glass, one of them yells "Opa!" or "Another Chianti!" It isn't Greek cheese, and it's not Chianti—it's just a red. I've already explained several times that I'm breastfeeding and don't drink, and it's met each time with "One isn't going to hurt you, just pump and dump," first by Evan, then Julia. Ben just looks at me in a way that makes me feel like he pities me. All I can think about is the baby furniture Elsie saw. Clearly Julia isn't pregnant, and I have yet to see them with a child. I want to ask them about it, but there hasn't been a natural opening for *What happened to your baby?* Or, *You said you're planning a family.*

"We've been together for . . ." Evan is pretending to count the number of years and months and days. Right down to the hour and minute. It's a charming party script he's mastered. My mind drifts to the beginning of us.

When I met Evan, everything moved very quickly. We moved very quickly, too quickly. One date led to two dates, led to three, and so on. He was charming, mysteriously reserved, and smart. I was open and open to acquiring all his emotion. I was empathetic to a fault. Evan learned his traits through practice and mimicking others. I earned mine—my job required it. My mother, the house I grew up in, required it. Evan's personality gives him an advantage; mine gets me in trouble—gives me panic attacks and anxiety.

Like many relationships, the beginning consisted of lots of dinners where there was a lot of wine. After a glass, often two, I'd be lightheaded and giddy, and I listened with so much intent while Evan poured out his pain in a broody, rugged, *very* masculine way. I'd nearly taken him in the back seat of his car the first time we shared a meal. His broody, dark openness was hot.

There was a time when he told me about his previous two relationships. He'd been in love with women who didn't appreciate him. They didn't appreciate the amount of time he invested in his future, or his needs. And, that was something I understood—the men I had dated weren't interested in my career goals either. There was no value to what I did, just how I made them feel. Instead of hearing what Evan was saying, though, I related to it. Made our stories match. That was my first mistake.

These were clues, and I admit I'd been guilty of ignoring them. It was easy to ignore things when the sex was so good. In bed we didn't talk. We both worked long hours, loved our jobs, and when we met up it was instant chemistry. Work, sex, repeat. The oxytocin was addictive.

I didn't want to see the bigger picture. The one that was the narrative he kept selling me. Live together, where we could fuck all the time and then immerse ourselves in our work. A house, we could buy a house together. Own something in Los Angeles. I should have left right then. I should have recognized that invitation for what it was: a monstrous debt that would bind us permanently and would forcefully rearrange our goals and priorities—especially mine. But I didn't, because we had a trip planned, and we had a house-hunting budget, and we had just bought tickets to the Hollywood Bowl, and well, there were so many commitments already made.

The thing is, I didn't listen to the warning signs because I wanted to believe this was it. And when I lost my job at *LA News First,* I needed his support. When we got married and he asked for a baby, I should have left. I wasn't ready to commit to a family. Then I got pregnant, and we had Jacob, and I'm so thankful to have my baby. I should have left. Left before things became complicated. But, I didn't. Instead I had panic attacks and took a job teaching spin classes. And now, as I rebuild my career as an investigative reporter and the panic attacks are under control, and I can handle this all on my own—I remember who I always have been.

Evan wants me, though. Damaged and hurt and broken. He won't let go.

The truth is, Evan wants the picture-perfect family. A wife that will support him and his career, whether she works outside the home or not. And before Jacob, maybe I was doing that. I can't remember, to be honest. So much has changed since Jacob came into our lives. The biggest realization being that I'm not in love with Evan. I love him—he's Jacob's father, but I'm not *in* love, and I can't force myself to be anymore. And, if he would be honest with himself, he's not in love with me either. He just cannot handle the idea of failing. If he walks away from this marriage, that's exactly what he'll be doing—failing.

His complete arrogance and the sense of entitlement he feels over me makes me feel like a hostage. I keep the peace for Jacob. And I pray all the time that Evan will get so sick and tired of it all that he'll break up with me because I know if I were to leave, it would wound him too deeply to let me go without a fight. There is only one thing in this world that I cannot bear to lose, and I am terrified Evan would try to take Jacob from me. I need him to walk away and realize that he doesn't love me.

"So it was love at first sight then," Julia says.

I realize Evan's been deep in conversation with our neighbors about our relationship, and I've not heard a word. Do I tell them we're separated? Jacob's been in Evan's lap since the pizza arrived. The two of them still have a natural way with each other. Jacob looks like an extension of Evan's body. He sits still in Evan's lap, hugs, bounces, and high-fives on demand for him. I'm glad they are this way. The guilt I'd feel if I created a chasm between them would be insurmountable. Enough for me to beg Evan to come home. But it's getting late, and I have work to do, and I can't sit here all night waiting for coyotes to come or not come. It's a stakeout, but I'm not prepared to move from humans to wildlife. And then on cue, proving to me one more time that he is definitely a mama's boy and my best partner, Jacob starts to whine. He's tired and probably needs his diaper changed at this point.

"Well, that's my signal it's time for me to pack it in," I say. "It's been an eventful and long Monday."

"I can stay and keep watch, if you don't mind?" Evan asks me. It's awkward. Ben and Julia side-eye each other.

Ben peers under the car, using his phone as a flashlight. "I think she may be done with labor," he says.

"No, of course I don't mind. But, I may suggest more distance, so she feels safer moving herself and her litter." Oof, if that wasn't a dagger in the heart. Evan looks pained. It was not a metaphor for our relationship. It was the truth. "I mean, like our porch." Because it is our porch still. He's just not living here at the moment.

"That's a good idea. I'll put the lawn chairs away and wrap up out here," he says to me. He gives Jacob a huge kiss good night and hands him to me.

Ben looks at his watch and says, "I didn't realize it'd gotten so late. We should get to bed. It's one a.m. New York time. Plus I'm wiped from moving."

"And wine," Evan cheerily chimes in. I catch Julia flashing him a quick glare, but it softens before anyone else can notice.

It was dark, but I had no idea we'd made it—no, I'd made it, to ten. Jacob had two naps today. I'm not at all surprised he managed.

"Have a good night, Julia, Ben," I say. I look at Evan. "And, I'll see you in a bit." With that I head inside as quickly as I can. I think about the mama cat under the car. Trapped by her babies. Tethered to the creatures she's brought into this world of high stakes and demands. Unable to guarantee that any of them will be okay. It was only a month or so ago that one of her feral pack members had been hit by a car and left for dead right in front of Elsie's house. Another white one, male. His stomach bloated. He didn't make it, but Elsie did take him to the emergency vet. They found cancerous tumors all over him and decided it best to put him down. Just like that.

Instead of a bath I wipe Jacob's face and ears with a warm, soft washcloth. Change his diaper and put on green-and-navy-striped footy pajamas. He still smells baby delicious. I inhale his head deeply as I sit in the oversize armchair in his room and read him *Are You My Mother?* He's already asleep, but I don't want to put him in his crib, not while Evan is still hanging outside. Jacob has become a shield in that way. It's unfair, but it's the truth. "It is what it is," my grandmother used to say.

I hear the front door open and know Evan will be waiting for me downstairs. I relent and put Jacob in his crib and go down.

"Hey," I say.

"Hey, it's getting cold out there. I'm going to go grab a jacket if that's okay? I didn't want to rile up Jacob if he wasn't asleep yet."

"He's out. You can go up." I really don't want Evan in my room, or even on the second floor of the house. My nerves have never felt so calm as they have since he's been gone. "I have work to do, and I have to get up early tomorrow. How late do you plan on staying?" I ask.

"I could stay the night, if you'd like me to," Evan says. He steps in closer to me. The look of longing stretches across his face.

"I'm tired, Evan. I just want to get some research done and head to bed."

"Are you working on something new?" he asks.

"Sort of, there's a woman missing. Hasn't made the news yet. That fire behind the Groceries for Less, a body was found. Plus, I'm still working on the cold case that Lopez gave me. Though that is proving difficult, and it's frustrating."

"Okay, then, maybe I'll take off. If a coyote does come, it'll have a hard time getting under the car where she's positioned herself. Plus, I think she'll be moving that litter to a bush soon, if no one is out there watching."

"I agree," I say.

Evan comes a little closer until he's an inch away. "I love you, Corey," he says and kisses the top of my head. Without hesitation he wraps me up in his arms and hugs me. I get my arms up enough to pat his back. Then, after a few seconds, he lets go and leaves. I lock the door between us.

10

I get up before Jacob and stop quickly at the window to peek out and check the driveway. Ben and Julia's car is still there. I wonder if the cat is. I read the brief news about the house fire. Only one station mentioned it, and only on their online page *Local News That Counts*. The story is considered old just twenty-four hours later. It's brief, just a recap of the one minute of screen time the street reporter gave:

> A house fire in the Northeast Los Angeles neighborhood of Highland Park is said to have been started by faulty electrical wiring. A neighbor called 911 when she saw the flames rising at the back of the house. There was one casualty, a woman whose identity is still unknown. The house had been vacant for quite some time, according to the owners, who live out of state. Fortunately, no other structures were damaged.

Faulty wiring in a vacant home. How would a faulty wire in a vacant house catch fire? I need to text Chris and Detective Lopez this morning. And, I plan to go to Anne Silva's house. Monique would like me to work Tuesdays, but I remind her, I'm part-time. Today, I'm only on the hunt for answers. And Sonja Hart has officially been missing for twenty-four hours.

Me: Detective Lopez, it's Corey. Do you have time to meet today? I can come to you.

Detective Lopez: Lunch, one p.m.

Me: See you then.

I hear Jacob rustling in his crib and jump up to get him. He's not quite awake yet but in the in-between stage where he's trying to wake himself up. Or, wrestling to go back to sleep. I have no idea. He looks like he's trying to get into a full down-dog yoga pose.

"Good morning, my love," I say. He grumbles and half whines, half cries. Little waking-up sobs erupt from him in a pattern that sounds like a song's chorus. I pick him up, and he's wet. I feel the bed. It's wet. Did I give him too much water yesterday? Or not enough? Will he be dehydrated? I give him a quick change. Wipe off any residue on his belly and legs. "I promise you a nice soak in the tub later, okay?" I wrap him in a fresh diaper and onesie and head downstairs.

"We have a big day again," I say. "We need to go see Detective Lopez at the police station. Do you remember Detective Lopez?" Jacob's response is more grumbles. He looks like he woke up on the wrong side of the bed. "That's okay. How about some banana? *Buh-na-nuh?*" I ask. This snaps him out of his morning mood and excites him. I tear up a banana for him and some baby oatmeal, which he'll eat about a tablespoon of, but at least I'm trying. I sit next to Jacob's highchair and watch him out of my peripheral vision while I type in the address to Anne Silva's on Google. It's not far—I look at the clock. How early can I show up at someone's front door on a Tuesday? It's almost eight a.m. It seems reasonable enough. I fill a sippy cup that is a cross between a baby bottle and water bottle for Jacob and a traveler mug of coffee for me. The alarm on my phone goes off. It's time to take my anti–panic attack pill, Paxil. I turn off the alarm. I've been snoozing it since I woke up. I'll grab the pill next time I run upstairs—maybe. I feel fine. I want to stop taking it, but I'm scared. It's the anticipation of ripping off a bandage. I must decide to do it, and that's it. It's done.

The drive to Anne's takes us down one of the main strips in Highland Park, York Boulevard. A new brewery in an old billiards hall, a seating area in what used to be a few metered parking spots outside a purple brick coffee shop that also serves milk tea. Every other eating spot or drinking spot uses the name Highland Park some place in its name: Highland Park Eats, Highland Park Drinks, Highland Park Coffee. The street is narrow, one lane in each direction, and it's always busy with cars, it doesn't matter the time of day. The street, the stores, all the buildings are old. The new paint strategically excludes the preserved original signage of former businesses, long since shuttered. There's a park on the corner that used to be a gas station.

It's the second park I took Jacob to when he was just a few months old. A Northeast LA mommy group was hosting a meetup. Evan encouraged me to go, even offered to come with me. I showed up with Jacob but didn't see any groups, just a lot of women with their kids not talking to each other. After a while a small group started to form, and I approached, my anxiety high, and asked, "Is this the mommy group?"

"Yes," a small, pregnant, red-haired woman said. She smiled but didn't say anything else.

"I'm Corey. I registered for the meetup online."

"Oh, okay, that's you," said another pregnant woman. A brunette in denim overalls and a baseball cap. "So, to join the outings and the group, there's a fee, and I didn't receive that from you. Before you can participate, we do ask that you pay for a membership."

"I'm sorry, I must have missed that. I thought it was just a park meetup."

"Yep, you can pay online any time," the brunette said without telling me her name. She turned back to the women gathered and continued the conversation I had previously interrupted. I walked away, pushing Jacob in his stroller, not understanding if I was supposed to stay or leave. By the time Jacob and I got home, I was completely over mommy groups.

Since then, the community has had the park tested for toxic chemicals since it was built on top of decommissioned petroleum tanks. The city and the residents are at odds with the results, and that mommy group still meets there. I won't quickly forget their faces or their Facebook group anytime soon.

It's not unusual that Sonja's place would be on York Boulevard. There are still a few residences before and after the commercial buildings. I cannot see the street numbers on the buildings, but Google says I'm here. I park on the side street, grab Jacob and the tote bag I use as a diaper bag and purse, which I've filled with necessities for both Jacob and me: a baby book, stuffies, diaper, wipes, sippy cup of water, emergency Klonopin, Sharpie, and thermos of coffee. I start walking back in the direction I came.

I come up on 7936, and it's a hair salon. I step in with Jacob.

"Hi, welcome to York West Salon," says a woman at the front desk. She's too put together to be younger than thirty, but guessing her age would be difficult and embarrassing. She is stunning. Long, dyed red hair that could be a wig or extensions, as it is stunningly healthy. Her makeup makes me want to sit in her chair for a full makeover. And her clothes look tailored to her body.

"Hi, I'm looking for Anne Silva," I say.

"You're in luck. I'm Anne. Did you make an appointment, honey?"

Nope, I've never seen this woman at Cyclone. Ever. And her Facebook posts now make sense. They were of her clients. It's all coming together. I blame the Paxil for my not figuring it out more quickly.

"No, I was referred by Sonja Hart?" I say. I wait for a reaction, anything that may indicate she knows about Sonja.

"That's great, okay. Well, let's look at the books and see when we can get you in," she says. So far, there's no implication that she and Sonja know each other at all.

"Do you have any openings now? I'm a mess. You can see that. I haven't had my hair cut since I was pregnant. And, he's"—I gesture to Jacob—"just full-time. And, work, and life. Would it be possible to do something now? I'd be so grateful." I don't want to leave until I know who this woman is to Sonja. Was she the one filming Sonja's reading? I'm working the sympathy-mom card hard and hoping that the lack of morning clients only means she was planning a slow day, not that she sucks. It's pretty high rent to open a business on York. Oh god, what is this haircut going to cost me? Right on cue, Jacob grins so wide I can see a tooth just starting to crown. He throws his arms at Anne and speaks the most beautiful, joyous babble.

"You're good," she says. "The baby is a nice touch. My morning client rescheduled, but normally I don't do walk-ins. Take a card and call or text me to make an appointment next time." I grab a card from the front desk and follow her back to a chair. I sit down with Jacob in my lap.

Anne pulls the hair scrunchie off the top knot I threw my hair in this morning, and my dirty dishwater-colored, blonde locks cascade down in a frizzy but straight mess.

"Your hair is super healthy. Not cutting or using any dyes on it for a while was smart. You gave it a break from breaking," she says.

"Thank you," I say. It makes me feel good. I realize she's making me feel good as part of her job, and I like it. "How long has Sonja been a client?"

"About a year."

I wonder if she likes her as a client. Does Sonja tip well? She's a community volunteer. I'm sure she treats everyone well. Talented, beautiful, generous—these are the things that should be on her missing-person poster. I'm going to have to tell someone to update it immediately.

Jacob is fussy, and I need to distract him for a bit. I pull out his favorite book, *The Pout-Pout Fish*, to suck on. That achy, itchy crowning tooth will appreciate the cardboard pages.

"So, what are we doing with your hair today?" Anne asks. She's brushing it out to its full length, and I honestly haven't paid attention to just how long it's gotten. "Do you want me to do some color?"

"Oh god, no, I don't want to take up your time. Maybe just a couple inches? You don't even have to wash it," I say, and a second later Jacob throws the book in my face and screeches. I taste blood on my lip.

"Little man, that wasn't nice," Anne says. "Mama, stay here, I'll be right back."

When she returns, she has a blanket and some folded towels, plus a child's wooden sensory toy. She lays out the blanket next to me, sets the toy up, which opens like an easel, and she gently takes Jacob from my lap and puts him in front of the toy.

"Don't worry, you're not the first mama to come get her hair cut," she says. "Now, I think, we can do better than a trim. Look at your face, it's so pretty. We should let it show. How about some fringe and angles?"

"How about a pixie-cut?" I say. It comes out of nowhere. But I am oddly resolute. "I want to take it off."

"I think that would look perfect on you." Anne smiles and winks. "But, you have to let me lighten the whole thing up. I promise, with the pixie, it won't take long. Now, you tell me how well you know Sonja. And, can you text her and ask her why the hell she missed her appointment without canceling?"

Anne drapes a salon cape around me and snaps it behind my neck. I look at Jacob, who is invested in a phone receiver that is attached to the sensory toy by a cord, looking like an old rotary phone. Then I look back at Anne.

"I met her at the Cyclone Spin Studio, where I teach. I don't know her well, but she gave me your info when I asked the class for referrals."

"I've been to a spin class there! I love Cyclone, especially Monique—she's fun," she says. "Honestly, Sonja is a hoot when she's here. I didn't know she took spin." Anne takes a large paddle brush to my hair and starts brushing from the bottom up. It feels amazing to have my hair brushed by someone else. There's that touch sensory firing off again. When she gets to the top, she sets the brush down and takes a rubber band and wraps my hair in a low ponytail. "Sonja is full of surprises. Did you know she writes poetry?"

"I didn't," I say. I need to keep this conversation going. "I know that she volunteers in the neighborhood." I'm hoping to get the gossip train rolling.

"Did she tell you about the guy she's dating from her class? Gurl, he is twentysomething. And listen to me, she's the one keeping it on the down-low."

"No, I didn't know." Okay, Sonja is seeing someone. She's in college. She performs poetry. She's friendly and funny and open.

"I couldn't do it. Listen, I'm forty-five. I do not have time to waste on these babies. It's not worth it to me. But, more power to her. We can all live vicariously through Sonja. Make her tell you about the time he followed her home with two dozen roses. Lovesick."

"What do you mean *followed her home*?" I ask. That's an odd way to phrase something, *followed*. That sounds less like dating and more like stalking.

"She never let him pick her up for dates. Like I said, low profile. But, gurl, he is obsessed with her. He followed her home after class one night, all incognito, and surprised her at her door with all these roses."

"Did she like that?" I ask.

"I don't know. I think she was flattered. I mean, between you and me, I think she low-key loves it. And you know what, good for her. She said he's been talking about marriage and a family with her. I was like, he better hurry and ask you, or you better let this one go, if you are not trying to have more babies."

"Yeah, I can't imagine going through another pregnancy. I mean, because I know she has a grown son."

"Okay, see, you know more than you let on. I can see her having another one with the right person."

"Did she ever say this guy's name?" I need a name from Anne. It's easy to like Sonja's personality from her video and stories about her, but I wish I knew her in person, and I'm hopeful to, but I need names right now, Anne.

"Gurl. Yes, I've seen his Instagram. He's hot. Like, hot—hot. Mike something." She stops cutting my hair for a moment, but I'm afraid to look. On the table next to me is a ponytail of hair no longer attached to my head. Anne pulls out her phone from her apron. "I know his handle. Don't tell Sonja, but I looked him up again to show the girls after she left. Hang on."

I try to maintain a look of captivation on my face as I scrutinize this woman—this stranger spilling her guts to me about a missing woman I'm pretending is a mutual acquaintance. It's all coming too easy, isn't it? The specific details about Sonja's love interest. His name, his social handle, all this oddly specific information I need but haven't asked for . . . yet. Does it feel rehearsed? And if it is, do I believe it? Maybe she's protecting Sonja. Or maybe she has something to hide. Or maybe it is all true, and I just can't read this situation right.

As Anne scrolls through, looking for Sonja's boyfriend, I peek at Jacob still happy with his temporary toy. Then I sneak a peek in the mirror at myself. My hair has been severed into a very short bob, and I begin to panic.

"Here he is! Mike Lee. Listen, you'll know when you see him why I didn't forget and needed to show everyone."

Anne hands me her phone to look at the Instagram page of Mike Lee, a.k.a. @matmastermike. The whole page is Mike doing jujitsu. Is doing jujitsu even accurate for what I'm describing? I don't know. There are reels of him pinning opponents on mats. Pics of him winning trophies. Pics of him holding an armful of medals. And even more shirtless photos than are necessary for anyone on Instagram. He's definitely got a body to rival an action hero. I hand the phone back to Anne and pull mine out while she answers a text. I open the Notes app and discreetly type *Mike Lee* down and drop my phone in my lap.

"Okay, time for color and then a wash, and then the real work begins," Anne says.

I look at my watch and see we've already been here for thirty minutes. I'm worried Jacob will be bored soon and start fussing again. Anne spots me looking at him.

"Don't worry, I've got more toys, and he's fine. Relax. You've earned a little time to pamper yourself," she says. To be honest, the Paxil has worked wonders on my ability to calm down and not overstress about anything. Too many things, actually. For a moment I relax. I have a lead, Mike Lee. Maybe a new hairstylist if this doesn't go bad, and she doesn't turn out to be Sonja's kidnapper. Another hour isn't going to deplete the day.

Two hours later, I'm staring in the mirror at a woman who has my eyes but a pixie of platinum blonde hair that shows off her defined cheekbones and jawline. I look incredible. I've never felt stronger and more feminine than I do in this moment. Jacob is in my arms, trying to tug at my hair, but there isn't enough for him to grab anymore. I am speechless.

"You like it?" Anne asks.

"I-I." It's all I can mutter. But I do. I absolutely love it, in fact, and feel all kinds of power in it. "I don't know what to say."

"Say nothing, but make an appointment by texting me next time. Also, you'll need to see me sooner than one year. This cut requires maintenance. Probably a little trim and touch up in six weeks. Okay?"

I nod. It's the only thing I have left in me. The tears of joy sting behind my eyes, but I'm a desert, the part of me controlling the release of emotion still numb from the Paxil. How long will the side effects of the medicine last if I stop taking it? Something I probably shouldn't look up on the internet but ask Dr. Rosenberg. I hand her my credit card without even asking. When she's done, she hands it back, and Jacob and I head back to the car. I'm walking a little straighter now. My chin is raised. I can do this, all this. Raise a baby, have a career, solve crimes. I can be me, and it will be fine—but is it only because of the drugs?

11

It's a few minutes past noon. I just had a way-too-long haircut while Jacob contented himself with toys and not my breasts the entire time. I feel relief and then guilt for the relief. I dig through my bag for his sippy cup and find a smoothie packet. I unscrew it and hand both things back to him.

"You hungry, bud?" I ask Jacob as he grabs for the smoothie pack first. He hesitates for a moment, then sucks on the plastic mouthpiece with what appears to be enjoyment. I twist my body more into the back seat to put his sippy cup of water next to him. "We have to run another errand before home. We're going to go see Detective Lopez," I tell him in my most fun mommy voice I can make without feeling fake. Jacob is too busy with the smoothie to care.

I check my messages and see Evan has texted several times. Now that we're not living in the same house, he texts me more often than he had before. Since he pays the phone bill, I don't see the numbers, but I'm positive it has to border a thousand a month at least.

Evan: Dinner tonight?

Evan: I really miss you guys.

Evan: I hate not seeing Jacob every night. I'll plan on being there around six.

Evan: Is everything ok? It's not like you not to write back.

Evan: Seriously, just let me know you're okay.

How much could he miss us when he spent last night with us? Sometimes I think he writes what he thinks will elicit a reaction from me. Or, a faster response. The last message he sent came in about thirty minutes ago. I'm getting sweaty just reading his texts. The impatience. The overworry. The expectation that I should jump when he calls, texts, says to. I don't want him to come over, but I'm trying not to fight. I'm trying to make everything easy during this separation. I hear Evan's voice in my head correct me, it's only a trial. A break—space for us to regulate after so many little, angsty, daily arguments.

The marriage therapist we're seeing, Dr. Kelley, referred to us by Dr. Rosenberg, has asked us to practice boundaries during our trial separation. She didn't simply say *trial*, she said *separation*. It's not a break if Evan comes over whenever he wants—it's not even a trial. Our homework for the past week was to write down our boundaries and discuss them at our next session. I pull up my Notes app on the phone and type.

> Boundary: stop blowing up my phone with non-emergency texts.

I stare at my phone and scroll back to Evan's text chain. How do I sound not angsty in my response?

Me: Sorry. My phone wasn't available. I was getting my haircut. We're fine. Running errands now. Six sounds good.

I wait for Evan to reply before I pull out of my spot. There aren't any dots letting me know he's even attempting to write back. Fuck it. I pull out and head in the direction of the police station to see Detective Lopez.

The police station is not a busy, fast-moving, high-traffic building. There's always street parking. And the architecture looks more corporate than crime. Maybe it is. Maybe crime is a corporate business, our prisons are. I find street parking easy enough and not far from the front doors. The only way anyone would know definitively that this is a police station is the parking lot of cop cars tucked next to the building. When there's a shift change, it reminds me of an anthill, just a line of like-looking cars coming out of the gate in a steady stream.

I collect Jacob and my bag, double-checking it and Jacob's car seat to ensure I've grabbed his sippy cup. And once I've done that enough to settle something in my brain, I head up and into the precinct.

It's clean, sterile. Chairs are nailed to the floor so they cannot be lifted and thrown, but otherwise they look like any other waiting room chair. The front desk is behind bulletproof glass, but otherwise it could be the post office—folks in uniforms waiting to be of service to the next guest. But the vestibule is empty, except for Jacob and me.

I walk up to the window and wait to be acknowledged. The man behind the glass is not even looking at us. He is visibly focused on the computer screen that I cannot see. Jacob shrieks, mostly something he does when he's tired of waiting, not necessarily upset. The man jumps, startled by the outburst, I assume, and not that we've been waiting for five minutes. I assume he knew we'd been there waiting because he is a police officer.

"How may I help you?" the officer asks. Hughes, Officer Hughes, his name badge says.

"Hi, I'm here to see Detective Lopez. She's expecting me," I say.

"Your name?"

"Corey Tracey." Leaving off the Lieberman is easy.

"Have a seat, I'll let her know you're here. And that you brought a child."

It's hard to place Officer Hughes's age, but I'd put him over thirty. He's muscular, but not the kind of muscular that bulges through shirt-sleeves. I can see he works out by the cut of his jaw—it's strong and hard. He's the man women like in uniform—if that's seriously even a thing. It's such a stupid saying. My yoga pants and T-shirts are a uniform. Does that make me sexy? No.

"How about you, baby? I put you in a onesie every day, does that make you a man in uniform?" I ask Jacob. He grins. His cheeks have been filling out. They're so puffy and round, and red when he laughs.

"Ms. Corey Tracey, you are early," Detective Lopez says as she enters the vestibule from a pair of heavy-looking bulletproof doors. "Come on back with me."

With Jacob on my right hip, which has been aching a lot, we follow Detective Lopez back through the doors she entered from. Walking through the precinct, I recall all the intrusive thoughts I had the first time I was here. My eyes dart to the police in uniforms, their guns strapped to their waists. Before the medicine, I thought about how long it would take me to grab a gun and start shooting if I needed to. Today, nothing. My brain is so quiet it's almost terrifying. No internal voice asking me what I would do if I was standing on the edge of the cliff. Would I jump? Just nothing at all. Is this how everyone else's brain works? Are they completely silent too?

"Have a seat, Ms. Tracey," Lopez says. "Are we permanently dropping the Lieberman?"

I pause. I had not anticipated being asked about my last name by anyone. It could have just been an error made by the officer, which informed her I was here and not me only giving my maiden name. A hyphenated name like Tracey-Lieberman, it could happen they just drop the Lieberman. I cannot remember an instance when that's happened, but Lopez doesn't know that.

"Nope," I say. I don't want to discuss my personal life, not with a cop. "Have you heard anything about a missing woman? Name is Sonja Hart."

"I have not. Has she been reported missing? If so, who reported it?" Lopez asks.

"Her son reported her missing. Lives in a different state. Hasn't heard from her. She's not answering calls. He posted it online, and the Highland Park Facebook group has it reposted. She was a student at South Pasadena Community College." I pull my phone out of my bag with one hand while I hold a drowsy, almost-napping Jacob in the other arm. I scroll through to the text from Chris about Sonja and click on the link that takes me to the Facebook missing-person post and hand it to Lopez.

Lopez studies my phone. It looks like she's reading the comments under Sonja's picture, as she uses her finger on my sticky dirty screen, swiping up. I'm tempted to pull a wipe out of my bag and offer it to Lopez when she hands me back my phone.

"I agree with the commenter that says it looks like a fake."

"No, she's real. I went to her hairstylist today and—"

"And asked about her disappearance?" Lopez asks like she's questioning me.

"No, I asked for a haircut and told her I was referred by Sonja Hart. She confirmed Sonja is her client," I say.

"The hair looks good. It suits you. But you know the drill. Just because her grown child isn't getting his mom to answer the phone doesn't mean she's missing. They may be arguing. He may want money from her. She may have taken a vacation from him and shut off her phone."

"What about missing an appointment with her hairstylist without canceling?" I ask. I know it's not related—Sonja was fine, or at least alive until yesterday morning, but I need to convince Lopez of the urgency.

"Are you telling me you've never missed an appointment?"

Lopez had me there. I've missed more than my share. Usually I call and cancel, but not always. Still, something is there. I feel it.

"Why did the police go to her apartment then?" I ask.

"A wellness check, likely. Do you know what they found?"

"A witness stating he saw her leave with a suitcase."

Lopez nods at me. "Listen, Corey, not everything is a crime." I can't make my face look happy with that answer. She shakes her head and says, "I'll make a call, see what's up, when I have a minute." I nod and force a smile. I know she will, but I don't know if anything will come of it. "Do you have anything new on the Renee Flores case?"

"Not yet." The guilt hits me that I haven't yet, and that I can't get a sense of Renee like I can Sonja. The old police interviews aren't thorough enough, and there's no one left to go back to except her parents. Both are well past retirement age and hesitant and distrustful of not just a nonpolice investigator but a former TV news journalist. They're pissed that more wasn't done for Renee and their grandson at the time of the murder, and the only person that will talk to me is a cousin who wasn't even born when the crime occurred.

I can't find Renee's widowed husband yet, James Flores. I've made it through at least two dozen James Floreses online and haven't nailed down the one I'm looking for. The whole case is making me question my ability to investigate. Part of me wants this Sonja Hart case for pure selfish reasons—a win.

"Remember, I'm paying you for the Flores case." This time I nod at Lopez. "But, keep me posted on Sonja Hart if you continue to follow up, since I know you won't listen to me. Okay?"

"Absolutely. Question, what about that fire behind the grocery store, any leads on who the person is that died?" I ask.

"Neighbors have already told us there was a squatter living in the house. Had been there for a while. Looks like the squatter started the fire, trying to heat the house up using the gas stove."

"The news said it was faulty wiring," I say.

Lopez cocks her head in a way I can only interpret as *Really?*

"When will you have confirmation on the body?" I ask.

"It has been confirmed to be a woman, but the body was burned bad. We'll see if dental records come back with anything. If not, I don't know that we'll be able to figure out who she was with one hundred percent certainty." Lopez looks down at the file on her desk. I can't read the label from where I'm sitting. "Not unless someone knew her and can verify she lived there."

"So, someone would need to claim her." I'm saddened by the idea that a woman could die without anyone knowing who she was. Without a ceremony to honor the life she lived, even if it wasn't all good. At some point in her life she was someone's daughter, and that has to count for something. Anything. What if she had older children searching for her all their lives? My stomach twists in knots, and I feel the beginning of anxiety. I'm sweaty, my armpits already creating wet circles on my shirt. I'm finding it difficult to swallow, and the saliva in my mouth won't stop coming. I need to spit it out. I grab a few tissues from the box on Lopez's desk and discreetly spit into it.

"Are you okay, Corey?" Lopez asks. I'm thankful that Jacob is out, but his heavy head and body are killing me, and I'm trying to keep myself together in front of Lopez.

I touch my head as a sharp zap that feels like an electric current buzzes through my brain.

"I'm fine, yeah." What if it was Sonja Hart in that house when it went up in flames? What if someone dumped her dead body there and intentionally set the fire to cover their tracks like someone did with Renee Flores? Why not? It's the perfect cover. It wouldn't be the first time—the mob has been cleaning up this way for decades.

My mind is racing. Why would someone kill Sonja? At what point does the story become a homicide, and why isn't she answering her phone? And if that were true, then who and where is this squatter? Someone is in the morgue, but someone is still out there unaccounted for. God, let the latter be Sonja.

"Can you let me know when you've identified the body?" I ask.

"I will." Time is my enemy now. It wipes away everything: evidence, facts, people, feelings. Time is the great reset. It's the thing we cannot stop from coming, and it takes no prisoners—good or bad, time gets us all.

Lopez rises from her desk to walk me out. I drape my large sleeping baby over my shoulder and follow Lopez back to the heavy bulletproof doors. I look around the precinct and notice how empty the desks are. Not just of officers and bodies, but of stuff. Most desks are bare, but for a phone and computer. A few are like Lopez's—there are pictures in frames, trinkets, and paperwork. But there are more empty desks than those lived in. A problem for the community and the overworked officers.

On the other side of the doors, I turn back to face Lopez.

"How long has arson been a problem in the neighborhood?" I ask.

"Arson is always a problem. Last year there were just shy of five hundred reports of arsons in Los Angeles. Seven since January in Highland Park, not including Monday's, and it's only March."

"Can you send me the arson reports for the year Renee Flores was murdered?"

"Sure. In fact, there was one serial arsonist around that time. Get this, he was active LAFD—Los Angeles Fire Department. Not a murderer, though. Got off on setting fires and then putting them out and *pretending* to solve them. Even won an award for distinguished service."

"How did he get caught?" I ask.

"Camera. It was just around the time some businesses in the area were getting cameras—not many, security cams were not mainstream market or affordable like they are now. Anyway, he hit a building—new construction that had big investors behind it—and the camera caught him."

"Did he admit to the fires?"

"He did. They all happened when he was on active duty. Matched all the reports."

"Was he incarcerated before the Flores murders?"

"I'll have to look it up. But the fire doesn't match his style. The Flores fire was to cover up the bodies—it was amateur. You've read the file. The fire was started with a pack of cigarettes being lit and tossed in the living room. The fireman arsonist used a highly flammable polyurethane product."

"Understood." Would it be the craziest thing for an arsonist to fantasize escalating his behavior to murder? I need to review the Flores autopsy report again. I must be missing something. The neighbor said a man walked in behind her, but why didn't she scream or run outside immediately? Because she had to have known him.

"If I hear anything on Sonja Hart, Ms. Tracey, I will let you know. I promise. And, I mean it, the haircut suits you."

To be honest, I'd completely forgotten about my hair.

12

I head home with Jacob, who has managed to stay asleep even when I buckled him into his car seat. I know he's going to wake up when I attempt to smuggle him, still sleeping, up to his crib to finish his nap. The idea of alone time to spend on the computer working sounds too good to be true.

I turn onto our street and head toward our driveway. I want to see if the neighbor's car or the cat have moved yet. I hear screaming. It could be a loud car radio. I roll down my window to get a better listen. Shouting, not screaming. Someone is shouting about something. It's so loud, but I don't see anyone, and I can't make out what they're saying. It's not uncommon to hear arguments from different places—the sound, the yelling, it bounces off the hills and canyons and travels all over. But this yelling sounds less like a distant echo and more present. I slow down to a creeping pace in the car, which makes me look obvious. But to who? I can't see any people.

As I get closer to our house I park in the street and turn off the car with the windows down and listen. I look toward the giant picture window, still undressed, of the new neighbors. Julia is gesturing wide with her arms, her upper body slightly leaning toward Ben where he stands about a foot away from her. Her mouth is open wide like she's yelling her words to him, no, at him. I look at their front door—it's open. Only the screen door blocks any strays or bugs or little lizards from running in.

I turn the car back on and find a spot in front of my house. When I close the door, I notice Elsie on her porch, listening to Ben and Julia shouting. She gestures for me to come over. I grab my bag and lift a sleeping Jacob from his car seat and head over to Elsie's porch. Jacob is slowly waking. I take a look around to see if there's anyone else watching, listening, and notice Pete standing just out of the line of sight from most passersby, staring at Ben and Julia through their side window. Pete, the neighborhood's self-appointed block captain, is more like a Peeping Tom than a security guard. The windows on the right side of his house match up to the windows on the left side of Ben and Julia's. Privacy is a premium in these old neighborhoods.

I wonder how long Pete's been outside, listening and watching. I wonder if he's met the neighbors. I wonder what Ben and Julia think of him. A former convicted weed dealer who now passes out crisp single-dollar bills to all the kids on the block. A token of good faith. Something to motivate their loyalty to him. He's slick, has his hand on the pulse of the block, sharp as an eagle. I can't stand him, but I also need him. At his age of somewhere around pushing ninety, Pete poses little threat. He's a nuisance, and I can cope with that.

"Hey," Elsie says as I make it up her porch. She holds out her hands, asking for Jacob. I pass him over in his drowsy state, just awake enough to see me. It's a huge improvement from just a few months ago when I wouldn't let anyone hold him. Now I can let Elsie take a turn.

"Hi. How long has that been going on?" I ask, motioning my chin toward Ben and Julia's house.

"On and off all day."

"Anything to be concerned about? I see Pete is invested."

"I think it's just louder in his house than it is out here," Elsie says. "I don't think this move was about a career pivot. I think there's trouble in paradise, and you were right: It's not because of that oversize couch."

We watch silently for a moment, until I can't help but ask, "Why did you hold out on me?"

"Huh?"

"The squatter. You said you didn't know anything."

She shifts Jacob to her other shoulder as she turns to me. "I didn't—I don't. I just clued you in on what the whole neighborhood already knows, Corey. I don't know who was in there, but everybody knows which spots are boarded up, and when nobody's living somewhere in Highland Park, people move in. Just the way it always is."

She breaks eye contact and glances up at my hair. I'm suddenly self-conscious. "You look shiny and new."

"It's a good haircut, right?" I say.

"It's a good haircut," Elsie repeats back to me, nodding her head. The emphasis of the words as she says them gives me an immediate boost of confidence, and I feel my dry lips crack from the grin spreading across my face.

A truck pulls down our street and stops in front of Ben and Julia's house, blocking Elsie's and my view. "Well, that's my sign to take this guy in and get him something to eat," I say. I want to get back to my house, where I'll have a view. I can see the neighborhood go by without anyone noticing me in the window, watching.

If Pete knew I didn't need to stand outside on the curb and pay off the kids for the gossip on the street like him, there'd probably be a turf war.

My large front porch with its low-hanging roof and eaves makes me even more incognito. And all I have to do is run up to my second floor and stand on our little Juliet balcony, where Julia and Ben can't see me at all, I am positive. I've checked every angle on the block, and it's hidden. I'll still be able to see over the truck and right into their front door.

"Jacob, are you hungry?" I ask.

"No. No. No," Jacob says.

"Are you tired?" I ask.

"No." He motions with his arm outstretched and fist opening and shutting. I look into his room across from the Juliet balcony and see his giant building blocks. Each one just the size of his head. No choking hazards and no sharp pointy corners to step on.

I take Jacob in his room and plop him down in front of his building blocks.

"I'll be right back. Mommy is going to look outside for one minute," I say. He just looks at me. I close the baby gate Evan installed on the outside frame of Jacob's door and head out the door of the small balcony.

The truck is already pulling away from the front of the house, giving me an even clearer view of Ben and Julia.

Julia is standing about a foot away from Ben. He's using his hands and arms to emphasize whatever he's saying. Julia stands there, arms crossed, still—so still she looks like the Buddha statue that was dropped off outside the house. Yes, there's a Buddha statue, at least six feet tall, on their front concrete lawn. I lean over the balcony to make out what Ben is saying. They're not shouting but they're also not happy.

"Mama!" I hear. Jacob has pulled himself up to standing at the baby gate. His yell sounds more frantic than gleeful. His nose is running, his cheeks look red. I thought whatever it was had passed, but maybe he is sick. I try to think back to the hair salon. He was very patient, but not lethargic. I think about him at the police precinct. He was drowsy, wasn't it nap time? What have I fed him today? Do colds happen like this—one minute okay, one minute not, on repeat? I'm trying to think through the pages of the baby book of the first five years, which our health insurance company sent us. I read it front to back but can't remember most of it.

I hope it's not an earache. The last one was painful and caused him to bite my nipples during feedings until they bled. Dear God, please don't let it be an earache.

I run to the baby gate and lean over to pick up Jacob when a loud boom outside shatters my nerves.

"Mama!" Jacob yells, again, and the crying starts. I pull him up in my arms and turn around toward the balcony. I need to see what's happening outside. *"Mama!"* Jacob sneezes, and his nose explodes a yellow-greenish hue of liquid all over his face. I want to go outside for

just a second, but I should go to the bathroom and clean off Jacob's face first. Outside or tissues? The thought feels eternal. I choose Jacob. I will always choose Jacob.

"Let's clean you up, baby. Mama is here."

"Owie," Jacob says. The giant tears wetting his face break my heart in a million pieces.

"Where is it owie?" I ask him. He tugs on his ear.

I set him on the counter, holding him there with one hand as I pull out a fresh, soft baby washcloth and run it under the warm faucet. Then I clean off his face, giving his nose a gentle squeeze to empty it a little further. I feel Jacob's head, no fever. I pick him up and head downstairs to get him some juice mixed with water to sip on. As we head down I stop at the window.

"Did you hear the big boom? Want to go see outside with Mama?"

"Owie," he says and now holds his belly, and then it comes, a mountain of puke. Shit. And there it is, a giant diaper blowout. And then he's fine. Everything is fine except for the giant mess of additional fluids I now need to clean. "Mmm, Mama, mmm," Jacob says as he points to the window.

"You want to see outside?" I overpronounce the word *outside*. We go to the window to find clues to the boom. The warm vomit turning cool as I walk. A reminder I have a huge mess to clean. It smells. Everything is running down my arms and legs. It's fine. We look out and see the giant Buddha has fallen over. Julia is still standing, arms crossed, while Ben collects broken pieces of the statue and puts them in a brown moving box. "Uh-oh," I say to Jacob. "Uh-oh, broken."

Jacob laughs a little as I say uh-oh. "Uh-oh, we have a mess to go clean up. Uh-oh." The giggles are contagious. And to be fair, it is a funny-sounding word. I take Jacob upstairs to the shower, and I strip us both naked. I hold him in my arms while I rinse us both off. As the water pours over us, I keep circling back to Julia, standing quietly over Ben. So incongruous with the cartoonish person I'd met yesterday, or the hysterical woman mewing over feral cats. Each time embodying a different trope—like she was filling out one of those trashy magazine quizzes, trying to get a specific outcome.

The windows in our house are thin. They're the original windows with new glass. Nothing double paned or storm proofed. When it rains, as rare as it is, I know I will be laying towels underneath them. And when it stops, I set up fans and space heaters pointed at the walls to dry out any moisture that's seeped in from the shitty old windows to prevent the mold that is inevitable. So I know if there's more to hear, I'll hear it.

Inevitable. The things I know that are inevitable: Evan coming to see Jacob and me this evening. Every evening is inevitable. I will ask him if Jacob has been sick around him. If he noticed any symptoms on Sunday. Inevitably he will say no.

I feed Jacob applesauce and white rice and a bottle of breast milk from the freezer. Breast milk cures everything, my doula told me. I wonder why I never drank it to cure my anxiety. All the bland things to help his belly. My pants buzz, and the more often it happens, the less I notice that it's uncomfortable.

Chris: Are you able to meet up today?

It is the message I am always waiting to read. A message from Chris. I look at the time. It's already four p.m. Evan will be here at six. It's close, but Jacob has been fine since the giant sneeze, puke, poop incident.

Me: Yes.

I need to write to Evan, confirm he still plans to be here at six. Make sure I'll be home before he arrives and not give him any reasons to take Jacob away with him today to his house. As long as I'm always available when he wants to see Jacob and me, we don't have a problem. As long as Evan feels like we're spending time as a family, I can see

Chris with my baby for work purposes. I don't want to be without Jacob. I want him to be with me. I want to be with him. I want to be with Chris too.

Me: Hi, I have to go out for a bit to run some errands. When are you planning to come over?

Evan: I thought we said 6 so we could do dinner together, does that still work for you?

Me: Is 6:30 okay?

Evan: See you then.

I finish re-dressing Jacob: diaper, onesie, elastic-waisted, denim-colored baby pants. They look more like jeans than anything I've been wearing lately. I am inspired.

"Come on, Jacob. Help Mommy find some jeans that might fit." And match my new haircut. Something that says I'm trying again.

I start with the maternity jeans first. It's as if my ass, hips, and stomach have all dropped several inches lower than they were when I was pregnant. I put on a pair from before Jacob, since I've bought nothing new since giving birth. They're easy enough to pull up, but the zipper doesn't close. Defeated. I am defeated. Maybe I'll add *Buy new jeans*, or any pair of hard pants, to my list of errands for the week.

I slip on my favorite pair of black yoga pants, but instead of my usual workout-gear top, I opt for an oversize, thin-striped oxford, a denim jacket, and sneakers instead of my usual bare feet and Birkenstocks.

Me: Are you free now? Diner?

I write to Chris, hoping he isn't thinking dinner.

Chris: See you there in fifteen minutes.

I grab my mesh bag that doubles as a diaper bag and throw it over my shoulder. I look in the mirror. I look a little bit like the woman I was before Jacob. She's there. I see her when I look hard. Jacob is on the bed watching me. I dig through the big mesh bag and find a sheer red lip gloss and add it to my lips. Just one light-handed swipe. A quick run of my fingers through my new hair and finally mascara—I never forget to wear mascara. I step away from the mirror and look at myself in full length. I am put together. I think maybe even pretty.

"Jacob, how do I look?" I ask. He squeals with excitement. Like a dog, and I hate saying that, he sees our bag on my shoulder and knows we're leaving the house. An adventure awaits.

13

I take a different route to the diner than normal so I can go past Sonja's apartment. I pull into the parking lot and look for her Prius. The apartment building is small, twenty units total. The lot for the cars is adjacent to the building and even smaller—I count only ten available spots for tenants. The blacktop of the lot is cracked, the lines for the spaces faded, and weeds are pushing through the ground with a resilience I admire.

I'm glad Sonja has a spot. The street parking in the area is limited, and she would have to walk alone over the tracks and past the alley. I've walked the alley between the tracks and the buildings before, and it is often littered with needles, pipes, and old mattresses. The safest thing coming out of the alley to attack after dark is a coyote.

Sonja's car isn't here. My stomach drops. She was reported missing on Monday. It's late in the afternoon on Tuesday, and no one has spoken to her since Saturday. I need to find the café she performed at, and I need to see Mike Lee. Someone must know something.

Jacob and I arrive at the diner, and I don't see Chris's black Honda. I like arriving first and watching him arrive. It's awkward when he's waiting on me. I hate that he has to watch the not-so-graceful display of me carrying a large baby, big bag filled with supplies for the large baby, a body that just doesn't feel like I own it. I think about the video I watched of the baby giraffe standing up and walking for the first time, and that's what I relate to. New body, new conditions, first-time walker.

The diner is slow when I walk in and the sign **PLEASE WAIT TO BE SEATED** is turned around to: **PLEASE SEAT YOURSELF**. I grab our favorite booth and slide in with Jacob. Jacob is standing on the bench seat of the booth, bouncing. He's only mastered the knee part of the bounce. Bending and unbending his knees very fast. His balance not always 100 percent. He looks at the napkins and silverware and makes an immediate choice to grab the spoon. I grab the butter knives and reach across to the empty table next to me and drop them. No knives ever. The one thing I haven't gotten over is knives. I just don't want them around me.

In the moment it took me to drop the butter knives on the empty table, Jacob has found the salt and pepper shakers and is now raining pepper and salt all over the booth and the table. I take them away, and the shrieking begins. Dumb move, Corey. I dig in my bag for a toy he can shake and find a bottle of pills. I make sure the cap is on tight, childproof, and I hand the bottle to him. I'm sure the pills will turn to powder and dust after he plays with them, but they're just my emergency Klonopin. I keep a few of them on me, five to be exact. Enough to walk around with in case a panic attack finds me. I didn't take my Paxil this morning, and the sliver of anxiety or guilt that I had skipped it is gone. The rest of my Klonopin are hidden in my sock drawer. Hidden from me so I won't take them all. And hidden from anyone that comes over and may want to steal them.

"Hi," Chris says. He's at the table, and while I positioned myself to see him first, my baby distracted me enough to not even notice him arrive.

"Hi," I say. Chris is wearing his usual: a T-shirt that is fitted, jeans that unintentionally hug his thighs, and sneakers. The way his hair naturally falls around his face is lip-biting sexy, and I wonder if he knows it and wears it that way on purpose. I wonder if he uses a leave-in conditioner. I never intentionally lean in to smell it, that would be weird, but I'd like to accidentally touch it. See if it's crunchy from products or soft. He takes my breath away every time I see him. "Everything okay?" I ask, trying to mask my internal dialogue.

"I think I have a lead on Sonja Hart," he says. There's no time for a catch-up this time. We're headed straight into work. A missing woman, and I know that's exactly what we're supposed to be talking about.

"Me too. I met with the person I found on Facebook today," I say. Part of me is completely devastated that he hasn't noticed my hair or anything else. I've been so overthinking that there's something between us I'm immediately embarrassed. Embarrassed I'm even upset he hasn't noticed. Jesus. There's a missing woman.

"Tell me everything," he says.

"Her name is Anne Silva. She cuts Sonja's hair. She gave me the name of a guy that Sonja has been seeing. Actually she showed me his online profile. She didn't seem to know that Sonja was missing, but at the same time alluded to the idea that this guy was maybe stalking her." As I say it out loud, it sounds funny to me, off. "I don't know if she was bullshitting me to be honest. I know there's more to Anne's story."

"What's the guy's name?" Chris asks.

"Mike Lee."

"Okay."

"Okay?" I say it so forcefully Jacob throws a sugar packet down onto the table. The sugar packet lands with a small thump, sopping wet where he'd been sucking on it.

"We know she's attending South Pasadena Community College, and I may have found out that she may have been seeing someone there—it could be the same guy." He looks at Jacob. "Hey Jacob, my main man. How are you doing?"

"And?" I ask. I'm pulling the new sugar packet Jacob has acquired out of his balled-up fist, and he's meeting me with a vicious grip. I finally relent. I need to know more from Chris. "Is that it? Any name for this source or person that told you? Get a name of the guy? When did they last see Sonja? Yesterday? Today? In a class or around campus? Is she missing? What are you saying?" I'm demanding. I see he's trying to include Jacob. I see the look on his face when he's processing the information, and I may be a little irritated with him for not noticing the glaring change in my appearance at the table. It's all coming out way too fast and far too much.

"Sorry, that was a lot. It's just time sensitive—we're quickly approaching forty-eight hours missing. I know you know that." Jacob likes when Chris, when anybody, includes him in the conversation. His need for the attention is as pervasive as my own when it comes to Chris.

"What I know feels like gossip—it's a smallish campus, large enough that not everybody knows everybody, Corey. But not so large that rumors can't be spread. Take this information with a lot of skepticism. And remember, I knew her. I want to find her, alive, as much as you do. The student she was secretly dating is someone she's in class with. Apparently, they started out as study partners. She's been known to tutor other students as a part-time gig. A classmate says she saw them kissing in the parking lot once. Or, she thought she did. She wasn't close enough to be entirely certain. I don't know where that guy is, and I don't know if they're together." Chris drops his head, looking down as water Jacob spilled inches toward him. "From my experience with Sonja, she was always solo, never showed up with anyone."

I nod. "Okay, do you know the guy's name?" I ask.

"Maybe Steve? The kid I spoke to didn't have a clue. Didn't know Sonja's name either, only ID'd her from the pic I showed him. Precisely why I'm hoping you're in the mood for a ride to the South Pasadena Community College registrar's office. We need to get a copy of Sonja's classes and a class list for all of them. Or, maybe you can audit her classes tomorrow and see if the professors know anything, saw anything?"

"Do you think I have some sort of magic authority?" It comes out snarky, and I mean it to be teasing. I sound petulant. I feel my face turning pink. One Paxil missed, and I'm showing embarrassment again? That's not possible.

"I think Lopez has some pull," he says. His tone is neutral, gentle even. There's no question he didn't hear my snark.

"What about your cousin?" I ask. His cousin is on the LAPD. He's a beat cop but has put in enough years to have some sway. "Do we need to ask Lopez for every favor?"

"My cousin is working on something right now. He's unavailable."

"Is he undercover?" On what, I wonder. What aren't the police telling the community. I hope he's working on some kind of fentanyl bust. People, kids, have been dropping left and right from the epidemic, and I worry about Jacob at sixteen experimenting with marijuana someone laced with fentanyl and dropping dead before I can rescue him.

Chris shakes his head at me. He'll never tell, but I doubt he knows. I wonder if they've ever been out of communication before.

"I have to be home by six thirty. Evan is coming over for dinner with Jacob," I say.

Chris nods. He smiles. There's a beat that is more of a pause before he says, "You look good. Your hair, it, it suits you." The smile he gives is so kind and genuine it reaches all the way up to his eyes.

"Thanks." I try not to read into the compliment. "I think it's time I start looking like I care. It generally works better when I want something from someone."

Chris laughs with me. He has a big, full laugh that has Jacob bouncing, clapping, and shrieking.

"Well, let's pay for this coffee and get going. We don't want my favorite guy, Jacob, and his mom to be late for their dinner date."

He's not even a bit judgmental as he says it. There's no passive aggression. It's simply a statement.

"No, it's not a date—"

"I'm happy for you both," he says. I don't know if he's talking about Jacob and me, or Evan and me. I guess it doesn't matter. As far as Chris goes—we're work partners, nothing more.

"Are you?" The words are spilling out with no forethought or restraint. "I'm sorry, if this is too personal, you don't have to answer, but, do you have a girlfriend?"

"That's a first, you asking me about my dating life."

"I'm sorry. I didn't mean to be intrusive. You don't have to answer that." I struggle to apologize for asking. I'm so on display in every way with Chris, I want to hold a little more power or at least knowledge of him, his life. Online he's all business—his personal life guarded. It's frustrating to have to ask.

"It's fine. I like that you asked. I do," he says and then stops. "Well, I'm not sure if girlfriend is the word we use at this age, but I am seeing someone. She's a lawyer."

In one swift moment my spirit is crushed. I feel stupid for putting on lip gloss, and my hair, god, I didn't even do it for him, but I wanted him to notice. I'm embarrassed for thinking he cared for me as more than anything other than his partner. I feel like such an asshole I want to crawl away. I'm so thankful I was able to tell him that Evan was coming to dinner. Good. Maybe he'll think I'm dressed better for my *date* with Evan that I already denied was a damn date. Because we're married, separated, and working on something I don't even want.

"Do you want to take two cars? Or, do you want to drive and drop me back here after?" Chris asks. His question pulling me out of the absolute spiral I've spun out into.

"Yeah, let's take two cars in case we run long. I don't want to keep Evan waiting." I regret the last comment the moment it comes out of my mouth. "I'll follow you over."

Chris gives me a nod and a wink, and I open the car and put Jacob in his car seat. After strapping him into the harness, I lean in and give him a kiss. "I love you. You are my whole heart." I pop open a baby smoothie pouch and hand it to him. I shut his car door and see Chris watching from his driver's-seat window.

"Sorry, I'm almost ready," I call.

"It's fine. I like watching you with Jacob. You're a natural," he says.

A natural? I'm a mess. I'm on medicine, which I didn't take today, to protect me from my own brain panicking every time I think about the possibility of my baby being hurt. The ball of despair I've become since having Jacob. Curling into the fetal position under the dining room table, waiting for the panic and fear from the intrusive thoughts. The inability to breathe, the closing of my throat—if Chris had ever seen me like that, he wouldn't think I'm a natural. I don't believe anyone would. I am not the picture of perfect mothering, or influencer mothering. I am trying to survive every day. I am checking in on the intrusive thoughts to see if they're there. I still don't keep knives in the home, and my husband lives in a separate house. I'm not even a very good spin instructor. I'm tolerated because I'm the only person Monique likes to work with at the studio—at least that's what I tell myself. And, I have no problem teaching at seven a.m. Everyone else competes for the afternoon and evening classes. The only thing I know I can do is help find people. Help tell their story. Help give closure to the families and friends that love and miss them. That's all I'm good at—and yet, I've produced no answers on the Flores case. And at this moment someone is missing, and I'm mentally wrapped up in this childish crush on a loop in my head. This is the intrusive thought now. Fuck.

I jump into the driver's seat and pull out of the spot behind Chris. And we're off to South Pasadena Community College.

14

Driving to Pasadena on the 134 Freeway east from the diner is making me anxious. The traffic is at a standstill. Not because there's an accident in sight, no, because there are a lot of people living in the city. It's always congested at all times of day. I exaggerate, but it does feel like I haven't been on this freeway when it hasn't backed up in a really long time.

I look at the clock and it's five fifteen p.m. Every minute sitting in this traffic gets me closer to Evan and not Chris. I cannot be late for Evan. I need to make sure I can get back on the freeway and get home in time. I don't like the idea of Evan hanging around inside the house without me. Going through the bedroom that doesn't feel like ours anymore, but mine. I shouldn't be worried. He has every right to be there, for now.

I look in the rearview mirror at Jacob. He's dozed off in the warm car. That's good. A little nap before seeing Evan is perfect. I look at the car in front of me, at Chris's black Honda. He waves at me through his back window. I wave back, not sure if he can see me. He puts his blinker on, merging in stopped traffic to the right lane. Are we getting off?

I follow Chris off the freeway. He calls me on the phone.

"Hey, this isn't going to work," he says. "I know you're pressed for time. Why don't I see what I can get on my own."

I look at the clock again. It's 5:35 p.m. Relief floods over me, and I feel the muscles begin to relax in my shoulders and neck. "Okay," I say, "can we talk tomorrow?"

"I'll text you tonight."

"Okay, but if you have plans with your girlfriend, you don't have to. I can do my own research too—online." I cannot believe I just said that. I brought up his girlfriend. What am I, twenty-five years old? What is wrong with me?

"She's in New York for the week. I'll get in touch tonight."

We hang up, and I don't know if I'm embarrassed or relieved.

I take surface streets home from where I left Chris. Thinking about getting back on the freeway has my throat reacting like it does when I'm anxious. It tightens, making swallowing nearly impossible. I know I can make it on surface in thirty minutes in this traffic. I look back at Jacob. He's awake now, watching out the window. I'm thankful he's not fussy after a long day and an upset everything earlier.

The March days are getting longer, but they're not long enough yet. The sun is still out but setting quickly, and the colors are hypnotizing—reds and pinks paint the sky and clouds. Even with the cell towers, phone lines, electrical wires that run the length of the city blocks, it's still beautiful. The colors of a Los Angeles sunset are brilliant. I've not seen anything like them.

I pull up to the house and see Evan on the sidewalk chatting with Ben, but his car isn't in the driveway. I park in the street in front of our house, just in case more cats are readying themselves to birth under someone's car. I pull Jacob out of his car seat and walk over to where Evan and Ben are talking.

"Hey," I say, announcing my presence and startling both men.

"Corey, I didn't—where's your car?" Evan asks.

"I parked in the street." I point toward the car, but Evan is staring at me, jaw open. I cannot tell what kind of look he's giving, and I'm not sure if it's because it's getting to be too dark or if I've never seen this one before. "What's wrong?" I ask.

"Your hair. What did you do to your hair?"

Once again, I'd forgotten about my haircut.

"I think it looks great," Ben says. "Good call. You have a nice face for it."

What the fuck kind of thing is that to say? Jesus. "Thank you," I say to Ben anyway. "Hey, you wanna go inside? This guy needs a diaper change."

"Yeah," Evan says. He looks to Ben. "Nice to see you, man. Maybe tomorrow night we can grab that beer?"

"Sure. You guys have a great night," Ben says to us both.

Jacob is excited to see his dad. He reaches his hands out to be taken by Evan, but Evan is pulling a roller suitcase behind him and up the driveway. I say nothing.

"Wait until we get inside, big guy, and then Daddy will hold you," I tell Jacob. "What's with the bag, need more things?" I unlock the front door and am relieved it was still locked, and Evan hadn't already let himself in. Once we're inside Evan parks his suitcase on the stairs and takes Jacob from me.

"Well, I was hoping you would have noticed, but it's been a month. My Airbnb stay is over. I'm home."

Fuck, fuck, fuck.

"Are you okay?" Evan asks.

No.

My head zaps. He's still looking at me with some sort of pity or disgust on his face. He wants to be here so bad, but he can't stand me, the look says it all. Or does it? I can't think. My brain isn't getting oxygen. I try to take a deep breath, but it goes nowhere. I cannot fill my lungs. I cannot swallow the saliva that pools in my mouth. There's a lump in my throat. I need a Klonopin, now, before I spiral. This is too much.

"I'm surprised."

"I thought you'd be keeping track," he says.

"I thought we would be discussing your moving back in with Dr. Kelley."

"I miss you. I miss Jacob, and we can talk about it this week with her."

"Why wouldn't you wait before coming back without the go-ahead?" I'm trying not to raise my voice. I count to ten in my head, then twenty.

He reaches for Jacob, and Jacob reaches back. I don't want him to take my baby, but Jacob is making his own decision to go with Evan.

"Let's not do this in front of Jacob, Corey." He kisses Jacob's big rosy cheek and makes a show of giving him a huge hug.

"I'm going to get a glass of water. I'll be back." Instead of going into the kitchen, I run upstairs to my bedroom. I dig in my sock drawer for the bottle of Klonopin I hide in an allergy pill bottle so no one will know. I grab one and go to the bathroom. I can barely swallow my spit—I'm not even sure water will go down at this point, let alone a chalky white pill.

I put my mouth under the bathroom faucet and swallow the pill with more water than necessary, and I start to cough.

"Corey?" Evan calls. "You okay?"

"Yep, just swallowed water wrong." I shut the door and bang my hands against the edge of the sink. Why, why, why did he come back?

I flush the toilet to make Evan believe I had to pee. I turn the faucet back on and wash my hands. The pill is in me. I know it will take effect in a few minutes. I also know the calendar starts over with how many days I've gone Klonopin free. I go back downstairs to Evan and Jacob.

"Are you okay?" Evan asks from the floor, where he's changing Jacob's diaper.

"I'm okay. Just getting home, needed to pee, wash my hands, put my stuff down," I say.

"What did you do to your beautiful hair?"

"I cut it," I say.

"It's not you." Evan sits on the couch with Jacob in his lap.

"Mammma," Jacob says and points, as if to tell Evan he's wrong.

"I don't know, Corey, is this because of your anxiety? Why would you do something so dramatic without talking to me about it?"

"I don't need permission to cut my hair, Evan. I didn't go out and buy a car without telling you. I cut *my* hair." I'm defensive and feel savage. I want to ask him who the fuck he is to judge me. It's the first time I really feel my anger so acutely toward Evan. Dr. Rosenberg has been working with me on intensive short-term dynamic therapy. We've concentrated on the anger I refuse to let consume me, so instead I push it down, all the way down, until the guilt eats away at me. That turns into anxiety, and that turns into panic. I think I may be having a breakthrough with my anger, and I need to shut it down. Now is not the time.

I see Jacob watching me—us. I can't help but project all the *what if* onto him. Is he waiting for us to be nice? To fight? And if I'm not nice, will Jacob grow up to resent me? Instead I just let Evan know with a smile. "I like my hair."

"I'm just not used to this version of you you're becoming. You're different."

"I think I'm getting back to the person I was before," I say. I keep my voice neutral and throw in a smile for Jacob.

"You're nothing like the woman you were before. And, that's not bad. It's just going to take me some time to adjust to her."

"To me."

"Yes, to you. But the good news is, I'm home, and we can start learning each other again." He gently tosses Jacob up in the air above his head. "And this guy can have us all day and night in the same place again. Are you so happy about that, big guy?"

Jacob giggles in the air, and I know he loves the feeling of flying above his dad's head and free-falling back into his waiting, strong hands. He knows Evan will never hurt him. I wish I felt that way too. I watch Evan toss Jacob again. The giggles flooding all my senses. Did I ever feel that way when Evan's hands were all over me? Did I giggle and cherish the time he made me feel like I was floating in the air? If I did, I don't feel that way anymore, and I can't force it even for Jacob.

Evan walks over to me with Jacob in his arms and bear-hugs the three of us together. "Aren't you going to welcome me home?" he says.

"Welcome home," I say. He looks at me and smiles, but something is different with his smile. He doesn't smell the same either. A new shampoo or aftershave. He squeezes my upper arm tight as I pull out of the embrace.

"You're so muscular, and that short hair—maybe you could have a new career as a stunt woman. Maybe you can throw me around," Evan says. He looks at me suggestively.

"Is that a compliment?" I ask. What an asshole. It's exactly something my mother and father would say. I want to throw up. I wonder if Jacob is telepathic. They say children and their mothers can read each other's minds and feelings. I try to turn off my brain. Dial it back to neutral.

"It's a joke. I was teasing, lighten up. I just need time to get used to this new look." Evan locks eyes with me again. I see something different—it's hesitation. Maybe distrust. "Listen, I'm going to take my bag upstairs and unpack. I'll take Jacob with me. Then, let's go out to get some dinner, okay?"

I watch him hold Jacob and lift his suitcase with his free hand. He's right. I could probably hold Jacob and carry that bag too. I am strong, and I do like that about myself. I lie down on the couch and close my eyes for a minute. The Klonopin is working. I'm light and floaty. I could sleep.

Evan just moved back in. It takes effort to lift myself up when I just want to lean into the calming cradle of the antianxiety pill. But I push myself off the couch and walk up the stairs. One step at a time with purpose. I'm concentrating, holding the wrought iron banister as I go. I get to the top, and I see Jacob on my bed, staring at his dad with adoration and love. I sit on the top step of the staircase and cry. This is it. This is the rest of my life. I did this to me, to us. All of us.

15

I walk back downstairs to make myself some coffee. I have to work. There's work. I need to find Sonja Hart. And, I need to find what I'm missing in the Flores case. I won't let anyone's story go untold or unfinished. It's my mission to make sure every murdered, missing, undetermined woman's case is heard. I want to believe that if I disappear, someone would finish telling my story.

Sonja is current, so she has to come first. Before she disappears forever.

I'm startled by the doorbell. I can't remember the last time anyone rang it. I carry my open laptop to the door with me as I hear Evan come down the stairs with Jacob. I open the door, and Ben is standing there without Julia.

"Hi," I say. "Can I help you?" The Klonopin is slowing me down. I shouldn't have taken a whole one. I need to sit.

"Yeah, is Evan—" Ben starts when Evan lands next to me with Jacob.

"Hey, man, what's up?" Evan says. It's like the two of them have been friends for years. Their energy with each other is so casual and familiar. "Come on in."

Ben slips by me, and I sit down on the couch with my open computer resting in my lap, a mug of coffee on the table in front of me. Evan sits on the floor with Jacob. Ben opts for our blue velvet wingback chair. A purchase I will never regret even if it never matches anything in the house.

"I hope I'm not interrupting. I was wondering if I could borrow Evan for a couple hours. Go get a beer or something."

"Yeah, man. We were going to get some dinner, but it looks like you're getting to work, Corey?"

Evan's assumption is correct, but still it feels shitty to be dumped in an instant. At the same time, I can pump Evan for information on our new neighbors and their fight today, if I let him go now. "Yeah, I need to work, and Jacob needs to get to bed soon. Go, have a beer. Enjoy."

"Thanks, Corey. I promise to have him back before bedtime," Ben says.

I'm positive it's supposed to be cute or quirky or funny. It is none of those things, but I go through the motion of smiling at the statement. Evan gives Jacob a kiss and pops up from the floor. Jacob starts crying and pulling at Evan's pants. I get up and go to Jacob.

"Hey, buddy, you and Mama can play. Do you want some dinner? We can eat on the floor like a picnic," I say to Jacob. I pick Jacob up and stand. I sway slightly. No one notices. Evan is at the door with Ben, ready to go. That was fast. I didn't even see him grab that jacket.

"Thanks, babe. I'll text if we're going to be late," Evan says.

"Sure," I say. Babe? "Have a nice time."

They leave, and Evan shuts the door behind him without locking it. I flip the deadlock over and grab my phone from the side table and text Chris.

Me: Anything?

Chris: I was just about to write you. Nothing. It was dead on the campus. Registrar office was closed.

Me: I'm going to DM this Mike Lee guy on Instagram. Keep you posted.

I rock Jacob, still whimpering about his dad leaving, on my hip while I open my fake Instagram account, @amberdawn. I use a picture of a sunrise as my profile pic and had previously loaded my account with free pictures from the internet. There's art, theater, and dog parks. I don't want anyone to think I'm a bot. Jacob's sobs are calming. "One second, baby. Let Mama write this one message, and then we'll go get some noodles. Do you want some noodles? Yeah?" I say to Jacob as I type and stare at my phone screen. I find @matmastermike and send a quick message.

> *amberdawn:* Hi, I'm a friend of Sonja Hart. I was wondering if you'd seen her recently? I'm trying to track her down for her son. She hasn't been texting back.

I hit send and pocket my phone. Time to feed my baby and put him to bed, so I can work before Evan gets back.

Jacob fell asleep so quickly I hardly believe it. The Klonopin hasn't completely worn off, but coffee is helping. @matmastermike hasn't written back yet, but I can see that he's read my message, so I know he's been active online. I look him up on other platforms. He's not on Facebook, but I find an older YouTube account from what looks like his high school days when he was competing in martial art meets. Even in high school he was completely ripped and looks older than most of the kids he's competing against. I watch the first video. Damn. He could kill someone. He's lethal. He strikes and doesn't miss. I watch as a young man turns purple in the face, pinned to the mat by Mike Lee. Later in the same video, Mike receives a first-place trophy and medal.

Part of me would like to train with Mike Lee, and part of me is terrified that Sonja may have hooked up with the wrong dude, and another part of me cannot picture the poet I saw doing anything with this man. I watch another video of Mike taking out an opponent and wonder if he's ever trained for MMA fighting. I wish I could kick a fraction as well as his front kick looks. Damn.

Ding.

There's an Instagram message for @amberdawn. I open the app on my phone.

matmastermike: I don't know a Sonja.

amberdawn: Do you go to SPCC?

matmastermike: I don't know who you're talking about or what SPCC is, lady.

Did Anne mean Sonja was seeing someone from her workout classes? Did I misunderstand? I check the notes in my phone. I didn't write down college class, just class.

amberdawn: Do you teach Martial Arts?

matmastermike: Yeah, first class is free. Jujitsu Center in South Pasadena. Interested?

It's a universal thing—free first class. That's how everyone hopes to hook you.

amberdawn: Can I send you a picture of Sonja and can you tell me if she's ever been there for a class?

matmastermike: If you promise you'll come in for a class Amber Dawn, sure.

Flirting is also a universal language. I upload the missing-person picture of Sonja to the chat and wait. Mike Lee has suddenly disappeared.

He hasn't even read my last message—the picture of Sonja. Dammit. I wait a few more minutes, but I may have lost him for good.

Something's not adding up. Either Anne got it wrong, or Sonja showed her Mike's profile page as a fantasy, or Mike Lee is lying. But, was he training her, and did he know anything about her whereabouts? I'll find out tomorrow. God, I'm so tired.

I start doing a person search on Sonja and each person that "may be related to her" from the search finder. She's lived in three different homes in her forty-two years. That's not many. That tells me she settles down and likes to grow roots, as people say. She has only one child listed. Everyone else is a cousin or sibling. One deceased mother and no listed father. There is an uncle. I don't have a great fondness for uncles after my last case.

I look into Sonja's son. All his accounts are set to private. As a mother, I approve, but it's not helpful to my investigation. I log into Reddit and cross my fingers when I put *Sonja Hart, Highland Park, Los Angeles*, and *Missing* into the search engine. One post by a Reddit user handle L00tHunt3r001reads:

MISSING: SONJA HART PLEASE KEEP EYE OUT

Under that is the same picture and stats floating around social media. But, underneath that are plenty of comments, including from the poster L00tHunt3r001.

Redditussser1: Were they taking any hallucinogens? Sometimes people are prone to psychosis and when they play around they find out.

CosmicCaffe1nator: Yo that happened to this kid I went to college with, bro. Scary shit. Full on.

HyperHiveM1nd: Report to LAPD, there's no limit to how long they have to be missing.

CosmicCaffe1nator: Do they have any mental illness? What did the police say? Where have you looked?

It just goes on and on with a lot of armchair psychiatrists diagnosing a missing person without ever once suspecting that someone may have taken her or suggesting that it's a scam. That she must have done something to herself to end up missing. The cynicism of even the most sympathetic people has me reeling. I scroll through a full page of people arguing with each other in the comments about which drugs could cause psychosis. Or, others commenting how they'll pray and how badly they feel. And then, one comment from L00tHunt3r001 letting everyone know that he is in fact her son and that he just wants to find his mom. She just moved back to Highland Park. She is taking family counseling courses at South Pasadena Community College, and she doesn't do drugs. *She's a good person with a big heart,* he wrote last.

I copy his handle and paste it into multiple search engines to see if it's used anywhere else, but only Reddit posts come up in my search, and they're all about gaming. Nothing illicit or weird. My eyes are getting blurry, and I'm surprised how tired I am after so much coffee.

I look at the time. It's late, eleven p.m. I need to get to bed. I start to head up the stairs with my laptop. Maybe I'll get a few more minutes of searching in before I pass out. I'm halfway up when I hear the front door. I jump. Is this it? Is someone breaking in? I start to run to Jacob, until I hear Evan's voice.

I forgot. Evan has moved back in, and now he's home. I wish I was asleep already. I'm not ready to get into bed with him. To share that space doesn't feel comfortable and hadn't for a long time before tonight.

"Corey?" Evan whispers loudly up the stairs to me.

"Hey." I head back down to see him. "How was your night?"

"Well, that guy is not doing great. This move was a Hail Mary—is that the right phrase?"

"I'm not sure because I don't know what you're talking about." Evan gets closer. I can smell he's had more than he usually does on a work night. He's moving in like he wants a kiss or more. I put my arms out to stop him. I push into his chest and ask him, "What is the Hail Mary?"

"Right, yeah. They're way worse off than we are. He hasn't worked in nearly a year. She's not going back to work because she wants a baby. A *baby*. Like Jacob. He said they've done, like three rounds of IVF and nothing. So, they're going to try with a doctor here."

Interesting—no job. Three rounds of IVF at what, twenty thousand or more each round? Plus, a new house with a million-dollar price tag. Sounds like a million-dollar problem.

"I heard them fighting earlier today. Did he say anything about that?" I ask.

"She sucks. That's what he said. She sucks, and this is it for them. He doesn't think she's going to stay. She's crazy, Corey."

I hate that he's calling a woman crazy. I hate that it's his go-to word for *women*. He always called his ex-girlfriends crazy too. I never stopped him. I was complicit. It haunts me now.

Evan puts his hand through my hair before I can stop him. "You know what your hair makes me think of?" He's so close to my face, his breath is hot and reeks of alcohol.

"Okay, I think you've had a little too much to drink tonight. Why don't you go shower and see if that helps get some of the liquor smell off you," I say. His lips are brushing up against mine now, and I can smell something else. Perfume, or maybe it's Ben's cologne. It's definitely not Evan's scent.

"I'm not ready to sleep," he says in my face, almost a whisper, almost seductive, but he's drunk, and it sounds more like he's being petulant again.

"Okay, well, I need to get up early, so I'm going to go to bed. If you're going to be up late, do you mind sleeping on the couch? I don't want you getting into bed and waking me."

"Why don't we go get in bed together?" His voice is so low it's taken on the gravelly, seductive quality that would have had me naked before we even made it to a bed, when I was drinking with him.

"Evan, I'm not going to sleep with you. You're drunk. You just showed up tonight, and you decided you're moving back in without talking to me first. You didn't even give me a heads-up. I'm not ready for this. I need time, and we need to talk to Dr. Kelley. I need to talk to Dr. Rosenberg, alone. And, you're fucking drunk. You need to sleep it off."

"Fuck you, Corey. This is still my home too. I'll go sleep in Jacob's room." Evan stands in front of me. This is his Hail Mary. Waiting to see if I'll pity him and feel enough guilt to say *Fuck it. Let's go to bed together*. But, I don't budge. "Fine, good night," he says.

I wait and watch Evan climb the stairs to Jacob's room, where he'll either sleep in the overstuffed, oversize rocking chair or on the floor. I don't want to follow him too closely. I don't want to instigate a fight. While I wait, I look at my phone. It's eleven thirty. I think about texting Chris while I wait on Evan, to tell him what I've found. I worry when Evan's near that if he catches me texting with Chris, he'll freak out. That will be the fight of all fights. The constant feeling that I'm one text with Chris away from losing everything.

It's irrational. I work with Chris, and Evan knows that. He just doesn't like it, never has. Evan has always sensed I had feelings for Chris, even when I didn't know I did. If the roles were reversed, I probably would feel the same way. I hear Jacob's door close. I let out a deep breath. I am relieved. My legs feel wobbly. There is so much emotion built up inside me, my body doesn't know how to physically process it all. My brain needs drugs to calm it. My phone vibrates. I look at the screen.

Chris: Any luck tonight?

I collapse onto the couch. This is what I needed. Chris and work to get me through this moment.

Me: I have a lot to tell you. I don't think she was dating another student. This Mike guy doesn't know her name. He's a martial arts instructor not a student at the college. I don't know who is lying Anne, Sonja, or Mike Lee. I need to go over to the studio he works at tomorrow and show him Sonja's picture. See if she ever took classes there.

Chris: Want me to come with you?

Me: I can handle it on my own.

Chris: I know you can. Diner after?

Me: Yep. I'll go early. They have a nine a.m. class. I can make it over there after I teach.

Chris: Sleep well. Talk to you tomorrow.

I close my eyes and hold my phone against my chest. I can almost smell Chris. It's always the fresh scent of laundry or soap. It's so soft and clean. And the peppermint of his breath—after our accidental kiss, the flavor would appear phantomlike in my mouth for months. It's specific and delicious. I love when the mint mixes with his coffee, and all of a sudden, he smells like a peppermint mocha. I open my eyes and snap out of the dream before I'm too affected to go up the stairs. I don't want to sleep with Evan because I'm turned on by my fantasies of Chris. Fuck, fuck, fuck.

16

Evan is leaving for what looks like a run when I get up at six a.m. I hear the front door close and head to the window to check. I don't need a calendar to keep track of the days when I live with Evan. It's Wednesday, and he's putting out the trash cans. I would have forgotten. I'm sure he thinks he's moved home just in time to rescue me. And there he goes for his run. He'll do three miles and will be back in thirty minutes. Thirty-one if his shoes come untied. I have to get Jacob up and ready to go teach with me, which means he needs a small breakfast that will keep his belly sated for most of the class. Sometimes he sleeps through my seven a.m. classes, sometimes he's ready to party.

I peek into Jacob's room. The sound machine is still going, and he's out. I wonder if he woke up at all during the night, and Evan took care of it. I throw on my prescribed uniform—black leggings and a Cyclone T-shirt in black. Monique is fond of black. Kat had been the partner that ordered bright colors and tie-dyes.

I check my phone to see if Mike Lee ever wrote me back on Instagram. He did not. No worries, I have the address to his studio and the class schedule. I want to be gone before Evan gets back, so instead of waking Jacob and taking him to the kitchen with me, I run downstairs and prepare a bottle for him. No time for nursing this morning, plus I took a Klonopin yesterday, and I do not trust nursing him this soon after I take one. I throw a bunch of baby-food pouches into my bag and a sippy cup of water. I race back upstairs and pull out my brush until I realize, no brush needed. My hair looks even more awesome this morning. I run my fingers through the short strands and make it look styled. I look at my bottle of Paxil and leave it. No pill today. By the time I'm ready, Jacob is up and bouncing as he stands and smiles in his crib.

"You ready to go to work, buddy?" I ask him.

"Mama." He claps for himself, or me. He is my own one-person cheering squad.

"That's right, Mama and Jacob"—I point at him when I say Jacob—"are going to go to work." I pull him out of the crib and work like there's a fire under me to change his diaper, get him in a cute onesie top and leggings, and get us out the door before Evan returns. I just can't get into last night with him.

We're out the door, and I see Ben and Evan running together up the block. You've got to be fucking kidding me. I race to my car like I don't see them and get Jacob strapped in.

"Corey!" Evan says from a few houses away. I can't pretend I don't hear him. He's too close.

"Morning, good run?" I ask both Evan and Ben as they approach now.

"Greatest way to clean out the alcohol from the pores," Ben answers.

"I'm glad I caught you," Evan says. "I'd like to make up for missing dinner last night. What do you say you, Jacob, and me go out tonight?" Evan takes my hands in his and looks at me with pleading eyes. I don't want to put on a show for his new friend and my new neighbor.

"Sure. I'll send you a text later. I'm not sure when I'll be getting home from work yet," I say.

Evan gives me a quick kiss on the cheek and leans in to give Jacob one too. Then he opens my car door for me and almost tucks me inside. He closes my door. It's weird. Ben looks on in what looks like admiration for our relationship, but it's all fake, and I want to let him know that. But, I can't tell if he deserves to know. Did he call his wife crazy, or is that how Evan interpreted it? I smile and wave at them both as I pull off the curb and head to the Cyclone Spin Studio.

I head in the back door and push Jacob in his stroller behind the six a.m. spin class to the front desk. Monique is teaching this morning, so the room is dark. The window shades are down instead of up letting the sun do its thing. Monique always teaches in the dark. In the evening classes she turns out the lights, but she has battery-operated candles lighting herself on the instructor podium. Admittedly, it's pretty cool.

As Monique ends her class with a cooldown, I greet the seven a.m. riders on their way in. Each person checks in on the iPad that sits on the front desk, but I like to watch, put a name to a face so I never forget. The six a.m. class is trying to exit as the seven a.m. riders continue to file in. I look at the list of riders who signed up for the morning class, and I see Anne Silva's name. She hasn't shown up yet, but sure enough her name is on my list.

"Lieberman," Monique yells from the middle of the room. "Holy shit, your hair."

I keep forgetting my hair is different. I smile and give a thumbs-up. I'm staring at the riders coming in, looking for Anne. Did she get in touch with Sonja? Shit. I lied about knowing her.

"I didn't peg you for a pixie girl, Lieberman. I like it," Monique says as she bends over the stroller to greet Jacob with a high five. "This is the first time I think I've ever seen you come in here looking . . . what's the word—"

"Styled?" I say. I feel like I've been styled.

"Groomed." Leave it to Monique to find the most offensive way to say the same thing. "What are you waiting for? Those riders may nominate one of themselves to lead the class if you don't get up there, Lieberman."

"It's Tracey," I say.

"Okay," Monique gives me a half smile, like she's proud or tickled. "Tracey-Lieberman and her new hair throwing down already."

"Just Tracey," I say, and I walk off, pushing Jacob in his stroller to the podium with me. I don't look back at Monique, but I sense either bewilderment or delight. I wonder what she's thinking. She's only ever met Evan once, briefly, but I doubt she cares about our relationship or my personal life. She doesn't like gossip or being in the middle of anyone's business. But she does like strong women. She does support independence. And after Kat's death, she's leaned more in to her work relationships than I'd previously ever witnessed. I hope I made her happy today.

Anne still hasn't arrived, and I'm already five minutes into the first hill. The disappointment I'm feeling has my legs working faster up the incline, and as I look out into the room of riders, I see that everyone's pace is off because of me. It's hard not to make everything a metaphor for my relationships. My timing with Chris has never been right. Evan and me . . . there is no pulse left. Ugh, I need to get out of my head, out of this class, and to the South Pasadena Jujitsu Center.

"For this final climb, I want everyone up and out of the saddle. Take that dial and crank it as far to the right as you can. It's going to be hard, it's going to burn, but what goes up must come down. Let's earn the downhill reward. On three we climb. One, two, three!" I look at Jacob after I yell three into the mic and see that he is staring up at the blue and green lights I put on at the beginning of class. I make a mental note to purchase baby sunglasses for him. I feel a familiar grip on my chest. The anxiety is there, brewing. It can't be from skipping my pill already, too early. I'm okay—day two, and I'm still okay. Two days isn't going to change things that quickly. I just need to change what I'm thinking about, and I'll be fine—where is Sonja Hart? Yes, I need to think about Sonja Hart and not me and not my baby and not the damage I'm doing to my relationship. Sonja needs help. She's somewhere out there with god knows who, and she is my focus now.

Monique let me leave again without taking out the trash or wiping down the bikes some riders neglected to clean themselves. There are always a few. She took care of it, partly because I told her I was in a hurry and likely because she appeared to be mesmerized by my new haircut.

Me: Hey, I'm heading to South Pasadena Jujitsu Center to hopefully see this Mike Lee Sonja Hart may or may not have been dating I'll text you after I'm done and on my way to the diner.

Chris: . . .

I'm left hanging, with those three dots, but at least Chris knows where I am going, so if I never make it to the diner or home, he'll have a place to start if I disappear.

17

The South Pasadena Jujitsu Center is a modest storefront next to a coffee shop, the Gold Line Coffee and Pastry, and a nail salon named Nails by Sabrina in a fancy cursive font. The jujitsu studio has a large front window with decals of jujitsu athletes in poses and the name of the studio in block letters, and it all looks fresh and new. The brick of the building is blindingly white with black trim. So white it looks newly painted. The whole exterior looks new, but the building has to be old. The brick is too beautiful for the new construction I see around Los Angeles. There is a small parking lot for employees only, so I find a spot on the side street next to the building. The sign reads **One Hour Parking**, and I cannot imagine the stress I'd feel taking a class and knowing it cannot go a minute over or I may be ticketed. An adverse feature of Los Angeles—the notorious parking tickets.

I grab my bag and Jacob and head up to the front door. It's locked. I look at the schedule printed on the glass: **open 9 AM – 8 PM, Monday – Thursday**. I look at my phone—it's 8:36 a.m. I decide to take Jacob next door to the coffee shop and wait.

There isn't much foot traffic on this street. It's a destination street, meaning you come and park your car at the business you're attending, and then you leave. Even the coffee shop is quiet for a weekday morning during rush hour. Maybe it's a weekend-crowd kind of place. The lack of a parking lot for customers is the most LA feature—it wouldn't deter Angelenos in the slightest.

"Good morning, what can I get started for you?" the woman behind the counter asks. She's wearing all white and looks more like a pastry chef than someone dealing in coffee beverages.

"A large coffee with cream," I say. "It's pretty quiet. Is that normal?"

"It depends. We're pretty busy on the weekends. I think it's just that all the businesses are less than a year old. I like to say we are building a new clientele. The building was sold, old tenants out, and then it was rehabbed and sold again. So, all new everything. We usually get a little rush after the classes let out next door."

I notice the woman looks close to me in age. She wears a simple wedding band, white gold or platinum maybe. Hell, it could be silver. She, expertly and with confidence I'm familiar with but not used to in a coffee shop, grabs my coffee, then adds a pastry from the display to a plate. It looks like a cheese and some light-colored fruit Danish. Then she comes back with both items.

"You two"—she points to Jacob—"look like you may like a fresh guava-and-cheese Danish."

"Thank you."

"You are welcome. I make them fresh daily—Danish is my passion."

"Is this your place?" I ask.

"It is, well, mine and my husband's. He's on dad duty—our little one woke up with the sniffles."

"I'm so sorry. That's scary."

She gives me a sympathetic look. "It's okay. Mine's five. We're past the freak-out stage of every little cold." She winks at me and Jacob. "I'm Tara."

"Corey, and this is Jacob." I pull my phone from my purse and pull up the picture of Sonja I have saved to show Mike Lee. "Can I ask you a question?"

"Sure."

"Have you ever seen this woman in here before? Likely with the group that comes in after a class next door." I hand my phone over to her. She pinches the screen, and the picture zooms in more. "Do you recognize her?"

As the woman stares at my phone, I look toward the front door and window, and I recognize the view. The little stage is missing, and there's no mic right now, but the window view is spot on from the inside. The tree planted in a pot instead of the ground, the small parking lot, the metallic backing of the window stickers.

"Do you host an open mic here?" I ask.

She looks up from my phone. "Not so much an open mic, but a poetry, storytelling, comedy mic once a month. Had to nix the musicians. Not enough room for their equipment. Man, they all bring so much stuff."

"That woman was here. She read poetry at your event a few weeks ago," I say. Jacob burps and a little spit-up trickles down his chin. I wipe it off with my hand and then my hand with my pants.

"She looks familiar, yeah, but her hair is very different. I do remember her. Mostly because she's so damn talented. Have you heard her stuff?" I nod. "But also, she asked me for a job application. I had to tell her I was staffed up and"—she gestures at the empty café—"I did feel bad, though. I liked her. She helped bus the table after her group finished."

"Do you remember anything about the group she was with? How many people? Was she more intimate with any of them?" I ask.

"No, not really. I'm sorry. I think there were maybe five or six. I was pretty busy working the floor alone." She hands me back my phone and bends down under the counter. "I had her fill out a job application just in case. I might still have it." She stops mid-search and comes up empty handed. "Wait, who *are* you?"

"I'm Corey Tracey. I'm an investigative—" What am I calling myself these days? "I used to be an investigative television journalist—I was on *LA News First* years ago. Now I work independently. I'm freelance." I hate that I am revealing myself. It's vulnerable and yucky.

"I thought your face looked familiar." Tara cocks her head to the side and looks at me for a beat. "You have different hair now too." She continues to pull out a plastic filing bin and sets it on the counter. "These are all the resumés I'm hanging on to in case." In case someone quits or in case they get busy, I don't want to ask. "Let's see, what's her name again?"

"Sonja Hart." As I watch Tara flip through the pile of applications and resumés, I tear a small piece of the guava-and-cheese Danish off and feed it to Jacob. He scrunches his face in disgust, spitting out the pastry. "Not your thing?" I ask him. I take a bite and let the warm cheese and sweet guava melt in my mouth. It's absolutely fresh and the best thing I have maybe ever eaten. I want to ask for another one to take home for dinner.

"Yep, here it is." Tara takes a look over the document. I hope she doesn't have a black marker she can start redacting information with.

"I already know where she lives, and I have access to her phone number," I say. Hoping the honesty prevents any secrecy. "She's missing, and her son is trying to find her." I'm playing the mom card and pray for more sympathy.

I watch Tara hesitate. She looks at Jacob and me once more and then says, "Do the police know you're looking for this woman? I want to make sure this isn't some kind of scam happening. I mean, you look trustworthy, but I can't be sure, and I—"

"No need to explain, I get it." I guess the mommy-and-her-baby duo isn't working on Tara. It's the first time someone is questioning my intentions when I have Jacob in my arms. "Yes, they do. I work as a consultant. Hang on." I set Jacob on the counter and keep him there with one hand while I dig in my bag for Detective Lopez's business card. I know I have it somewhere in this abyss of a bag. I feel its bent, pointy corner and pull it out. "Here, I work with Detective Lopez. You can call her and verify." The card looks so used. It's been through a few bottle leaks in my purse while floating at the bottom under a pile of mommy-and-baby debris. "Sorry, it's seen better days, but it is legit."

"Okay, thank you," Tara says, and she takes the card and hands over the job application. I quickly scan the minimal document. It's a homemade job application. The standard name, pronouns, phone number, address, and then a few lines to put down previous experience. I see that Sonja has worked in food service for what appears to be her whole life, but not here in Los Angeles. One of the three locations listed is in the Central Valley of California, Visalia. That sounds wrong. I thought her kid lived in Oregon. Maybe her son left Visalia, and that's when she moved back here to LA? Did someone follow her down here?

"Oh no, no, buddy. You'll burn yourself, hot—hot," Tara is saying to Jacob, who I now notice is trying to grab my cup of coffee. I watch as his fist knocks the cup right over.

"Oh god, I'm so sorry," I say to Tara. I look around for napkins to wipe up the spill. Tara caught the cup and righted it before the spill could be bigger than a small counter puddle.

"No worries, it's all good." She has already cleared the spill with a towel from behind the counter and is refilling the cup. I watch her put a fresh lid on the top, the previous lost to the floor.

"Jacob, buddy, I'm sorry. Are you hungry?" His eyes give him away. He's about to cry. I don't know if it's because he wasn't allowed to have the coffee, because the coffee spilled, or because he's actually hungry. I go back to my bag and pull out a smoothie pouch. This one has a green lid to indicate it has spinach in it hidden among the apple, pear, and mango. I twist off the cap and hand it to him. He takes it and starts sucking on it. I watch him pucker up his face with the first taste. A powerful punch of flavor. "Is it yummy?" I ask. He nods and continues to suck.

"Mm, that one is yummy," Tara says, looking out her front window. I follow her eyes and see a very well-built, muscular man in black workout pants and a black tank top walking toward the jujitsu center. He has a gym bag over one shoulder and is carrying a set of keys in the other hand. He looks up and sees us watching and gives a wave and smile to Tara.

"Is that Mike Lee?" I ask.

"I don't know his name. He doesn't drink coffee or eat pastries. But he teaches next door."

"So, he wasn't here the night Sonja read her poetry?"

"No, I would have noticed him," she says.

"Do you mind if I take Sonja's application with me? I'll bring it back, promise."

"Sure, but I'm going to keep Lopez's card and add your info to it." I watch Tara write my name on the back of Detective Lopez's card. "Number?"

I rattle off my cell, and she catches it all on the first try. I dig out my wallet to pay.

"On the house, this time," she says.

I thank her again. I like her. I wonder if we can be friends—Lord knows I could use one. Jacob drops his near-empty smoothie pouch on the floor near the exit. I scoop it up off the floor and smile goodbye to Tara one more time. Outside I shove Sonja Hart's job application in my bag and walk next door to the jujitsu studio, ready to speak to whoever the *yummy* man of Tara's dreams is.

I try to pull open the door, but it doesn't budge, so I push, and it still doesn't move. The good-looking guy that waved moments ago runs from the back of the studio to the door.

"We're not open yet," he says through the glass door.

"Are you Mike Lee?" I ask. He unlocks the door and opens it.

"We're not open yet. Class starts in ten minutes, but we don't have day care either," he says.

"Yes, I mean, no, I'm not here to work out. I actually just finished teaching a spin class." I don't know why I just told him that. I'm flustered, sweaty, holding a baby in one hand and a hot coffee in the other. "No, are you Mike Lee?" I ask again.

"I am, yeah. What's up?"

"My name is Corey Tracey, and I'm looking for a woman named Sonja Hart. I think she was a student here?"

"Weird, you're like the second person to ask me that. Is she dead or something?"

"I hope not, but she is missing."

"Shit, I'm sorry, I didn't . . . The name doesn't sound familiar, but I get a ton of one and dones," he says.

"Here, can I show you her picture?" I have no free hand left. My coffee is in one, Jacob in the other, and my phone is floating in my bag, hopefully on the surface. "Do you prefer to hold a hot coffee or a baby for one minute?" I ask as I shove my coffee toward him. Mike takes the coffee in what looks more like obligation than courtesy. I find my phone on top, thank god, and pull up Sonja's picture. "She would have longer hair now."

"Honestly, she looks like a lot of the middle-aged moms that come in to try out martial arts. I mean, maybe?"

Middle-aged moms? Sonja is forty-two. I want to smack him. We do not all look alike, sir. "Okay, I'm not going to ask you for an apology on that one, but for reference, we do not all look alike. Thank you. Second, do you keep a record, like a sign-in or waiver people sign for the class? Maybe we can look her up? See if and when she may have taken a class?"

"Listen, I don't know what's going on here, but I'm not just going to give some rando lady and her baby private information on someone. Again, who are you, or whatever?" He's gesturing while still holding my hot coffee, and I fear it may spill all over him or me and Jacob. I set my phone back on top of everything in my bag and take back my coffee.

"You're right. I apologize. My name is Corey, and I'm privately looking into Sonja's disappearance. Her son hasn't heard from her and has filed a missing-person report. You don't have to give me anything personal. I just want to know if she's been here recently. If I can narrow down the last time someone saw her or the last time she signed into a class, maybe it can help."

"Isn't that what the police do?"

"It's complicated, but I am a private investigator."

"Show me some identification that says that. Prove it to me." This guy knows his stuff. I wonder if he teaches self-defense. I should ask before I go. I hand my coffee back to him and pull out my phone again. I don't have business cards, but I do have old YouTube videos, story credit on Chris's website, and while all my headshot pics are pre-Jacob and prehaircut, I sort of look like me still. I wonder if I look like every other middle-aged mom in them too.

I hold the phone up in his line of sight. "This is me. Corey Tracey."

"Oh shit, my mom loved you." He pauses and gives me a once-over. His body visibly relaxes from the defensive stance blocking the entryway to holding the door open now for Jacob and me to enter. "Come on in, I'll check the computer. Like I said, I can't remember her, but I get a lot of women in here for the free first class. Out of those, only a quarter of them sign up for more."

The space smells mildly of bleach and sweat. The floor is one large mat with a laminate wood perimeter. We walk in a wide circle, and somehow I know it's to avoid the mat with my shoes on. The far wall is all mirrors, and as I walk toward it I cannot help but look at myself. At the woman I've become. My reflection across the room is different from what I imagine it is. I'm not lumbering and awkward like I feel. I'm sturdy and sure footed. My biceps are flexed and powerful as I carry Jacob, and my disheveled leggings and Cyclone T-shirt look like they fit me well, showing off this body, this person I've become. The desk area is behind a counter, just like at Cyclone Studio, but instead of a desktop computer, the jujitsu center has a laptop, a small sleek printer, and a tray of waters behind a sign that says **WATER $2**. It looks like the water is self-serve and pay. There's a small money receptacle next to it—it's just a square metal box with a lock on the front and a slit on the top for bills and coins.

Jacob leans across my chest, reaching for a bottle of water. "No, no, Jacob, I have your cup in my purse," I say. But, before I can dig it out, Mike is twisting off a cap and handing the open bottle to Jacob.

"On the house, little man," he says to Jacob. "Wait, that's okay, yeah? He looks at least a year—he can have a water?"

"Yes, he can. Thank you." And then Jacob dumps the water in his mouth and all over himself. I pull the bottle gently from his hand and set it back down, nearly empty.

Mike sits behind the counter in front of the laptop. "Okay, what's her name again? Sonja what?"

"Sonja spelled with a *J*. S-O-N-J-A. And Hart, H-A-R-T. No *E*."

Mike types the name and then hits the mouse. I watch his pointer finger scroll the mouse in a down motion. He stops scrolling and presses the mouse with a heavy tap.

"Yep, she's been here. It looks like she's come twice. Both times were free trials, weird. It happens, but rarely. Looks like she was here about four weeks ago."

I set my coffee on the counter and pull out the job application and look at the date. It's dated four weeks ago as well. "How many instructors do you have?" I ask.

"Just me and the owner at the moment. It looks like Sonja would have taken both classes with me. I'm sorry I don't remember her. Like I said, I get a lot of women in the mom age range. The class she came to is very popular and gets crowded. It's a hybrid beginner and self-defense."

I believe him. He's not hiding a secret relationship with Sonja Hart. My gut is loud on this one—not the guy.

"If you want to come to the class, the first one is free." He grabs a sheet of paper and hands it to me. It's a printed calendar of the month with every class listed. "My classes have ML next to them."

"Thank you," I say, shoving the calendar into my bag. I grab my coffee off the counter and make to leave. "Mind if I come back if I have any more questions?"

"Only if you take a class." Mike smiles at me, and it's more boyish than before. Is he flirting with me now? Is this why all the women come to his class? The women that are all *mom age* and *look the same*?

A little quid pro quo. "I'll think about it, thank you. And, if she comes back in, would you text me if I leave you my number?"

"Sure thing." I rattle off my cell and watch him add it to his phone.

"Hey, can I get a picture with you for my mom?"

"Next time," I say.

I head out the door and back to the car. I set my coffee on the hood while I strap Jacob into the car seat. "You want to go to the diner, buddy? See Chris?" I ask him. He looks relaxed, and I recognize the face all too quickly. He's making a mess in his diaper. "Okay, well, let's change it when we get there, okay?" And with that, a large gas bubble erupts from his seat. Jacob giggles. "Yes, kid, I bet that did feel good."

18

I get in the driver's seat and pull out of the parking lot. I need to text Chris we're on our way. I can't get the voice function to work to text him. I discreetly pick up my phone and do it by hand.

Me: On my way to diner.

I hit send when I see the police lights in my rearview mirror. Shit. I pull over to the curb and roll the window down and wait.

"Morning, license and registration, please."

I start digging through my bag. I hope I don't get a ticket, and I hope he doesn't run my plates. I had enough run-ins during the last case. As I'm working on scooping out my wallet, Jacob is letting out more gas, and all I can think is, Please don't let it be a blowout.

"Good morning, Officer," I say to the cop. I wouldn't know him. He's a South Pasadena cop, not part of the Northeast LA division. "I'm just trying to get this guy home to change that diaper. We had spinach this morning."

"Ma'am, do you know why I pulled you over?"

"No," I say. I lie, but I'm not going to admit to texting while driving. My phone was practically in my lap. No way he saw it.

"You left a large coffee on the roof of your car that flew off about a block ago and could have caused damage to another car. I'm going to have to give you a ticket for littering."

I look down at the cupholder in the middle console, and sure enough it's empty. Dammit.

"I'm so sorry, Officer, I was distracted with the diaper. Can you let this be a warning? I promise I won't make that mistake again." I hand him my license and registration and insurance card just to show that I'm legally allowed to be behind the wheel. Jacob's diaper is starting to permeate the car. I look at the South Pasadena badge the cop is wearing and don't see a name. He's white, around my age, maybe, and neither attractive nor unattractive. His demeanor reminds me of an actor's interpretation of playing a cop. Maybe he was an actor in a former life. It is Los Angeles.

"I will give you a warning this time, Ms. Tracey-Lieberman. But you've got to be more careful. Good luck with that diaper."

The Lieberman stung a little. He hands me back the three pieces of identification I had passed to him: driver's license, registration, and insurance card. I am so thankful, I take my time putting them away. I check my phone for any texts *before* I pull back into traffic. Nothing back from Chris, but I'm sure he's at the diner waiting for me. It's just a feeling I have.

I get to the diner and know two things are true: First, I smell like shit, literally, and second, Jacob's diaper has exploded. I'm going to have to try to clean him up in the back seat of the car before going in. There's no way I can carry him all the way to the restroom with the explosion he's had. I park and jump into the back seat to begin the arduous task of changing a diaper blowout in the car. I lock the doors, always. I dig through my bag and pull out a half-emptied bag of wipes and a changing pad. I pull Jacob from his seat and see that it's halfway up his back. I'll have to wash the car seat when we get home too.

I sit Jacob up and strip him out of the onesie, taking it all off, piece by piece, down over his legs instead of over his head. Jacob is finding the entire ordeal hilarious and bouncing himself around. I have to use one hand to hold his arms up over his head, so he doesn't end up touching any of the mess.

Ten wipes in, and the box is empty. I grab the water bottle Jacob took from the jujitsu center and pour it onto some napkins I keep in the center console in case I need to blow my nose. I get as much off as I possibly can. "I promise a bath as soon as we get home."

The extra outfit in my bag is a size too small for him, but I make a mental note to update that as well. His chubby legs are squeezing out of the onesie, and I can only snap one button shut over his diaper. I scoop the soiled clothes, diaper, napkins, and baby wipes up in one hand and Jacob in the other. We walk up to the House of Pies diner, our makeshift office, and I throw out the entire lot of soiled items into the trash. He would grow out of the onesie in a month or less anyway. No need to hang onto what I don't even think I could put in the washing machine, as soiled as it is.

We walk in, and Chris spots us before we see him. He gets up and waves us over. A booth in the back, not our usual spot. I walk to the back with Jacob. I swear I can still smell his dirty diaper.

"Hey," I say, "sorry I took so long. I was in the car, changing a huge diaper." I make a wide-eyed face at Jacob when I say huge, and he bursts into a fit of laughter. It's contagious and has me laughing with him. But even though I'm laughing, I have a pitlike feeling in my stomach.

"I think," Chris says and dips a clean napkin into his water glass, "you may have missed a few spots." He takes the napkin and rubs my neck and then my upper arm.

"Well, I guess that explains why I was still smelling it." I'm not even embarrassed. Two days off the Paxil and still subdued, mostly. I am feeling fine without it.

"How did it go with *Matmastermike*?" Chris asks. The smile on his face when saying Mike Lee's online name spreads all the way up to his hazel eyes. His teeth are on display, perfect and so white against his tan. There's a small dimple on his chin usually covered by facial hair, but he must have shaved today. I would ask, but that would definitely be over the line, I think. Everything about his current demeanor makes me relax, and I don't ever want that to change between us.

"I wouldn't make too much fun, *NelaScanBoy*." Chris's former social media handle was something of the past now that he had revealed himself with an online paper that reported on the stories he and I worked on—crime in the northeast area of Los Angeles. I never minded his screen name, but Evan absolutely abhors it. I mean, he abhors everything about Chris.

"That's not fair. I was incognito." Chris laughs despite the truth. "Now, are you going to share what you know?" I start to when the waitress comes by and delivers a table of food. Everything I usually order for myself: a grilled cheese, soup, french fries, and coffee. Plus, a bowl of fruit and a plain scrambled egg for Jacob.

I wait for the waitress to retreat. Then I say, "Thank you."

"You can thank me by telling me what we know."

"Right, so, Sonja took two classes with Mike Lee. He doesn't remember her. I believe him. It looks like she took his free trial class, and those are usually filled with a lot of people, if it's anything like Cyclone. I also found out she applied for a job at the coffee spot next door." I reach into my bag and pull out the job application and pass it to Chris. "The date she filled it out matches the date of the second class she took at the jujitsu center. That was last month, about four weeks ago." I take a bite of my sandwich. "The coffee shop is also where she read her poetry. At their monthly open mic. Doesn't sound like she had a date there, just friends."

Jacob is standing and leaning into my shoulder for support while I cut the squares of honeydew and cantaloupe into smaller squares he can pick up and gum, so he doesn't choke. In his hand is a fistful of scrambled eggs. Half the eggs make it into his mouth, the other half pour out into my lap and onto the booth's bench.

"Okay, so she's not dating Mike Lee," Chris says.

"But why make that story up to your hairstylist?" I take a sip of coffee. "Unless she didn't. Who would you lie about dating if you were a student in college?" I say. "Your professor."

"We need a copy of her classes."

"I also need to speak to Anne Silva again. She knows more. She also signed up for my class this morning but didn't show."

"Which I would say has absolutely nothing to do with Sonja, except that it obviously has everything to do with Sonja, and it's not just a coincidence," Chris says.

I take a mouthful of food. I can't think, and that's all I need to do, think. Once the Paxil had kicked in to its full effect a few months ago, my brain began getting gluey. It's like being stuck at the end of a sentence and not being able to finish it.

Sometimes it feels like there are shelves of information, but cinder block walls have been erected in front of them, and I have no access and no tools to break through. Two days no Paxil, and that hasn't improved yet.

I thought that was good. I wanted that because the panic attacks were physically and mentally unbearable. The obsessive thoughts were a constant fear that I can only remember as dangerous.

"What are you thinking?" Chris asks.

"I'm not," I start to say when Jacob hits me in the face with a balled-up hand of honeydew melon. The moment is passing in my brain. The restraint and grip on my emotions lessening as I smile and laugh at Jacob. "I should not be laughing, little dude, but Mommy needed that." I want to tell him that hitting Mommy in the face is bad, but I can't bring myself to do it. It's been two days off my medicine, and so far, no panic attack. No stirring of impending doom when I think, Knives. That's good. Maybe I am better. Maybe I don't need them anymore or ever again. If I have the Klonopin to catch them before they start, like last night, and the cycle has been broken from having the Paxil in my system for six months, maybe I'm better.

I'll call Dr. Rosenberg tomorrow and tell him. I should write it down, set a reminder. There are so many little tasks, to-dos that I can't remember. Do I blame the Paxil, or is that just motherhood.

"Let's check in with Sonja's son," I say. "Maybe something has changed. Maybe he's heard from her today. When is the last time you spoke to him? Are we sure their relationship is solid? He's not trying to scam someone into telling him where his mom is, and she's not trying to get away from him, right?"

"No, but I'll check in with him when we're done. I have to head out soon. I have to pick my friend up from the airport."

I know he means his girlfriend. No one picks up their friends from the Los Angeles International Airport. We send a car service. It's absolute mayhem and takes hours. But, a lover, most of us make the trip for a lover.

"Yeah, I should get this guy home for a proper nap. I'll see what else I can find out online. I'll call Lopez. Maybe she did me a solid and looked into it a little." I look at the time. It's barely noon. I should head over to South Pasadena Community College. You can't rack up a bunch of absences and not have the professor send a warning or something. It would be noted, somewhere.

For the first time I'm able to snatch the bill and pay while Chris is in the restroom. It's a power move. Or I'm just tired of feeling like everyone is taking care of me. I hate that he usually grabs it before me, and shoving money at him is getting embarrassing when he never accepts it.

"I'm this way," I say, pointing to the right of the parking lot. I don't see his car, and I pray we're not near each other. Since he brought up going to the airport, I cannot get the picture out of my head of him with a woman. All those flirty smiles working their magic on her. Peppermint kisses saved for her. I wonder if they were together when we kissed. Oh god, I hope not. I hope I didn't make him. I can't even say it.

"I'll walk you," Chris says.

Fuck.

"Great, so are you heading to LAX then? Or Burbank Airport." If he ends up saying Burbank, I may have gotten the whole thing wrong in my head. Anyone would pick up a friend from Burbank. It's basically like going through the drive-through. Two terminals and no waiting. And it's only twenty minutes away. Please say Burbank.

"LAX, I'm picking up my lady friend, Megan."

She has a name. Megan. What do I say? Something kind and not snarky. I don't want to show my hand.

"Wow, you must be pretty serious. Picking someone up at LAX is a big deal." Fuck. That's not what I wanted to say. Fuck. Fuck. Fuck.

"Yeah, I tried to set up a car service for her, but she's been gone awhile and wanted to see me right when she landed."

"That is serious." I feel my shoulders droop a little.

"It's only been a couple of months, but we've known each other since college. There was this reunion, and we both ended up at the bar talking. She's not in the market to get married again. She doesn't want anything serious. Bad divorce that she's still going through. Too many assets. That's actually why she was out of town. Probably wants me as a palette cleanser when she gets off the plane." Chris chuckles softly.

It's more vulnerable than I'm accustomed to seeing him. I like it. I'm jealous of Megan. I wonder if she gets this soft, shy, insecure side of him often. "And what about you? Do you want to get married?"

"I was married before," Chris says.

"What?" No. I would have known, wouldn't I?

"It was right out of college. In fact, we were college sweethearts. We were young and thought we were old enough to know we'd love each other forever."

"What happened?" Did they have kids? Does Chris have a child? A teenager? I'm crumbling. Why don't I know about this?

"We only lasted a year. Bought a little house in East LA, played house in it, but we didn't play well together after a few months." We are in the middle of a parking lot, walking, and Chris pauses. He just stands there and pauses. "It was a long time ago. There were some hurt feelings, mostly sadness. I think because you only get to do it the first time once, you don't want to fail." He starts walking again until he reaches my car, and we stop. "Anyway, she's in San Diego now. Married, three kids. Happy."

"I'm so sorry. I can't believe I didn't know."

"When we met, Corey Tracey, my marriage had been long over. It lasted less time than most first dates." Chris laughs at his joke like it can erase the admission. "And, I admit, I had a little crush on you when we met. I didn't want you to think of me as the young divorced guy, so I never told you."

"That doesn't make me feel any better. I investigate everyone—I didn't know." I am suddenly insecure. How had I been so casual about Chris that I never took a deep dive into his life? "You did not have a crush on me. But, I appreciate you trying to make me feel better for being a shit friend after all these years of not knowing or asking." I open the car door and get Jacob strapped into his seat. "Did she cheat on you?" I don't know why I ask it. Inappropriate, personal, obtuse. It comes out more accusatory than curious at the same time. Shit. "I'm sorry. I didn't mean it like that. Did either of you meet someone else, and that made it easier to say, 'This isn't working'?"

"I don't know if she did, and it didn't matter. I know I didn't, and I was willing to try, but we weren't meant for the long haul. Not everyone is. We were fighting over nothing all the time. She wasn't happy. In the first six months of our marriage, she bought three new cars without telling me. She'd drive one, not like it, and return it like it was a T-shirt that didn't fit. Just kept returning them for a new one. The third time I came home and saw a different new car in the driveway, I knew we had a bigger problem. She wasn't happy with me, with the relationship, and no matter how many cars she bought and traded, she was not going to ever be happy."

I understand too well. It aches in my chest how much I understand, and I have to go home and live with the person I said I'd spend forever with, knowing we aren't right.

"Did you two have children? Are any of the three in San Diego yours?" I want to know. I'm furious I never took the time to ask him before. Or, maybe I'm mad I've been so vulnerable in our work relationship, and he hasn't trusted me enough to be the same.

"No, no kids. I tried, though. I thought maybe if we had a baby, she'd be happy with us. But it didn't happen."

The admission makes me think of Ben and Julia. It didn't happen for them either or hasn't yet. The empty crib they schlepped across the country is really the only thing that makes me think they might still be trying. Is he trying to give her this baby to save their marriage? And is Julia so unhappy that she just wants out? Is the guilt over pushing him out of her life consuming her, the way mine consumes me? What if it hadn't happened for Evan and me? What if there was no Jacob . . . I would be free. The thought drops from my brain straight down my spine and explodes in my heart and guts. I desperately try to unthink it—to reframe the thought as *Ben and Julia* might be fortunate that they can't conceive, because if they do, they won't ever be able to extricate from each other. But I can't shake the guilt of what I've just done: wondered if my life would have been better if my son hadn't been born.

"What about you, any marriages before Evan?"

The question snaps me back to the present moment. Thank you, Chris. You don't know the hell you've just rescued me from.

"No. One reckless, premature proposal that resulted in an immediate breakup, but no marriages. Honestly, I didn't think I was the marrying type."

"Why?" Chris looks at me with so much care and patience there's a part of me that feels I may be able to be honest.

"Another time. You have to get going, and this guy"—I nod my head toward the passenger door—"needs a nap."

"I'll let you know what I find out from the son."

"Sounds good. I'll talk to you later."

I watch Chris walk away for a moment. I wait to see if he'll look back at me. He doesn't. I get in the car and turn to Jacob.

"I'm so sorry, baby. There is nothing I wouldn't give or go through to be your mommy."

I stretch across to the back seat and kiss Jacob on his nose, and he lets out a giggle that lets me know that in his eyes I have done no wrong. But I know what I did. I slide back into the front, start the car, and leave.

19

I park outside the college in a visitor spot near the registrar's office. I grab Jacob, asleep, and tuck him into the baby carrier I pull on over my shoulders. He doesn't even flinch at the transfer from seat to carrier. Every time he sleeps through being moved from one location to the next like this, I tell myself it's because of a growth spurt—nothing else. Not the medicine I still fear leaks into my breast milk. Not the on-and-off cold he seems to be battling this week. Not the separation of his father and me. No, it's just a growth spurt.

The door to the registrar's office is open. It's an unremarkable office. More like walking into a bank. The waiting chairs are blue vinyl with a wood frame that reminds me of a kitchen from the nineties. Not the kitchen in the house I grew up in, but in the fancy subdivisions where you chose from four different house models and had to ask an HOA if you could paint your front door a different color. Every house was designed to match or complement each other.

There is only one person behind the front desk. She looks like a student.

"Hi," I say, "I'm wondering who I need to speak to about getting a copy of a current student's class schedule?"

"Hi, are you the student? Do you have your student ID with you?" she asks.

"No, it's a friend of mine." I doubt this is going well, but she's young. Maybe she won't be able to say no to me as a threatening older woman.

"I'm so sorry. We do not release the schedules of our students. That's confidential. Have you asked her to print you a copy?"

"No, the problem is she's missing."

"Missing? Like, kidnapped? I should call the campus police—"

"No, no. I just haven't heard from her in about a week and would like to chat with her professors to see if she's been attending classes. Or, when the last time she did attend a class was."

"Have you filed a police report?" she says, giving me a hard stare.

I look at Jacob and stroke his back. He lets out a small whimper of a sigh, perfect timing. I am hoping to draw the young woman's attention to him, so she'll stop looking at me like I'm trying to scam someone. College students today are far superior to when I was a kid. The access to technology and television and films on demand make them savvier and more intuitive. If she can see me as her own trustworthy mom and not a predator, maybe I have a shot.

"Yes, her son has filed a police report."

"And who are you to this student?"

I don't know if I should tell her the truth or make something up.

"I'm a friend." I decide to pivot. "Okay, I'm not a friend. I'm an investigator."

"Oh my god, do you have a podcast? I'm obsessed with true crime podcasts."

I think quick and pull out my phone. "I was a TV news investigator." I pull up clips from my past. "That's me." I show her the video.

"No way, that is so cool." She snatches the phone from my hand and turns up the volume. The sound of my voice makes me cringe a little.

"Is there any way you can help me?" I am pleading a little as she watches, engrossed, at the next clip of me.

"Okay, so, I can't help you, but I'll leave a note for my boss." She pulls out a clipboard and pen and hands them to me. "And I'll tell her that you're a famous true crime reporter. Fill out the top part of this sheet. Just the section to give your name, telephone number, and email, and I'll make sure she gets the information about the student and you." I watch her pull an index card–size sticky notepad out for herself. "What did you say the student's name is that's missing?"

"Her name is Sonja Hart."

She jots down the name in blocky print, all capital letters, and then draws a box around the name. Going over it not once, but three times. I hand her back the clipboard, paper filled out, and pen.

"Thank you," I say. "May I have a business card or a number I can call to check back in?"

"We only have a general line for the public." She hands me a card that says *REGISTRAR'S OFFICE*. Underneath that is a phone number and email that reads: *registrar@southpascc.edu*.

"Who should I ask for when I call?"

"Just explain to the person who answers. I'll make sure the office knows who you are and what you're looking for." She hands back my phone. "It's so cool to meet you."

"Thank you." I leave with no goodbye. There's no wishing me luck or hope that we find her. I play the entire exchange back in my head and cannot get over how completely sterile it felt.

I sit on a bench outside the office and pull out my phone. I need to tell someone. I need help, and no one wants to be the person to give any.

Me: It's Corey. Did you hear anything about Sonja Hart yet?

Detective Lopez: No—and I checked, but there's nothing you don't already know.

Me: No one will tell me anything. Can you make the college give you her class schedule, anything?

Detective Lopez: At this time, no crime has been committed. It's completely up to the institution's rules. If they told you no, they'll tell me no. Corey, use the resources you have. I know you, dig deeper.

Me: What about Renee Flores? Did you get the dates the arsonist was incarcerated?

. . .

I hate those damn dots. No response. Think, Corey, what do you know? I know that Sonja Hart left with a suitcase Monday morning, and it's now Wednesday afternoon. Too many days to end well. I know Anne Silva knows more than she told me. And, I know Lopez is right, I need to do something more.

I get home with Jacob and don't see Evan's car in the driveway. I look at the clock and see I have at least an hour before he gets off work. Jacob has been asleep for just shy of an hour. If I can get in the house without waking him, maybe I'll have a good thirty more minutes to work.

I make it as far as the front door when I hear Julia's voice from across the street. I turn to look. She's not talking to me. She's on her cell phone. Sitting on the front steps of her porch. She sounds erratic, but she's not pacing around or standing. She's seated calmly. She's not even flailing her arm around while she talks. But her voice is chaotic. Switching between worried, annoyed, angry, sad—erratic.

I can't process it right now. I slip inside and gently tiptoe upstairs to get Jacob in his crib. I have a plan, and I need as much time as he can give me.

Once Jacob is down, curtains all the way closed to keep his room dark so he sleeps longer, I open my computer at the dining room table and create an account under my own name on YouTube: Corey Tracey

Investigative Reporter NELA. NELA is short for Northeast LA and a nod to Chris's old handle.

I type out a script because I'm not ready to improvise. I know what I need to say, and it has to come across with sincerity. I can do this. It's been a few years, but you never forget how to be sincere on camera. If there's anyone out there that remembers me from *LA News First*, that's all I need.

I turn on my phone's camera and start to record:

"Hi, my name is Corey Tracey. Some of you may remember me from *LA News First*. I'm hoping you remember me as the person that always told you the truth and didn't embellish a story to make it sound better. I need your help. There's a missing woman from the Highland Park neighborhood of Northeast LA. Here is what we know—her name is Sonja Hart. She's five feet, four inches tall. She's forty-two years old. She used to wear her hair short and bleached. Currently it is dark blonde to light brown, about shoulder length. She is a student at South Pasadena Community College. I'd like her to know that her son is very worried about her. If you know Sonja or have any information about her whereabouts, please reach out to me. My email and a picture of Sonja Hart is in the description below. You don't need to leave your name, but please send any information that may help us locate Sonja. Thank you."

I stop recording and don't bother to watch it back. I'll end up deleting it if I do, and I don't have time to record it again. There is only now. My finger hovers over the "Post" button, and then I pause. What if this is the wrong move? What if someone has Sonja and feels safe, but my video puts pressure on them to act? What if they hurt Sonja because of me? I admit to myself that these are all real possibilities. But most of what I've just said is on the Facebook post already. And it's also entirely possible that if I don't take this chance right now, it might be the reason Sonja Hart doesn't come home to her son. I post the video. I tag Chris's news blog. I create a Reddit account under my own name and post it in the Northeast LA subreddit. I email it to my old news station. The worst that can happen is they delete it. The best, they email me back and ask questions.

I put my phone away. I don't want to give myself any opportunity to delete what I've posted. I'm going to wait and see if anyone even watches it and comments. I'm stalemated, and it's all I've got. I should text Chris and let him know, but he's picking up his girlfriend. Shit. I wonder what she looks like.

I open Facebook on my phone and start scrolling through Chris's profile. I look at his friend list and search for a Megan, but there aren't any. I look through the past few months of posts, but there aren't any pictures. Typical Chris. What kind of lawyer did he say she was . . . or did he? No. I can't remember. The stupid Paxil erases so much short-term memory it's wild. If it took six months to fix the problem, maybe it will take that long to make things less gluey and blocked.

"*Fuck you!* I want you to leave!" I jump at the sound of Julia's voice outside. My front door and windows are all shut, and I can make out every word she's saying. She's screaming at the top of her lungs.

I run outside to see who she's screaming at and see Ben. He's just standing there while she shoves him in the chest away from the house.

"I don't want you here. *Leave*," she says.

I debate running across the street, but I would have to abandon Jacob alone, asleep, vulnerable in his bed. I can't do that. It's too far. What if he falls out of his crib and needs me? I watch Julia continue to shove Ben, and he takes it. No arms raised in defense, but he's also not leaving. He's not trying to calm her down either. Two things run through my head. He's letting her humiliate herself in front of the neighbors. He wants to look meek and like the victim of his *crazy* wife's actions. Or he's not trying to do anything. Maybe he is defeated and tired. I grab my keys from inside and lock the door. I give a quick plea to the house. "Please protect my baby. I'll only be a minute. And just across the street. Thank you." I kiss my hand and place it on the door, and I'm off the porch, crossing the street to Julia and Ben's front yard dispute.

"Hey, guys, how are you?" I ask them at the same time.

"Hey, Corey," Ben says. "We're just having a hard day. Don't worry about us."

"Julia, is that true? Are you okay?" She doesn't look at me. She keeps her head down, eyes to the ground. I can't tell if she's crying or not. Her face is red from shouting. "Julia, do you want to come over for a cup of coffee?"

"I think it's best we take our conversation inside. Corey, thank you, but we have some things we're in the middle of," Ben says. He walks over to his wife, puts his arm around her, and guides her up the porch of their home.

"Julia, if you need anything, I'm home. My door is always open," I say. She doesn't even acknowledge that I'm there. She's gone completely still as she steps into the house, Ben behind her. He shuts the door without even so much as a small wave goodbye to me. I stand and watch their front window for a full minute, but neither of them makes an appearance. I assume they've hidden themselves in the bedroom to finish their fight away from the prying eyes and ears of the neighbors. And we are prying, every last one of us.

I head back across the street, hoping that Jacob hasn't awoken alone and scared because I closed his curtains all the way.

"Mrs. Evan," Pete calls. I didn't notice he was outside watching the fight as well. He calls all the women on the street by their husband's first name, and the unmarried women he doesn't address at all. A sign of respect for the men and disrespect for all women.

"Hi, Pete."

"They're not good, huh?"

"I don't know, to be honest. Have you heard anything besides that outburst? Do you know what started it, Pete?" I ask.

"He's always leaving. Doesn't say where he's going. Mrs. Ben doesn't like it. She yells at him when he goes, when he comes back. She sounds a little . . ." Pete whistles while rotating his finger in a circle pointing at his head.

"That doesn't make her crazy, Pete. Maybe he's the one that's crazy, always leaving and not telling her where he's going. Who he's seeing. Why he's going."

"Not a woman's place if you ask me. I dunno. I keep to my own business." I'm so sick to death of that narrative. It's no use arguing with Pete. He's too old to reeducate and never going to change his views at this point. Any harm he's caused was years ago. No one listens to him now anyway. His influence is limited to the crisp single-dollar bills he passes out to the little kids when he can get close enough.

"I need to get inside. Jacob is napping," I say. Pete looks up at the house. At the upstairs windows, like he knows exactly where Jacob is. I'm mad at myself that I let him know I left my baby alone in the house, asleep.

20

I get inside and run up the stairs to Jacob's room. He's still sound asleep, and I know he's going to be up all night now. I end his nap by pulling open his curtains and letting the late-afternoon sun pour in. He stirs a bit at first. His strawberry-blond hair is poofy on top and flat on the sides. I love watching him stretch, rub his eyes, catch sight of me, and smile. He pulls himself up, so he's standing with the support of the lip of the crib.

"Mama," he says, smiling and bouncing. "Mama!"

"Yes, buddy, did you have a good nap? Are you hungry? Want a snack?"

"Okay." That's a new one. It's not a crisp, clear *okay*, but it is definitely *okay*. A new word.

"Okay," I say. "Okay, let's have a snack, okay." He bounces, trying to launch himself into my arms as I lean in to pick him up.

"Hello?"

I stop on the second step down.

"Corey?"

My anxiety stirs, roiling through my intestines. Evan is home.

"Hi," I say. I'm frozen at the top of the stairs, not wanting to move. Maybe he'll leave, and that will be that. I don't know. This is panic but not the kind with the intrusive thoughts. No, intrusive thoughts aren't giving me this panic, Evan is. His voice, his being here, his letting himself into the house without telling me he's here by text after a month of separation. I'm not ready for this. I feel the sweat from the anxiety and panic pooling under my arms and at my lower back.

"Dada, hi, Dada, hi," Jacob says. He's squealing and rocking himself in my arms, trying to squirm his way to Evan.

"Let's go see Dada," I say. My voice cracks as I say it. I'm trying to keep myself together. I do not fear Evan. It's just . . . over. We are over, and I'm too much of a coward to tell him—maybe Ben and I have more in common than I thought. I'm afraid of what it will do to Jacob, and this house, and my life. Is this regret? I do not regret my baby. I cannot articulate the feeling. I'm searching and pulling the threadbare strings in my brain, trying to get it to work like it did before the Paxil and postpartum anxiety.

"Hi," I say to Evan again, now that we are face-to-face. He leans in and kisses me on the cheek. I almost back away so he can't reach me, but Jacob nearly leaps out of my arms and into Evan's, pulling me forward with the force and strength of his small body.

"You just waking up, little man? You look like you had a long nap today."

"Okay," Jacob says. It comes out with so much glee and pride.

"Okay," Evan says back. "Do you want to have dinner? Should you and Mommy and Daddy have dinner?"

"Okay," Jacob says again.

"We have a new word," I say.

"Nah, he's been saying that on the weekends with me. We've been working on *okay* for a while, right bud?"

"Okay," Jacob says and bursts into a fit of giggles. Why didn't Evan share that with me? Why didn't he tell me that Jacob had another word? And why is this the first time I'm hearing Jacob use it? It's my fault. I get so wrapped up in work, I don't listen enough. The way Evan would relish in hearing me say that out loud. It would be so validating for him. Exactly what he's spent our entire marriage complaining to me about, my devotion to my job. When we dated, he liked it. Once we became a family, it was off-putting. Once we had a baby, it was a crime. Unmaternal.

I look for my phone. I'd left it when I went outside to see the commotion between Ben and Julia. I find it exactly where I left it on the table with my laptop. I wake the screen, and there are multiple notifications stacked up. I open YouTube, and it's a free-for-all of comments and wishes of luck. There are already over two hundred comments. It will take me the rest of the night to get through each one. I check Reddit, and it's nearly the same.

"Corey?" Evan says.

I flip around from the table and spot Evan in the kitchen, next to our dining room, staring at me. "What?" I ask.

"Everything okay?"

"No. I have a missing woman to find."

"Did you crack your cold case?"

"No. I haven't done shit on the cold case. The local missing woman I told you about. I've been moving through sludge, trying to think my way through it, but I'm starting to see a little clearer now."

"How's that?" he asks.

"I quit taking the Paxil."

"Did you talk to Dr. Rosenberg about coming off it?" Evan asks. There's a hint of something in the tone. An energy shift—he says it not with contempt, but there's ice, and it bites.

"Dr. Rosenberg said I can come off it whenever I want, no problem." I wasn't lying—he did say that. The caveat was and is that it wouldn't be without his direction first, but Evan no longer has privilege to my sessions with Rosenberg. Patient-client and all that follows. Technically he never had the privilege. I chose to let him in. I am now choosing to shut him out. "Are you okay feeding Jacob? I'd like to go upstairs and do a little work on this case."

"Of course. I think I'll take him out and let you work in a baby-free house for a bit if that's okay with you?"

No, no, no. I want to control the environment, not lose my baby. I have to think quickly of a reason to say no. Think, Corey, think.

"Corey?" Evan says. I'm staring at him and not saying a word. I cannot feel if my mouth is frozen in a frown or a straight line. Neither one great for this moment. Evan can read my expression, and I don't want him to. I'm stuck giving in. I have to play my cards right all the time, or Evan could take Jacob from me permanently. What if I'm the one living in a short-term rental or an RV full-time while he and Jacob are here in the house together. A nanny or another woman coming in and taking care of my baby full-time. What if Jacob starts to call her Mommy. I'm spiraling. My throat is tight, and swallowing is difficult. I would take a Klonopin right now, but that would give Evan receipts of my mental status. *Too fucked up to take care of our son, stopped taking her medication without authorization. She's a crazy person.*

"Yeah, yeah, that would be great," I say. I smile until I feel it reach my eyes. No misinterpretation. "Sorry, I was zoned out for a minute. I think I had déjà vu—like we've done this exact moment before." I softly chuckle. It is fake, but I've had a lot of practice in the news business giving a false chuckle when I needed to get out of a potentially bad situation. "You guys go. Enjoy some dinner together."

"Want me to bring you something back?"

"No, I'm okay." I don't want him to be out any longer than necessary with Jacob. Knowing Evan, he'd place me an order after he and Jacob had finished, requiring them to wait longer for my food to be done. No. I don't want that at all.

"Okay, I'll check in with you in a bit," he says.

"Do you have a diaper bag?" I ask.

"Yep, packed and ready in my car. I'm all set."

Of course, he's Evan, and there's never a situation Evan isn't completely prepared for.

I get to work on the comments from my post as soon as I hear the door shut and lock behind Evan. So many posts are just prayers for Sonja Hart. If not prayers, prayer hands. There are several hundred about me and my current appearance versus the last time I was on the air. I am chubby, old, and trying too hard, according to the most brutal. That's good. No one has called me a hag. Then there are the typical pile-ons of Sonja. The type of things you see all over socials when there's a victim: *Was she on drugs? Is she an addict? It was the husband, it's always the husband. Did her family give you permission? Probably a scam.* Nothing with any firsthand knowledge of Sonja and no friends.

I switch over to Reddit to see if there's more. A lot of the same, plus the armchair psychologists claiming Sonja likely had a mental breakdown, as in psychosis. I can't rule it out, but if that were the case, and if she were on medicine that she needed to take daily, the police may have taken the disappearance more seriously. And her son, her son would know that, right? He would have said as much to Chris. I think about my own mental breakdown just six months ago. The panic attacks that ruled over my body. The intrusive thoughts that drove the panic attacks. The constant loop that something, someone would hurt my baby. That if I were left alone, I may harm myself. None of that was true. I didn't want any of that, but fear was driving me until the Klonopin and the Paxil and Dr. Rosenberg. But that can't be Sonja. She didn't have a new baby, no postpartum anxiety and hormones fueling her.

No, I think she had a suitcase, got into her car, a white Toyota Prius, or so the custodian said, and she left. *Why* is the best question I can ask right now. I continue to scroll through the subreddit page and click on every comment, opening a new stream of commenters, commenting on the original comment. And, if I hadn't read every single subcomment, I would have missed the one that was specifically addressed to me:

> Corey Tracey, I know Sonja. I will email you.

Whoever the commenter is, they are taking their time emailing me. I make a mug of cereal and add a scoop of peanut butter to it. The house is so quiet when I'm alone. I don't remember anywhere I lived alone being this quiet ever. What did I do, play music? Run the TV? I can't remember. Maybe my thoughts were always so loud and demanding I didn't notice the quiet. Maybe the Paxil has muted so much of that mental noise that it simply wasn't loud anymore.

I look at my phone to check the time. Evan and Jacob have been gone for well over an hour now. They should be on their way home. I expect Evan will text me any minute to make sure I don't want him to bring me any food. I take a huge bite of cereal and peanut butter as I lean against the counter to eat. I can't be bothered to sit, too agitated and on alert until Jacob is home.

I jump at a pounding on the door. It's urgent, and then I hear, "Corey? Are you home? It's Julia." I leave my mug of cereal and answer the door.

"Julia, is everything okay?"

"It's Ben. He's left, and his phone is turned off, so I can't reach him or find him on the app, and I don't know if he's—" Julia stops, looks at her phone that is currently trying to ring Ben, but a voicemail answers instead.

"You've reached Ben's phone. You know what to do next. Make it urgent." What a weird thing to say. Maybe it's an inside joke, but what would make that funny?

"Julia, what do you mean Ben is gone? I saw him with you just a couple of hours ago. Do you remember? You two were outside arguing."

"We weren't arguing. I hate when people say that."

"Okay, I'm sorry. It appeared you were upset," I say. I change my tone entirely. She's distressed but lucid. "Why don't you come inside and have a seat?"

Julia nods and moves toward the couch and drops down into the seat with the weight of the world in her lap. The phone in her hand a brick weighing down her wrist.

"Ben and I lost a baby last year. Did he tell you?" I shake my head. "I didn't want to move here. I wanted to stay near my friends and family. I just haven't really felt like myself since the miscarriage."

"I'm so sorry, Julia. I can't imagine how hard that must have been."

"No, no, you can't because you have your baby. You get to hold him every day. Put him to sleep. Hear him call you Mama."

I can't argue with her. All those things are true. It's also true that I feared the worst. That I would lose him. That he wouldn't wake up one day.

"Don't look at me like that. I don't need pity. I just want to know where my husband is. Do you know?" Julia's face is like magic. One minute she was in distress, eyes filled with tears and frantic. Now she's firm, angry, but composed. It's fascinating to watch the absolute extreme of both emotions within seconds of each other.

"Julia, I don't know where Ben is. I don't even know why I would."

"Ben was out drinking with your husband last night. I assume your husband tells you where he's going. Or am I overestimating your relationship?"

She is overestimating. I feel my mouth hanging open. I'm in awe of this person sitting in front of me. Moments ago, I wanted to give her a hug and tell her it would be okay and that I'm sorry she had endured so much pain and grief. "My husband is out to dinner with our son. I'm sure he'll be home shortly."

"Where?" Julia asks.

"Excuse me?"

"Where did your husband go to dinner with your baby?"

I don't know. I don't think I asked. Evan asked if I wanted him to bring me back something. Did he say what? Shit. I don't know where my husband is, and I don't care except that he has my baby. I don't know where my baby is.

The panic sets in. It's full blown. I jump up from the couch and grab my phone. I text Evan.

Me: WHERE ARE YOU?

...

...

What is he typing? Is he trying to type me back? Do those dots appear if he's typing someone else, or can only the person he's texting back see them?

Me: Evan, I mean it. Where are you? Where did you and Jacob go?

Before I can hit send, the front door is opening, and Evan and Jacob walk in, followed by Ben.

"Hello, we're back!" Evan stops and catches sight of Julia before landing on me.

"Ben, I'd like to go home now." If I didn't know that she had just arrived at my house out of the blue and been here for all of five minutes, it would have sounded like I'd been babysitting her all day, and she was over it.

"Of course. Did you get the note I left you?" Ben asks. Julia shakes her head. "I'm sorry, I didn't mean to worry you. You were napping, and I thought you needed the rest." Ben reaches for Julia's hand, and she allows him to lace his fingers through hers. "Evan, thanks for dinner. Appreciate it, man. Run in the morning?"

"Definitely, see you outside at six."

This is weird. Read the room, men. I take Jacob out of Evan's arms and follow Ben and Julia onto the front porch. "Julia, thank you for stopping by. If you need anything, I'm around."

"Thank you. I'm sorry I came by unannounced."

"It's fine," I say. Ben looks at her. I guess it could pass as sympathy or irritation, frustration, desperation.

Inside I close the door behind me and look for Evan, but he's not in the kitchen. I run up the stairs with Jacob in my arms and find him changing in the bedroom. I immediately apologize for barging in on him and step out to the hall.

"It's okay, Corey. It's nothing you haven't seen before. We're married."

"Right." But, we haven't lived together in a month, and our relationship has felt over for much longer than that. I cannot remember the last time we were intimate. Was it six months ago?

"Where did you go tonight?"

"What do you mean? I took Jacob to dinner."

"Did Ben go with you? You didn't tell me that."

"No, actually, I ran into him outside. He'd been out at an interview for a gig. He saw Julia in the window and asked if I could just vouch for him. He doesn't want to get her hopes up about the job in case it doesn't pan out."

"There's something off about him," I say.

"C'mon, he's a good guy—"

"You've known him for three days?"

Evan pulls on a pair of sweatpants and a clean white T-shirt. When he's done, he comes over and puts his arms around Jacob and me and says, "Listen, you can trust me. I'm a pretty decent judge of character. I married you, for Christ's sake, didn't I?" He pulls my chin up so I'm looking in his eyes. We both stay for a beat until I pull my chin and body away. I sit on the edge of the bed with Jacob, leaving Evan standing in front of us. He drops down into a squat and leans in, his arms resting on my thighs. "I can tell you this. She's on drugs, but don't say anything."

"Drugs? What do you mean?"

"She's on pretty heavy antidepressants. An SSRI."

I start laughing, almost hysterically. There it is. The way he feels about women on medicine. "Wow," I say. I get up, which throws Evan off balance a bit, and I take Jacob into his room to change him.

"Corey, what the hell?" Evan says, coming into Jacob's room and pulling out a pair of pajamas for me to change him into.

"I'm also on an SSRI," I say.

"You're on it for anxiety. And that's totally normal. Your hormones are whacked from having a baby."

"Well, if that's the case, she's on it for depression because she lost her baby, and her *hormones* are, quote, whacked," I say.

"I can't talk to you when you're like this, Corey."

"I don't want to talk to you, Evan." I hesitate to raise my voice or speak like I'm mad because I don't want Jacob to feel or sense my frustration.

"Why don't I read Jacob a story tonight and put him to bed, and you can go chill out," Evan says.

Are you fucking kidding me with this guy? "That's okay. We have our weeknight routine down to a science. Don't we, Jacob? Want to read our book?"

"Okay," Jacob says and smiles up at me from the changing table I have him sitting on.

"Why don't you go relax," I say to Evan. "You're probably exhausted from your day." I honestly don't care if he's exhausted or not. I don't want to be in the room with him a second longer.

21

Evan ended up on the couch. We didn't speak the rest of the evening. This morning he was out for his run when Jacob and I left for spin class. I checked my emails all night, waiting for this mysterious commenter to explain how they know Sonja Hart and what they know about her disappearance. Still no message as of five minutes ago.

"You look like shit, even with your new haircut," Monique says. She's just finished auditioning another new could-be instructor, and at this point she's just going to have to pick someone and train them to teach the way she wants them to.

"Thanks. It's not going great."

"Which thing, your marriage or the missing woman?"

"Both, if you need to know. When are you going to hire one of these instructors and be done with it? Frankly, they've all been better than me up there. And, we need help. You haven't replaced anyone." We lost too many instructors six months ago: Liz, Kat, Diane.

"Correction, I need help. And you're right, they are all better than you. But don't worry, I like this one." She looks directly at Jacob and gives him a light tickle to the tummy. He laughs the minute Monique touches him. "And before you think to ask it, no, they will not replace you, as pathetic as you are on the bike. I know you're still riding without any resistance."

"Well, the twentysomethings don't even ride the bike, they just walk around the room. I'm better than that." I smile. I like the easy banter with Monique. I couldn't imagine we'd be like this when I started at the studio—she was just too prickly. When someone like Monique lets you into her inner circle, you know exactly where you stand, and it's the most validating experience. No matter how much I complain about teaching classes, it really is a sanctuary of peace for me. "Tell me what it is you like about this one?"

"She's hot."

"Seriously? That's why you're hiring her? That violates so many ethical—"

"Relax, I'm kidding. She's good. And I like her taste in music."

Monique slips behind the front desk, and I greet my riders as they enter the studio.

"Julia?" I say a bit too loud. She doesn't blend into a crowd, but I think that's probably true of most beautiful actresses. Her oversize sunglasses give the impression she's hiding, but who would she be hiding from, me? I am shocked at the understated black leggings and oversize new, vintage-style T-shirt, but the Louis Vuitton weekender doubling as a gym bag offsets any attempt at subtlety.

"I hope you don't mind. I was going to run with Ben this morning, but his back is hurting. I know you mentioned you teach spin, and I've been missing my Pilates classes. I just thought maybe I would give this a shot." She says it with such sincerity I want to believe that maybe this is who Julia really is. But I can't ignore my gut telling me that this is who she wants to be, or who she needs people to believe she is. Who she needs me to believe she is.

"Hi, I'm Monique, and it looks like you're new. Can I get you to fill out a waiver?" Julia darts her eyes back to me after a quick glance at Monique.

"Monique, this is my new neighbor, Julia," I say. "Fresh blood all the way from Brooklyn for you." I wink at Julia, hoping it alleviates some of the tension that is radiating off her. "Julia, this is my boss, Monique, Cyclone's owner."

"I don't want to sound like I'm fangirling or anything, but my mom used to watch this soap opera all the time, and you look just like the girl that was on it. I think her name was Cynthia?"

Julia blushes and smiles wide. "That was me. I can't believe you recognize me. I didn't think anyone would when we moved here."

Behind them I watch as another familiar woman comes in to ride, Anne Silva.

"Um, Julia, you're in great hands. I'll be back," I say and slip past them.

"Anne?"

Dressed in black leggings, a black tank top, and a black duster, there standing in front of me, is Anne Silva. She rips off her large black sunglasses and looks at me without smiling.

"You have to style this haircut. I told you that when I cut it. You can't just wake up and go, Corey. You're going to give me a bad reputation."

"Are you here to take my class?" I ask. She looks more in distress than I would say is normal for seeing my bedhead pixie. "Or are you here to talk about your friend Sonja?"

"I know, I know. We need to talk."

I look at the sea of riders until I find Monique finishing up getting Julia settled onto a bike, and I wave her over.

"Good," I say. "I want to hear everything you know. Just give me a second to get my class covered."

"What's up?" Monique says, looking at me and then Anne.

"Monique, this is Anne Silva." Monique doesn't register who or what I'm talking about. "She's a friend of Sonja Hart." It clicks, and Monique nods. "Can you teach my class?"

"You owe me."

I nod. "Thank you."

I grab Jacob's stroller and motion with my chin for Anne to follow. We don't speak outside. She follows me across the street to the boba coffee shop we all go to before and after classes for a hit of caffeine or team meetings when we don't want to stand around in the lobby of Cyclone.

Once we're seated, with coffees, I take Jacob's headphones off his ears and pull him out of the stroller into my lap. I open up a smoothie pouch from my bag and let him suck on it. When I finally look at Anne, without her sunglasses hiding nearly her entire face, and under the harsh morning sun blazing into the coffee shop, I can tell she's been crying or hasn't slept—probably both. I ask her, "What do you know?"

"I listened to your post last night online. I reached out, but I thought it would be better if we talked in person." She takes a sip of her coffee, and when she sets it back on the table she stares at the cup, turning it in circles, distracting herself.

"Anne, what do you know? Where is Sonja?"

"She's been questioning her relationship with this guy she's been seeing."

"Not Mike Lee," I say.

"No, I made that up obviously. It was just a joke between Sonja and me. We took his free class twice and—well, you saw him." I realize right then that I should have asked Mike if Anne had been on the class list too. "You were asking a lot of questions, and it spooked me. I was trying to protect my friend."

"So why are you talking to me now?" I ask.

"I knew who you were when you came in, asking for a haircut. This is a small community, Corey Tracey. I didn't trust you. But I do think my friend is missing. I'm really worried now." The tears come hot and fast and fall into Anne's coffee. I hand her a napkin.

"Tell me about the guy she is seeing," I say.

"He's aggressive—not physically, not violent. That's not what I mean." She sighs. "He's just always around. Wants to be with her all the time and it's only been, like six weeks. He love bombs her, shows up uninvited with dinner and wine and plans all the time. It all sounds really sweet and thoughtful, and you think, like, *Wow, what a catch.*

That's what we'd all love in a guy. But, honestly, it's been exhausting her. She's told him to scale back, but then it's texts and voicemails, and in general it's been getting difficult for her."

"Did she break things off with him?" I ask.

"I don't know. She's a private person. It's weird. I haven't met him. He hasn't come to any of her poetry readings, but she probably hasn't invited him either."

"Understood. Why are you worried now and not two days ago?"

"She was going away for a few days. She was supposed to go camping in Joshua Tree."

"With this man? Does he have a name?" I ask.

"I'll get to that." I nod. "So, she's going camping in Joshua Tree with him for two nights. They're supposed to talk about their relationship. She wants to tell him . . ." Anne stops mid-sentence. She shuts down completely, her eyes on her coffee or on her nails tapping the side of the cup.

"Anne? What does she want to tell him?"

"She was at my house crying about it the whole day and night on Sunday—she's pregnant, and she wants to keep the baby, and she was going to tell him—about the pregnancy and keeping the baby. He doesn't know. She wants to keep the baby and raise it together, but she doesn't want to be in a romantic relationship right now. She really likes him. He's just a lot. She's trying to kickstart this next chapter of her life with a new career and everything."

"Anne, who's the man?" I ask. Jacob is squeezing his smoothie pouch. It only half makes it into his mouth—the rest is on my shirt and in my lap.

"He's one of her professors. His name is Ryan Moore," she says. "Get this, it's hilarious to me. He's her poetry professor. She's going back to school to get a degree in family counseling, and she's taking a poetry class. But that totally sums her up, pragmatic and romantic."

"Okay, I'm trying to understand, Anne, but I guess I'm a bit confused. Why are you concerned now? What has changed with Sonja's plan?" I attempt to not sound demanding, but I'm impatient while swiping smoothie off my body. I don't want to break eye contact with Anne, so I'm swiping with the napkin blindly.

"There's no cell service in Joshua Tree National Park. Have you been? It's a whole different world. It's vast desert and boulders, and these trees, Joshua trees, that look like they're from another planet. It's huge, the park. I read yesterday that it's bigger than the state of Rhode Island. Also, it's quiet—like you don't even know other people are camping there." Anne stops talking. She watches Jacob flailing around his now-capped, empty-ish smoothie pouch.

"What's changed, Anne?"

"She was supposed to be back yesterday. I tried her cell, and it's still off. None of my texts have been read all week. They were supposed to be back yesterday morning. It's Thursday, and I haven't heard from her since Sunday. It doesn't feel right."

"Why do you think her son reported her missing on Monday?" I ask.

"I don't know. I guess maybe she didn't tell him where she was going. I've been trying to message him on Facebook, but they've gone unread. I've never met him before. I knew of him. Sonja is so proud of him. She's been trying to give him space so he can be independent, she said. I don't know." She is frantic in her delivery.

"Okay. This is good. When is the last time you called her?" I ask.

"I texted her while you and I have been talking—it hasn't delivered."

"What do you know about Ryan Moore?"

"I've never met him. It's been a whirlwind of an affair."

"Anything about his personality? Is he married, kids, divorced?"

"I only know what I've told you already." She looks up like she's thinking—about what she remembers and probably trying to keep out all the private things that would embarrass her friend to have shared.

"He got her address. She didn't give it to him. Probably from school records, I don't know. This was before they were dating, like he was just her professor. He sent her flowers and had desserts delivered and not in a creepy way, she said, but he did sign them *From a secret admirer*. Just, he knew how to get her home address from the school."

Creepy. Anne definitely agrees—it's creepy.

"Then after class that next week, he walked out with the students, and she said after everyone else had disappeared he was still walking with her and chatting and making her laugh. When they got to her car, he brushed her hair out of her face, and she said it was instant, she felt so much heat from him. It was like a movie, she said. He asked her what she was doing right then, and the next thing that happened, they had dinner, drinks, and sex." Anne grimaces after the word *sex*. She takes a gulp-size swig of her coffee, now that it's cooled down.

"Since then he texts her every morning to see how she slept. He brings her coffee before class. It's dinner, drinks, and more texts—always with the texts. They're pretty graphic, so I'll just say—in front of the baby—that they're explicit in what he wants to do with her and to her. It's always about pleasing her. It's too much." Anne takes a break from talking. I see tears welling up in her eyes. "Why hasn't she gotten home yet? Joshua Tree is, like two hours from here. Once you're out of the park, you have service again. Do you think she forgot her charger?"

There is so much guilt in her voice I extend my free hand and cover hers with it. I give it a squeeze.

"I don't know. Maybe she did forget her charger," I say. I give us a beat. Let her adjust before I ask, "Can you tell me what you're thinking about right now?"

"That I should have said something to her, like don't go." She lets out a stream of tears, and I claw through my everything bag for tissues. I always have tissues. I know I have a tissue. I find a wad of them I had shoved in my bag when my travel pack ran out. I pull one out, iron it flat with the side of my hand, and pass it to Anne.

I give her a minute to let it all out before I start asking more questions. I know this isn't good. I know Anne knows it, too, but there's nothing she could have done to intervene. No matter how much guilt she'll carry for a long time, there was nothing she could have done.

Sonja is a grown woman. I can only hope I don't have to start using the past tense . . . *was* a grown woman.

"You saw her on Sunday?" I ask.

"Yes, she came over, crying. All day, all night—hormones. She just got one kid out on his own, her son, Jonathan. He's starting his adult life, and now she's starting again, and she was so ready for it."

"Tell me more about Jonathan," I say.

"As far as I know they have a normal relationship. He lives in a different state. I remember she said he's doing like a gap year or something. He's working for his dad, maybe?" Anne takes another long drink of her coffee. Her finger traces the groove of the table we're at. "I met Sonja a little under a year ago when she came in for a haircut. We hit it off, and we've been friends ever since. But, it's haircuts, drinks, workout classes. She's great, and I love her. I just don't have a long history with her, ya' know?"

I did know. In so many ways. I didn't know the man I'd been having happy hours with in my friend group in my twenties was a rapist, until he raped me. Some people hide secrets. Some people never let people know who they really are. Some people just don't share the hard stuff because it keeps a friendship at arm's length, and that helps keep the relationship fun and easy.

"Anne, I need to get to work and make some calls. Would you like me to give you a ride home?"

"Are we done? Just like that?" she asks. "I thought you'd jump into action and give me some orders or direction. What can I do? I can't go home and just sit there. My shop is closed today, and I need to be busy. Give me some direction, please. Tell me what to do. Should I drive out to Joshua Tree?"

"I can't tell you to do that. Where would you even begin if you drove out there? No. You can start by calling the"—I dig my phone out of my bag and search for local police departments in Joshua Tree—"San Bernardino County Sheriff's Department in Joshua Tree and tell them you'd like to report a missing person."

I pull out an old receipt from my bag and a pen, and I write down my cell phone number and pass it to Anne. "Text me or call me the minute you have any new information. Tell me what the sheriff's department says to you."

"What are you going to do?"

"I'm going to find Ryan Moore. And I'm going to call Sonja's son."

22

Me: I know where Sonja is.

Chris: I'm coming over.

I get home and don't see Evan's car, which I shouldn't because he works, but lately I have this nagging feeling like he's always going to be at the house when I'm there. Or, he'll just show up in the middle of the day to catch me doing something. The only things I do are work and mother. I don't have anything to hide, but it feels like I'm hiding everything, and I'm always about to be caught.

Just thinking about it has my anxiety poking me in my stomach. It's palpable. My throat feels tight, and there's that electric zap in my head again. What is that? I definitely have to look that up. Shit, I was also supposed to call Dr. Rosenberg. And it's now been three days I haven't taken the Paxil. Everything is fine. I'm on top of this case now, and that's all I need.

"Hey, buddy, let's go take a nap, you ready?" I ask Jacob. He had all but fallen asleep in the car. I wouldn't let him—I wouldn't have been able to transfer him without waking him, and those ten-minute power naps in the car always give him more juice. He rubs his eyes and lets out a giant yawn with a sweet sigh at the end. "So sleepy, huh? That turned out to be a very long morning, huh?" Before I make it to the top of the stairs, Jacob has fallen asleep. His head rests on my shoulder, and I don't want to let go of him. I hold him and sway back and forth, searing this moment into my memory forever. I press my nose to his head and inhale deeply. I want to remember the smell of him forever.

Before I'm ready to let him go, there's a knock on the door. Chris. I gently lay Jacob in his crib and close his blackout curtains. I leave a space for the sun to shine through. I hope he wakes up sooner than later. I'm right here with him all the time, but sometimes I miss him even when he's napping.

I run downstairs and open the door, and it's Julia.

"Hi, Corey. Um, I wanted to stop by and apologize for last night. I was acting poorly, and that's not how I want you to think of me. I'm sorry."

"You were fine. I can't say I wouldn't have felt the same way waking up in a new house, a new city and state, and my husband missing. I probably would have called the police and reported it." It's supposed to be funny, but it's not. At least not to me. Too soon. "Did you enjoy the spin class?"

"Yeah, I look forward to going back. Monique is a hoot. She signed me up for monthly unlimited classes—so, looks like we can carpool." Julia fumbles with her hands and looks at the keys she's holding. "Ben was in an accident last year. He fell down some stairs, banged up his shoulder and neck pretty bad. Anyway, after surgery, a year ago, they gave him oxycodone. He's been off and on when the pain is just too much. The move has acted up the pain, and he's been taking his pills again, and they can make him drowsy and not act like himself. So, yeah, it's been a hard year for both of us. Anyway, I appreciate you looking out for me."

"I'm so sorry. God, that's a lot. I'd invite you in, but I'm working and—" I want her to come in so I can ask more questions, but I can't right now. It will have to wait. Sonja is my priority.

"No, no, of course, I didn't want to interrupt. But, I did want to show you something." Julia reaches into the oversize quilted bag on her shoulder and pulls out the tiniest black-furred kitten.

"Oh my god, that can't be one of the kittens from the litter? Is it?" I ask. I have no idea how fast kittens grow, but it's been, like four days?

"No, I don't know where they ended up. I hope in someone's backyard under a bush. But, I felt so strongly attached to them, to her. Watching her birth those babies. I went to the shelter and adopted him. This is Oliver."

"Well, that is something. Oliver, you are very lucky."

"I'll let you get back to work. Let's have coffee soon." Julia practically skips down my driveway, holding Oliver. Before she heads into her house, she turns and waves. There's something wrong there, and I can't figure it out. I don't think Julia is crazy, but she's definitely something.

"Hey," Chris says. He comes up the opposite side of the porch, taking me by surprise. "Tell me everything, from the beginning."

I fill Chris in on everything that's happened. We sit in silence while we sip coffee. I check my phone and see Chris watching me.

"I'm looking to see how many homicides occur in Joshua Tree National Park every year and how many people go missing there. But, it doesn't make sense to me."

"What doesn't make sense?" he asks.

"Why would she go camping with the guy she's about to break up with? While she's pregnant with his baby and about to tell him she wants to *just be friends*? Something's not right. Hang on."

I open my laptop, which is conveniently always left on the dining room table these days. I look up the faculty directory at South Pasadena Community College. I find Ryan Moore's information and pick up my phone and dial.

"Hello, this is Ryan." I look at Chris and nod. Success on the first try. That almost never happens—I assume Moore hangs out in his office a lot.

"Hi, ah, my name is Corey, and I was given your information by the registrar's office? I was calling to inquire about auditing your poetry class?"

"Sure, that's no problem at all. Are you a current student?"

"No, thinking about taking a few classes, and this one caught my attention," I say. I wonder if my voice sounds eighteen or forty, inquiring about college classes.

"Well, I'd love to have you. I have a class this evening you're welcome to attend. It starts at five ten p.m. and goes until seven forty. If you give me your email, I'd be happy to send you directions."

"That sounds perfect." I give him my email before saying, "I look forward to meeting you." I look at Chris and cannot read his expression. My stomach hurts. I can't begin to imagine what this man has done to Sonja Hart.

"It's obvious, he must be married, having an affair, and the baby Sonja wanted to keep would ruin his life," Chris says.

"But what did he do with her?" I ask.

"He didn't take her to Joshua Tree."

"Or he did and came home without her."

"I'm going to find out tonight," Chris says.

"No, I'm going. You're not going to show up at his class and just ask him. Then what? Think, Chris. I need to go see Lopez before the class. Fuck."

"There's no way anyone's going to find a body in Joshua Tree anytime soon unless some hikers just happen to stumble off a path and accidentally bump into one. And, the rate of decomposition with the wildlife there . . . goddammit," he says.

"I don't think she's in Joshua Tree," I say.

"What do you mean?" Chris asks.

"Tell me again what her son said to you or what he said in the missing-person report."

"His mom has been missing for more than twenty-four hours," Chris says.

"Why would he lie?" I ask.

"He wasn't lying—last time he spoke to her was Saturday, and everything we're taught is twenty-four hours, and he didn't want to wait that long." I nod, smart kid. "Her phone has been off or going straight to voicemail. She hasn't read any texts he's sent, which is unlike her because they usually text continuously throughout the day."

"We need to find out what was said the last time they did text or speak. We need to call him. Right now," I say. I wait while Chris puts in the number and puts it on speakerphone.

"Hello?" The voice of a man child. Young but assertive.

"Jonathan, it's Chris Villar."

"Hey, sorry I haven't called you back. I picked up some extra gig work, so I can get some money to get down there. Have you heard anything? My mom still hasn't turned on her phone, and the police haven't called me back. I'm trying not to freak out, man."

"Good, keep busy. How short are you on the ticket?"

"I don't know, the prices keep changing—"

"Well, when we hang up, why don't you look and text me what you need. I'll see how I can help." I can barely hear the thank-you through the heavy breathing now. I recognize that sound. That is the sound of crying by a young man trying to hold it in. "Hey, Jonathan, I have my friend here with me. I told you about her, Corey Tracey. We'd like to ask you a few more questions. Would that be okay?"

"Yeah. Is she going to find my mom?"

"Hi, Jonathan, I'm Corey. I am going to try very hard to help find your mom, I promise, okay?" My heart breaks hearing him cry softly on the other side of the phone. I don't know if he's alone or has someone to comfort him. "Hey, Jonathan, tell me about your mom. What is she like?"

"She's funny, really funny. She's kind, and she cares a lot about everything and everybody. She used to have this route to and from work, where she passed a church that fed the unhoused twice a week, right? So, she worked at this restaurant forever—they loved her—and on her way home from work she would always take all the leftover dinner rolls, bread loaves, a huge vat of soup, and desserts and dropped them off at the church to serve. That's just who she is. She's always thinking about other people."

"She sounds awesome, I can't wait to meet her. I watched the video she posted of her poetry reading. She is very talented," I say.

"She is, she wanted to be a singer-songwriter when she was young, but she kind of got sidetracked with me. That's why she's taking poetry now."

I think of Jacob taking on the burden of my life choices, and it breaks my heart. "The sidetracks are where we live our lives, Jonathan." I want so badly to reassure him his mom made the choices she did because she loves him more than even herself.

"So, you're up in Oregon now? Is that right?" I ask.

"Yeah, my dad's here. I'm taking a gap year before I start college. My dad owns a construction company, so I'm working for him and saving up."

"That's great. I wish I had done the same thing. Why did your mom move down here to LA? Do you know?"

"Her family had lived there for a little while when she was a kid, and she always wanted to go back. She said she wanted to change things up, start the next chapter in a new place. I'm planning to move there next year and go to Cal State LA. I already got accepted. My mom always has a plan. She got there first to set up a place for us while she found work and enrolled in school. She's just a really good mom."

"She sounds incredible." I wait a beat because my heart is breaking. I am breaking. There's the zap in my head, and I'm having trouble breathing. Oh god. I can't swallow. No, pull it together, Corey, not in front of Chris and this kid and oh fuck. I jump up and start doing jumping jacks. I count in my head while I say to Jonathan, "Jonathan, did you and your mom talk every day?" . . . ten, eleven, twelve, thirteen. Okay.

"We text every day. We FaceTime on Sundays. That's our routine. And she didn't call me on Sunday. She texted in the morning that she was going to her friend's house. I know she was talking about this guy she's dating—I just knew because she never says *a friend's house*. She says their name, like, *I'm going to Natalie's or Sara's*. But she never says his name. I don't even know his name. My mom was not a big dater when I was a kid. She was really all about being my mom."

I'm still standing, pacing. Chris is looking at me, and I cannot tell if he's worried or even notices. He's just calm. Always calm, not indifferent, just calm. If I had to put his energy into words, it would be safe, strong, and calm. "Jonathan, can you tell me exactly what was said in your last communication with your mom?" I ask.

"Hang on, I'm going to put you on speaker, so I can pull up my texts." I hear the outside clearly now. There are men calling to each other and a radio in the distant background.

"Are you at work?" I ask.

"Yeah, they're cool, though. My dad's the boss. Okay, I have it. My mom texted me on Sunday and said, 'I'm going to be late for our call today. I need to go over to my friend's house for a little bit. I'll call you from the car when I leave.'"

"And she never called you?" Chris asks.

"No. And she never read my response text either. I told her I was going to be at work, but to call anyway. Dad said he'd give me a break."

"You often work on Sundays?" I ask.

"No, but we're trying to finish this job, and it's time and a half on Sundays."

"Jonathan, one last question, did your mom talk about any of her friends here? Do you know their names?" I ask. I want to see if he knows his mom has a friend named Anne. A friend whose house she spent her Sunday at, crying about a new baby coming into her and Jonathan's life. I want to make sure he doesn't think she was all alone here in LA while he took a gap year and lived with his dad. And why wasn't his dad helping him with a ticket? Maybe because missing a phone call doesn't feel like a big deal. Would Evan be dismissive about my well-being if I left him? Would he help our son out if he needed to get to me? Stop it, Corey, not now. Breathe in for, fuck I can't remember. I go for seven, then out for five or six. I just need a Klonopin. I need to end the call.

"Yeah, she has a friend named Anne. That's who she spends most of her time with. I think she had some friends from her classes too, but they were mostly around my age, so she didn't go out clubbing or partying with them or anything, just like school friends. That sounds weird, I know. And she has some sort-of relatives, not close but good for a holiday get-together, ya' know?"

I desperately want to comfort him, to tell him she missed their call not because of a man she was dating, but because she was at Anne's house, but I can't, not yet. I need to keep everyone's story separate while I put together Sonja's victimology.

"Hey, man, you did really well. Thank you. Why don't you look at those ticket prices and let me know if you need assistance, okay?" Chris says.

"Thank you, I will. I'm hoping my dad will float me, but I'll let you know. Mrs. Tracey, thank you for listening to me. I know my mom would like you. Really, thank you."

Chris hangs up the phone, and I'm crying. I didn't even realize it had started. One more set of jumping jacks, and I feel okay to sit down for a moment.

"Corey, what's going on?" Chris says. He brings me a glass of water and sits next to me on the couch, placing the water on the table in front of me.

I wipe my face with the back of my hands. "I'm just feeling a lot right now. I was taking Paxil, but I came off it a few days ago. I'm just adjusting, I think." I take a sip of the water. I can barely swallow it, but my breathing is under control for the moment. "I don't think I will ever be able to tell that child his mother is dead."

"We don't know that she is," Chris says.

"Think about it. Her son reported her missing the day she was supposed to go to Joshua Tree—according to Anne. But she didn't even tell her son that she was going on a trip. She missed their Sunday call and never texted him even Monday to tell him she was okay. The custodian at her apartment saw her leaving with a suitcase in *her* car. Moore didn't pick her up. She was driving. She would have called her son at some point and told him she was going camping, or sightseeing, or having a baby with Moore, or that she was okay."

Chris looks at me, confused. I'm not making sense, but the lines are connecting like threads in my brain. The threadbare yarn is full again. I can follow the trails in my mind. "She never told her son she was pregnant. I think she planned on going to Joshua Tree, but I think she told Moore before they left. And, I think Jonathan never heard from her, because she never made it out of Moore's house." I stop. I realize at some point I'd gotten up and started walking in circles. "No, I don't think they ever went to Joshua Tree. I don't know where Sonja is, but I don't think she ever left Northeast LA."

23

Me: Lopez, it's Corey, I need to talk to you asap

Detective Lopez: I prefer Detective, Ms. Tracey. I've got some interesting new information on our Jane Doe from the fire. I'm out—I'll stop by in a bit.

"Okay, Detective Lopez is stopping by. What are you going to do?" I ask Chris. Before he answers, Jacob is calling from his crib. I look at the clock on my oven. He slept for just over an hour. That's good, perfect actually. "I need to go get him before he thinks I've left him." I'm only slightly joking. What if he really did think I left him because I don't appear right away when he calls me? What would that therapy look like when he's an adult? Abandonment issues? I don't want to think that far into the future. Sonja. Sonja is my immediate need.

"I'm going to get going. I want to do some digging into Ryan Moore, and I have a person who can help me."

"Who? I thought your cousin was—"

"Megan, did I mention she's a lawyer?"

Oh, right.

"I don't remember if you did or not. How is her divorce going? Any headway?" I will admit to remembering that part.

"No, it's not going the way she hoped. I'm going to head over to her office and see what she can find out about Ryan Moore."

"See if she can access any records regarding past stalking charges, restraining orders, juvie records—all of it." I'm pacing and counting off items on my fingers. "I'll let you know what Detective Lopez says, and you do the same with Megan. I want to get to the class at five," I say.

"What about Jacob?"

Oh my god, Jacob! How did I forget to go get him, and why don't I hear him? I run up the stairs, two at a time, and find Jacob on the floor, playing with some letter blocks my mom sent him.

"Jacob?"

"Mama!" He holds a block up for me to take. He is smiling from ear to ear.

"Jacob, did you climb out of your crib?" He crawls over to the crib and pulls himself up using the slats on the front side. Once he's standing, he holds one hand out to me and starts walking right to me. Walking, not crawling. I fall to my knees to catch him. "My love! You are walking." I scoop him into a hug, and then I pick him up and stand. I head back downstairs, and there's a note from Chris. He left to go see Megan.

I don't know what time or how long Lopez is going to be, and I need to get Jacob fed and changed before we head over to South Pasadena Community College. I haven't breastfed Jacob in an entire day, and my breasts haven't leaked either. I don't have time right now to think about it, or I may start mourning the near end of this closeness between my baby and me. I pull some precooked noodles out of the fridge, some applesauce, and an egg to scramble for him quickly.

I serve Jacob in his highchair while I sit next to him and work on the laptop. Before I can get onto the video and read new comments, Lopez is at the door.

"Hi, come in," I say. She's alone, and I'm glad. Her partner, Detective Marks, doesn't like me. I don't think he dislikes me either. I think he doesn't have time or trust for anyone that isn't a cop. Marks has to be close to retirement, unless he's the type to stay at a desk and never retire. His skin is scarred and marked from teenage acne or whiskey. His shirt collars are always a little yellow. His badge is worn, scuffed, and marked all over, and his shoes look older than him.

Lopez sits on my blue velvet wingback chair. "Can I get you something to drink? Water or coffee?" I ask.

"No, I'm fine, thank you." She leans back before saying, "Have a seat."

"Let me just grab Jacob first." Our whole house is open. The kitchen, dining room, and living room are basically just one giant square distinguishing their individuality by furniture and appliances. "He took his first steps today," I say. "Just before you got here. I can't believe it."

"Oh, I feel sorry for you. That baby is about to be the busiest part of your life, Corey Tracey. I hope you're ready. Once they start walking, they never stop."

I pull Jacob from his highchair and a little too roughly clean up his hands and face with a paper towel. He complains and swats at my hand doing the cleaning. I bring him out to the living room and give him a few toys to sit and play with. "Okay, tell me, what's going on with the Jane Doe?"

"Well, we still don't know who she is yet, but we can rule out the woman that was squatting in the home," Detective Lopez says.

"How? Did you find dental records?" I ask.

"No, better, she came into the police station to report that her home had been torched."

"What does this mean?" I ask.

"It means we have a dead body with no identification," she says.

"Do they know yet what caused the fire?" I ask.

"Nope, that's why I am investigating it as a homicide. I have a Jane Doe, whose manner of death is undetermined, but cause of death is fire," Lopez says.

"What does that mean, her manner of death is undetermined, but cause is fire?" I ask.

"She was alive when she burned to death, but it could have been an accident, suicide, or homicide." Lopez gives a look to the kitchen to check on Jacob, I assume. "Corey," she says, looking back to me, "the body is burned so bad, there's no way to identify her except the hope of dental records. We'll have to go through missing persons and get the information for local missing women and then apply to get dental records for those individuals," Lopez says.

"How long will that take?" I ask.

"Several weeks, if we're lucky. Months if we're not."

Jacob pulls himself up again, this time using the coffee table for leverage, and starts toddling over to Lopez. I watch with pure fascination. I am beaming with pride. Like this accomplishment is unique and my kid should be up for an Olympic medal. I let him continue to explore his walk while I watch him and talk to Lopez. "I believe Sonja Hart is dead and not missing."

"Tell me more," Detective Lopez says.

I grab Jacob to keep him still in my lap while I break it all down—big mistake. He arches his back against me, trying to free himself from my lap and arms, shrieking, and flailing around. I'm embarrassed. I feel entirely out of control, and I'm the parent. If the internal effects of my panic attacks could look like something externally, this would be it. Jacob, in this moment, would be the visual representation. My god.

"Corey, put him down. He can explore while we talk. I've got my eye on him, too, don't worry," Lopez says.

I gently set Jacob on his feet. He wobbles a little and then takes off toward Lopez. Instead of stopping, he moves right past her to his toys, which are in a hamper-like basket. One by one he begins to pull the toys out. That will definitely take him some time.

"Okay," I say. "I'm ready."

"Sonja Hart. You're going to tell me why you don't think she's missing but deceased."

"Right." I sit back against the couch, tucking my left leg under me and tell Lopez about the past four days. I inform her of every person I've spoken with and met, up to today's conversation with Jonathan and my pending conversation with Professor Ryan Moore. By the time I finish, Jacob has lost interest in his toys and is pulling out the pans from the bottom kitchen cupboard. We'd held off on babyproofing the drawers and cupboards because it was cumbersome and time consuming. But at the rate of speed Jacob is curiously getting into everything right now, I guess I will have to. "What do you think?" I ask Lopez.

"I was hoping for some hard evidence. The story is compelling, but you're operating on feelings, and I need some concrete evidence. You know this, Corey."

"I'm heading to his class in"—I grab my phone and look at the time—"an hour."

"You're taking Jacob with you, I assume?" she asks.

"That's my plan, why?"

"Well, if he's attracted to women your age and you bring that baby, I'm not sure you're going to be able to flirt your way into a confession," Lopez says.

"I've never flirted my way to or through anything, and I've always managed to get what I need," I say. "Can you request a copy of Sonja Hart's dental records too?" I ask. "She is officially on the missing-person list."

"I will see what I can do. Do you have her next of kin's information?" she asks.

"It's her adult son. 'Adult' is a joke. He's eighteen or nineteen. I will get his contact information from Chris and forward it to you. Sonja and her son, Jonathan, lived in central California before she relocated here. City called Visalia."

"Got it. Is the kid still there?" Lopez asks.

"No, he's not even in the state anymore. Lives in Oregon with his dad," I say. "He's trying to get a flight down here this week. I don't even know if that's a good idea. Maybe his dad should come with him. On the other hand, he should be able to give us access to the apartment to look around," I say. "The possibility of finding something in Sonja's apartment that would tell us what happened or give me hard evidence, since we don't have a body, could be everything."

"Careful, Ms. Tracey, the last thing I need you doing is ruining evidence I may need to use."

"Understood," I say. A loud crash followed by a delayed cry of distress from Jacob has me darting across the room to the kitchen. Jacob is sitting on the ground, his hand closed in the cupboard door. I set him on the counter and run cold water over his hand and fingers. There are no marks. Thank god for slow-closing, light cabinets.

"Is he okay?" Lopez asks from the living room.

"He's okay. More scared than hurt." Then to Jacob I ask, "Are you okay, little man? I'm so sorry I wasn't paying better attention." I feel the guilt like a wave, and it yells at me from some place in my head I cannot identify, *Bad mom, bad mom, bad mom.*

"Corey," Lopez says, standing in the kitchen five feet from Jacob and me, "I'm going to take off. Please be careful tonight. Mind yourself, play it cool. I do not want to come looking for you and our man Jacob here. Do I make myself clear?"

"Crystal. I'm not going to say anything. I'm there to audit the class my friend Sonja spoke very highly about," I say.

"That's right. Keep it upbeat, light, casual, innocent," Lopez says. I nod. She lets herself out the front door, and I scoop Jacob up off the counter for a diaper change and a car ride to South Pasadena Community College.

24

Parking at the college was easy, too easy. I never trust good parking in Los Angeles, but Ryan Moore's email gave me directions to an uncovered lot that opens for students at five p.m. and has on duty security guards. When I pull up, I give them my name and the class I'm attending, and I am free to park. Nothing in LA has ever been this easy.

> *Evan:* Hey, I'm going to be late tonight. No need to wait for me for dinner. You guys do your thing.

I completely forgot to let Evan know I'd be out. I hadn't thought of him since leaving this morning, hoping I wouldn't have to see him on my way to work. I didn't.

> *Me:* No worries, I'm taking a class tonight with Jacob. See you later.

No guilt, and technically I didn't lie. I feel fine, no anxiety. I decide to take Jacob in the baby carrier. He should be tired from a full day of first steps. Fuck. I need to tell Evan he's walking. I'll do it later when we're both at the house. It's not a text at this point. I can't record it right now either.

The interior of the building could definitely use some color, new carpeting, and in general a facelift. But, as far as community anything—center, college, arena—goes, this is pretty great. I find the room Ryan Moore listed and don't know if I should knock on the closed door or just walk in. There's no window allowing a peek inside. I don't even know if there's another class in session. I look at my phone to check the time—it's 5:05 p.m. Class starts at 5:10. I can't wait for someone else to come along and open the door first. Especially if Moore is in there alone, I could miss an opportunity to catch him off guard before the class starts.

I tap lightly on the door before pulling it open. The room is smaller than I expected. Enough seating for about twenty to twenty-five people. At the front of the room is a table with a tabletop podium sitting on it and a dry-erase board behind. An old desk chair with wheels has been stationed in the corner away from the professor's table, and there, standing at the podium, skimming through papers, is a man with reddish-brown hair, about five feet, nine inches tall, ruddy skin, thin, late thirties to mid-forties-ish. He's wearing jeans and a button-down. When he sees me, he smiles. It makes him appear charming and friendly.

"Corey Tracey?" he asks.

"Yes. Professor Moore?" I ask.

"You bet. I'm so glad you could make it. I can see it was probably too last minute for a sitter? I'm so sorry, I didn't realize. What's this guy's name?" he asks. He doesn't miss a beat. It's one long warm greeting, and I'm swept up in the frenzy of it.

"I'm sorry, I should have asked you on the phone if it would be okay to bring my baby. We're an item—wherever I go, he goes these days," I say. I try to match his smile with my own. Keep it light, nonthreatening.

"It's completely fine. If he gets fussy, feel free to leave and come back in as needed. I'm just glad you're interested in poetry. We're not a very large class, and a lot of the students are adults coming back to school," Moore says.

"Yep, that's me. I'm interested in exploring new and different opportunities. I currently teach spin classes. In fact, one of my riders,

Sonja Hart"—I look right at him—"told me about your class." He doesn't flinch, doesn't let go of the smile.

"Sonja is an incredibly talented writer. I've been trying to convince her to submit some of her work for publication."

"I would have told her I planned on auditing, but she missed my class this week," I say.

"Yeah, she must not be feeling well. She missed an office hours appointment she scheduled with me," Moore says. He's slick, I'll give him that. Easily convincible, the way he says Sonja missed an appointment with him. You don't go to office hours when you're fucking the teacher. I can't tell if he's testing me or thinks I don't know anything. Obviously, Sonja would never have brought my name up because she doesn't know me. But did she bring up Anne's name to this guy? How much of her life did she share with him in the fast, hot and heavy relationship they had? "Do I know you?" he asks.

"I get that a lot," I say. "Have you ever been to the Cyclone Spin Studio? That's where I teach."

Two people walk into the room, chatting as they enter, thank god. Anne's words replay—*Everyone knows who you are.*

"I'm going to grab a seat in the back, if that's okay?" I say.

"That's great. Anywhere you'd like," Moore says.

I head to the back corner nearest the exit, where I can watch each person closely as they enter and exit. More folks enter the class and take a seat. And then, Moore begins the class.

"Friends, we have a visitor in our class this evening. This is Corey Tracey. Let's try to make her feel safe and heard, and maybe she'll share a bit of her writing with us at some point this evening. Welcome, Ms. Tracey," Moore says, and the students give me a little clap. It's weird, I feel like I'm going to have nightmares about midterms and finals tonight. It's a mixed group of race, age, and gender. I'm not nearly the oldest in the class, or the youngest.

"Corey Tracey?" A woman with gray hair and more mature skin says. "Are you the lady that helped solve the murder of those girls a few months ago?"

I shake my head. "Common name," I say.

Fuck. Dammit. Anne told me everybody knows me. In fairness, I thought she meant in Highland Park.

"Still, you look familiar," she says.

"Are you from Highland Park?" I ask. Avoiding the question until I can think of something clever to say in response.

"I am, why?" the woman asks.

"I think we shop at the Eagle Rock Trader Joe's at the same time a lot," I say. Please let that make her drop it.

"You know what, that may just be it. I'm there every day, honestly," she says. It's just enough for her to drop it. I'm sure Moore is filing it away in his memory to look me up after the class.

After the introductions and a reading of everyone's work in progress, it's time for a coffee, email, restroom break. I'm not sure I can take another hour of this class. Jacob has been kneading my chest with his head, trying to sleep, wearing down the tender skin at my décolletage. The clunky reading style of the unfinished poetry is painful. The good poetry I would prefer to read silently at my own pace. The one thing I have learned in the first hour is that Moore is adored by his students, and that he admires them in return.

He comes off almost as an idol that the class worships. This is not a typical undergraduate class—a room full of eighteen-year-old freshmen would not be enamored the way this group is. No, it makes sense why this class fills with older students. I wonder if Sonja idolized Moore as well. Did the trance of that idolization wear off once they had slept together and he became an ordinary man to her? Did love bombing, or his worship of her, change the dynamic that originally won her over? I forgot to check if he's married. I look at his hands but cannot tell from where I'm sitting. And not wearing a ring doesn't qualify him as unmarried anyway. I know that firsthand. Between my work on the news, and the swelling since pregnancy, the amount of time I didn't wear my wedding ring is far greater than the amount of time I have ever worn it.

The other students are gone now. It's just Jacob, Moore, and me. I want to engage in a way that will be less alarming than *When did you last see Sonja Hart?*

"I'm sorry, what do you prefer to be called, Professor Moore, or do you prefer Ryan? I should have asked earlier," I say. I usually like to take power away from people in interviews, but in this case, Moore is used to being idolized, the students have been addressing him as Ryan, and he seems to respond positively to the adoration. I want him to feel like he has the power here, so he'll feel more comfortable talking.

"I prefer Ryan, actually. I don't subscribe to the formality of titles in the classroom. We're all the same here, working adults looking to learn something different," he says. Interesting that he's leaning into his teaching pedagogy as though that's going to excuse him from me grilling him about Sonja. "That's great. So, Ryan"—I look down at Jacob and stroke the top of his head softly while he sleeps, making sure Moore is watching—"do you have kids?"

"Not yet. I hope time doesn't run out on me before I have the opportunity," he says. "Is this your first?" he asks. Good, he's comfortable. My earlier mention of Sonja hasn't scared him, yet.

"First, yep. He's great, my husband and I had to try for a while also. Tell your wife not to give up. It'll happen," I say. I wait for his face to respond. He looks at me and tilts his to the side.

"I'm sorry?" he asks.

"Oh no, I'm sorry, I assumed you were married because of the conversation about having kids." I fake embarrassment, but I know I can't make my face turn red any more than I can control it from not turning red when I am embarrassed.

"No, I'm not married." He smiles, chuckles lightly. He's not offended or angry or indifferent. He thinks it's funny.

"What's so funny?" I ask.

"I don't know. You mentioned Sonja, and so I assumed you knew that she and I have been seeing each other recently." Shit. What is happening? Is he going to admit to everything? Too much guilt can make people do weird things.

"Is that allowed? I mean, aren't you her teacher?" I ask. I want to tread lightly and not rock this boat of trust we have going.

"She applied to transfer into someone else's class so it wouldn't be an issue. Obviously, it wasn't planned. It just happened. I don't know if she's shared her work with you, but it's passionate, and the slow burn of love that she writes about, I couldn't help fall for her," he says. Moore looks lovesick. Like he can't wait to scream that he's in love with Sonja Hart. I wonder if he's kept her locked up and alive just so she won't leave him. Oh god, I need to get Lopez over to this guy's house. I need to keep him talking.

"How long have you and Sonja—" I say, but people are starting to reenter the class, and Moore cuts me off by welcoming everyone back. Shit. The conversation is over.

"Oh, you know Sonja?" A white-haired woman with young skin asks. The hair is deceiving. She can't be more than thirty, but there's also something about her energy that says *I'm older than you think*.

"Yeah, she told me about the class," I say. "Are you a friend of hers?"

"We're all friends in here, Corey. You can't expose your vulnerability in your poetry if you don't feel safe. We're exploring sides of ourselves that we've never shown to the world. Friendship feels too underwhelming of a word. I'd say we're more like lovers," the woman says.

"I'm sorry, I am terrible with names these days, mommy brain. What was your name again?" I'm going to have to take everyone's name down because, my god, did she just say they were all like lovers?

"I'm Antonella. Are you working on a piece? Multiple pieces?" she asks. She isn't being rude, just inquisitive and maybe trying to act supportive. I get the feeling she'd have a lot of constructive feedback if I read anything out loud. I don't think the lady with the baby in poetry class is Antonella's style, but I could be making assumptions.

Before I can answer, Moore takes back the class's attention. He looks back at me and gives me a wink I may have missed if I wasn't watching him like a hawk. It was so quick and masterful, like he does it all the time. I smile in return and nod and sit back against the most uncomfortable, hard plastic chair I've ever felt and wait for the class to end.

By the time the last person leaves, it's nearly thirty minutes after the class has ended. I've had riders at Cyclone try to stay late but having Jacob has worked to my advantage. It's always a diaper change, nap schedule, feedings. I've used it all to excuse my quick exits. Moore, however, looks like he enjoys the postclass comradery and indulges the students. He engages with them like they're old friends hanging out. For them, I still sense awe and adoration. There is a power dynamic, and Moore is at the top.

"Corey, what did you think of the class?" Moore asks while gathering his things.

"I thought it was great. Really strong work from the students. It's obviously a testament to your teaching style," I say. I have no idea because I wasn't listening most of the time. I was contemplating how to ask Moore if he killed Sonja Hart. I was imagining the room he may have her locked up in. I'm now wondering where he lives—somewhere close by, or does he commute, and am I going to have to involve an entirely different division of the LAPD?

"Are you sure you weren't trying to not fall asleep?" he asks.

"I'm not sure anyone would be able to fall asleep in these chairs, even an overtired new mom." He starts to walk slowly toward the door, and I follow. "Can I walk out with you? I was hoping to chat a little more, if that's okay?"

"Yeah, of course. But, I don't have anything to say about Sonja if that's what you're here to talk about." Moore pauses at the door, his hand on the knob, and I start to worry I've made a mistake staying until I'm alone with him in a windowless classroom at night. Who would still be here? Are there even later classes happening? Maybe a custodian?

Maybe a security guard that roams the halls? I didn't see a desk at the front when I entered. Shit.

"What are you going to do, lock me in?" I ask. My eyes point to his hand on the knob and back up to match his stare.

"Oh god, no, I'm sorry, I wasn't, no—I just have to close the door and lock up after we leave. I'd be happy to walk you to your car if you're nervous about predators. I'm so sorry, I'm not. No." Moore ushers Jacob and me out and does exactly what he said. He closes the door and locks it from the hall.

Neither of us says another word until we are outside.

"I'm sorry again for the misunderstanding back there," Moore says. "I was not trying to give off predator energy. That's not me, I swear."

"Where's Sonja?" I ask. It's demanding, authoritative. Now that we're not in the classroom, his domain, I take the power back, and I won't relent until Moore tells me what he did with Sonja.

"I don't know."

"I'm her friend, and she hasn't returned my phone calls," I say. I don't want him to know that anyone suspects anything is wrong yet. Better that he thinks that someone in Sonja's life is here, overmomming the situation.

"Listen, I don't know where she is. We haven't spoken all week. We had a plan Monday, but she said she was running late and wasn't sure she'd make it. She wanted to slow things down between us until minimally she had an opportunity to switch classes." I can't tell what Moore is feeling. He's indifferent, but he could be masking his anger.

"Did you notice anything different about her behavior?" I ask.

"You sound like a cop."

"I'm not, but I haven't heard from her since Saturday, and I'm concerned," I say.

"You know what's interesting about this conversation is that she told me she hadn't mentioned me to anyone in her life yet. I thought she was embarrassed because she was dating her professor, which at our age is ridiculous. But, I understood. Yet, here you are asking questions about our relationship. I'm not going to tell you another damn thing about Sonja until you answer a couple of questions of mine. Again, who are you?" Moore says.

I debate his stance in my head. I see he's struggling to gain some leverage here, but I don't think giving him any will be helpful. "I told you, I'm a friend of Sonja's, and I haven't heard from her in a week. She told me about you because she wanted advice on how to proceed with her relationship with her professor. You could have failed her if she dumped you, and believe it or not, even women at this age take their academic careers seriously, so yeah. I'm wondering what you know about where she is." Moore doesn't flinch. He doesn't show anything on his face.

"Ow, shit," I say. The zap in my brain or head or skull is back. I can feel this one in my teeth. Do I have a brain tumor? Is all this—the panic, anxiety, obsessive thoughts—are they all because there's a tumor and—

"Corey? Are you okay?" I hear him ask, but nothing registers until I feel Moore's hand on my shoulder, shaking me. "Corey, can you hear me? Raise your hand if you can hear me."

I raise my hand and say, "I can hear you. It's just . . . a headache." I want to puke but not in front of Moore. I need to go, I need to go, I need to move. Please don't let it be cancer. Is cancer better or worse than knives? No, no, no. Shut up. No! I get to the car and walk around to the back and double over as best I can to avoid my sleeping fifteen-month-old baby, who is not tiny like he was six months ago, and I vomit, followed by a fit of dry heaving. It's dark, and the lot is nearly empty now. I see some people look, but they're far enough away to not involve themselves.

With my hands shaking, I manage to transfer Jacob to his car seat with little fuss. Before I leave, I dig through my bag for the emergency Klonopin and take it, using Jacob's sippy cup of water. I sit for just a few minutes longer, put my headphones in my ears, and turn on a podcast on my phone. I turn it up loud enough to block the thoughts in my head until the Klonopin can start working. This is only a small setback.

I knew there would be setbacks. Dr. Rosenberg said that it wouldn't just go away, but I'd learn to cope with the attacks when they happen. I'd learn to prevent them. I'd deal with unresolved anger and push the fear and guilt that eats me up inside away. "I'm okay. I'm okay. I am okay." I say it out loud, over the blaring podcast in my headphones. Loud enough so I can hear the sound of my voice. "I'm okay. I'm okay. I am okay."

I need to get home and get Jacob in his crib, safe and sound. I need to sit down and think. Think about Sonja Hart. Sonja is in real danger. What if she isn't dead, and we can somehow find her alive? I need to get home and find out where Ryan Moore lives. I need to look at his social media. I would bet anything he's on LinkedIn, but who would he be on the socials? How many DMs has he slid into? Has he ever dated a student before, or is Sonja really unique? I'm not even sure I'm right about Moore. His energy is not what I thought it'd be. And with the number of students adoring him, why would he need to hurt Sonja? He's not married. He wants a family. She intended to keep the baby and include him. They could have been a family. I can't exclude him, though. He may have been the last person to have spoken to her. Ever.

I take a deep breath. It hits the bottom of my lungs. I'm ready to drive home.

25

I try three times to change Jacob's diaper without waking him, but each time he stirs, fusses, and pushes my hands away. I pause until he drifts back off, too tired to fully wake him and push my diaper agenda onto him. I finally succeed and put him in his crib, where I know he is almost completely safe. My anxiety over him reduced to a speck in my stomach.

Now I'm mostly anxious because Evan isn't home. I was glad not to see his car when I pulled up. But now that my baby is safely in bed, the Klonopin has slowed my racing heart and mind, and I am acutely aware of Evan's absence and know he'll be arriving at some point, and that ratchets up the tension in my already-shattered nerves. I want to close my eyes for just a bit before I settle into digging through Ryan Moore's online presence, but I can't. My nerves won't allow it when I know there will be an interruption, an Evan interruption, at any moment.

I wonder if I should text him, see when he'll be here, but that would just unsettle me in other ways, the knowing. The clock watching instead of working. I jump on the computer and start with the search engine: RYAN MOORE. My god, there are over two thousand Ryan Moore listings on LinkedIn. I need to narrow in on my search, so I add South Pasadena Community College. Of course, his listing on the college faculty registry is first, but I needed something less safe and more personal. I try the white pages to get his last known address. Shockingly, nothing in Pasadena, so I start to create a wider circle and put in Alhambra, then South Pasadena, which feels impossible on a youngish community college professor's salary. Nothing. I put in Eagle Rock, Altadena, Sierra Madre. I want to skip San Marino because if Ryan Moore lives in San Marino, then I have bigger problems—he would have to be loaded. Generational money, likely, and could easily pay someone to have taken care of Sonja. Shit.

Nothing. Last, but never least, and I don't know why I put it in last, I just wanted it to be different, I put in Highland Park:

> Ryan Moore, age 40s, Los Angeles, CA 90042 — Highland Park.

I map his address. He's on the border of South Pasadena and Highland Park, on the Highland Park side of Monterey Road. Less than ten minutes, all surface. I could get there tonight in probably four to five minutes. My phone vibrates on the nightstand. I forgot to toggle the silence switch back.

Chris: How'd it go tonight?

Well, I had a panic attack, there's this zap or electric current that feels like it's rocking something in my brain, and then I puked, but right before the puke I let Moore get away.

Me: It went. Too much to text. Tomorrow?

Chris: Do you teach in the morning?

Shit. I almost forgot.

Me: Yes. After?

Chris: No problem, I'll come over to you, okay?

Me: Perfect.

I hear the swoosh of my text being sent and then the closing of the front door from downstairs. "Evan?" I call out. I want to alert him that I'm awake. I want to make sure it's him. And, I want to caution him, let him know that I know he's here. I look at the clock. It's nine p.m. Where would he be this late? I've never known him to keep late work hours.

There's the sound of the familiar creak on the third step. I once made a joke that someone should oil it, and I used to laugh out loud at the stupidity of the whole thing, but now I appreciate it's tried-and-true notification that someone is coming. Like an alarm or a booby trap. I need to take a deep breath before he gets here. The feeling of butterflies in my stomach is more like the pit at the top of a roller coaster. I can't swallow—the anticipation is that palpable. Thank god for the Klonopin.

Evan stops on the landing and looks into our room. When my eyes meet his there's only silence. We stay there for a beat too long. It feels like an understanding. We're both too tired to try tonight. Too tired to argue and too tired to try not to argue.

"I'm going to sleep on the couch," Evan says.

"Okay," I say. I don't know if I should ask how his day was or his night, or how he is. I'm confused and the Klonopin's full effect makes it easy to not care. It doesn't even feel shitty. It feels fine. Evan doesn't even come in to change his clothes. I watch him walk away toward Jacob's room. He's a good dad. A great dad. I will always love him for that. I get up to close the door all but a crack. I don't want to watch him walk back downstairs. It's all easier if I don't have to witness it.

26

The couch is empty when I get up with Jacob. A blanket neatly folded with a pillow on top are the only signs that Evan slept there. His car is still in the driveway, so he's still around and will end up back at the house before work. Instead of the Sunday scaries, I have the Friday frights—a whole weekend of Evan here all day with Jacob and me. I wonder if Ben joined him on his run again. I also wonder if he's avoiding me this morning as much as I'm trying to avoid him by hurrying to get out the door and to work.

I rush to the car with Jacob. The only things awake and out this early are me, Jacob, Evan, and the coyotes. There's one coyote the neighborhood refers to as el lobo, or the wolf. He's huge and lumbers through the area during foggy mornings. From far away he could be mistaken for a large German shepherd, but when he closes in, el lobo is a massive, wild coyote. I've only seen him once, before I had Jacob, and he stopped me dead in my tracks. We had an old-fashioned stare down that he definitely won. He took the win and left in the opposite direction, and I swore to never be outside in the morning fog again.

This morning Evan is even more intimidating than el lobo. I don't want to have another staring contest with him, like we did last night. The silence between us is causing me to confuse tension with anxiety. The Klonopin in my system last night helped, but I don't want to take another one, and I'm not ready to start the Paxil again. The panic attacks are still gone, the intrusive thoughts fleeting and not a broken record that plays all day, and the fogginess is just beginning to lift. I want to get through this on my own.

"Mrs. Evan," I hear Pete say from across the street. I turn around and see him walking toward me and the car. I shut Jacob's door and walk around to the driver's side so Pete doesn't have access to him.

"Pete, how are you this morning? Kind of early, no?" I ask. I know the man doesn't sleep. He's up all night and all day, hawking the street like private security.

"I thought I saw you go running with Mr. Evan this morning?" Pete poses it like a question, but it sounds more like a statement.

"Nope, he was out before me. This week he's been running with your new neighbor, Ben." I like to add that detail since Pete is right next door to Julia and Ben, and I know he hates it. I know he was hoping no one would move into that house. He hates sharing space, and their houses are so close the easement between them can barely fit a watering hose. Yet, Pete made sure to plant a row of pepper bushes there just to claim the space as his. Such an asshole. I would have planted roses or Australian lavender bushes—something tall and flowery.

"No, he was with a lady. But, nah, it couldn't be you anymore. She had a ponytail." So Pete noticed my haircut. How lovely for me.

"Are you sure it was Evan?" I ask. Pete nods. I'm positive that all of us white gentrifiers are starting to look alike to Pete. I'm more positive we all cause him the same amount of grief the way we liberally park in front of his house, open endless amounts of artisan coffee shops that only serve pour-overs or French press for six dollars a cup. I do not blame him for being irritated or impatient. "Okay, well, I need to get to work. I'm teaching class this morning." Pete waves instead of saying anything else and slinks across the street to sit in his car and watch.

I know Evan's running route. I can drive it quickly before I head to the Cyclone Studio. Maybe see if Evan is running with someone, or if Pete had just been trying to cause trouble. I make a right on Monte Vista Street and head north. I realize I don't even know what time Evan had gotten up and left. He could already be circling back home. I slow down as I hit the independent fruit market and coffee bar. No one is seated outdoors, and they're not even open for another fifteen minutes. I drive down a little farther, because Evan doesn't make his loop until he gets to Avenue 61. I slow down as I approach Lola's Coffee. Lola's opens at five a.m. The front of the café is all windows, with only one table inside to sip coffee and then four tables outside. They make delicious morning pastries too. I nearly slam on the brakes when I look in the window and see Evan sitting at the table, coffee in hand, beside a woman I've never met before.

I put my foot on the gas and speed off. I head straight to Cyclone like I should have in the first place. Dammit, Pete. I do not need to know that Evan is with a woman this morning. Who is she? What does this mean? I thought he came home because he wants to work on our relationship. I'm not even sure I care, but I'm mad and embarrassed and . . . fuck, territorial.

When I get to Cyclone I'm on the verge of crying or screaming. If Monique looks at me wrong, I will say the wrong thing.

"Tracey, you good?" Monique asks. "You look like you already took a spin class."

"I'm fine." I look up at the podium, and the new instructor is just finishing. "How's she working out?" I ask.

"Great, this is her fourth class, if you can believe it." I want to scream at Monique, *What's not to believe? This is probably her only job! She looks eighteen, probably is. Probably lives at home with her parents!* And, so what if she does, Corey? She has every right. You're not mad at her. She doesn't look anything like the blonde, tan, thin female runner in a sports bra and matching shorts that Evan is having coffee with.

"Dude, your phone is vibing," Monique says.

"What?" I ask. It's more of a snap.

"Your phone is vibrating." She points to my cell phone bouncing in the cupholder on Jacob's stroller.

I snatch it off the stroller. It's too early for anyone to be calling.

> *Evan:* Hey, I was hoping to catch you before you left this morning. I wanted to say sorry about last night. Give Jacob a kiss for me. Will you be home for dinner tonight?

Fuck him. I slam the phone down on the front desk. Monique cocks her head and squints her eyes at me. She looks like she's trying to weigh if she should ask what that was about. Instead, she greets the riders from class as they enter and check in. I avoid turning around and allowing any of them to see my face.

The new instructor is mobbed by her riders while making her way to the desk where Monique and I are. Typical, everyone loves the new person. Isn't that right, Evan? New is just new. It's not different or earth shattering, it's just new. Shiny, unmarred, and new.

"Hi, are you Corey?" She's made her way to us and is smiling so wide I can see a filling on a back tooth. On closer inspection she's not as young as I had thought. In fact, she looks older than Monique. She's sweating so profusely it's obvious she puts all the resistance on while she teaches and rides. Her energy is too much for me in this moment, but I don't want to be an asshole on a first introduction.

"Yep, Corey. I'm so sorry, I know you're our new instructor, but I haven't caught your name?" I say.

"Amanda." She holds her hand out ready to shake mine. I grasp it and notice how firm her grip is. "It's really so great to meet you. Monique said I should do everything you say or ask, and that you're the best person to know." Amanda looks at Monique and winks. Dammit, Monique. Are they already fucking each other?

"Well, now I know you're a liar," I say. Monique and Amanda burst into a fit of laughter.

"I told you not to even try. She would know you were full of shit," Monique says. Then she looks at me and says, "I told her you're lazy and late. Now go teach your class, Tracey, or I'm going back to calling you Lieberman, because Lieberman always jumped when I said to."

One way to get rid of a bad mood is to just hang out with people who like you. I'd go so far as to say that I think in a couple more years, Monique may even grow to love me. The thought of it makes me laugh. I park Jacob next to me. His headphones are on, and he leaves them while he plays with the light-up toy I brought him. Every time he pushes a button, another one glows, and he chases the lights around the board. And just in case that doesn't keep him interested, I've tucked in a board book that's filled with pages of different textures and giant pictures of animals with googly eyes. At least I did something right this morning, and it was for the most important man in my life, Jacob.

"Okay, riders. I hope you're ready to push those legs this morning because we're going to ride like we're being chased by all the feelings we never want to feel again. Let's take it up and out of the seat, turn that dial up twice, and let's pick up that pace." And for the first time in a long time, I turn the dial with my class, and I feel my legs burn. Burn like the anger inside me is setting them on fire. I look out to the front desk, and Monique is watching with a half smile tugging up the left side of her face.

At the end of class my riders are too tired to hang out and chat. Most of them grumble as they walk out.

"What was that about?" Monique asks.

"Are you fucking the new girl?" I ask.

"Let's just say both our questions were rhetorical, and neither of us needs to answer them," Monique says. "Instead, let me say this, 'Good class, Tracey.' But, maybe ease into this new class energy. I don't think your regulars were expecting to work that hard."

"I don't get it. You're always telling me I need to go harder. Now I'm too hard?" My energy is still hot. The ride only did so much. Dammit, I don't want to push Monique. She's right, and I'm angry.

"Yeah, I want *you* to work harder on your bike. Your classes are great. What's wrong?" she asks.

"I thought you don't like to know people's problems, so I'm sparing you mine."

"Well, I also don't want you biting my head off, so out with it," she says.

"I saw Evan this morning having coffee with another woman," I say.

"In your house?" she asks. The look on her face tells me she's going to kill Evan herself.

"No, god, no, no. He left early to go for his morning run and apparently ran to coffee with this woman."

"Tracey, you're not using your married name anymore. Do you actually care?" Monique asks, and she has a valid point, and it's the one I'm trying to figure out. Monique switches playlists. She's about to teach the next class, and her riders are pouring in where mine are sprinkling out.

"Yeah, I know. I'm confused, and I'm pissed at him and myself for caring."

Monique nods her head in understanding. I'm so glad she isn't jumping into armchair-psychologist mode like so many others would if I told them.

"And, no, I'm not fucking Amanda. I think she has a boyfriend." Monique smiles and winks at me. "But next time you're jealous of who I'm going to bed with, you could ask a little nicer." I take the used, sweaty towel I'm holding from class and throw it at her. "When were you going to tell me your new neighbor is Julia *fucking* Palmer?"

"I'm glad you know who she is," I say and laugh.

"She was like this salty teenager on this soap I grew up watching. I'm pretty sure she turned me gay."

"Wow, did you tell her that?" I ask.

"Oh, I took her out for coffee and signed her up for ongoing monthly classes. She should be here any minute. It's a shame she has a husband, but she's got a real hard-on for you, though."

"What do you mean?"

"Nothing, just that she feels bad about your situation—shit like that."

What the fuck? Did Evan tell Ben about us? What game is this woman playing? "Okay, tell me more. What else do you know about her?" I say.

"I mean, just gossip from the rags at the checkout counters, but I remember she made the covers a few times—she had some issues. Child-star shit."

"What else about me?" I ask.

"Corey." I spin around and see Julia entering the studio in a beautiful teal-on-teal sports-bra-and-leggings set. She does look like a TV actress.

"Hey, Julia, I'm glad to see you back."

"I didn't know you'd be here today," Julia says, tucking a strand of hair behind her ear like she did the first time we met. That overrehearsed tropey move I recognize from any given girl next door on TV.

"Me too," Monique says. "Corey, take your kid and get out of here. He needs playtime, and I mean it." Monique used my first name? What power does Julia wield?

"Agree," I say. "Thank you. You make a really okay friend," I say to Monique. She scowls at me immediately. "Have a great class, Julia." I smile and roll Jacob out. We have an appointment with Chris. And I need to call Lopez. And I need to drive by Ryan Moore's house. And there's a woman's burned body in a morgue with no name, and Monique is right. My baby needs to play and be a kid.

27

I park in front of my house, where I can see the driveway and that Evan's car is gone. A few times, before he moved out for a month, I would see his car in the driveway and just keep driving. I wouldn't park and go in with Jacob. I'd drive around the neighborhood until I couldn't any longer.

I look in the back seat and Jacob is out. Must be another growing spurt. I don't want to wake him up. I'll let him sleep a little longer and drive over to the house that burned down behind the Groceries for Less.

There isn't anybody around. Just yellow police tape marking off the property—as if the flimsy material and words of warning are enough to prevent stupidity or scare off thrill seekers. The tape doesn't reach the curb, so I park directly in front of the house and stare at the remnants of history. There's nothing much to look at. The house isn't gone, but it is destroyed. The front windows are all blown out, probably from the water hoses trying to get the fire out before it spread. I learned that from my deep dive into fire investigation techniques. Initially detectives had posited the Flores fire might have been a result of a break-in when they found the broken glass in the living room, but a rep from the fire department had clarified that the high pressure of the water from their hoses frequently blows the glass inward. Next door there is a little girl, maybe three or four, playing in one of those plastic, red cars with the yellow roofs you can get in and out of. I wonder if the air is okay for her to be breathing. She should be at the park instead—but not the one built over an old gas station in town. I guiltily look back at Jacob. "You should be at the park too, huh?" I say so softly, hoping it doesn't drop into his psyche and haunt him the rest of his life.

Someone honks behind my car. I look, and the driver is telling me to go. I realize I'm parked on the wrong side of the street in the wrong direction. I just wanted to get as close to the house as possible. I take off to circle the block. When I turn the corner, I see the neLA Living signs have been vandalized with spray paint. Maybe it's old, maybe it's new. Signs are always spray-painted or vandalized. I drive slowly, looking, watching. Across the street from the neLA Living condos are two houses right next door to each other, being gutted. And on the dumpster, set in the driveway separating the two homes, is a neLA Living decal.

I have to turn, or I'll drive down into a dead end. Instead of going home, though, I turn into the Groceries for Less store parking lot. I look around to see if the man I'd met here the day of the fire, Dave, is still around. I pull up to an RV that looks like it's been through several apocalypses. I'm not sure if it's his, but it's the only one in the lot today. I drive up alongside the RV and debate getting out of the car and knocking. I don't want to leave Jacob alone in the car, even if I am right beside it. I also don't want to honk and have the entire lot of people look and Jacob wake up. I let my Subaru idle next to the house on wheels for a few minutes. If anyone is home, they'll come out or at least peek through a window. Nothing happens. No one's home.

"Mama." Jacob is awake. Perfect timing as I park along the side of our house opposite the driveway.

"Well hello, my precious. Did you have a good nap?" I ask. "Are you hungry?" I need to text Chris and let him know he can come by. I need to call Lopez too. But, I choose Jacob right now. I want to just be present with my guy. Monique was right, he needs playtime, and he needs a chance to work out his legs again. Oh shit, I forgot to tell Evan he's walking. In fairness he didn't show up until late, and neither of us had spoken at all. I pull Jacob out of his car seat and I can feel how heavy his diaper is. It's soaked. "Let's get you changed, buddy. That can't feel good." I should have checked before leaving the studio. Bad mom, dammit. I'm trying to focus. Focus on all of everything—and my husband may be cheating on me. This whole time he worried and accused and pointed the finger at me and what I was, transparently, doing with Chris while he's off sneaking around with another woman I've never seen before. I can't let the image of her go from my head. I feel sick.

Jacob screams and pushes his hands against my chest as hard as he can. "Do you want down?" I ask.

"Okay," Jacob says. It's got to be the best sound I've ever heard. I set him on his feet on the sidewalk, and he takes off to the steps that lead up to our house and stops. I jog after him, and when I get to the steps, I stop right next to him and take in why he didn't try climbing them himself. Chris is sitting on the stairs, waiting for us.

"Hi, I'm so sorry. Did you say you were coming? I thought I'd text you when I got home. Shit, I'm sorry," I say.

"No, I was in the neighborhood over at the fire site earlier. Decided I'd get breakfast on the corner and then come meet you. You're right on time. I've only been here a few minutes," Chris says.

"Do not believe that man," Elsie says from her porch. "That man has been waiting for you for half an hour. I told him to leave until you texted him, but he refused." Elsie sounds defensive, but also maybe a little flirty. "I had to fix that man a cup of coffee just to keep him from pacing around the sidewalk, letting Pete get all up in his business. Corey, have a conversation with your partner. He cannot just go loitering around this block, someone is going to—"

"Going to what?" I ask with a smile.

"You know, call the cops or, I don't know, have him over for breakfast," she says. My jaw drops. She winks at Chris, and I see him blush. He *blushes*. My god, it's amazing to see him get embarrassed. What is actually happening here? "Corey, do you know that Chris's cousin went to prom with my sister?" I did not, but nothing surprises me in Northeast LA. Everyone's cousin, sister, brother, aunt, uncle is related, married, dated, or something to someone else. It's absolutely a small town in the big city.

"If you two are done with whatever this is that's happening here." I'm not sure if it is flirting at this point, but it is something. The energy Elsie is giving off is electric and needs water, fast. "I'm going to change my baby's diaper."

"No," Jacob says and hits my leg. "No, Mama."

"You don't want to change your diaper?" I ask.

"No," he says, again, and I start laughing. I've been waiting since Jacob was in my belly kicking for the day that he and I would be able to have a two-way, verbal conversation, and here it is. I'm at a loss for words, and I feel tears forming in my eyes. They're warm and happy and wow.

"Amorcito," Elsie says to Jacob, "let your mommy change your diaper, and then you can play."

"No." Jacob's face is turning red like it does before a meltdown, which is absolutely rare for him.

"Hey, little man, can I come change your diaper with you?" Chris asks.

"Okay," Jacob agrees. He then turns to me and lifts his arms for *up*. I scoop him and his soggy diaper into my arms and carry him up the steps, turning around once to wave goodbye to Elsie. She winks at me, and I have no idea what she's indicating by the smile she gives with it. What does she think is happening? She knows I'm married to Evan. I wonder if she saw Evan with the other woman earlier. I wonder if the whole block knows because of Pete. I wonder if Evan knows I know.

"Okay, let's go upstairs and change your diaper, then you can visit with Chris," I say.

"No," Jacob yells. He's really loving the word, and I regret him learning it. He pushes against my chest and screams. His diaper is so full and heavy, and he has become so strong I'm both astonished and proud. I have to put him down before he slips out of my arms. He runs around the living room, his little jeggings falling down from the weight of his diaper.

"Um, can you watch him for a minute while I run upstairs and grab things to change him?" I ask.

"Of course," Chris says.

"He just started walking yesterday. I need you to promise to watch him. I haven't babyproofed the corners of the counter or the tables. The cupboards aren't locked or the drawers. I haven't done anything, I-I need you to really follow him around, okay?" I say, and Chris looks at me with that smile that reaches all the way to his eyes. It is unmistakable that something I've said pleases him, or I've reminded him of something funny, I don't know—I wish I knew, but I like when he looks at me like this. "Why are you smiling like that?" I ask.

"You're a good mom, Corey Tracey. I enjoy seeing the woman I knew stalking predators around a news station being the most attentive, protective, and capable mom." He takes a beat to look over at Jacob, who is trying to climb onto the coffee table. I start to move toward him when Chris says, "Let me, you go get that diaper." Chris springs forward and swoops Jacob up, gently giving him a ride in the air. It's followed by a gurgly laugh by Jacob.

After changing Jacob and running around playing chase for fifteen minutes, I'm exhausted. Chris and I have been tag teaming, but Jacob is fast and just keeps going, and I'm not in the shape I thought I was from spin . . . I am going to have to start running again. I put Jacob in his highchair for lunch, and, of course, he wants down. He wants to run. "Look, buddy, banana, noodles, melon." I also pull out a meatball from a box of leftovers Evan brought home the other night when he was covering for Ben. I taste it for spice and freshness. I chop it up and put it in front of Jacob. Where did he go that serves meatballs? I run through the local restaurants in my head: Mexican, El Salvadorian, Mexican, Mexican, Mexican. This is Italian, definitely Italian. I cannot think of a single spot we've ever been in the neighborhood that serves Italian meatballs.

"What are you thinking about?" Chris asks.

"Nothing," I say. "Let me fill you in on last night."

I watch Jacob make a mess of himself as I fill Chris in on my conversation with Lopez and everything that happened at Moore's class, leaving out the panic attack and head zapping.

"How did Lopez find out the body was not the squatter?" Chris asks.

"She showed up at the police station to fill out a report that her house had burned down," I say.

"And, how can they confirm she's the same woman that was actually living there and not another unhoused person in Highland Park?" he asks.

"Shit, I didn't ask." I cannot believe I didn't think to ask Lopez. The distraction level was high, and my thoughts were on Moore and Jacob running around the house for the first time.

"Corey, you are doing just about a thousand things all on your own. You're allowed to miss a question. I'm not doing all this." He gestures to Jacob and the house and maybe the spin clothes I haven't changed out of yet. "And I miss things too."

"Yeah, but there's no excuse. I used to be better." I'm still trying to get my focus back, and I need the brain fog to clear. My head is, like zapping since I came off the medicine, and it's freaking me out. I can only hope it's not a brain tumor, and that's freaking me out. And if I think too much, the thoughts come back. The ones that circle and don't shut up, and I can't, I cannot go back on the Paxil.

Chris takes my hands in his, like he has in the past when I'm spiraling, and he pushes his thumb and forefinger into the space between my thumb and forefinger. I take a deep breath and drop my shoulders immediately. I hadn't realized I was holding them up at my ears. It's such a relief, I slouch in my chair and close my eyes. I feel the hot, wet tears, but I won't let them out. Not today, tears, not right now—wait, the tears want to flow. Maybe the effects of the Paxil are wearing off. And then I feel something wet and solid hit my face, and I open my eyes. Jacob is throwing cold, unsauced spaghetti noodles at me. Chris is laughing, and I pull my hands from his, grab a noodle off my shoulder, and throw it at him. It lands right on his nose, and Jacob giggles that deep, rich, hysterical giggle only babies can make. It's intoxicating. It's the moment I thought I'd be sharing with Evan but could never picture us here, like this.

Evan would find this too messy, too encouraging of bad manners, too distracting from Jacob's feeding time. I can imagine him saying, *Food is for eating, not playing*. I would sigh, he would question my sigh, and then we'd be in a debate for the rest of the night surrounding appropriate and inappropriate behaviors for a child, which were all based on hypothetical scenarios. The energy would be drained from me, but he'd be revved up for multiple more rounds. I'd leave the conversation to put Jacob to bed, and then I'd sink into a semislumber in my clothes, too tired to change or wash my face, but Evan would sneak into the bed beside me and try to wake me for sex. The absolute audacity of the scenario makes me laugh out loud.

"Oh, you think noodles on my face is funny, Ms. Corey Tracey-Lieberman," Chris says and throws a noodle at me that lands on my forehead. Jacob laughs that deep, delicious, hearty giggling laugh again. And, when Chris says Lieberman, for what feels like the first time ever, I realize it's the name that Jacob has too. He will always be Lieberman, and I will always be his mom, so maybe it's not so bad to keep the hyphen.

I clean Jacob up, and after a late morning of running around and a big lunch, he's ready for a second nap, and I'm ready to work.

"Why don't you make some coffee while I put this guy down for his nap, and we'll get started," I say to Chris. He's already been here for two hours, and we've barely done any work. My guilt starts to gnaw at me. If I'm not feeling guilty that I'm not enough for Jacob, then I'm feeling guilty I've ruined my marriage, and if I'm not feeling guilty about my marriage, I'm feeling guilty about the imposition I'm putting on Chris by always needing to be a mom first. And if I'm not feeling guilty about that, I feel guilty that I'm not working hard enough, fast enough, or smart enough to find Sonja—or every other victim.

Jacob is so tired he falls asleep in my arms after one short verse of "Twinkle, Twinkle, Little Star." I gently set him in his crib and kiss his head. "You are my whole heart, my love." I look at the monitor on his dresser. The one that Evan and I both have connected to our phones. I wonder if he's watching me put Jacob down for his nap. I wonder if he listens in on my time with Jacob when he's not here. I walk over to the device and turn it off. And, instead of closing Jacob's door on my way out, I leave it ajar, so I can hear him call me when he wakes up. The way my parents did it, and the way theirs did before them.

Chris already has two cups of coffee waiting on the table. My laptop is closed but placed next to my coffee cup, and Chris has his open. I see his earbuds are in and on his screen is me. He's watching and listening to the message I posted regarding Sonja's disappearance and information. I had forgotten to tell him about my plea to the community. I tap Chris on the shoulder to get his attention. I sit down at my computer and watch him.

"Do you know you have over a thousand views on this?" he asks while removing his earbuds. "That's more viewers than I get readers. Who is the person that had information?"

"It was Anne. I sat down with her yesterday morning, remember?" I say. "But I can't figure out why her information, Moore's story, and

Jonathan's are all just a little bit off." I take a sip of my coffee, and again, it's perfect. Just the way I like it. A splash and then one more of half-and-half, the color of a caramel candy and sugar, but not enough to remove the flavor of the bitterness of the coffee. I would keep Chris around for as long as possible if he always made my coffee this well. "By the way, is Jonathan coming down? Did you give him the money?"

"No, his dad is coming with him. They're driving. I think they're going to leave today after work." Chris looks back to his screen and then up at me. He pinches his face in concentration, staring at me and not saying anything.

"What is it?" I ask. "You're making me nervous."

"You need to keep making these videos. People want to help, they want to see someone with your authenticity on their screens again. They want to know someone is fighting alongside them, and it's the new generation, too, this is how they get their news, selectively by trusted sources on their socials."

"So you just want me to start my own news channel on social media?" I ask.

"Yes. We, *we* are going to start our own news coverage on social media that will be an extension of *The Eastsider Times*." Chris isn't emoting anything. He is still, his hands clasped together, elbows resting on the table. "Now, you tell me how the stories make sense if you break them down, person by person."

"I think Sonja wasn't entirely honest about her plan with Anne. I think she gave the gist of it to her. I think Sonja did have a plan to get away for a few days to think about all the changes that were about to happen. I think she wanted to be alone. I think Anne is the type of person and friend that would never have let Sonja go away solo. Especially if she knew that Sonja was going camping alone. I used to have a friend that did this sort of thing all the time—go camping alone," I say.

"And?" Chris asks.

"We *used* to be friends. It was nerve racking. I never knew when she'd be back, if she'd get lost. Sometimes she'd go to Mammoth in the winter to camp—there are avalanches and bears, and I couldn't do it. I couldn't stop worrying, so I pulled away." I do that a lot with friends, actually. For all sorts of reasons. "She's still a friend on social media. Last I saw she was living in a van, on the road full-time. I don't think Sonja is that kind of a nomad, but I do think she needed space to think and be still."

"Okay, so she tells Anne she'll be out of range, she's going camping with her boyfriend, and she's going to tell him she's pregnant." Chris recaps it so simply it sounds like a fun getaway.

"Except, he's not yet her boyfriend. It's been casual, and technically he's her baby's daddy. At this time, she's revealing that she's pregnant and wants to cool things way down. Build up their friendship, keep the baby, and raise it together," I say.

"Okay, so if Sonja is going alone to Joshua Tree, when do you think this conversation is happening with Moore?"

"I think Sonja put her suitcase in her car, but she wasn't leaving on her trip right away. I think she planned to go to Moore's house first to tell him she's pregnant. I think she probably planned to call her son since she missed their Sunday call but never got the chance. Two things could have happened here. One, say we believe Moore, and he's not lying, that would mean between the time she loaded her car with her suitcase and before heading to his house, she made a stop. During that stop something happened, and now she's missing . . . but where's her car? It's Highland Park. She could have parked her car on the street somewhere, and as long as there isn't any street cleaning, it could be there for a week or more. Right?"

"Two days is the limit, but someone would have to call to report a car being left for two days. If no one does that, a week, sure, maybe longer," Chris says. "We'd need to canvas the streets of Highland Park block by block—"

"For white Priuses. Does Jonathan know his mom's license plate number?" I ask.

"No, I already asked—was hoping to call in a favor from a friend to find the car. When he gets here, we need to go through paperwork at her apartment to see if we can find it. Or, you could ask Lopez if she can look it up for you." Great, another favor from Lopez on a case that isn't hers. She'll want me to find the car first, and then she'd look the plates up, that's how Lopez works. She needs a reason, tangible evidence, to proceed.

"Okay, possibility two. Sonja made it to Moore's, and Moore is lying. Again, where is her car? Did he put it in his garage? It's a Prius. Can it fit inside a storage unit?" I ask. "We need to find Sonja's car."

"Do we think that there is any chance Sonja did leave town?" Chris asks.

"I don't think so. If she had, she would have called Jonathan—it's a two-hour drive," I say. Anything is a possibility, but I don't believe she leaves town without calling him at some point.

"What makes you so positive?" Chris asks.

"Because he's her baby. The most important person in her life. She would call to tell him she loves him and that she's going to be out of reach for a day because of the service. She wouldn't want him, her baby, to worry about her the way she's spent his lifetime worrying about him." The way I feel the words in my whole body resonate. I would never leave Jacob. You couldn't pry me away from him. Especially without saying goodbye and that I'd be right back. I will always fight to get back to him, no matter how old he gets.

Nothing is getting clearer. I'm only certain now that I don't have a clue. I need to get over to Moore's place. What if Sonja is there, locked in a room, alive. Maybe I can get the license plate number if I give Lopez something in return. "Hey, can you give me Jonathan's phone number? I want to give it to Detective Lopez," I tell Chris. "I'll see if she can get me Sonja's license plate number. And as soon as Jacob wakes up, I'm going to drive up and down this side of York to look for her Prius. You take the west side of York, okay?" I ask. He nods and hands me his phone with Jonathan's number pulled up. I text Lopez immediately.

Me: Hey, forwarded you Jonathan Hart son of Sonja Hart phone number. I need Sonja's license plate number. Kid doesn't have it. White Prius, California plates registered to Sonja Hart, I assume.

I cross my fingers. Usually Lopez is a quick responder, or minimally I see the three dots and know she's usually trying to get back to me—there's nothing right now, and the waiting, even for a moment, feels condemning as hell.

"I'm going to start canvassing. I texted you my location, so you can follow me, and we don't double up where York and Figueroa meet," Chris says. "I'll talk to you in a bit."

I walk Chris to the door. After he leaves, I press the link to his location on my phone and watch the dot on the screen move as he leaves my street. I wonder if he'll forget to turn his share location off, so I can watch him whenever I want. Do I actually want to know where Chris is, especially if he's with Megan? I don't know yet.

My phone vibrates, and it's Lopez.

Lopez: One favor, one time: California plate number 728JBS4, white Prius. Find me that car, Corey Tracey.

Me: I will.

First, I'm going to post a video to my thousand viewers and see if we can get a little assistance. This is what social media should be used for—helping find the missing members of our community. We don't need milk boxes—we need the internet.

> Hi neighbors of Northeast LA, I'm Corey Tracey. I am still in search of information on the missing Highland Park resident, Sonja Hart. With your help, I am hoping we can bring good news to her family. We are currently looking for her vehicle, a white Prius with California license plate number 728JBS4. If you see this car, or think you saw it, please comment immediately. I will have notifications turned on. Spread the word as far and as loud as you can. Please share this video. Please tell your neighbors and your friends. We need to bring Sonja home.

And on cue, Jacob is awake and calling me by name. "Mama!"

28

After a very quick diaper change and snack of breast milk, five minutes on each side, Jacob and I head out to the car for a ride around. Instead of the stairs, which Jacob has no practice on, I let him walk down the, albeit steep, driveway, holding my hand. The trouble he's giving me about being picked up is outrageous. Out of nowhere he only wants down now.

As we slowly edge our way down the driveway, I look across to Julia and Ben's house. The screen door is wide open, as is the front door. I look around but don't see their car. Oh god, their new kitten, Oliver, is probably already on the run and adopted into a band of feral cats by now.

"Jacob, up, Mommy needs to pick you up. We need to cross the street," I say. I point to Julia and Ben's house with my free hand. Jacob raises his arms, and I am relieved. My guy. He does love me, still wants to help his mommy, thank god.

I walk up to the open door but refrain from walking inside. Instead I call out, "Julia? Ben?" No one answers. I extend my head forward to look around without going inside. "Julia?" I ask again. The entire house is an open floor plan, just like ours. They are two very different houses, but both have a living room that opens to the dining room, and straight through to the kitchen. There is no one. I can see that the back door is closed, though. I'm not sure if that's good, bad, or indifferent. "Ben?" I call, and Oliver jumps from out of the shadows and onto the dining room table. The table takes up the entire dining room and part of the kitchen. It's a thick wood table, rectangular in shape, with a wooden bench for seating on one side and chairs on the ends and other side. I imagine the two of them testing it out in an overpriced New York furniture store, Ben arguing for comfortable chairs with backs but relenting when Julia insists that the low profile of the bench fits their aesthetic. The living room barely contains the oversize couch the movers brought in, and the kitchen is filled with moving boxes. "Oliver," I say, "where are your people?"

Jacob reaches for the cat with desperation. He pushes off my chest and yells, "Down, down!" I reach in and pull the heavy door closed before I have to give in to my son, and then tightly close the screen door.

I look up and down the street as if I'll see Julia or Ben at any moment coming home, smiling, having forgotten they left their house wide open. What if someone is home and needs assistance because they've fallen and hit their head? I swoop up Jacob and run back up their front steps and throw open the front door and march in like I own the place. "Julia? Ben? I'm in your house, and I'm coming to see if you're okay," I say loud enough into the empty space. I don't want to alarm an intruder or Julia. "I'm now entering the hallway that appears to lead to your bedroom." I look left and see a room full of boxes and check it out, nothing. I walk to the bathroom, which is located in the area between the two bedrooms. I enter the small space and open the curtain, nothing. I walk to the second bedroom, where there's an unmade king-size bed. A small wood rocking chair in the corner and a six-drawer double dresser at the foot of the bed that leaves the thinnest amount of space between it and the bed frame. I slide open the mirrored closet, a violation of their privacy that I will regret later, I'm sure, but I can't help myself. It is filled to capacity with women's clothing. Jeans, linen drawstring pants, T-shirts, and button-downs, all Julia's. Half the items still have tags on them. None of it screams

Hollywood actress, and there is no room to hide the body of Ben or Julia inside it.

It must have been a mistake. They left in a hurry, and the door didn't close all the way, and it opened itself up.

I walk back to the front door, double-checking my steps and turning around to make sure there isn't a secret nook I haven't explored. "Julia, I'm leaving now. I'm going to close the doors behind me. I will check back later to make sure I didn't miss you." I say it for the sake of any ghost I may have also missed. Or, Pete if he's listening at the window. I am thankful Jacob stayed calm enough while we walked through the new and strange house we'd never been in. I'm glad Oliver had enough sense not to leave out the open door. He sits by a wastebasket he has tipped over, gnawing on a piece of paper.

"No, baby, that's not good for you." I bend down to take the crumpled paper from his mouth, but he darts away, dropping it on the floor. I should leave it—it's not my business, but I'm already in motion, picking up the crushed yellow Post-it and unfolding its many wrinkles to read its secret message: *Going out. Back in a bit. Love you.* Ben's note from the other night, crumpled in an angry ball of rage and thrown out. Why lie, Julia? I promptly recrumple the paper and toss it into the tipped-over can. Hopefully Oliver won't go trash diving again, but something tells me his feral instincts will die hard.

My anxiety only starts to peak as I leave. The last time I walked into a house with an open door, someone had been shot and killed. Jacob was with me then, as well. I swore then I would never take him into a house like that again, and here I am, having done it. The tears I've felt well up so many times this week shed uncontrollably now.

I look down at my free hand, and it is shaking. My phone is vibrating, and I pull it out of the pocket of my spin class pants that I still haven't changed out of yet. It's notifications from the video. I wipe at my eyes with the back of my hand. Trying to clear the watery vision. I cross the road back to my side of the street. I open the app on my phone, and there are already four comments:

> White Prius on the Monte Vista St corner of Avenue 59 west of Monte Vista. Didn't get the license plate!
>
> White Prius seen off Fig by the old pharmacy Avenue 57 not too sure it's still there
>
> White Prius parked around Aldama St and Avenue 54-ish
>
> Try the old motel off York. I saw a Prius there a few nights ago. Weird to see that car there.

I screenshot the messages and send them to Chris.

Me: I'll take the first two, you take the second two locations, okay?

Chris gives my message a thumbs-up. I get a very-upset-about-going-in-the-car Jacob into his car seat. Buckling him in is a chore, but he is secure and calming down with a smoothie pouch in his hand. I take one last look at Julia and Ben's house and let my mind wander for only a second about where they could have gone in such a hurry to leave the house open before I put the car in drive and take off in the direction of the old pharmacy.

I circle the block looking for the white Prius, but there's only a silver one parked about three blocks north, and the license plate does not match. I pull over and text Evan.

Me: Do you have Ben's number? Our neighbor?

Evan: Yep, what's wrong? Julia looking for him?

Me: No, I am. Their house was wide open, and no one is home. I went in to check if someone was there, hurt. But the house was empty.

Evan: Corey! You could have gotten yourself killed. What if it was a robbery in progress? Jesus. What is wrong with you? Was Jacob with you?
Fuck.

Me: Can you just give me his number or text him and find out? I don't have Julia's number.

. . .

Those three dots that force me to wait. Not today. I take off to the next Prius sighting. I've already overshot Avenue 59, so I head west up the first street and turn south on Monte Vista, going under the speed limit, keeping an eye out for anything that even looks like a parked white Prius. I hit Avenue 59 and turn, heading west. The street is crowded with parked cars. I slow way down, paying close attention to each car, forgetting for just a second what color car I'm looking for, and I put the car in reverse and go backward two driveways, *white Prius, white Prius, white Prius.*

"Mama," Jacob says. I hit the brakes and pause in the middle. I turn my body around as far as it will twist.

"Yes, buddy?" I ask, and he hands me his empty smoothie pouch. "Thank you," I say, "do you need anything? Want your water?"

"Okay," he says. I twist back to the passenger seat and dig through the bag for his sippy cup. It's half full, plenty, but I can't remember if the water and sippy cup are from today or yesterday. I try to remember if I made him a fresh water this morning or this afternoon. Shit.

I wipe the top of the cup off and hand it back to him. "Water," I say. Jacob grabs it from my hands, and I sense he'll be good for maybe five or ten more minutes. I drive down the rest of the street and don't see a Prius at all. I pull over and text Chris the news. I have one new message waiting.

Evan: I called and texted Ben, no response. I'm going to leave a little early and meet you at home.

No. That is not what I wanted. I check when the message came in and glance at the clock. Just five minutes. I text him back.

Me: No need, really. I'll keep an eye out when I get home and let you know.

Evan: Walking to my car now. See you shortly.

Would I go home and have to confront Evan about the woman I saw him with this morning? What would I even say? I text Chris to let him know my status and then head home. I need to call Lopez, check the comments on my video, see if Julia and Ben are back, and figure out how to confront my husband about the woman I saw him on a date with. And a huge part of me just wants to say fuck it to everything and go back to South Pasadena for a guava-and-cheese Danish.

I call Lopez while I still have Jacob distracted and buckled in, and I'm not racing around the house, preventing an accident.

"Detective Lopez," she answers.

"Hi, it's Corey Tracey-Lieberman."

"Oh, are we back to the full name?" she asks.

"I don't know, not important. So far none of the leads on cars has panned out. I'm frustrated."

"I'd like you to meet me at the station in the morning, eight a.m.," Lopez says.

"Okay, I'll be there. I have a question. How do you know the woman that came in and said her home burned down is the woman that had been squatting there? Couldn't it have been some other unhoused person? There's no way to confirm without identification, is there? I mean, do you even have the woman's name that was squatting?"

"We have a cell phone bill addressed to the house with a driver's license that matches the name on the bill. Her name is Carol Ellis, and you'll want to meet us here in the morning at eight, because Carol wants to tell us about her friend Sonja Hart."

I slam the brakes in the middle of Monte Vista Street. I find space in front of a fire hydrant to pull over and throw the car in park. "What are you saying?" I ask.

"I'm saying that Sonja Hart's missing-person case has moved to homicide."

"Is that her body in the morgue, burned to nothing?" I ask. I feel vomit forcing its way up and then back down. I want to cough from the burn but bite it back.

"I'm saying that Sonja Hart's case is now being investigated as a possible homicide, and I need you to come to my office first thing in the morning, Ms. Tracey-Lieberman."

"Did you make contact with her son?" I ask.

"We did. He will be meeting us at the precinct tomorrow as well," Lopez says. "I will see you in the morning. Don't let anything else come up until then, do you understand, Ms. Tracey-Lieberman?"

"Understood," I say, and the call is ended.

I'm five minutes from home, but it's taking me forever to get there. I'm racking my brain, trying to think over everything Moore said last night. If he was lying about anything. He'd make a terrific poker player. There weren't any signals that he was holding back, but I wasn't being me. I was pretending to be someone else. A friend who hadn't heard back from a friend. I can't go home, not yet.

I pull Moore's address up on my phone and head there instead. It should have been the first place I checked for a white Prius. I have to cross the train tracks twice on the way. I get caught waiting for the Gold Line to pass both times. I end up in front of his house at last, a tiny bungalow. Maybe not even legal to build these days but grandfathered in at some point. The street is traffic heavy, and there's little parking. I find a spot up the road a way and know I'll have to let Jacob walk, but I try to put him into the baby carrier anyway. It's a nightmare. I look like I'm abusing him. Thank god we don't have to cross the busy street. We walk down the slight hill to get back to Moore's house. I look up and down the street for a Prius as we go but don't see one.

"Jacob, Mommy has to put you in the carrier now," I say. "Please don't fight me. This is important, and it may be a little dangerous. Can you go in the carrier?"

"No."

"I promise, promise you can walk back to the car when we're done." Jacob stands rigid, looking at me with distrust. A look that reminds me of Evan. "Okay, I'm going to pick you up and put you in the carrier." He just keeps looking at me, a stare down. Before I can pick him up, he starts to waddle-run away. I chase him a few houses, and when I catch him, I scoop him up hard and fast and secure him in the harness attached to my chest. If motherhood were viewed as a magic show, women would be rich, I think. Jacob pounds on my chest with his curled fists.

"No, stop hitting Mommy," I say. He cries, maybe from guilt, maybe from not getting his way. "It's okay. I promise. Just for a minute, okay? I need you to be my helper for just a minute." This seems to work magic, the promise and the tone, perhaps.

I get to Moore's house, and there's a short driveway, no gate, so I walk up it to check out the backyard. Nothing but an untrimmed lemon tree and some succulents growing wild. There's a shed posing as a garage that I doubt any car can fit into, but I walk toward the window and peer inside. Maybe Sonja is there and wishing someone would locate her. I stand on my tiptoes to see in. There's no light, and it's so dusty. I pull my phone out of my pants pocket and turn on the flashlight mode and hold it to the shed window. There is only a bike, surfboard, and camping gear that I can notice. No Sonja.

"Corey?" It's a man's voice, but I know it's not Moore. I spin around and see Chris. "What are you doing here?" he asks.

"What are you doing here?" I ask.

"I came to look around for a white Prius, remember? I saw you and Jacob walking down the street toward Moore's house."

"I'm looking for a Prius and for Sonja," I say. "I know she's not here. I just wanted so badly for her car to be."

"Come on, before Moore gets home," Chris says.

"Lopez said Sonja's case has been elevated to possible homicide."

"Let's go, now. We'll get to him, I promise, but not here like this."

I agree and leave the backyard with Chris. I promised Jacob he could walk back to the car, but I don't want Moore to see us and need to hurry like Chris said. One house away from Moore's, a man, who looks a lot like Moore, is jogging right toward Chris, Jacob, and me, and he's staring right at me. I grab Chris's hand and spin him toward me. With Jacob squished between us, I grab Chris's face and start kissing him. He doesn't push me away or step back or fight me. He leans in, hands wrapping around my back, gently pulling Jacob and me closer.

I feel and hear the man pass us and see him running up the steps to Moore's house. I open my eyes to look. It isn't Moore. Maybe a brother? I pull back from the kiss but not from the embrace Chris has on me.

"I'm sorry," I say. "I thought it was Moore. It looked just like him."

Chris looks up to the house as the door is closing. "Brother?"

"Maybe. Or, cousin? Too young to be his father." Chris is still holding on to my waist and staring at me, and I'm staring at his lips. "God, I'm sorry." I shake out of his hands and start walking again. "I'm so sorry, I know you have a girlfriend and that was so inappropriate, I just—"

"You were thinking on your feet, like you always have. I love a good impromptu make out sesh."

"It was not a make out session. It was a kiss. And, please, if you tell Megan, tell her I'm married and deeply embarrassed and sorry, and it was just for the job. Tell her a woman may be dead." I say it with so much authority I can't tell if Chris is hurt or holding in laughter.

"We're not exclusive," Chris says.

"I'm sorry?"

"Megan and I are not exclusive. She doesn't ask, and I don't tell and vice versa. She just got out of a long marriage. She's working on settling her divorce, and I'm not sure she's looking to settle down again ever," Chris says.

"Oh, okay, good. I wouldn't want to be the person that causes you any problems in your relationship. God, I feel so stupid. I'm really sorry," I say.

"I know how that feels," Chris says. We've reached the car, and I unstrap Jacob and get him into his car seat. He fights me a little, but Chris does his magic and calms him down.

"Mommy loves you," I tell Jacob and kiss him on the cheek before shutting his door. "You know how what feels?" I ask Chris.

"Being the person that may have come between someone's marriage." He looks at me like I'm supposed to understand his coded statement.

"I don't know what you're talking about," I say.

"Corey, I kissed you, a few months ago. Evan moved out. You two have been struggling," he says.

"No, no, none of that is your fault. He doesn't even know about the kiss. No, we've been struggling long before we got married. We shouldn't have gotten married. I love our child, but we weren't meant for the long term. I'm trying to figure out how to coparent and not fail Jacob. But, no, you didn't come between our marriage. That kiss, that was—"

"What?" Chris asks. "That kiss was what?"

"A weak moment. I needed someone. I was scared and going through so much, and you were there and—"

"Got it." He smiles at me, but it doesn't touch his eyes the way his smiles usually do.

"Chris, no, that's not what I meant."

"Corey, you do not need to explain it to me. You are married, and we are working a case. There is plenty of time for us to have this conversation when we're not in the middle of fuck all. I'm not going anywhere. You're kind of stuck with me now."

I want to say it back, but I don't. I smile and look at my phone. I have three texts from Evan. "I've got to get going," I say. At least it's something to break the silence. "I'm meeting Lopez at the precinct in the morning. The squatter—Carol Ellis—and Jonathan Hart will be there. I'll be in touch when I'm done."

I don't say anything else. I leave Chris on the sidewalk, get in my car, and leave.

29

It's a ten-minute drive home, and that's going just below the speed limit, taking the long way with all the lights and two railroad crossings that always hit right when I get to them. I park in the street in front of the house and directly across from Julia and Ben's. Julia is sitting on the couch, their large picture window still open for the world to see in. She's petting Oliver and reading. I don't see a car in the driveway or on the street in front of their house. I assume Ben is out. I grab my phone and type Julia Palmer into the search bar. I cannot believe it's the first time I'm searching her, and they've been here for five whole days. I've been off the Paxil for four whole days, and I'm starting to see how many things I'd let go of.

"Mama," Jacob says. I turn around to look at him. "Mama."

"You ready to get out? You want to go see Daddy?" I ask him. I close my phone on the Julia Palmer search. It will have to wait a little longer.

"Okay," he says. Jacob is paying the price of being locked up in a car seat or baby carrier every time I need to go ask questions or investigate again. When I pull him out of the car, he wants down immediately. Evan's car isn't in the driveway, so Jacob starts to climb up the slope to the gate. I look at my phone and open Evan's texts.

Evan: Almost home.

Evan: Where are you guys?

Evan: Dammit Corey, let me know everyone is okay.

Shit.

Me: I'm so sorry, I was driving and couldn't text you back. We're home. We're fine.

I hear Jacob cry, and I look up. He's taken his first tumble and scraped his hands. I scoop him up and hold him harder than I have in a while. "It's okay, my love, it's okay. Walking can be hard. Just remember to slow down. We all just need to slow down." While I hold Jacob, I do a quick scan of the block from my position above it and don't see any white Priuses. I don't see Pete, Evan, Ben, or even Elsie. So I let it go and take Jacob inside for a bath and some dinner.

After a quick but messy dinner of beans, carrots, and peaches, Jacob has a nice long soak. I comb his hair and smell all the soft-oatmeal-and-lavender scent of his shampoo, and it is as delicious as newborn baby smell. "Do you want to read a book tonight?" I ask in a funny voice and smile. I give his belly a little tickle and then give him a huge kiss on the cheek and a squeeze. We pull out a book together from his little shelf and just as we settle into the overstuffed chair in his bedroom, the front door opens.

"Corey?" It's Evan.

"We're upstairs, getting ready for bed," I gently call back.

"Dada!" Jacob yells. He is overjoyed to hear his dad's voice. I wish I felt the same.

I hear Evan take the stairs two at time, and he's standing in Jacob's room in a flash. "Where have you been?" I ask.

"I had to go out for a bit," Evan says.

"Did you have an after-work meeting?" I ask.

"No, but I did promise a few folks I would meet them at happy hour on York for a quick drink. And since you weren't home when I got here, I figured you wouldn't mind," he says. Convenient of me to not be home yet, so he could go out.

"You were out early this morning. Did you go for a run?" I ask.

"Yep."

"Did Ben go with you?" I ask.

"No, I went on my own. I've only gone running with him once. Hey, lay off the guy tonight, okay? I don't want to fight or argue about the neighbors."

"Did you meet up with anyone during your run or after?" I ask.

"No, I went running, came home, and then went to work," Evan says. "What's wrong with you? You know my routine and the path I run. It's the same thing every day."

"Nothing, I just drove past Lola's today on my way to Cyclone, and I saw you having coffee, very early, with a woman I didn't recognize," I say.

"Oh shit, I totally forgot that was this morning. Yes, she's a new work colleague."

"What's her name?" I ask.

"Lynn. She's a nice girl, you'd like her. Anyway, I'm catching her up on all the ins and outs of the accounts and whatnot," Evan says.

"She did not look like a girl. I'd definitely categorize her as a woman." I take a beat. "So, you were just meeting her for coffee before work? Why wouldn't you be meeting her at work. Especially because that's where your computer is and probably hers is too."

"Yeah, but it's nice to meet outside the office. It gives her the opportunity to speak openly. Anyway, I told her to meet me at Lola's since it's on my running path."

"She's just a colleague you met for coffee before work?" Evan nods. I'm not going to ask why Pete saw them running together. Not now, not yet.

"Corey, if I was having an affair I wouldn't do it in our town, at our coffee shop, where you'd see me. It's not anything. Don't get crazy and start overthinking it."

Crazy. There it is again. Evan's favorite word to call his exes, our neighbor, and probably me, behind my back, to Lynn. Why didn't I see it in the beginning of our relationship? Why did I blame his exes too? Fuck you, Evan. As soon as Jacob falls asleep, and Evan leaves or makes his bed on the couch, I will find Lynn on the internet.

"Don't look at me like that, Corey. I love *you*."

"Are you in love with me, or do you just love me because we have history? I saw you with Lynn. I saw the way you were smiling. You were happy. I haven't seen you look like that with me, not in a long time. What are we doing?"

"We're fixing our family and figuring it out, Corey."

"We're not broken. I'm not broken. And I think the more *un*broken I am, the more you want to break me, so you can keep me hanging in there. Every fight feels like a rope tethering me to you. Is that what you want?" I ask.

"I'm not going to argue with you. You do sound crazy. I'm going to record you next time, so you can hear yourself. I didn't force you into this marriage, Corey. Remember that," Evan says.

"I know, but we don't have to stay together to be a family, Evan. You can go be happy. We will always be a family because of Jacob. We do not have to be together to figure it all out."

"Is it him, Corey? Are you together?"

"Who?" I ask.

"Don't do that. Do not. Do. That."

"It's not Chris, if that's what you're asking. It's us, Evan. I don't make you happy. I can't even make myself happy right now. I need to figure me out. I should have done that before we got married. I will always love you. You are Jacob's father." Relief and dread wash over me simultaneously. I still wish I could take the Klonopin to slow down all the feelings bubbling just under the surface. I don't need it. I want it to stay ahead of the panic that is sure to come up the moment this conversation is over, but I don't need it.

This stretch of silence from Evan feels wonderful. He's not locking me into a battle I don't care enough to win. We're there now. The end. The period at the end of the feeling that was too scary to share before. It's out there, and the silence feels like relief.

"Are you going to keep working with him?" Evan asks.

"Yes."

"I can't leave you if he's still in the picture."

"That's, what? Do you hear yourself? That, that has nothing to do with us. That's my job." I stop before I escalate into a so-called irrational tone of dismay that will end with Evan calling me crazy, again. "And, I can't even believe I'm telling you this because, honestly, Evan. But, Chris has a girlfriend. There is nothing between us." I look at Evan's hand and see that his wedding ring is still on.

The thing is, I would have been fine if it was a date, I think. It hurts, but I think I just want him to be honest. Stop fighting for me to be all in when he's not even all in. I want him to be happy, but I also don't want to feel guilty for not wanting this anymore. For not wanting to try to make the effort in this relationship anymore. If Evan moves on I will be able to just be. I'm learning that Evan won't leave unless it's his idea. And he won't leave until I'm completely broken.

30

Even though Evan slept on the couch, the fact I knew he was somewhere in the house, possibly seething, left me restless all night. Unrested and up at five thirty a.m. on a Saturday. I can still feel Evan's seething anger, or maybe it's my own guilt. I don't want to go downstairs until he's left, but he can be a fucking mouse when he wants to be, and I'd never know he was missing. At six a.m. it's light enough outside to go see if I can catch Dave in his RV at the Groceries for Less. I gently pick up Jacob and change his diaper. He's just barely awake when I grab a few baby breakfast goods from the cupboard for him.

Evan isn't on the couch. The blanket folded and pillow on top. I clock the driveway on the way out. His car is still there, and I have half a mind to drive by Lola's Coffee, but it's not quite on the way, so I skip it. I do not want to find out he'd be dumb enough to go there two days in a row with this woman. I wonder how crazy he's told her I am. Or if he's told her how wounded he is by my constant rejection and what a bitch I can be. And I wonder how much she believes him. Has anyone taught her not to listen to men who talk shit about the mother of their children, the women they're married to, or that, given a fraction of an opportunity to work on their marriage with their estranged wife, they'd take it and then call you, the mistress, crazy.

I look across to Ben and Julia's house to see the front door open, screen closed, no car in the driveway. I look through the front window but can't see anything past the couch at this time of day. They need to get their shit together. I will not take Jacob back to their empty house like that ever again. I buckle Jacob in and catch a glimpse of Pete in his car. I gently close Jacob's door. I'd love him to fall back to sleep if possible.

I walk around to the driver's side and wave Pete over.

"Mrs. Evan, I saw Mr. Evan leave for his run half an hour ago," Pete says.

"That's great, Pete. Did you see Ben, your new neighbor, leaving this morning?" I ask.

"No, I haven't seen him come home or leave since yesterday morning."

"Did you see Mrs. Ben leave?" I ask. I cannot believe I've called Julia "Mrs. Ben," but I want Pete to give me everything he knows.

"Yeah, I saw her come home yesterday, saw her up all night too. Lights on, music loud."

"Have you seen her this morning?" I ask.

"Nah, only Mr. Evan this morning. Running alone," Pete says. I appreciate the heads-up and wonder if it's Pete's way of signaling me to watch out for Evan, or that he is keeping an eye on Evan for me? I don't know, too convoluted for Pete.

"Thanks, Pete. I've gotta get going," I say.

"You don't teach on Saturday mornings, Mrs. Evan. Where are you going?"

I hate that he knows my schedule from watching me. "To check out the fire behind the grocery store," I say. "You know anything about it?" I ask.

"I knew the lady who lived there. We both got coffee and fresh-baked loaves from the back of the grocery a few times a week. Nice lady, a shame her home is gone now."

"What do you mean? The homeless lady that lived there?" I ask.

"She wasn't homeless then. She is now." He laughs, but it isn't funny at all. Apparently when you squat, you technically are no longer homeless. That made sense. Couldn't argue with Pete or anyone else about that.

"The grocery store was passing out bread and coffee?" I ask.

"Nah, some people, you know, get the coffee and bring the bread and give it around. Nice folks," he says.

"On what days? What time?"

Pete looks at his watch and says, "They should be there sometime today. Maybe tomorrow."

I pull out my phone, and it's still the search results for Julia. I pull up my pictures and shove the picture of Sonja on my screen into Pete's face.

"Did you ever see this woman there passing out coffee and bread?" I ask.

"Maybe, don't remember. I see a lot of people."

"I gotta go, Pete. Will you be around later?"

"Yeah, maybe. You know I got people I need to see. Why? You need something? Want to come see the peppers growing? Real spicy ones."

"Yeah. I'll come by, okay? Check if you're home." He nods and walks back to sit in his car.

I get to the Groceries for Less and look around the loading dock first. No coffee or bread yet. I see what I hope is Dave's trailer. It's in a different spot, so I can tell he's definitely taking it out and driving it. Which may be scarier than the idea that he lives in the near-dilapidated thing. It's so old there's duct tape wrapped around the hood and undercarriage. There's only one windshield wiper, and the back bumper appears to be attached by maybe chicken wire? It's a mess, and I fear Dave driving in it and all the folks on the LA freeways behind it, next to it, and in front of it.

I park in a spot right next to the RV, separated by inches, and no one else is in the parking lot. I glance at Jacob asleep in the back seat and make the decision to allow him to stay asleep. I'll be right outside his door while I talk to Dave. I grab the MAGLITE out of the trunk of the car and hold it down by my side. I have my keys tucked between my fingers in my fist. I knock on the RV door with the toe of my right foot, careful not to scuff the already-damaged door, but loud enough to make an impression on whoever is inside. I should definitely take a self-defense class at the South Pasadena Jujitsu Center.

I hear footsteps the second after kicking on the door.

"I'll move, I'll move. Just give me a second to warm her up," the voice says.

"It's not the police or towing," I say. "I'm Corey Tracey-Lieberman. Are you Dave? I met you the day of the fire. Monday, I met you Monday and left you my number?"

The door unlocks, and I realize just how flimsy it is. The man from Monday stands in front of me, holding the door open. He's cleaner than he was then, and I wonder if his RV shower works, or if he has to drive somewhere for that.

"Hi, Dave, I'm so sorry to bother you so early in the morning, but I was hoping I could ask you a few questions?" I say.

"Yeah, I'm up. Don't sleep much anyway," Dave says. He is younger than he appeared at first. Again, the shower has done him wonders. He's white with a tan that can only be explained by years of time spent outdoors. "This about the lady in the house?"

"Yeah, did you know her?" I ask.

"Which one?" Dave asks. I'm confused but don't want Dave to know.

"The one that was in the house when it burned down."

"She was a nice lady, always bringing around coffee and bread for those that needed it. Didn't matter if you were housed and in need or unhoused. She knew people are people. Coffee and bread for all the folks," Dave says. I nod, prompting him to keep going. "Ya' know if Carol hadn't gone to the clinic that day, no one would have been hurt. I'll tell ya' that much." Dave sounds stoic, but the slightest amount of water begins to pool in his eyes, and I know he's not.

"What do you mean?" I ask.

"It isn't like Carol not to be there getting her fill of free bread. She's like that." Dave pauses to cough. A wet, sick cough from the lungs.

"Someone said they saw Ms. H heading over to the house with a loaf and some coffee."

"Do you know Ms. H's name, Dave?" I ask. And if he did, why the hell had he not told the police?

"Listen, I didn't know she was in there. I thought it was Carol, until she showed up around here yesterday, asking for a place to stay. I swear it."

"Is Carol here now?" I ask.

"Hell no. I'm so pissed off at her I sent her away. She's afraid of being arrested for the fire and the dead body. Believes they'll pin it on her somehow and lock her up. She just found out the lady was in there too. Dammit, I wish to hell she wouldn't have been such a fucking do-gooder."

"Who, Dave? Who is Ms. H? Do you know her name?" I ask.

"We only knew her as Ms. H. Don't know her full name." As Dave says it, I already know, I feel it deep inside me, the confirmation that Sonja was burned to death. How, why, who?

"Dave—" I start when I hear a thump on the window I'm practically leaning against. Jacob has woken up and is yelling, "Mama!" and hitting the window with his sippy cup. I put my hand on the window and smile and yell, "One second." I know this does not compute, but I need to know. "Dave, did you ever see Ms. H's car?" I ask.

"Yep, she drove a white Toyota, what's it called? The environmental ones."

"A Prius?" I ask.

"Yeah, that's it," he says.

"And do you know where her car is now?" I ask.

"Probably towed. She always parked it here in the lot, and they always tow," he says.

I pull my phone out from my pocket and pull up the picture of Sonja Hart I'd shown to everyone I'd asked so far. "Is this Ms. H?" I ask Dave.

"Yeah, that's her. She looks different. Her hair is different, but that's her," he says. I put my phone back in my pocket. My keys and MAGLITE nearly drop. The weight of the confirmation that it's Sonja hits me. Hits me that a young man has to find out today that his mom is dead.

"Dave, I need you to stick around and not drive off. I'm going to be back with a Detective Lopez. If you have to leave because of a tow, please call me. Do you still have my number?" I ask.

"My phone is out of commission at the moment. But, I don't have any work today. I'll try to be around."

"Do you have any idea where Carol may have gone?" I ask.

"Probably back to her house. It didn't all burn, and she can be stupid as hell," he says. I hate him for saying that but totally understand his need to. To push people away that he cares about because they were too disposable in this world.

"Thank you," I say. "I'll be back." Dave doesn't even wait until I leave before the cardboard thin door springs closed, and I hear the lock click into place.

31

I drive over to Carol's burned house to see if she's around. "Jacob, are you hungry, buddy? I brought you a yogurt." I pull over to the curb a few houses before the burn. It's interesting that there are any street spaces available at all. With the condos and townhomes around the corner and the multigenerational homes in the area, street parking is in high demand. Then again, it's the site of a police investigation. I pull out a squeezy tube of yogurt and rip the corner off and pass it back to Jacob before I get out and put on the baby carrier.

"Hey, buddy, hold on to that yogurt tight. We're going in the carrier this morning, okay?" I hope the distraction of food will prevent him from screaming to walk this morning. I need to be quick, and I need him to be close.

The worst mistake I've made so far this morning is opening the yogurt before getting him into the carrier. Dammit. With yogurt squished between us both, at least there's enough to keep Jacob sated. I walk quickly toward the house. When I get to the police tape, I see two people inside. Both dressed similarly and not at all what I think Carol would be wearing.

There's nowhere to hide and watch, and if Carol is in there, dammit.

"Hello!" I say. One head raises and looks out to Jacob and me. I see the familiar slump of the shoulders and the tight, low bun of Detective Lopez. Then I see her partner, Detective Marks. His large stature now fully visible as they walk out toward Jacob and me.

"Ms. Tracey-Lieberman, our meeting isn't until eight at the station. What brings you out this early to the scene of a crime?" Lopez says.

"I'm looking for Carol. Did you see her inside?" I ask.

"No, there isn't anybody inside, and definitely no place to hide inside anymore," Marks says. His face hasn't gotten any prettier, still scarred, definitely from childhood acne, and deeply furrowed by his expression of distrust.

"What do you know, Corey?" Lopez says.

"I know the body is Sonja Hart's," I say.

"How can you confirm it?" Marks asks. "What proof do you have?"

"I have a source. Says he knows 'Ms. H' went into the house to find Carol because she didn't show up to the coffee-and-fresh-bread service that morning."

"What's a bread service?" Detective Marks asks.

"There's a group of volunteers that come out a few days a week to serve coffee and hot loaves of bread to whoever needs it. Carol must be a regular. Then, Carol showed up yesterday to my source's home, asking him for a place to stay. Carol is alive. Sonja Hart is missing—escalated to possible homicide, and there's an unidentified body in the morgue." It's not hard to put it all together, but Marks is looking at me like he's doing math or sizing me up as a possible threat.

"Where is this source, Corey? Did he say anything about the fire? Did he see who started it?" Lopez asks.

"I thought it was faulty electrical wiring," I say. It's sarcastic at worst, honest at best.

"We're not sure," Lopez says. "It has not yet been determined what started the fire."

"Is that why you're out here so early? Canvassing for an accelerant? Let me help." I start to step over the yellow police tape, but Marks catches my arm and holds me back.

"No," Lopez says. "Corey, you've done enough. Why don't I meet you at my office at eight, like we said."

"I haven't done anything useful yet."

"Ma'am," Marks says, and I know it's not going to be good. "Were you aware that you were trespassing yesterday in Ryan Moore's backyard?"

Shit.

"I don't know what you're talking about," I say.

"Give it up. You're on his cameras in his backyard, looking in his shed," Lopez says. "He wants to press charges. As of right now, I am putting you on warning."

"I'm trying to find Sonja Hart. He was dating her, and she was pregnant with his baby. Not to mention she told him she needed space the day she went missing. Did you know he was her teacher?" I say to Marks. I say it all so fast, I don't know if any of it made sense. Jacob throws his yogurt wrapper on the ground. I squat to pick it up, but Marks beats me to it.

"Yes, we know Sonja was in Moore's class, and we know about the relationship," Lopez says. "Mr. Moore was very cooperative and transparent when we spoke to him yesterday."

"You questioned him and didn't tell me?" I ask.

"I am not required to alert you how and when I am doing my job, Ms. Tracey-Lieberman," Lopez sighs. It sounds like she's doing it at me, but then she looks at me while Marks is scanning the street surrounding us, and she winks. She does not smile, but that wink tells me a million things I need to know.

"Got it," I say. Jacob starts whining. It's time to go, and I agree. "I guess I will see you at the precinct in an hour."

"Corey, bring what you know about this source of yours. I mean it," Lopez says, making me question if we're on the same side or not after all.

32

I swing home before the precinct to feed and change Jacob. "Jacob first, think of Jacob first," I say to myself over and over. I need to keep Jacob at the top of my mind this time. Not Sonja, Carol, Dave—just Jacob.

I pull down the street and see Julia outside, shoeless, in sweats or pajamas. She is leaning into the window of a car that is not hers and Ben's. Their car is still not in the driveway. Maybe Ben slept at a hotel. Evan has done that in the past during the hardest times we've had. I'm nearing the house and watch Julia climb into the car, and it drives off. I park and quickly pull Jacob out of his seat. I look up at Julia's house, and the door is wide open again. What the fuck is going on? I see Oliver looking out the front window, and I run across the street with Jacob to shut their door before the cat notices it's open.

"Let's go get some oatmeal and apples," I say to Jacob. "Mmm, Mommy wants some apples and oatmeal too." Jacob gabs back excitedly, and so much of me wants to have a full conversation with him in more than baby speak, no and okay.

There's a warm pot of coffee on the counter, so I know that Evan had been here, but his car is gone now. I help myself to a cup. I grab the instant oatmeal and plop a big bowl of it in the microwave and set out to cut up an apple. I open the utensil drawer, completely forgetting that I don't have knives. I'm almost shocked when I see it empty.

"Change of plans, we're going to have banana and oatmeal," I tell Jacob. And that's all there is to it. I scoop some hot oatmeal out of the large bowl and add it to a small plastic babyproof bowl for Jacob. I put the bananas on the side and add a small baby spoon—even though Jacob will still fist the oatmeal into his mouth.

I sit down to eat with him and am about to open my laptop when Evan bursts through the front door.

"Oh good, you're back. I wasn't sure if you were teaching this morning," Evan says.

"No, it's Saturday," I say.

"I know, it's my day with Jacob," he says.

Right, of course. I guess we are keeping our rules about time with Jacob. After last night's conversation, it makes total sense. I don't want to deny Evan or Jacob time together. We agreed when we separated that Evan would get Saturdays and half days on Sundays.

I feel my throat closing and my heart racing. I try to swallow, and it catches, my throat too restricted. I don't want to be separated from Jacob today. I can't let Evan see me this way. I can't.

"Okay," I say. "I have a meeting at eight this morning, so I should get ready."

"When you're back maybe we can do something as a family," Evan says.

I can't breathe. I need to get up and move, but anything I do will signal to him that I'm having a moment. I just want to feel the anger, but it's coming up as panic, and I—my phone vibrates, and I pick it up.

Chris: Everything okay this morning?

I look back at Evan and say, "Okay." I stand up because I'm dying inside, and I give Jacob a big, long kiss on the head. "I'll be back soon," I tell Jacob. "Mommy loves you more than anything else in the world. You are my whole heart." I carry my bowl to the sink and look at Evan and smile. I drop the bowl and leave the room. I need to go before I break down in front of him. I run up to the bedroom and grab a Klonopin out of my dresser drawer and chew it. It's time to go.

Lopez meets me in the interview room that's located in the front lobby area of the precinct instead of her desk behind the bulletproof doors.

"Something going on in the back today?" I ask.

"You could say that. For a Saturday, we're pretty damn busy." She stops and tilts her head and asks, "Where is Mr. Jacob?" I'm surprised it took her this long to notice.

"He's at home, spending time with his father," I say. Lopez looks at me. I think she knows I took Klonopin. Am I slurring? "Why are you looking at me like that?" I ask.

"How am I looking at you?" Lopez says.

"You're squinting like you're trying to see into my head and read my thoughts," I say.

"No, you're the one squinting at me, and your eyes are dilated. Plus, you're not demanding answers from me, what's up?" Lopez asks, and I know she knows I took a Klonopin. Or, that I'm on something. Dammit.

"I felt a panic attack coming on and took a Klonopin. I'm fine now. And I will remind you that they are prescribed to me for exactly how I take them."

"What's wrong?" she asks.

"I'm pissed that Evan took my baby."

"Corey, Jacob is Evan's baby too. You've got to learn to separate from him. He's got to grow and learn the world for himself. What are you going to do when it's time for him to go to school?" Lopez asks.

"Homeschool is always an option," I say. Lopez bursts into laughter. I can't remember her ever finding anything as funny in the six months I've known her. Her laughter is contagious. I start laughing too.

"Girl, you are funny. I didn't think you of all people would make me laugh that hard. You couldn't homeschool."

"Why? That's not fair. I could too," I argue, but she's right. My work is too important, and once school starts, Jacob wouldn't be able to go with me . . . would he? "That's years away. Why are you talking about school already?"

"Corey, listen, it's a good thing to let him take some time with his dad. You need this space. I need you fully invested here right now. Let's talk about this source of yours."

Shit, Lopez is good. She didn't miss a beat segueing back into the case. The way I attack people is much more jarring, abrupt, go for the jugular. Lopez has the upper hand here.

"His name is Dave, no last name." I start with Monday and meeting him in the parking lot during the fire. I let her know he lives in an RV often parked in the Groceries for Less parking lot. Regular at the coffee-and-fresh-bread handout. Knows Carol as a regular and "neighbor" and Sonja as a volunteer. "Dave doesn't have a phone right now, so we need to go meet him at his house on wheels. Where's Carol?"

Lopez looks at her watch. "It's eight twenty. I don't think she's going to show."

"What time is Jonathan Hart going to be here?"

"Not until noon, with his dad," Lopez says.

"Going to be hard to identify the body, isn't it?" I ask.

"Our victim has evidence of a fractured femur likely from an injury when they were quite young, considering how it healed. There's also a piece of jewelry we recovered. So, no, no body images. We have enough to move forward and when her dentals come in, that will be the period at the end of the sentence."

"Why isn't Moore at the top of your list of suspects?" It comes out slow, not slurred, but I am fully lucid. I hate that the medicine slows me down.

"I'm not saying he's not." Lopez does that look again like she can read my mind. "What are you not telling me?"

"Sonja Hart was pregnant."

"So you said."

"She was, according to her friend Anne Silva, going to tell Moore on Monday. But she was also planning on slowing things down with him. She wanted to tell him she needed some space, things had moved too quickly, and now a pregnancy at forty-two, a kid going off to college. Plus, she was starting a new career. I don't know. Did the autopsy show a pregnancy?"

"No, but if it was new, and how badly her body was burned, it wouldn't be a high probability the pregnancy would show. We're waiting for access to her apartment. Maybe there will be evidence of the pregnancy there. Do you want to give me Anne Silva's info, or do you want me to locate her on my own?"

"She's not hard to find. She's not even hiding. She wants her friend found. She owns a salon on York. Her car!" I spring up in the seat, not realizing how laid back I had been. "Have you checked the tow companies? She parked it at Groceries for Less, and Dave, the RV guy, told me they tow all the time."

"Good, that's good, Corey. Now, why don't you go home and take a nap and let me do my job today," Lopez says.

"I'm coming back at noon to talk to Jonathan with you," I say as I stand up to leave.

"Are you going to be okay to drive?" Lopez asks. "I'm happy to give you a ride."

"I'm fine, I promise. I've learned my lesson. I know my limit. I could use a bottle of water if you're offering, though."

"Sure." Lopez holds the door open for me, and we exit to the lobby. She goes behind the bulletproof reception desk and comes back with a plastic bottle of water.

"Thanks." Lopez nods and walks back to the bulletproof doors that lead to her desk, a room filled with pictures of all the homicides Lopez is still working on with Marks.

I nod to the officer on "reception" duty and leave.

I get three blocks from the station and notice a police car following me. I make a few quick, unexpected turns, and they continue to follow. Lopez must have sent them to make sure I get home okay. I hate being babysat, but I appreciate her concern. I let them follow me the rest of the way without being a jerk. As soon as I park, they speed by me, and I wave and smile. It's met with nonchalance. I don't recognize the officers, must be new or transfers. Not that I know everyone, but I usually can spot a few familiar faces. My phone buzzes before I get out of the car.

Chris: Hey, you with Lopez? What's going on?

I forgot to write Chris back earlier.

Me: Just got home. Too much to type.

Chris: I'm around the corner. I drove by and saw Evan's car. Meet me at Lola's?

Yeah, that's where I want to go meet Chris. At the place I just found my husband with another woman. I check the time. It's been just under an hour. I should go inside and check on Jacob. Maybe Evan will let me take him to the coffee shop. Maybe I'm also so delusional on Klonopin that I believe that.

Me: I'll meet you there in a few. I need to check on something.

Chris: See you shortly.

I get out of the car to see that Evan is pushing Jacob in the baby swing on the porch.

"Hi," I say, announcing myself so I don't startle them. "How are you guys doing?"

"Oh my god, Corey, I wanted to text you. Jacob took his first steps! When I say steps, I mean he was running," Evan says. He's filled with pride and joy, and oh my fucking god, I forgot to tell him that Jacob took his first steps two, three days ago. Technically, it's not even my fault. He hasn't been around. He's been on dates with other women. But I don't want to spoil it for him.

"Wow, that's so great. Did you record it?" I ask. I had not been so thoughtful.

"I did. Don't worry, I got it all." I smile and nod at him.

"So, I have one more thing I have to work through for Detective Lopez today," I say. Which isn't entirely a lie. I plan on heading back to the station at noon to meet Jonathan and his dad anyway. "What were you thinking for the rest of the day?" I ask.

"Well, I tried Ben, but he's MIA. I was thinking of going on a run with Jacob. Do you have any interest in a run with us?" Evan is using all his charm. He's in such a good mood, and I get it, he's been with the best guy for the past hour, Jacob.

"How about you go on the run, and I'll take Jacob with me to finish up this work I have to do." I say it with so much sincerity and no hostility, or as if I'm trying to get away with something. It just is what it is, me giving him time to himself to go run.

"I thought I would take Jacob in the jogging stroller," he says.

Corey, you need to be okay with this. Give him this time. It's okay.

"Great, that sounds like fun. Why don't you two do that, and then the three of us can meet back here for an early dinner." I know he'll call it a family dinner, but early dinner is the only way I could get it out of my mouth. I open the water that Lopez gave me and take a giant gulp. I'm so thirsty, my mouth is dried out, probably the Klonopin.

"Thank you," Evan says.

I scoop Jacob out of the swing and plant a huge kiss on him, squeezing him until he laughs. "I love you so much. I missed you, my baby." His hand reaches out for the swing, and I set him back in it. "I guess I'm going to get going, so I can get this done and out of the way before dinner."

"Okay, we'll see you soon." Evan looks at Jacob and says, "Say bye-bye, Mama, bye-bye."

I want to fucking cry.

33

I get to Lola's, and Chris is waiting at an outside table for me with two coffees and two pastries. It looks like some kind of turnover and blueberry muffin.

"Hey," I say as I take a seat. I grab the coffee in front of me and take a large gulp. I want this Klonopin to wear off. I feel like I'm moving through cement. "Late breakfast treats?" I ask.

"Raspberry muffin and a peach turnover," he says.

I grab the muffin and dive in. I will eat, caffeinate, and water the pill out of my system as much and as fast as I can.

"It's Sonja. The body that was burned is Sonja. She's dead," I say.

"And it's confirmed?" Chris asks.

"It will be when Jonathan arrives at the police station in a few hours. They have a piece of jewelry and a childhood injury they need confirmed," I say. "Then dental records."

"And her car?"

"Maybe towed from the grocery store parking lot. Lopez is looking into it right now."

"Moore?" he asks.

"They don't know. Where's the motive? She was pregnant with his kid. He was in love with her. And get this, he wants to press charges against me for trespassing. Apparently, he has cameras all over his property."

"Super. Do I need to try and get ahold of my cousin to get that cleared up for myself?" Chris asks.

"I don't think so, Lopez didn't mention you, and neither did Marks."

"You saw Marks?"

"Yeah, I went over to find that guy I saw on Monday in the lot during the fire, remember? I gave him a water. His name is Dave. Anyway, Carol, the squatter, had gone to see if she could crash at his place. He said no, and he thinks she went back to the house, or what's left of it. And when I got there, Marks and Lopez were there assessing, looking for something. They're not going to find shit. The house was left to the looters the minute the fire was out."

"Was Carol there?"

"No, and I think she knows more than she's said. Why would a squatter go to the police to report that the house she had been illegally staying in was burned down?" I ask.

"Does she suffer from any illness? Mental?" Chris says. He's trying to be correct about the way he identifies it.

"Dave didn't say. He said the morning of the fire she was at a clinic. I assumed she's either clean and getting methadone, or she was sick and getting something for that at urgent care? Either way, that's not what an unhoused person suffering from a mental affliction would do, is it? Also, it seemed from the way he talked about it that Carol was a regular. Why would Sonja know where she lived and feel compelled to go check on her and take her coffee if she wasn't someone that came all the time and had a relationship with the volunteers?"

"Agree. There are a lot of threads to pull here. We can keep guessing, but we should go talk to Dave." Chris is already standing up. He inhales the last bite of his turnover and tosses his napkin in the trash.

"We need to find Carol. Let's see if Dave knows where she would have gone." My biggest concern now is keeping Carol alive. If someone suspects she witnessed something, there's no telling what could happen to her. I hope she hasn't permanently disappeared. "I can't stop thinking about the fact that she went to the police station to report that her house burned down."

"What would have been her motivation to file a police report?" Chris asks out loud, but I can tell he's answering himself in his head.

"To find a trustworthy cop you can tell what you know to." I say it with authority.

"Carol knows too much. Come on, I'm driving," Chris says. I check the parking signs where my car is, just to make sure I can leave it, and it won't be towed like Sonja's—if that's what happened. It's Los Angeles, likely it's exactly what happened.

We get to the Groceries for Less parking lot, and the RV is gone.

"He couldn't have driven far," I say. "I'm surprised the RV can drive at all. It is held together with chicken wire and electrical tape, and I'm not being funny."

"No, I've seen it before, or ones just like it. We'll drive around a couple of blocks, and I'm sure we'll find it. If I could only drive about a mile, and parking on the residential streets is a nightmare due to the homeowners hating my house on wheels, where would I park for a break?"

"Well, am I looking for work today? I would head down to the flower nursery or the hardware store. Both of those are about six miles. If I'm taking the day off and keeping within the mile radius, I would go to park streetside outside the Audubon entrance to Debs on Griffin Avenue," I say.

"Agree. I'm going to do a quick up and down on Fig, and then we'll head over to Debs."

We look at every fast-food restaurant's parking lot for the RV, but no luck. We head down Avenue 52 until it turns into Griffin Avenue, and we see a line of RVs just past the residential homes. There are six, and they look almost identical.

I see Dave sitting in a lawn chair outside his RV, talking with another man. "That's him. Pull over," I say to Chris. I look at how far the closest spot is, and it's a stretch. At least it's only six RVs. I've passed streets where there are twenty RVs deep in a line on one side and another twenty plus on the other. "Stop moving, and I'll jump out while you go park."

Unlike Evan, who would argue the motive, action, point ad nauseam with me, Chris pushes the button for his hazards, throws the car in park, and lets me jump out. He waits until I'm safely on the sidewalk and then pulls out to grab a spot.

"Dave!" I call out and wave, hoping the man he's speaking with will stick around too. I don't know how tight-knit the unhoused or RV community is here, but I imagine there's a sense of belonging and looking out for one another that goes without saying. It's human nature to commune. I don't see why these neighbors would be any different.

"Ms. Tracey, you found me. I was hoping if you came back, you'd know where to look. You're as smart as they say you are," Dave says.

"Who? Who says that?" I ask.

"Word gets around. You helped with those girls last year. Ya' know, we have internet, too, most of the time. We've been watching your vlog," Dave says. The other man looks at me in recognition too.

"Nice to meet you. I'm Richard."

"Hi, Richard. My vlog?" I say.

"Yeah, the videos you've posted about Ms. H, we've all seen 'em." Shit, I didn't want them talking to each other about Sonja. I needed them isolated before anyone could concoct an alibi. Dammit.

"Well, that's obviously why I'm here. I'm looking for Carol still. She wasn't at the house this morning when I went looking." I look at Richard, who is standing. He looks like a guy my father would have hosted at a backyard barbeque. He's trim with a small middle-aged belly. His clothes are clean, gym shorts, T-shirt, and a baseball cap. The only points I may be subconsciously deducting are for the beer he's drinking before noon, but I'm thankful it's wrapped in a beer koozie.

"I haven't seen her since last night. Listen, I don't let people into my space. It's not set up for another person. I can barely squeeze in myself.

And, I don't have any utilities to offer. Like I told her, go home or go to a shelter."

"What shelter would she go to?" I ask.

"To be honest, I don't even know," Dave says.

"Yeah, that makes sense. You're doing the best you can." I take a pause and see Chris jogging toward us. "You said Carol had gone to a clinic the morning of the fire. Is that part of her weekly routine, or did something happen?"

"Nah, it was urgent care. She said she had a chest thing. She'd been coughing for weeks, wanted to see if she could get an antibiotic. I was surprised she went before coffee. Never knew the lady to miss any free handout," Dave says, and Richard chuckles.

Chris jumps in at the break and sticks out his hand. "Hi, I'm Chris Villar, Corey's partner."

"Oh man, you're *The Eastsider Times* guy—man we can't thank you enough," Richard says. Chris brushes off the thanks with a flick of his hand.

"For what?" I ask.

"They write about neLA and the people here," Richard replies. This much I know.

"They've been dropping off new socks, underwear, and hygiene products around town to the fire stations, churches, and temporary shelters for people who need supplies and can't afford them," Dave adds.

I did not know that. I wish Chris would have shared this valuable information. I am humbled by his constant focus on others. I'm so wrapped up in myself and Jacob that I can't even breathe most of the time because I am suffocating myself.

"So you won't mind chatting with Chris here?" I ask.

"We've got nothing to hide. But, in terms of Carol, she got a part-time job on the custodial-services team at that nursing home up on Fig. She could be there today. Don't know, but if she wasn't at the house, burned and all, she'd probably be there looking for a way to move into one of those rooms without anyone noticing," Dave says, and Richard laughs. Carol sounds resourceful to me, and that's not funny at all.

"Which one of you has a working phone number," Chris asks.

"I do," Richard says. "Here, give me your number, and I'll call you right now so you can save mine." Chris rattles off his number, and instantly his phone rings. He silences it, and I watch as he puts in Richard's name and labels him *RV owner Highland Park*. It's a respectable and kind title.

"Dave, did you hear, talk, or see anything or anyone before the fire started?"

"No. Ya' know, there isn't a clear view back there. I've got the grocery store. Behind that is the car wash and the convenience store and then the houses. By the time I even saw the flames and heard the sirens, that fire was fully enraged."

Dave looks like he's seen too much in his short life. I don't envy the weight he's carrying around with him.

"Thank you," I say. "Also, so you know, I did give one of the detectives I work with, Lopez, your name. Told her she can find you at the Groceries for Less. So, if you want to keep a low profile, I'd say camp away from the store for a week."

"Thanks for the heads-up, but like I said, I've got nothing to hide."

We all nod at each other. Chris and I head back to his car. I look at each RV we walk past and wonder if there are children inside and what they would be doing. I think about Jacob and me. If Evan and I divorce, would I have enough to sustain us, or would I end up living this way? Barely able to make ends meet. Chris pays me what he can when I contribute to stories, and Lopez has a discretionary budget she uses for me, and it's not much. I teach spin classes only a few times a week, and adding all those sums together, I realize it's not enough. I start to panic. Fuck, please don't do this in front of Chris, please.

My throat, my heart, my stomach, my brain. I stop and start doing jumping jacks right near the car. I cannot get in that seat. I cannot be trapped inside that car. In fact, I need to run. Yes. I start running, and

Chris follows. He says nothing. He catches up to me and just runs beside me until I stop and catch my breath.

"Talk to me," Chris says.

"Can't talk, can't breathe," I say.

"Let's run a little more, come on," he says.

I run as hard as I can push. Chris stays beside me. I feel something burst, pop in my brain, and I can breathe again. I take a deep breath as I slow down and feel it hit the bottom of my lungs.

"Better?" Chris asks. I nod. "Want to run back to the car?" I nod again, and we set off at a steadier pace, but still a run, not a jog.

When we get to the car, I reach for the door handle and take another long, deep breath. I know the feeling will be back, but I use the deep breath to push it down. I start to chant Sonja and Carol in my head—*Sonja, Carol, Sonja, Carol*—instead of counting. I've got this.

34

Driving down Fig is a completely different vibe than York Boulevard. It's wider, bigger, and feels darker. There are mini strip malls with odd tchotchke shops, twenty-four-hour donut shops, and a rental furniture shop. The grocery stores are chains, but not the ones you ever see a commercial for—where people park their cars and walk around York to barhop and mingle, people on Fig walk or run to catch buses. And though there are more destination food spots opening on Fig, it's still not the social strip that York is, and I like it that way. Its authenticity to the roots of the area is holding strong, and it reminds me of the milk thistle flower that pushes its way through cement to survive.

We walk into the nursing home, and the foyer is more clinical than I anticipated. More like the reception area of a doctor's office than a place people live. The waiting area has one couch in a peach-and-pink floral pattern, almost like the decorator was channeling granny chic. The rest of the chairs are light blues and lavenders. I'm not sure if the aesthetic overall is Monet or someone's failed attempt at marketing to senior citizens.

"Good morning." A friendly woman behind the desk calls out. "May I help you?"

"Yes, we're actually looking for someone that works on your cleaning staff," I say. "Her name is Carol?"

"Are you family? Is something wrong?"

I realize I have no idea how old Carol is and whether I should lie and say I'm her daughter. Would sister be more accurate? Shit, why didn't I ask Dave or Lopez for a description?

"I'm her nephew—from her older sister. We're visiting the family and just wanted to say goodbye before we head to the airport," Chris says. Damn, he's fast. The receptionist smiles and blushes when Chris smiles back. Oh, this is going to be easy.

"Just a moment, and I'll see if she's working today," the woman says. I put her around thirty. A quick glance at her hands tells me she's not married or doesn't wear her ring, which is less common than I thought it would be. I'm nearly the only married person I encounter that doesn't wear a ring these days. I guess that's why it pisses Evan off. "I'm Gloria, by the way." She says it directly to Chris, not Chris and me. I get it, we definitely do not present like we're a couple. If anything, she must think we're friends or cousins . . . and what the hell, why don't we look like a couple? I'd like to tell her we are and see if she still feels flirty.

I walk around the lobby and peek down two separate hallways, I assume two different wings. I wonder how they divide the people who live here: assisted and unassisted. Memory loss? We may not be close in a traditional sense, but I never want to put my parents in a facility and hope that they age well, minimally to put myself at ease with how I may age. I don't want to live in a facility either and wonder if panic attacks can land you in one at an early age.

"Excuse me?" Gloria says. I hadn't realized that Chris was beside me the whole time I was wandering.

"Yes," I say and walk back over with Chris.

"Carol will have a break shortly. We have a picnic table around the back of the facility for the staff. You can meet her back there."

"Thank you," I say, but it's still Chris she addresses.

"We'll head back there now," Chris says.

"Okay, I'll let her supervisor know."

We walk out the front door, and I can't help myself from looking back and checking if Gloria is watching Chris still. She's not. One point for Gloria.

"Do you think she'll come out and talk to us?" I ask.

"I don't know. I doubt she believes she has a nephew and some woman here to say goodbye."

Just then, a gray utility-size door opens, and a woman, slightly round, short, gray haired, walks out.

"Carol?" I ask.

"Who are you?" she asks.

"I'm Corey Tracey-Lieberman, and this is my partner, Chris Villar. Your friend Dave told us we could find you here. We wanted to talk to you about Sonja Hart." That was it, that was all she needed to hear, and the waterworks spilled down her face.

"Are you cops?" she asked.

"No, we're investigative journalists," Chris says. I'm thankful he answered because I still don't know what I am. I used to be those things, but I'm still not comfortable owning the titles anymore.

"I don't know anything. There isn't much to say. She shouldn't have been in that house."

"Sonja? In your house?" I ask.

"Yeah, I don't know why the hell she went to check on me. I said I wouldn't be at coffee because I needed an antibiotic. Why the hell would she come bring me coffee? I wasn't even home."

"Did you tell someone to tell her you were sick?" I ask.

"I told Dave I wouldn't be at coffee and let Sonja know not to worry, I was just going to go get an antibiotic for this cough I have."

"Do you know how the fire may have started?" I ask. I want answers. Why the hell are the answers so slow coming. How many days has it been? I count on my fingers again—five, only five. Why does it feel like a month has passed?

"I don't know who started it. I wasn't home," Carol says.

"So, you think someone did this? Not any electrical wiring?" I ask.

"I moved in there about eight months ago. My apartment building was sold, and the tenants were evicted. I stayed on friends' couches for a bit, and the third time I was asked to leave I knew I had to find something permanent. I couldn't afford an RV."

"How did you know that house would stay vacant?" I ask.

"Dave knew. He's been around a lot longer than you'd think by looking at him. He said he knew the guy that had lived there a while ago, did some work for him, minor handyman stuff. Anyway, the guy moved to Florida and told Dave that he was going to wait out the market and sell high. Dave didn't feel right moving into it himself, being that he was still doing work on the place every now and again, mowing the lawn, flushing the toilets, running the water. Anyway, he told me I could move in until I was back on my feet, and that would be it."

"So, you were squatting until someone came to kick you out?" I ask.

"I took care of the place. Dave worked there a few days a week. I didn't bother anybody, showered here at work, never used the electricity or water there. I kept a camping bucket in the bathroom. I know you look down on me, but I'm just like you, just a few paychecks off."

"I don't look down on you," I say.

"Well, don't pity me either. I don't want it," Carol says.

"What made you go to the clinic when you did that day? From what I hear you never miss coffee-and-fresh-bread day," I ask.

"Dave was concerned about my cough. He gave me the money to go to the doctor and told me if I didn't go right away, then he'd kick me out of the house. I can be pretty stubborn. I wouldn't have gone otherwise. Dave's a good guy. He's always looking out for all of us." Carol sits down at the picnic table, and I follow and sit across from her.

"What are you thinking?" I ask.

"It's my fault that Sonja was killed. Dave will never forgive me. He told me as much. Told me it's my fault. I've got nothing. I've lost everything and the only two people that gave a shit about me."

"Where are you staying tonight?" Chris asks.

"I don't know. I may stay here in the locker room. I spoke to my supervisor. She can put me on for an overnight shift, and that way I don't have to leave."

"I have a friend that runs a private shelter not far from here. I can drive you there, get you registered. She can help arrange rides to and from work for you for the next week while you figure things out," Chris says.

"Thank you. Can I think about it?" Carol asks. I wonder why she doesn't jump on the offer, but it's not for me to understand right now. I need to figure out who killed Sonja, because that fire was intentional, and I need to figure out why.

"I know this is hard," I say to Carol. "But I have one more question. Is that okay?" She nods. "Why did you go to the police and report that you lost your house?" I ask.

"Rumor had it that they thought I was the one that died in that fire. The 'squatter' burned to death. I didn't want the person, and I swear to god I didn't know it was Sonja then, not until Dave told me, I didn't want that person's family to not know what happened to their loved one." Carol pulls a wadded tissue from her pocket and wipes her face. "You know, Highland Park is a small community. Sonja's mom was a friend of mine in high school. Isn't that funny? Everyone comes home at some point in their life. She was a good kid. I'm so sad she's gone." She blows her nose, and it barely helps. "Do you know if her family has been informed yet? I'd like to go to the service."

"Not yet," I say. "I'd be happy to let you know when they've set a date."

Carol pulls a piece of scrap paper from her pocket and a pen and writes her name and number down and passes it to me. Carol Ellis.

"Don't feel sorry for me," Carol says again. "I'm okay. I'm not a saint. I haven't been gray haired and old my whole life. I've made choices, and then some choices were made for me. But I'm a hard worker and a good person. Life hasn't always been easy for me, but I'm clean, and I don't drink anymore. Haven't for a decade. You can trust me when I tell you this, Sonja was murdered. There was nothing wrong with the house. Someone torched the place."

"I believe you, Carol." I cover the top of her hand with mine. "I believe you." I get up to leave, and something occurs to me. Ryan Moore has cameras in his backyard, and he lives there full-time. Wouldn't a guy that moved to Florida have cameras around his property since he's gone? "Carol, I'm so sorry, this is my last question. Were you aware of there being any cameras, like security cameras, around the property?"

"You know what, there were two. One was the doorbell camera on the front of the house, but when I went by the place to check the damage and see if there was anything left of my things, it was gone. Ripped off the doorframe. But there was one in the backyard that I noticed when I moved in. Dave told me it was offline, but I never believed him because I swear it looked like there was a light flickering on all the time. Anyway, I didn't want to get caught, so I always avoided it. Made a loop behind it, so it wouldn't catch me entering through the back door."

"Do you know if it burned in the fire?" Chris asks.

"I haven't gone back there. I haven't seen the back of the house since the fire. It's too much for me. But it was far enough away on an old fence post that I don't even think it was much use to whoever installed it."

"Thank you, Carol. Thank you so much."

35

It's almost noon, but I need to get to that fence post in the back of the house and see if there's a camera still there. Chris hauls ass back to the house. We park in the apron of the driveway and run. From this angle, the fire damage is so much worse. It must have started in the back. Knowing that Sonja, anyone, was inside and now looking at the damage is heartbreaking.

"How do you think Sonja died? I don't mean from smoke or fire, I mean, why couldn't she get out? She had to have what? Been knocked out? You see a fire, you start to run. And, I haven't met anyone that would have followed her to this house, knocked her out, and set her on fire."

"I spoke to my cousin. He sent me a little bit of the coroner's report. There was a skull fracture that could have been caused by the blast of an explosion, or possibly"—he points to the ceiling between the floors that is now open with exposed beams showing, some fallen, some looking precariously close to falling now—"she was hit by a beam trying to make her way out."

I turn around to face the back of the property. "What did Carol say she saw the camera attached to? A fence pole? I don't even see any fencing." Instead, there's an ornate cement wall, something out of another era, mid-century modern maybe. It runs the length of the entire back, what I assume is the property line. I walk carefully toward the back to walk the perimeter. I get to the northeast corner and still find nothing.

"Can you walk that side?" I ask Chris, who is looking around the blown-out back wall of the house.

"On it." Chris starts at the corner nearest the house, and we walk toward the middle together.

"I don't get it. There's no fence pole," I say.

There's a detached garage or unit of some kind that's blackened and damaged from what appears to be smoke and water. I look in the window. The property is empty. It looks more like an unused studio than a garage because the walls inside are finished. The interior looks unscathed by the fire. There's a lawn mower and several other supplies for maintenance. I walk the length of the structure, around the back, and up to the front again, and there, right in front of me, hugging the corner of the unit, is a metal fence pole that blends into the side of the garage like it's a part of the structure. I'll be damned. Attached to the bottom of the pole and held on by a black zip tie is the smallest security camera. "Found it," I call out to Chris. "I need scissors to cut it off this pole."

"Wait. We need to get some pictures of it first." I step back, and Chris photographs the camera. Then, he pulls a pocketknife out of his pants and in one swipe has the camera loose in his hand.

"Hey, all, did you find Carol?"

I nearly jump out of my skin. I spin around, and thank god Jacob is with Evan and not me as I stand, readying myself to fight.

"Dave, you scared me," I say. "We did find her, thank you."

"What are you guys doing back here?" he asks.

"Well, Carol hasn't been feeling comfortable coming back here, so we said we'd check if there was anything worth salvaging of hers," Chris says. Exactly what I would have said. I smile to myself, and if it comes off as a genuine smile to Dave regarding the situation, even better.

"Yeah, she's feeling guilty, I'm sure. I told her a million times to not mess with anything. To just pretend she was camping in a tent without the luxury of utilities. But I swear to you, she lit that pilot on the stove with a lighter so many times. I've been thinking about it all week, and

I bet she left something going on that stove, and it was because of the gas the place went up," Dave says.

"That's an interesting theory," I say. "You and Carol were pretty good friends, though, right?" I ask.

"What do you mean?" Dave asks.

"Well, you're the guy that helped her stay in this house when she was evicted from her apartment. Plus, you gave her the money to go to urgent care the morning of the fire. That sounds like a good friend to me."

"I try to help where and when I can. The guy that owns this place pays me pretty well to look after it. It's crazy. He doesn't even care about this place, ya' know. He's just sitting on this pile of money and not letting anyone benefit from using it as shelter. It's wild, man."

"Can I ask you a question?" I say.

"Sure, I told you, I'm an open book. I don't have anything to hide. I want to find out what happened so we can give some closure to Sonja's family."

"Yeah, me too. I appreciate that." I drop my head and look at the device I have fisted in my hand, hiding. I peek at Chris in my peripheral and see he's texting someone or calling someone. I see his phone doing something. Why did Dave force Carol to go to the doctor that morning of all mornings? It's an awful big coincidence. I remember when I saw him on Monday and handed him the bottle of water that his hands were black, slicked with oil or something.

"Do you know if the owner has any security cameras?" I ask. I don't want to scare Dave off. His eager openness is sitting funny with me. And why is he here right now when he said he couldn't come back. Not after someone he cared about died here.

"Just the doorbell camera on the front door, but that's gone."

"Shoot. Nothing back here that may have picked up an intruder?" I ask. I'm pressing him, but gently. I don't want him to know what I have.

"Nah, there was a decoy camera at one point, but I don't even know what happened to it. Probably stolen by kids." He shakes his head while I nod.

"We've got an appointment to get to," I say.

"If you see Carol again, can you let her know I forgive her?" Dave asks.

"Sure," I say. "You take care of yourself, Dave."

Chris and I walk past Dave to leave, and I start to feel a rush of adrenaline. I'm not anxious or panicky. I'm revved up and ready to fight or run a race. It's hard to tell what my body and brain want; all the signals are still crossed and trying to reorient themselves.

"What were you doing on your phone back there?" I ask Chris. We're on our way to the precinct because it's almost noon, and I don't want to miss Jonathan.

"Jonathan was texting me." It's all he says. I wonder if we're going to talk about what just happened in the yard. I need to break it down. Did Dave kill Sonja and why? He didn't want to kill Carol. What could be the motive? It's fuzzy, but I feel the why coming, I can almost taste it.

"Why aren't you saying anything?" I ask.

"I'm processing it all. I can't decide yet what I think about any of it, and I don't want to speculate. Not yet, not when we're going to go see this kid find out his mom is dead."

Shit.

People always say parents shouldn't bury their children. It's the deepest pain you can experience. But, what about young kids with young parents? Is that fair at all? Children shouldn't have to bury their parents either. Not until they're old and well lived. None of it makes sense. Only thing that does is that life is fragile. Human lives are fragile. Resilient, yes. But, oh so fucking fragile.

I pull out my phone to see if Evan has written me. Nothing. No missed calls, texts, or even email. There are tons of notifications that I have comments on my vlog, but I'll check those in minute.

Me: Hey, how is Jacob doing?

Evan: We're all good. Just stopped for lunch. Had a great run. You?

Me: Heading back to Lopez's office now.

Evan: Looking forward to dinner. We need to talk.

We need to talk could mean so many things from Evan. We need to talk about Jacob's schedule. We need to talk about the finances. We need to talk about our relationship. We need to talk about his affair. I don't want to talk about anything more than superficial conversation. The weather, running, his work, spin classes.

"Everything okay?" Chris asks.

"Yeah, fine."

"Sounds like it."

"You've been married. It didn't work. Well, I'm married. It's not working out, and I'm exhausted from trying. And I hate getting texts that say, *See you at dinner, we need to talk.*" I look at Chris, and he glances at me briefly. Long enough to make eye contact.

"I'm sorry. I thought you two were separated, and then I see him move back in this week, so I guess I'm confused," Chris says.

"You and me both." I sigh and look out the window. "It was a trial separation. One month. We were supposed to have a session with our therapist before he moved back in, but he surprised me with his suitcase and just let himself in. What was I supposed to do? It's his house, too, and his kid, and we don't have anything formal in place."

"You could have told him no."

"I could have told him no. You're right. It felt a lot more complicated than that."

"What part of it?" he asks.

"The part about Jacob. I don't want him to take my baby from me. I don't want him to be vengeful and do something that puts me in an RV on Griffin Avenue minus Jacob."

"Corey, if it's about money, I can pay you more now. I just found out we've been given a grant."

"Thank you. I wish it were just about the money. It's not. He calls me crazy, he tracks my medication. I'm afraid he will have me ruled unfit, and I'll lose full custody of Jacob. I'll receive weekend visitation, monitored. I don't trust Evan."

"I wish I could say that's not going to happen. If I can help, I always will. I know a few lawyers," Chris says.

"Thanks."

"You ready to go in?" Chris asks. I didn't even realize we'd parked.

"Let's go meet Jonathan."

36

Jonathan and his father are waiting outside the precinct for us. I assume that Chris planned it when they were texting during the exchange with Dave. Jonathan doesn't match what I had pictured in my head. He's larger than I imagined, like a high school football player or wrestler. He's got light-brown hair and fair skin. The freckles on his face make him look younger and more innocent. He's dressed well, khakis and a button-down. I want to believe it is all Sonja that made this young man appear stoic and brave, but Jonathan's dad is right beside him with his hand on his son's shoulder, looking like an older version of his son, right down to the khakis and button-down.

I know kids need their dads, and divorce is hard, and looking at the way Jonathan's dad has shown up with him today, I feel it.

"Jonathan, it's good to meet you," Chris says, pulling him into a brotherly hug. He turns to Jonathan's father and extends his hand. "You must be Mr. Hart. I'm Chris Villar. It's nice to meet you."

Jonathan's dad accepts Chris's hand, and they shake. "Call me Tim. I wish we were all meeting under better circumstances."

"Hi, I'm Corey," I say, jumping in on the beat that felt the most natural. I look at Jonathan, and he holds his hand out like Chris and his father had and shakes my hand. So young, but an adult at the same time.

"Should we head inside?" Tim asks.

"I'm not ready," Jonathan says. The mask of stoicism fractures as his eyes become glassy, and a hard swallow bobs his Adam's apple up and down. "Tell me if you know."

"What?" I ask him.

"Tell me, did my mom die?" Jonathan asks, his eyes pleading with both Chris and me. I look at Tim.

"Jonathan, I think we should let the police talk to us," Tim says. Jonathan bursts into tears, and Tim wraps him up in a bear hug. This is not the father I was expecting when Jonathan didn't know if he'd "float" him the money for a plane ticket. But, maybe that was a misunderstanding. Maybe he was trying to keep Jonathan safe from this exact moment. I see Tim is shedding tears as well, and I wonder if it's for his son or Sonja. Likely both.

"I didn't think one missed phone call would mean . . . I should have listened to you," Tim says into Jonathan's ear as he holds him close. His voice little more than a whisper.

"I think we should wait—" Chris begins.

"Do you want the truth?" I ask, interrupting Chris. Chris looks at me with nothing but support. If knowing what we know will help Jonathan make it up the steps and into the precinct doors to face what is waiting for him, then I'm going to give him that.

"I do. I don't want to lose it in front of a room of strangers. I want to know now, I want to know what's coming. I can handle it." He looks at his dad. Tim puts an arm around his son's shoulders and squeezes.

"I'm right here with you, kid. I promise we'll get through it together, no matter what it is," Tim says to his son.

"Okay, let's go sit on those benches, then," I say. I choose the bench I'd cared for my son on: changed Jacob's diaper, breastfed him, and nearly lost my mind during a panic attack. It feels like the right place to have this conversation.

"Your mom was doing great things while she was here as I'm sure you know."

"My mom is amazing; she never stops and puts everyone else ahead of herself. Especially me. She didn't want me to take a gap year. We were supposed to move down here together, but I wanted to spend time with my dad, and she made it happen. She was just like that."

"Yeah, I hope to be half that great of a mom to my son," I say. "Did you know that she was volunteering in the community? She was part of a group that would set up a coffee and fresh baked goods for the community. Anyone could come for a hot cup of coffee and fresh loaf of bread."

"That sounds like her. I mean she did so much. She was so busy, I just didn't always have the time to ask her enough questions about her day." The guilt washes over his face. He didn't need to have all the time, I knew this. Sonja loved him for all the time he did give her. It was enough. I know this because every smile Jacob gives me is enough, and it always will be.

"Before I tell you the rest, I want you to know that nothing is confirmed. You will be asked to identify some things today that may or may not be your mom's. Do you understand? I cannot tell you the rest unless you understand that nothing is certain yet."

"I understand."

"Your mom was serving coffee and bread. One of the women that usually comes didn't show up. She was at the doctor's, trying to get an antibiotic for a lingering cough. Your mom went to her house to check on her and leave her a loaf of bread and a cup of coffee."

Jonathan is silently crying. Tears stream down his face. I dig through my bag and pull out a folded stack of tissues and pass them to him.

"There was a fire in the house, and we think your mom may have been trapped inside by the fire." I rip it off like a bandage. I don't want to tiptoe around the rest. I don't even want to tell him she was pregnant. I wonder if Moore knows. Is he being called in as well? Jonathan turns into his father's chest and lets out everything he is feeling. An explosion of sadness that is heart wrenching. I must stand up before I succumb to it myself. I look at Chris and see he's crying softly too.

I need to know the list of suspects Lopez has put together as possibilities to who may have started the fire or trapped Sonja in that house. My list seems to be shrinking:

- Dave
- Ryan Moore
- Carol
- Richard
- The Custodian

I just can't figure out why anyone would want to hurt her. Who is telling Anne? Had Lopez brought her in too? I text Lopez to let her know we're outside, and all I get in return are those three annoying dots.

"I think we should head inside and see what the police know," Tim says. I nod in agreement. "You ready, kid?" Jonathan hangs on to the stack of tissues I gave him, using one at a time. I would have wadded them up and repeatedly smashed them against my sobbing face. Jonathan is far more together than I fear I will ever be again.

Lopez takes Jonathan and his dad into the back room, the same one they took me into with Kat's mom, Gilda, just months ago. I follow close behind.

"Why don't you wait out here with Mr. Villar," Lopez says. I want to protest, but on what authority?

"It's okay," Jonathan says. "I'd feel better if she came in too."

Lopez holds the door open and motions me in. I look at Chris, who takes a seat outside the room, and I understand. Some places are harder to be in than others.

"Show me what you're going to show me so we can confirm my mom is gone or not," Jonathan says. The bravado of his voice betrays the mask he's wearing to hide his emotion.

"Okay," Lopez says, "we can walk through the identification process first." Marks hands Lopez a folder, and it instantly brings back Kat's case. The difference for me is that Jacob isn't here in my arms to distract my emotions.

"First, I want to ask you, and maybe your father would know better." She motions her head toward Tim. "Are you aware of an accident in your mother's past that would have resulted in her leg being broken?"

"Yes," Jonathan and Tim both say. "Go ahead, Dad."

"She was in an automobile accident as a kid. The bone in her thigh was broken."

"Her femur?" Lopez asks.

"Yes, that's it," Tim says.

Lopez nods and writes something down on the pad in front of her, and Marks reads it over her shoulder. I should have stood closer to Lopez, but instead I played it neutral and sat in a middle seat.

"There was a piece of jewelry." I see Lopez struggle for the next words she says. "There was a piece of jewelry we collected, and we're hoping you can identify it." She pulls out an earring and a ring. The earring is a small plain diamond stud on a gold backing. And the ring is a simple gold band with an opal in the center and little diamonds surrounding it like petals. The opal and the diamonds make a perfect flower. It's stunning. "Have you seen this ring before?" Lopez asks.

Jonathan breaks character and is in full tears. Unable to speak between sobs. "That's Sonja's ring. I gave it to her when Jonathan was born," Tim says. He grabs his son and holds him tight. I see the tears flow from him as well, but he holds it together for his kid. Stoic.

"Let's take a break," Lopez says. "Ms. Tracey-Lieberman, may I speak with you outside?" I follow Lopez out of the room, and as I exit, I catch Marks walking a box of tissues and two bottles of water over to Jonathan and Tim. I guess he has a heart after all.

"I did not tell you to have a conversation with that young man before me," Lopez says. It comes out as scolding, and I'm not prepared for it.

"I'm sorry, but I don't actually work for you on this case. I established a relationship with him before you came onto this investigation, before it was a homicide. So, I had a conversation with him as my client, and you cannot tell me I did anything wrong."

We are in a stare down. If one of us crosses our arms first, I may burst out laughing. It's ridiculous.

"You're right, you're right. I apologize," Lopez says.

"No, I'm sorry. I should have texted you what I was doing. We do work together, and I do not want to fuck that up. It's been a tough morning. Are we okay?" I ask.

"We're okay," Lopez says.

"Listen, I found Carol, the squatter, and spoke to her. Did you know that the house had a handyman, caretaker? And it's the person that I told you about that lives in the RV, Dave. It's weird, right? Dave takes care of the property because the owner lives in Florida. Meanwhile, he lets Carol live there, slash squat, in the house. There's a lot to that, but no time right now." I wave Chris over. "We found a camera in the backyard that may have an SD card in it. And if it does, it might have captured the person who started the fire."

"It could also be a dummy camera, we don't know. Didn't want to tamper with it," Chris says. He pulls the camera out of his pocket and hands it to Lopez.

"Thank you," she says. "We haven't been able to determine how the fire started yet. There isn't a sign of an accelerant foreign to the environment. We're currently eliminating possibilities before we can home in on what happened. But my guess is, there was some sort of a blast that caused the skull fracture to Ms. Hart, and that's why she perished. It knocked her unconscious."

"Are you going to be able to tell Jonathan that she didn't suffer?" I ask.

"I will."

“Listen, I don’t know how long Dave is going to stick around, but he knows something, and I would get him in here before his RV decides to leave town for good,” I say.

“Tell me where he was last, and I’ll get someone out there,” Lopez says.

I write down Griffin Avenue, the license plate number of the RV, the electric tape, chicken wire, and the color and make—to the best of my ability. All items I memorized from this morning.

Lopez goes back into her meeting, and Chris and I leave. For now, we can’t do anything more for Jonathan. We’ll have to wait and see what’s next. I don’t know if they’ll discover Sonja was pregnant. I don’t know if they’ll meet with Moore or Anne. I hope so, and I’ll be there when they do. I just want justice for Sonja.

37

Chris and I drive back to my car once again in silence. I imagine Chris is writing Sonja's story for his feature next week in his head. I'm thinking about all the ways tonight can go with Evan. Chris pulls in front of my car and puts it in park.

"You okay?" he asks.

"Yeah, I'm just thinking about everything."

"Me too." He looks at me, and I want to hug him. Genuinely hug him, and I want that hug to say, *Thank you for being my friend.* I don't because there's too much in the way: steering column, coffee cups, windshield visor, and all my emotions for him. "You're going to be okay, Corey. And, if you want to, you can call me when the talk is over. Or text, I'll be on standby."

I give him the sincerest half smile I can muster. "Thank you."

I jump out of the car and feel excited to go home, if only to see Jacob. I've missed him all day.

"Hello? I'm home," I say into the void of our house. Evan's car is in the driveway, but I don't see or hear Jacob or Evan. I run upstairs to see if they're taking a nap together. Nothing. Weird. I text Evan.

Me: Hey, I'm home, where are you guys?

I hear a ding and vibration and look to the bedside table and see Evan's phone and watch charging. So, they're not here, the car is, and Evan never leaves without his watch. They can't be far. I run back downstairs and outside to see if Elsie or Pete are out watching the neighborhood and maybe know where Jacob and Evan went. But there's no one outside.

I look across to Ben and Julia's house, and the doors are wide open, again. I am so sick and tired of these people I can't begin to explain my frustration. This is not some idyllic countryside where your cat can roam free to be what, a barn cat? Where you leave your door open because there isn't another person for at least a mile? No, goddammit. This is the city. It's Los Angeles. There are rules.

I walk across the street and up Julia and Ben's porch and yell into the house, "Julia!" No one answers. I check the driveway again. Maybe I missed it. No, still no car. I see Oliver on the dining room table and what looks like a tall glass of wine. Oliver starts licking the contents of the glass. Before I can think better of it, I move inside to grab Oliver away from becoming one drunk tiny kitten. Can wine kill a cat?

"Julia? Ben?" I call out again.

Oliver is purring loudly against my chest. I dump the glass of wine in the sink and walk to the back door to see if Ben or Julia or both are in the backyard, but no one is there. It's just a large pile of moving boxes ready to be broken down and trashed.

I walk through the house to make sure, once again, that someone isn't wounded and unable to call for help. First the dump-all room. Which I assume will be an office, guest room, or baby room, nothing. I walk into the bathroom and check behind the shower curtain, clear. Then I head into Julia's bedroom. I open the closet, nothing. The bed is empty too. There's literally nowhere else they could be hiding.

"Julia? Ben?" I call out, but still silence in return. I wonder if, when she left shoeless earlier, she ever returned. She must have. I closed the door for her then, too, right? I can't remember. It's blending with the day before when I closed the door and the time before that. Wait. How many times have I found their door opened and closed it? I set Oliver on the back of the couch. "You be a good boy. I'll be back later if your parents don't get home tonight, and I'll feed you then, okay?" Oliver is still purring, and he swats at my face playfully.

I turn around to leave and instead of moving with legs and feet, I feel the hard knock of something against my head, and then everything is dark.

38

"I don't know. I felt something hit me upside the head, and then it went dark before I could understand or make anything out," I say. I am in a hospital bed, where I've been for two days now. The ill-fitted and unattractive, breezy hospital gown gives me gooseflesh.

"Corey, do you remember why you were inside your neighbor's house?" Detective Lopez asks.

"Yes, their door was wide open, and the cat, no, their kitten is there, Oliver. I didn't want the coyotes to get him, so I went to shut their door."

"Do you remember if you knocked before entering?" Lopez says.

"I'm not an animal." I think through the question, and it hurts my brain too much, so I stop. "I don't know if I knocked. The door was wide open. I know I yelled out for Julia and Ben, and no one answered. I walked through the house to make sure no one was injured and in need of assistance. And I remember calling out their names every room I went in." Or that may have been the time before. I cannot think. It hurts my head. "It's not a very big home. Someone would have heard me at the door when I yelled hello."

"I understand, but Julia says you barged into the house uninvited," Lopez says.

"C'mon. I had just left the precinct with you. I wasn't going around looking for trouble. Why would I do that?"

"She says you've been hostile toward her since they moved in, and that you were looking for your husband and baby."

I can't believe this bullshit.

"Are you kidding me?" I ask rhetorically.

"Corey, were Jacob and Evan home when you returned from the precinct?"

"No."

"And, have you had any *emotional* interactions with Mrs. Palmer?"

"Oh, that's rich," I say. "Can you pass me my phone?" Lopez reaches across the hospital food tray and hands it to me.

I open my search engine and, sure enough, there's my search from earlier on Julia. The first three headlines read like clickbait. They're old too. The first one is a picture of Julia barefoot and disheveled, and the title reads, Another Manic Episode in Central Park for Julia Palmer. I show the headline and photo to Lopez.

"I'm not the one with the problem," I say. "I have never been hostile toward Mrs. Palmer. She moved in a week ago. I haven't had enough time to breathe in her direction the wrong way. She showed up at my door a few nights ago, screaming that her husband was missing. And then he showed up with Evan and Jacob a few minutes later. I have no idea where he was. I swear to you, I know nothing about this woman."

"Except that you've been internet researching her."

"It's my job. Also, this is the first search I've been able to do, I swear."

"I believe you, but I also know you have a habit of running into houses you don't belong in," Lopez says. That's fair.

"I came here for another reason too," Lopez says. "I have some good news for you."

"I'm not sure I can handle a lot more right now. I feel raw."

"Welcome to the business. I promise this will lift your spirits, Corey Tracey. I looked up the dates our Highland Park arsonist firefighter was incarcerated. It was one year after the Flores murders. After a little more digging, it turns out that for his first acts of arson, a few small fires that he copped to, he used a pack of cigarettes. Because none of the fires were successful, we were able to match the brand of tobacco used in the Flores case with those from his early fires."

"So, he did it. It was him," I say.

"I'm afraid we will never get a confession because he died a few years ago, but we feel we do have enough evidence and information to conclude that it was him, yes."

"Holy shit. Of course she would let a fireman into her home. He probably introduced himself and said he was going around, checking everyone's smoke detector."

"I have an appointment tomorrow with the Flores family. I look forward to giving them some closure." Lopez puts her hand on top of mine. "You did that, Corey. You are giving the gift of closure to the Flores family, and I want to say thank you."

"I wish I could go with you."

"Me too, but you need to heal because I have your next case ready. Call me this week when your head feels up to it." Lopez stands.

There's a knock on the door, and a head pops in. "Corey?" I can't believe it. Someone has called my psychiatrist. Well, at least that's one thing I can cross off my to-do list now.

"Dr. Rosenberg, hello. I guess the word is out. I have been hit in the head and gone completely mad now," I say. He smiles, but the concern shows all over his face.

"I'll leave you to it. And, Corey, I'll be in touch later," Lopez says before leaving.

"I read your chart. Sounds like you took a hard blow to the head. Good news is your CT scan came back clear."

"Thank god." I don't have a brain tumor. "Dr. Rosenberg, before I was hit in the head by my neighbor, I was having these electric zaps, and I for sure thought I was dying." I half joke as I say it, but I'm also very serious.

"What do you mean?" Dr. Rosenberg asks gently and with concern.

"They started a few days ago. I stopped taking the Paxil—it's been about a week ago now. It was making me too foggy and stuck. I couldn't get the answers to process in my brain like I'm used to. And, it's been six months, I thought, well you said I could stop whenever," I say. I'm rambling for approval.

"I told you, you could stop whenever, but that we needed to speak first so I could guide you off them. You don't want to go cold turkey because there can be some side effects, like the 'brain zaps' you're talking about. How are you doing without them?"

"I've had a few anxiety attacks, not full panic, but the obsessive-compulsive thoughts aren't back. I've tried taking the Klonopin a few times to get ahead of the panic." He nods his head as I talk. "And now I'm afraid to go back on it because I can't let my brain feel that stifled. It's claustrophobic."

"Corey, we can try another pill. Something less strong and see how that does now that we have the thoughts under control. Would you be willing?" he asks.

"Yes, but I don't know why you're here and how it has anything to do with why I'm here," I say.

"Evan called me. He was worried. He said that things were stressful this week with him moving back in and your work. I hear a missing woman was found dead."

"My work is fine. Evan moving back in without permission or discussing it first with me or our therapist is not fine."

"I agree. I'm told you're going to be discharged today, so I'd like to see you in my office this week. I'm writing in a prescription for the new drug for you, and I'd like you to start that tomorrow, deal?"

"What is it I'm agreeing to take?" I ask.

"It's called Lexapro."

"Okay, I've heard of it. Will it take care of these zaps?"

"Those side effects do go away on or off medicine."

"Great." I extend my hand to him, and he takes it. "It's a deal."

"It looks like you have another visitor. I will have Scheduling call you with an appointment time tomorrow. Please go pick up the prescription this evening to take tomorrow."

"Will do. Thank you for coming," I say. I want to cry. I want to stand up and hug Dr. Rosenberg for coming and caring and listening to me. He gets up and pats me on my shoulder before walking out.

I take a deep breath and look down at myself. I am laid bare in this bed, a thin hospital gown hanging loosely from my body. I have no idea what I look like. It's the most vulnerable I think a person can feel.

"Corey?" I hear from the door. It's Chris.

"Yep, I'm in here, as decent as can be expected, so avert your eyes."

Chris walks straight to the windows and opens the curtains a bit more, so it isn't as dark, and I immediately squint.

"Oh god, too much?" he asks.

"It's okay. The headache is finally subsiding. I like the light. It makes everything seem far more cheery."

"How are you doing?" More generic questions. More pity. I cannot take everyone's sympathy anymore.

"I'm fine. I will be fine. That's the good news. The bad news is, my neighbor hit me upside the head and put me in the hospital."

"Did she hit you and then call you an ambulance?" Chris asks. He takes a seat next to the bed.

"I know she hit me. I've been told as much. And when I came to, EMS was putting me on a stretcher and hauling me out."

"Why?" he asks.

"Because I was unconscious."

"Well at least you're still funny. Why did she hit you?"

"I don't know, seriously. They've been acting odd. Fighting since they moved in, then she came to my house looking for Ben, said he was missing. He shows up, and they're all good. Then two or three days in a row I found the door to their house wide open. Which, whatever, but they have a brand-new tiny kitten. A week ago, I spent hours in my driveway with them, trying to protect a feral cat and her kittens from coyotes, so, yeah, I'm the person that went to shut their door when they were clearly not home. I went over and called out their names. I knocked. No one was there. This was the third time. I went inside to talk to the kitten, and when I turned to leave, bam."

"I hope she doesn't press charges," Chris says.

"What? I didn't do anything!"

"I agree, but my cousin told me she filed a police report on you." Chris looks at his shoes and says, "Technically it's breaking and entering."

"The door was wide open. I was being a concerned neighbor," I say. I'm so irritated with everyone. I know I sound whiny, but come on. What is wrong with Chris and Lopez?

Chris chuckles. "I agree. I'm on your side. I swear. You said it, there is something off with them. I was half joking, I swear."

"I don't want to talk about it. What's going on with Sonja's case?" I ask.

"Jonathan took Lopez over to Sonja's apartment yesterday to look for anything that may indicate there was motive. They didn't find anything. They also found her car at the impound. It's being searched as well. What I can tell you is, there was a suitcase in the trunk. And, in her bathroom at her house a positive pregnancy test. Jonathan looked at his mom's laptop and found a reservation for an Airbnb in Joshua Tree, so it sounds like she was going away for a little solo retreat."

"What about RV Dave?" I ask.

"He is MIA, but he couldn't have gone far. He'll be back. Guys like that stay close to home. It's like they're tethered here by an invisible string. Every time you try to leave, you're pulled back." It sounds like he's talking about himself as much as he is Dave.

"Here's some good news. Jonathan and Anne are having lunch today. Lopez set it up after interviewing her. Anne asked and was adamant about seeing her friend's grown baby. I hope it will be healing for them both. And, who knows, if Jonathan honors his admission to school here, at least he'll have some community to look out for him. Thanks to his mom."

"What about Moore?" I ask.

"He's not off the hook yet." Chris gets up from the chair and pulls it closer to me. I feel my heart rate speed up. "Corey," he says and takes my hand. "I want to tell you something. I always know the risk we put ourselves in is stupid, but we're not cops, and I take that for granted. You just got knocked out by a neighbor, not by a case or a story." He stops and looks me in the eyes. I have no idea if my eyes are bruised, if there's makeup smeared under them, if I'm bloodshot. It doesn't seem to matter to Chris because he's looking in them, not at them.

"I'm sorry, I should be more careful. I don't want you to worry so much. I don't want anyone to worry." I take another deep breath and close my eyes. "I would never risk losing my baby, so I know how far to push. Can't you tell I've calmed way down in the past six months? I'm focused on cold cases," I say and chuckle.

"That's not, no—Corey, I haven't wanted to interfere in your marriage. I want you to be happy, and if you found that with another guy, then I was heartbroken, but happy for you. But now, when Lopez called to tell me you'd been hurt. I don't want to lose you, having never told you."

My heart feels like it's beating out of my chest. I'm sweating. I look at the monitors I'm hooked up to and don't know which one is my heart, but I'm positive it's the one spiking all over the place. I turn back to look at Chris, but he's moved again. He's standing now.

Before I can say anything, he bends down and kisses me. It is different from both previous kisses. It's so soft, I feel a transfer of warmth from him to me. The kiss isn't long. He lets go and sits back down. I am speechless and terrified of what he's going to say next.

I hear someone clear their throat before I hear "Mama!" I almost burst into tears. My baby.

"Jacob, my heart." I swing my arms open to him, and he nearly leaps from Evan to me. "My sweetest boy, I have missed you so much." I squeeze him to my chest, and he holds on tight. Then Evan leans down and kisses the top of my head.

"I'll give you all some privacy," Chris says. "Evan, nice to see you. Corey, I'll check in later." I nod. I see Evan's jaw working, holding back what he'd like to say.

"You shouldn't be back to work yet," Evan says.

"No, of course, you're right," I say. I want to keep the peace. I don't know if he saw the kiss. "Can you get me my clothes? They say I'm being released." Evan brings my clothes over, and we switch. I hand him Jacob reluctantly, and he hands me my clothes. I pull all the taped-on monitors off. I don't care. I'm ready to go.

A nurse pops in, I assume because something alerted her to my monitor being disarmed.

"Mrs. Tracey-Lieberman, I see you're ready to get going, huh?"

"I am. The sooner the better."

"Okay, let me get your paperwork, and I'll be back." She leaves, and I plop down into the chair Chris had just been in, to pull on my leggings.

"Corey," Evan says. "I'm worried about you."

"I'm fine. The CT scan was all clear."

"Why were you in Julia and Ben's house?" he asks. I realize that he believes *crazy* Julia too.

"I told you and everyone else a hundred times already. Their door was open, and the kitten was going to run out. I called out for Julia and Ben, and no one answered. So I went in to check and make sure no one was in distress. When no one answered again, I was about to leave, and Julia popped me in the head. By the way, where were you and Jacob?" I ask.

"We were home."

"No, you weren't. I went inside, and your phone and watch were charging, but you were not there."

"I don't know. Maybe it's when I took Jacob for a quick walk around the block."

I nod. Liar. I'm 100 percent certain he was seeing Lynn, from work, with my baby. And he left his watch and phone so I couldn't use the Find My Location app on him. Fuck me, Evan is very good.

"Yeah, that makes sense," I say. I will not show my cards to this man. I reach out and take Jacob, who is ready to run the hospital halls. I grab my purse, the one constant in my life, my bag with everything in it. And I leave.

39

"How do you feel?" Evan asks. It was a long afternoon at home, just being stationary while Jacob ran around in front of me. My head throbs with every quick movement of my neck and my eyes.

"I've been better, but I'm okay,"

"Corey, I want to talk," Evan says, and I think, sure, this is the appropriate time. Catch me when I'm down for the count. "I'm leaving."

I shake my head once and wince. "What do you mean, you're leaving? Where are you going?" I ask.

"I've rented the same house but for six months. I can't do this anymore. I don't want to be the third man in line in your life." I feel myself nodding, and my teeth ache from the movement. "It's always going to be Jacob, Chris, then me."

"I'm sorry, Evan. I didn't want us to have this conversation like this," I say.

"I know, but when I saw you and Chris together in the hospital"—he drops off for a moment—"I can't unsee what I saw, Corey."

Okay, so he did see the kiss. Great.

"I'm going to leave tonight. I've already packed a bag for myself and Jacob."

"Jacob? You're not taking Jacob." I am firm, so firm about it I stand quickly and nearly fall back down. The shooting pain is intense.

"You're in no shape to care for yourself and for him tonight. Elsie is going to come over and stay with you. I will bring Jacob back in the morning before work, okay? It's just for the night."

I rub my forehead and start to cry. He's doing it. He's taking my baby, and it's my fault. I can't breathe. "Please, Evan, don't take my baby from me."

"Corey, I'm not taking him from you, I'm taking him for you. You can barely stand up. Your head is in too much pain." He stops and grabs Jacob as he zooms by. "Buddy, we're going to say bye-bye to Mama so we can go on an adventure tonight, okay?" Jacob falls into my arms, and I squeeze him. I stand up and nearly prepare myself to run with my baby. Run where? If I lock myself into a room the cops will come, and I'll look even more like a lunatic.

I try to pass Jacob back to Evan, but Jacob screams, "Mama, Mama, Mama!" He's screaming and crying, and Evan holds onto him tightly and leaves.

I follow them out onto the porch and continue to yell, "I love you, Jacob, my whole heart. Mommy loves you!"

I watch as Evan puts him into the car seat and buckles him in, still screaming. And then I watch them drive away. I am broken. I run upstairs and dig out my Klonopin. There is only one pill left in the bottle. Someone found my pills and took them. Who?

"Corey?" It's Elsie, my babysitter for the night.

I put the cap back on and keep the last pill in the bottle for when I'm desperate. I am not desperate. Who took my goddamn pills, Evan?

My head hurts too much to keep my eyes open. Elsie is already here. I didn't hear her climb the stairs even with the step that groans. She puts her arm around me.

"Why don't you go to bed, Corey?" Elsie says.

"It's too early. I just need to keep my eyes closed. Can you get me a new ice pack?"

I head downstairs with Elsie and plop back down on the couch, where I am determined to stay until Evan brings Jacob home. My phone starts vibrating on the table. I pick it up and don't recognize the number. I let it go to voicemail. My phone buzzes on the table, and I reach for it again.

Chris: RV Dave turned himself in.

I look at the new voicemail message that lights up my screen.

Hey Corey, it's Dave. I'm calling you from the police station. They said I could make a quick call. Someone has to do something about this. About these corporations that are hurting our community. They're forcing people out on the streets, into RVs. There are a lot of good people homeless now who shouldn't be, because of these greedy bastards. You need to check out neLA Living. Look into some of these unsolved arsons. There are bad people in Highland Park, Corey. I'm sorry Ms. H died, she wasn't supposed to be there, I swear. I'm never going to forgive myself for that. Not ever.

The voicemail ends there, cut off by time. I write Chris back.

Me: What happened?

The screen is a little blurry and hurts my head to look at anymore.

Me: Can you come over? I'm not supposed to drive for another twenty-four hours.

Chris and I sit on the front porch while Elsie pretends to watch TV inside. He brought chicken soup and rolls. I didn't realize how hungry I was.

"Start at the beginning," I say between spoonfuls.

"Dave showed up with the RV outside the police station. Walked in and said he wanted to report a crime. Hang on." He pulls his phone out of his pocket. "I'm just going to read directly from my cousin's text. He said the guy sat down with Lopez and Marks for an hour. He was hired by the guy who owns the place to torch it for the insurance money. I'm quoting here, 'Apparently the guy was the handyman and had a background as an electrician, unlicensed—he messed with the wires, made it look like an accident.'" Chris puts his phone down. "It goes on, he didn't know Sonja was in the house. He sent Carol to the doctor so she wouldn't be there when the fire started. Sonja being there was an accident."

"Why would he do that?" I ask.

"Money. The guy paid him a couple grand, and when you've been homeless for a while, a couple grand can feel like a huge win."

"I don't feel better. I was hoping I'd feel better if I found out the truth, but I don't."

"We don't work in happy endings."

We sit in silence for a few minutes, finishing our food. When I'm done, I set my take-out soup bowl on top of Chris's empty one.

"How are you with Jacob not being here?" he asks.

"At this moment, I'm okay. It will get hard, but I'm okay until morning, I think."

I stand up to stretch my legs and nearly fall down into my seat again, but Chris is up and catches me.

"Still a little wobbly too?" he says.

"Yeah, I keep forgetting."

Chris is still holding me around the waist, keeping me on my feet. He pulls me into his chest, gently kissing the top of my head and whispers to me, alone, "I love you, Corey."

I lift my head up to look at him. Our mouths find each other, and I sink into the kiss. It's all I can do not to entirely lose myself to him. To hold on to some restraint. I'm kissing Chris, and it's not a mistake. His kiss is soft, a gentle promise of the love he's offering: patient, accepting, slow, and steady. I lean in to accept more, my hands finding their way to his chest, where they rest for balance as I stand on my tiptoes to reach him better.

Chris smiles, and it reaches all the way up to his eyes as he stares into mine. I feel my face heat, and I can't hide it. "If I wasn't so tan, I'd probably be a little pink too." We both laugh. It's been so long. So long holding in these feelings and dancing around each other. And did he say he loves me? My god. Do I say it back now?

"Out of your head. It's all good. You're good, I'm good. This is good, and it's okay," Chris says. He pulls me in for a hug, and for the first time I don't feel guilty for my feelings.

Epilogue

It's been a few days since Jonathan and his dad arrived, and they've been packing up all of Sonja's belongings. Jonathan is having them shipped back to his dad's place for now. He's decided not to move to LA for college. But, before he goes, he wants to meet Ryan Moore. Turns out Sonja felt he may have been the love of her life. I set up a meeting for them and agreed to accompany Jonathan.

Moore chose a park that he and Sonja had frequented to picnic. He wanted to share that with Jonathan.

I spot Moore at a picnic table and wave. He recognizes me right away, either because I have a happy Jacob strapped to my chest, or because he's watched me too many times on his security camera. Though, he didn't end up pressing charges as soon as Lopez explained to him who I was and what I had been doing.

"Hello," I say. I am much more pleasant to Moore now that I don't suspect him of murder. "Ryan, this is Sonja's son, Jonathan."

"Hi," Jonathan says.

"Would you like to have a seat?" Moore asks. "Or I'm happy to walk around if that's better?"

"Sitting is fine," Jonathan says, and we all take a seat. "I wanted you to see a few things I found in my mom's apartment." Jonathan pulls out the journal from his backpack. "My mom loved writing poetry. She talked about your class all the time. She loved it." Jonathan passes the journal to Moore. "I found this journal in her desk, and you'll see all the poems in it are titled Ryan Moore." Jonathan looks down, a little embarrassed. Moore takes the journal and opens it immediately. His face turns pink. Poor guy has the same skin tone as me. We can't hide anything.

"Thank you for showing me this," Moore says. "Would it be too much to ask if I can take pictures of these?"

"You can keep the journal. I think she'd want you to have it."

"I am deeply sorry for your loss, Jonathan. Your mother told me about you all the time. She was incredibly proud of you and just, I'm sure you know, but she loved you so much."

"I do know, but it's nice to hear." God, this kid is remarkable. If Jacob grows up to have an ounce of this maturity in him, I don't know. It's all a testament to Sonja as a mother. "I also want to tell you something that she didn't have a chance to tell you. But I know she would have wanted you to know . . . I know I would have wanted to know."

Moore looks confused. I'm not sure if I'd want to know, but it's not my choice.

"My mom was pregnant. I'm pretty sure she was going to tell you that day. Anyway, I hope it's okay I'm telling you."

Moore looks broken. His tears are plentiful. His loss has doubled. Jonathan gets up and sits next to Moore and hugs him. "I'm glad you told me," Moore says. The two men hug for another minute before separating.

"My dad and I are going to go to dinner tonight to celebrate my mom. Would you like to join us?"

Moore nods. I excuse myself so they can finish up alone. I let Jacob out of the baby carrier and watch him run around the park grass. His legs are small enough that he can't outrun me yet. I feel a tap on my shoulder. It's Jonathan.

"I'm ready to go," he says. He looks back once to Moore and waves. "See you tonight."

Jacob fell asleep on the drive back to Sonja's apartment, where I dropped off Jonathan. Instead of heading home, I sit outside, parked, and look at my phone. I hesitate, but I want to know who will be spending time with my baby, so I plug in the company address for Evan's marketing firm and look at their employee roster. I look for all the Lynns. Only one pops up. Someone from the legal department. There aren't any employee photos, so I copy her full name and plug it into LinkedIn, and there's the woman I saw Evan with. I scan her bio, but it's generic, likely written by AI. I scroll through her previous work, and there it is, like a neon sign at night. Lynn used to practice family law.

My anxiety shoots off sparks in my stomach, and I'm glad I started the new pills Dr. Rosenberg prescribed because if Evan is already taking advice from a lawyer, that he may or may not be fucking—shit, the baby monitor. How many conversations of mine has he recorded without me knowing. I'm going to need a lot of help.

I head home with Jacob. I park across from Julia and Ben's. I haven't seen Ben since he came into my house with Evan and Jacob almost two weeks ago now. Julia is outside on her front porch. Their car has been in the driveway since the Monday I got home from the hospital. I get Jacob out of the car, and we wave to Julia—who has not yet pressed charges for my *breaking and entering*. If anything, it should be labeled trespassing. I didn't break the door—it was open.

"Hi, Julia," I say. She looks up from her phone and waves back. "Haven't seen Ben in a while, everything good?" I ask. This woman has knocked me out and called me confrontational. I'm happy to speak out and ask what I need to know. Plus, I've been on the Lexapro for seven days, and my brain is not sludge. I feel good. And I've had two appointments with Dr. Rosenberg. I don't think it's his place to approve my separation from Evan, but he has remarked twice now that I appear happier.

"Ben is fine, Corey, thank you for asking," Julia says. She goes back to her phone, but I'm curious.

"Yeah, where is he?" I ask.

"It's none of your business. He's fine now." Julia stands up and walks back into her house and shuts her door.

But it is my business. When someone goes missing in Highland Park, it's always my business, and as far as I'm concerned, Ben has gone missing.

Acknowledgments

Thank you, readers, for returning to the world of Corey and Jacob. Your support, messages, thoughts, and encouragement mean so much to me. I see you all, and I am incredibly grateful to each and every single one of you. Thank you.

Thank you, Dara Hyde, the best agent a person could ask for. You are a constant cheerleader, friend, collaborator, and a true Valkyrie. I could not imagine any of this without you. You are the best, and I am so lucky to have you as a partner on this journey.

To the best publishing team, Thomas & Mercer, thank you. Alexandra Torrealba, I could not have imagined a more wonderful, dedicated, joyful human to work with. You are a brilliant treasure. Michelle Flythe, you understand Corey so well and make her shine so bright. And Sarah Naughton, you have brought Corey to life with your beautiful voice, thank you.

To my friends that read endless drafts, answer all my texts, and pick up when I call, I cannot thank you enough. Your constant support and wisdom make it possible to keep going. To keep telling stories.

To my family, thank you. Thank you for forty plus years of support and character content.

And my dearest Jason and Jack, I cannot thank you enough for the unconditional love and support you both give me. You may have married a writer, Jason Beeber, but you didn't know just how many versions of every book you'd be reading, did you? You read them all, and you love them all, and your enthusiasm and edits are always the most precious. I cannot thank you both enough. My love for you is infinite.

About the Author

Photo © 2023 Joanna DeGeneres

Jaime Parker Stickle is the author of *Vicious Cycle* and *Take Hart*, books one and two of the Corey in Los Angeles series. She is a writer, actor, podcaster, and professor of film and television at Montclair State University. She is the creator and cohost of the true crime podcast *The Girl with the Same Name* as well as the hilarious podcast about side hustles *Make That Paper*. Jaime lives in Los Angeles with her husband, son, and four-legged babies.